The
White
Hare

JANE
JOHNSON

An Apollo Book

First published in the UK in 2022 by Head of Zeus
This paperback edition published in 2023 by Head of Zeus,
part of Bloomsbury Publishing Plc

9 7 5 3 1 2 4 6 8

A catalogue record for this book is available from
the British Library.

ISBN (PB): 9781789545234
ISBN (E): 9781789545197

Typeset by Divaddict Publishing Solutions
Photographs © Jane Johnson

Printed and bound in Great Britain by
CPI Group (UK) Ltd, Croydon CR0 4YY

MIX
Paper | Supporting
responsible forestry
FSC® C171272

Head of Zeus
First Floor East
5–8 Hardwick Street
London EC1R 4RG

WWW.HEADOFZEUS.COM

To Abdel, and the seals that swim
below the Allotment by the Sea

'There is no such thing as an innocent landscape.'

Anselm Kiefer

I

The body lies in the surf, lapped by the edges of the incoming waves. Each time the water falls back, little rills and whirlpools burgeon around the head and feet, making the pebbles rattle and the figure's long red hair undulate like seaweed.

A gull swoops in to examine the scene; it is not unknown for a seal or even a dolphin to wash up on this treacherous stretch of coast. The instinctive curiosity of the perpetual scavenger combined with communal memory compels it to fly low to investigate. But the dead thing is neither a seal nor a dolphin. It gives off no smell at all as the blackback glides over it, and so the gull flies on, catching an updraft at the western arm of the cove, which takes it soaring over the dark woods on the hillside.

Out on the eastern horizon, pale sun breaks through the mist, melding sea and distant headland into a single hazy shape, a fata morgana from which fortresses may rise and fall or ghost ships break free under tattered sail in search of their lost crews. It could be any time, or no time.

And still the body lies there, larger waves lifting one pale hand as if the figure is making a feeble attempt to summon help, but no one comes.

Oystercatchers fly past, skimming the surface of the ocean, their plaintive cries piercing the cool air. In the woods, rooks rise cawing in a sudden clatter of wings that echoes in the valley's dark cleft.

Sandflies buzz over the seaweed stranded further up the beach by the tide and drift lazily over the body as the waves gradually fall back towards the ocean. A small grey-green crab scuttles out of a rock pool and runs sideways over the sea-foamed stones and across the corpse's foot, pausing briefly to register the unfamiliar texture, then resuming its path, picking up speed as if disturbed by its discovery.

The sun climbs higher. The body now lies fully exposed, a clear landmark on the shore. It lies like a person in repose, on its side, one arm flung up above the head, face turned from the land as if spurning human interaction. The soles of its feet are white as lilies and beginning to wrinkle. One knee is drawn up, lending the figure a dancer's poise. The stains on the body's clothing contrasting with the muted colours of the natural world punctuate the scene like a shout.

Bruises have flowered like dark roses upon the pale limbs. There are many submerged rocks along this stretch of coast. It is a place where mariners thrown from storm-wrecked vessels think to save themselves by swimming to the apparently welcoming shore, only to find the currents fiendishly working against them. Few, if any, survive a shipwreck here. But this body is not the victim of a shipwreck.

It is told in these parts that for a short time a corpse's

eyes may retain the ghostly image of the killer, or killers, their gaze last fixed upon. But maybe those who found the body arrived too late, for the only reflection in its clear blue eyes is of empty sky.

2

1954

Summer winds cut through the trees, making them sway and sigh, as our Morris Oxford bumps down the narrow track to the house at White Cove, causing us to jolt and slide on the hard leather seats. A median of tall grasses peppered with dandelions and other bright weeds indicates that the track sees little traffic. I have never been anywhere so remote in my life. Even the so-called 'main' road off which we turned a mile back was so narrow it would require driving partway up one of the high hedges if you met the local bus coming the other way, which of course we did.

'Do you think the removals men will be able to make it down this track?' I ask, trying to be conversational, gripping the leather grab-strap.

'I'm paying them enough.'

My mother, Magda, maintains her concentration on the twisting lane, her expression set. My negative remarks have annoyed her but, even so, I can't help but compound my error. 'That farm we passed looked rather forlorn and unloved. This is quite a lonely place.'

Magdalena's gaze slides sideways at me. 'It's people we wanted to get away from, if you recall, *dear*.' She leaves a cruel pause, then adds, 'Perhaps you might show some gratitude.'

I flush. 'I've thanked you a hundred times. What more can I do?'

'*Nie bądź głupia*, Mila. Show a bit more gumption.'

Gumption is my mother's favourite English word.

In the back seat a small voice pipes up. 'Are we there yet?'

'Janey, darling.' I turn around to regard my daughter, all five-and-a-bit years of her, her short blonde hair tousled, her cheeks pink and creased from lying in a heap of clothing, her toy rabbit crushed to her chest, and suddenly everything seems fine again. 'Did you have a good sleep?'

'No.' She is emphatic. 'This car is very uncomfortable.'

'Now then, Janeska. We must cut our coat according to our cloth,' Magdalena scolds.

'It's too hot for a coat.'

'What Granny means, darling, is that we can't afford to waste what little money we have left on fancy cars.'

'Daddy had a fancy car.'

'Your father had a lot of things. Unfortunately, honesty wasn't among them,' Magdalena says sharply. 'And don't call me Granny. It makes me sound a hundred and two.'

Janey laughs. 'Granny's a hundred and two!'

'You need to teach your daughter some manners,' Magdalena barks, slowing for a bend.

'Let's not argue. It's not the way we want to begin our

new life.' My tone is wheedling. When did I become so... limp?

As we round the bend, a gap in the hedge affords a glimpse of a white house far below, backed by dark trees, and beyond it an expanse of lush vegetation leading down to a long, curved pale strand bounded by headlands into which grey waves roll. Is that it? It must be – it's the only house in view. The house at White Cove. This is my first sight of our new home; Mother travelled alone to Cornwall for the viewing, and to the auction where she ruthlessly beat off all opposition.

We could have bought a house in the countryside outside London, I think, not for the first time. Why have we come three hundred miles west to a place where the land falls into the sea? But by the time I found out that this was Magda's plan for our fresh start, it was a fait accompli.

The brakes screech and my left shoulder collides painfully with the door as the car judders and skates across the surface of the road. Magda swears loudly in Polish as the edge of the road comes towards us at alarming speed, and I am sure we are going to tumble nose over tail into those deep, dark woods. The engine coughs and smoke drifts ominously across the windscreen as if to cloak the view of our imminent demise. As the motor sputters its last, we grate to a standstill in the long grass of the verge, the bonnet of the car pointing out to sea.

Magdalena sits there, looking startled. Then she takes a deep breath and, as if nothing out of the ordinary has just happened, says chirpily, 'There. Look at that: our little corner of heaven.'

I take a deep breath and bite back the accusation that her

careless driving almost killed us. The house does look quite magical from this vantage point, its white walls contrasting sharply with the dark woods and the green foliage. 'See, Janey,' I prompt, turning around to check she is all right. 'It's our new home.'

But my daughter has her nose pressed to the other window and is looking not down towards the sea but back at the road. I wait for her to turn and examine the house and deliver her verdict, as if she is a child-oracle and her pronouncement will determine the future tenor of our lives. In the silence I can hear her breathing – is it a bit ragged, does she have a summer cold? But then she says urgently, 'Look, Mummy – just like Rabbit!'

I crane my neck. What does she mean? And then I see it, sitting utterly still in the middle of the road: an enormous hare as white as snow, its long ears pointed skywards, its dark eyes fixed on mine. My whole spine prickles. It is an eerie moment, uncanny, a tangible connection with a spirit of the wild, a sign of wonder arcing between the human and natural worlds. Then, in the beat of a heart, the hare is gone. For a moment my vision zigzags into crazed afterimages, as if from staring at too bright a light, and I blink and blink until it steadies.

'Well,' I say, breathing again. 'How incredible.'

'You saw it too!' Janey crows. 'Did you see it, Granny? Did you see the big rabbit?'

Magda doesn't turn her head, as if she hasn't heard us.

'I think it may have been a hare,' I correct my daughter gently. 'They're bigger than rabbits.'

'It was big! And white! Just like Rabbit.' To prove this, she flourishes her companion, a small and rather threadbare toy sporting a smart blue waistcoat that I ran up for him on the Singer sewing machine. It has three tiny buttons and is lined with a scrap of paisley silk, and a little red ribbon with a lucky knot in it, made to ward off evil spirits – a secret known only to Janey and me, and to Rabbit himself. My grandmother never let me go out without a piece of red string tied around my wrist or on my pram. I still have the one Babcia, my mother's mother, tied for me – and that is how these old superstitions pass from generation to generation.

'It's rather unusual for it to be so white. Maybe it got stuck in its winter camouflage.' The explanation sounds un-likely, even to me.

Magdalena makes no reply to this, but raises her small gold crucifix to her lips, then tucks it back inside her collar. She tries to start the car again, but the Morris resists her, coughing feebly, then dying. Swearing quietly, she tries again and again, and at last it comes to a sort of half-life with a belch of smoke. Wrenching it into reverse, she backs it onto the track and we putter down the final stretch of lane to the house.

3

The property seems larger than the photograph my mother showed me after she made her visit two months ago, when the spring sun had softened its lines and dappled the light that fell across its tall windows and unruly garden with its profusion of semi-tropical plants. Now, the bright summer light is unforgiving, and the place appears inhumanly large.

Magda manoeuvres the car around in an arc on the crunching gravel, brings it to a shuddering halt and cranks the handbrake. Two crows take off cawing, disturbed by our arrival, and alight on the roof of the nearby barn. They watch as we get out of the vehicle, their heads turning as one. The air is sharp, with a tang of salt; I take a long breath deep into my lungs, where it sits like something cool and solid.

Mother lifts her chin into the breeze, her eyes narrowed, in a state of controlled ecstasy. 'Being here will do us all so much good.'

'It's certainly bracing,' I agree.

Janey starts to scramble out of the back seat. 'Beach!' she

cries, pointing, and begins to make off down the sloping lawn.

I catch up with her and grab her arm. 'No! You are not to go on the beach without me or Granny. Never. Do you hear me?' I give her a little shake to drive the point home, then haul her back towards the car.

'But I *want* to!'

'We'll go for a walk later, if you behave.'

Janey turns lucent blue eyes upon me. 'Promise?' She does not trust the word of grown-ups – and who can blame her?

'I promise. You're to sit in the car for now, while Granny and I go into the house and check some things.' I hold the door open and watch as Janey settles herself and Rabbit with a copy of the *Eagle* she demanded from the newsagent in Penzance.

'But that's for boys,' Magdalena had said, disapproving.

'She loves Dan Dare,' I'd replied. 'Let her have it; it's better than the one full of ballet dancers and boarding-school princesses.'

With another admonition to Janey, Magda and I head for the house, where a wide, pillared veranda shelters a double-width front door. Magdalena deals firmly with the three – three! – mortice locks and bolts, and pushes the doors wide, past their creaking protest, and I follow her into the hall, craning my neck at the unexpected space overhead, for the staircase winds baronially to the upper floor. Despite the sunshine outside, cold seeps through my skin and into my bones – the sort of damp cold you find only in long-unoccupied dwellings. I rub my upper arms, wishing I'd worn a coat. Magda crosses the hall, her heels clicking on the flagstones, the sound echoing, and I turn in a circle, taking in the enormous dark furniture that must have come as part of the auction lot: a vast chest carved with hearts and thistles and running animals; an ornate hall-stand, its mirror spotted with desilvering; and a long settle arranged beneath iron coat-hooks.

First impressions remind me of the Sunday school in the Surrey village to which I'd been evacuated during the war – not a happy time; yet, for an empty house, it feels oddly full, as if there are eyes on me, but it's probably just my usual anxiety at being somewhere new. I will get used to it. I'll have to. I ignore the uneasy feeling crawling over me. I'm used to the sounds of habitation, of car horns and bicycle bells, of people shouting and children laughing. How will I adapt to such stillness and silence?

Magda turns back. 'I'll get rid of this old monstrosity and put the gilded mirror just there, and potted palms by the door. And we should restore the old panelling and deep skirting board. Are you paying attention? Perhaps you should take notes as we walk around.'

Only months ago I was living in a house of my own, decorated just the way I liked it, managing my own budget...

The formal drawing room off the hall is a handsome, characterful room that must have seen a lot of life. I can imagine a blazing fire set in its vast charred hearth, warming the chattering guests gathered with their sherry, and the thought cheers me, despite the view through the long windows that gives out onto the sloping lawn, beyond which, a hundred yards away, the grey sea laps at the beach stones.

Meanwhile, Mother is muttering. 'Awful, just awful, the state it's got into. Goodness knows how we make such a huge fireplace safe for guests. I'd hate to board it over, but maybe it would be cleaner and more practical.'

I watch her tap her way into the next room, bridling at her insensitivity to the house, as if I've been privy to her insulting someone to whom she's just been introduced. I want to reassure it that whatever renovations Mother carries out will be tasteful, that she has an excellent eye for design and a love of English history that runs far deeper than that of most natives of the country.

In the quiet she leaves behind I can hear a muffled thump, low and sonorous, like the pulse of blood of some huge animal. It takes me several seconds to realise it is the sound of waves striking the distant shore.

'Long curtains,' Magdalena is saying, clearly unaware she is talking to herself, 'in a mid-blue… no, a deep green velvet, to frame the scenery.' She turns to me, frowning. 'I don't think my couches are going to work in here – they'll be dwarfed, and I think they're just too modern. We might try the local auction houses for some good chesterfields. Make a note to measure the space.'

Sighing, I jot this down. Then I doodle a spiderweb and at the centre add a spider with Magda's face.

Towards the back of the house is a large slate-floored room with windows on two sides, an old range, and chairs and tables stacked up, like a boarding-school dining room out of term, an impression reinforced by the hatch in the wall connecting to the kitchen. Out of the side window I can see a distant headland across acres of bramble and gorse; out of the back window a slope of grassy bank merges steeply upwards into shadowed woodland.

The kitchen is uncompromisingly functional with its

acres of cold marble and two deep ceramic sinks, its rusting black range and a dozen abandoned pans hanging from an iron chandelier.

Magdalena stands with her hands on her hips. 'I don't mind old-fashioned, but this is positively medieval. We'll have to get it up to scratch if we're cooking for a full house of guests.'

You mean you, *rather than* we, I think, but do not say. The idea of running a guest house in such a remote location is a daunting one; the responsibility for feeding a crowd of strangers is positively terrifying.

'We'll have a big table here,' she indicates, 'and a Frigidaire.' She crosses the room to look through the doorway. 'Another expense.' She sighs heavily, as if to signal that this is all my fault.

Beyond lies a shelved scullery and a door to the outside passage, and the corridor past that leads back into the entrance hall. 'Just wait till you see the bedrooms!' Magdalena trills.

I tail her up the wide, winding staircase. At the tall, arched window halfway up, I look out towards the car and can just make out Janey's blonde head bent over her comic. For all her energy and spirit, she's an easy child to mother. Her love of reading has provided us both with respite over the past difficult year.

Reassured, I follow Mother up to the bedrooms. There are six of these, and two bathrooms. 'You'll have to take Janey in with you until we can partition one of these,' Magdalena declares. 'We can't waste such a big room on a little girl.'

From up here the view of the sea is inescapable: four of

the six bedrooms face out towards it. Today you can't even tell where the sea ends and the sky begins. Unseasonal for July, everything is a gradation of grey, though outside it is sticky, the heat trapped beneath dark clouds that are piling up on the western side of the bay, presaging rain to come.

'When are the furniture men arriving?' I ask, keen to fill these big empty spaces with familiar objects.

Magdalena consults her watch. 'They should have been here by now. Honestly, you pay top price and still they let you down. Decide which of the two back bedrooms you prefer.'

No sea view for me.

I wander along the dim corridor. The back bedrooms are darkly curtained and long unused. There is something defeated about them, as if, deprived of life for so long, they have simply given up. Opening the curtains of the westernmost room, I look out into the eaves of the woodland above the house, and feel briefly comforted. There is something intimate about the trees and the shadows between them, the scale of the landscape smaller and less exposed than the unending sea and sky. I want to shut myself and Janey away, to hibernate until I regain my strength.

I cross the room to an enormous wooden wardrobe. The doors are closed with an ornate silver key and when I turn it, they fly open. On the inside of one of the doors is a long oval mirror. I stare at my own reflection, something I've avoided doing for some months now. Gosh, I have lost weight. My clothes are hanging off me as if I've borrowed them from a larger woman; my hair is lank, my eyes ringed. I look pale and ill, and older than my twenty-six years. *You must do something with yourself*, I tell myself fiercely; and that's when I see the coat.

It nestles in the darkness of the hanging space, but when I pull it out, I disturb a stream of golden motes. Not dust, I realise, but tiny yellow moths. The coat is made of fur with a silvery gleam. It weighs heavy in my hands. Fancy leaving such a luxurious thing behind in a derelict house.

Holding the coat up against me, I angle my shoulders, arch my neck and make a mannequin's pout. I look ridiculous, but even so, I feel compelled to unhook its hook-and-eye fastenings and slip it on. The coat caresses me, the collar cool and silky against my cheek. I can just make out the faintest whiff of face powder and of expensive scent – Givenchy, maybe, or Chanel. In a sudden excess of delight I pirouette so that the skirts of the coat flare out then settle again, like big soft cats against my legs.

'What on earth are you doing?' Magdalena is standing in the doorway. 'Did you just find that?' It's an accusation, not a question. She's annoyed that I have stumbled on a treasure before she has.

'The previous owners must've forgotten to pack it. But it seems to be infested with moths.' I take the coat off and hang it back in the wardrobe. 'We should find out who they are and write to them.'

Magdalena strides across the room and lays hands upon the coat, examining it with the critical eye of a woman well used to such finery. 'Not bad quality. I'll take it into Penzance for cleaning.'

So, not finders keepers then. I feel a flicker of anger. 'I'll take this room.'

She looks taken aback by my sudden assertiveness. Then:

'It was probably one of the servants' rooms,' she says, and bustles out to continue her assessments.

I stroke the coat's sleeve as if it is still alive. The idea that it once was disconcerts me. How awful that animals have died just to clothe some rich woman in their beauty. For a moment I feel disgusted, then sad. Poor things. Trapped in a wardrobe, locked behind a mirrored door. I wonder who the coat's owner was and how it came to be left here when the rest of the property is so empty and bereft. She must have been tall, I think, for the hem swished just above my ankles and the sleeves came halfway down my hands. Was she old or young? Lovely or plain? Did her husband buy the coat for her as a birthday gift, or out of guilt, or had she purchased it for herself in a moment of extravagance?

As if prompted by my speculations, the scent of her perfume is suddenly stronger, filling my nostrils, swirling around the room, and I feel her absence. A terrible melancholy enfolds me and suddenly I can't bear to be in the room, or the house, any longer.

I run back down the carpeted staircase and outside onto the veranda, where I take deep breaths of invigorating sea air. Then, crunching across the gravel, I go to check on Janey.

Well before I reach the car, I know it is empty. My heart comes to a standstill, then skips rapidly. There is no sign of her. Maybe she has her head bent low over her comic, but I know with terrible certainty this is not the case, even as I wrench the rear door open and duck my head inside.

The *Eagle* lies discarded on the back seat, but Janey's toy rabbit is gone. I shoot back out so violently that I scrape the top of my head on the metal doorframe, barely registering the pain.

'Janey!'

Seagulls take off from the roof and go wheeling away over the garden, their high cries mimicking my shout. Shading my eyes, I stare down the expanse of lawn and shrubs that slope down to the beach. No blonde head, no red Fair Isle jumper. I spin around, looking up towards the lane and the woodland for a moving speck of colour, but see nothing. I run back into the house, calling my daughter's name. The sound is swallowed by the empty spaces, thinned out, enfeebled.

Magdalena appears at the top of the stairs.

'She's gone!' I howl. 'Janey – she's not in the car.'

'Stop panicking!' Magda descends the stairs in no great hurry. 'She's probably just exploring.'

'But she's only five years old.'

Magdalena purses her lips. 'You always were such a timid child. At five, I'd have been up a tree by now.'

We search the downstairs rooms, which takes very little time given the lack of hiding places, then go outside again, circling the house, calling out Janey's name. We check in the bramble-wrapped greenhouse, under bushes, among the lush of vegetation that borders the stream running down the side of the garden. I run further down, almost to the beach, and find a low stone bridge made from great slabs of granite laid on short pillars across the stream and call her name again. The profusion of plants swallows my cry. Onto the beach I run, my eyes playing over the long expanse of tumbled grey-white boulders, but other than a couple of oystercatchers dabbing in the seaweed at the water's edge, nothing moves.

In despair, I call Janey's name again and again but nothing

comes back but the sea sucking greedily at the stones, the crunch as they resist the drag of the waves. I run back up the path and find my mother beside the stone barn, calling, 'Janeska, come out now! No one is angry with you, but the game is up.'

I catch up to her, breathless. 'You haven't found her?'

My mother points to the little window above the barn door. 'I saw a movement up there.'

I stare up at the dark square but see nothing. Below, the barn doors open onto an interior as black as sin. From the car I fetch the torch out of the emergency breakdown box and shine the beam in wild arcs into the obscure spaces inside the barn, illuminating scads of cobwebs, thick ropes and old nets hanging from hooks in the wooden beams, above stacks of tools and bits of machinery.

A ladder leads to the upper level. 'Give me the torch,' Magdalena demands, and snatching it out of my hand, secures it between her teeth. Pulling her pencil skirt above her knees, she starts to climb the ladder like a fearsome pirate with a cutlass.

'Be careful!' I call out, imagining woodwormed rungs and broken legs, or worse.

The bobbing circle of torchlight disappears into the loft, and then there is a yelp, followed by voices. One of these is unfamiliar and distinctly male.

4

'Who in heaven's name are you, and what on earth are you doing in our barn?'

Magdalena glares at the stranger who has just climbed down the ladder out of the hayloft, following her and Janey. Her gaze is flinty. I look around for a weapon. There is a spade just over there, leaning up against the wall. Could I get to it in time if he makes a move to attack her? Could I bring myself to use it? He is much bigger, and no doubt much stronger, than either of us: tall, broad-shouldered, with powerful features. His expression is hard to read, even when he puts his hands up in a gesture of surrender.

'Sorry, I didn't mean to alarm you. I'll leave now.'

'Not so fast.' Magdalena is adamant. 'I want to know who you are and what you're doing on our property. There is a trespass law, you know.'

Is there a flash of emotion in those deep-set eyes as he looks at her, then away. I think I catch something – anger? Wariness? I take Janey firmly by the hand and haul her close. My daughter has questions to answer too, disobeying my order to remain in the car, but she looks entirely unabashed.

'He's called Jack,' Janey pipes up. 'Aren't you?'

'Yes, mam.' He sweeps off his cap, gives her a little mock bow. He transfers his gaze to my mother, his chin tilted in defiance. 'I had no intention of trespassing. I was walking, and then I heard your car coming down the track – didn't sound too good, if you'll pardon me making such an observation – and when I saw it was two ladies travelling alone, I ducked into the barn, not wanting to make you uncomfortable. But maybe that was a poor decision and I should have stood my ground and said hello. Then, when you went into the house, I thought the coast was clear – but just as I was about to leave, your daughter spotted me and rather than making my getaway, I climbed up into the hayloft—'

'That's not my mummy, that's my granny,' Janey interrupts sternly.

'Thank you, darling.' Magdalena taps Janey's hand a shade more sharply than is strictly necessary. 'I've asked you *not* to call me that. And quite what you thought you were doing climbing that ladder… it's not at all ladylike.'

'You climbed it,' Janey points out with faultless logic.

Magda purses her mouth and returns her attention to the man. 'Why didn't you take Janey back down again at once? Surely you can see it's not right for a strange man to be alone in such a place with a child?'

He looks over Magda's shoulder, out to the vista of sea and sky beyond, a gesture at once diffident yet somehow arrogant; as if he feels she does not have the right to question him, she being the stranger here. Then he looks down at his hands, which are strangling his cloth cap, and I can see that his knuckles are white.

'Give me your full name,' Magdalena demands of him, peremptory.

He shoots a look at me and I'm sure I can see panic on his face. I know what it's like to be on the receiving end of Magda's sharp tongue.

'It's Jack,' he says. 'Jack Lord.'

'Jack's not a name for a formal introduction,' Mother says. 'John or Jonathan?'

He doesn't appear inclined to answer this and Magda purses her lips. 'I am Magdalena Prusik, and this is my daughter Mildred.'

'Mila,' I correct. 'My name is Mila.'

Mother rolls her eyes. She returns her attention to Jack Lord. 'And, of course, you've met Janeska.'

'Your daughter, ah, granddaughter, was most determined to come up and say hello to me.'

'Yes,' Janey concurs. 'I wanted to introduce you to Rabbit.' She proffers her stuffed toy.

Rabbit is in rather a sad way: one of his ears is tattered and an eye hangs on a twist of cotton, but Janey will not allow anyone to mend him.

'It was an honour to meet you and Rabbit,' Jack Lord says solemnly.

I feel my anxiety ebb into a degree of abeyance; the stranger does not seem to be immediately threatening.

'And it's very nice to meet you both,' he says. His smile transforms his grim features, makes him look younger, even handsome. 'I'm very sorry to have alarmed you.' He holds out a hand to Magdalena, who looks at it for a long moment, then folds her arms.

I stretch out my hand; my mother is so rude, no matter

the circumstances. When he shakes it, I feel an unexpected flutter of anxiety in my stomach. I haven't touched a man since Dennis.

Jack Lord withdraws his hand gently and I realise with embarrassment that I held on to it for just a moment too long.

'I'm sorry if I startled you,' he says. 'I won't trespass any longer.' He looks around wistfully. 'It deserves some care and attention, this poor old house. No one's loved it for years.'

'Do you know its history?' Magdalena pounces.

Two beats of silence.

'Not really.' He gazes around at the water-stained ceiling and peeling paint. 'It's a big place for three ladies, if you'll forgive me saying so...'

Janey stands up straighter, having just been numbered as one of the adults.

'It won't be just us when we've carried out the work,' Magdalena says crisply. 'Tell me, Mr Lord, are you familiar with the area?'

'Passably familiar. I like to walk and explore.'

'I'm an explorer!' declares Janey. 'That's how I found you. Will you show me where you've explored?'

'Quiet, madam,' Magdalena chides, before returning her attention to Jack Lord.

'I know the footpaths around here – up through the woods. They are full of bluebells in the spring, you know, and there are some very picturesque strolls out along the headland. I could show you some time, if you like to walk?'

Magdalena regards him steadily, still chilly. 'Maybe when

we know you better. What do you do down here, Mr Lord? Do you live in the village?'

He looks away. 'I live nearby and do a bit of this and that.' He sounds evasive, and perhaps realising this, he adds, 'After I was demobbed it was hard to find the sort of work I like, so I've been going from place to place doing odd jobs, and I fetched up here. Like driftwood.'

'What sort of things do you do?' I ask, but when he turns to look at me, I look away. He makes me nervous, with his penetrating eyes and his strong chin.

'Repair engines mainly – that was my job during the war. But I can mend all manner of things, paint walls, dig gardens, cut wood. A lot of women lost their menfolk, and I like to lend a hand.'

'A Jack of all trades,' Magdalena declares, pleased with her English pun.

He laughs. 'You could say that.'

'Do you work on your own account or under contract?'

'I'm not keen on working for others,' he admits. 'I prefer to take my own instructions.'

Magdalena seems put out by this. 'Are there any local firms you can think of that might be trusted to take on our project?'

Jack looks thoughtful. 'I could ask around for you. Getting some of the bigger firms to commit to spending a block of time in such a remote spot might be difficult. The access isn't the easiest, and the house has a... reputation.'

'What on earth do you mean?'

He looks uncomfortable. 'People say it's an unlucky place. Not just the house, the whole valley. It has a long, dark history.'

Magda waves this away. 'I'm not interested in gossip and fairy tales. We're making a new start here.'

Jack Lord nods. 'I apologise.' He looks suddenly up towards the hill as if his ears have picked up something the rest of us haven't heard. 'I'll take my leave.'

He makes to turn away, but Magda says sharply, 'Did you say you were a mechanic?'

Jack turns back. 'Yes, I'm pretty good with most engines.' His eyes narrow. 'Your Morris did sound rather unhappy coming down the lane.'

As if on cue, a horn sounds. The removals van has arrived up at the top of the hill. Or, to be precise, two British Road Service trucks with tarps strapped over the contents piled into their trailers come grinding down the lane.

Jack Lord puts his cap back on, draws it down over his eyes. 'I'll leave you to it, then.'

'I'd so love it if you could lend a hand with the furniture,' Magda says, unexpectedly. 'And then perhaps you could look at the Morris.' And she offers him a sudden devastating smile.

I frown. At fifty-one, my mother has an excruciating habit of flirting with attractive younger men, no matter how inappropriate the circumstances.

A second of hesitation. Jack Lord looks down, then up again. He says quietly, 'I'd be delighted to.'

A grim-faced man climbs out of the first truck, and a younger man gets out of the second, wiping blackened hands on his overalls.

'You took your time,' Magdalena says pettishly. 'And what do you think you're doing transporting our belongings in such a shoddy fashion? I paid for a proper pantechnicon.'

'Pantechnicon!' The elder of the men rolls his eyes at his companion. He is squat and balding and his face is red. 'The lady ordered a pantechnicon!' He strings the word out mockingly, makes it sound absurd and exotic.

'You couldn't get no pantechnicon down that lane!' the second man says with a laugh.

'We had to go back into town for two smaller vehicles.' The first man enunciates each syllable separately – *vee-hick-youles* – a parody of a posh English voice. 'And then we had to unload and load everything up again. And then Bobby here got a puncture.' He indicates the younger man. 'It'll cost you extra.'

'Nonsense,' says Magdalena briskly. 'I expect some local knowledge and a bit of gumption when I pay such an exorbitant amount. And if anything has been broken I shall be calling your manager.' She folds her arms and glares, and the men go grumbling to unload the trucks, furious to be bossed about by a woman, and a foreign woman putting on airs at that.

My mother can be imperious and looks as if she has stepped straight out of the pages of *Vogue* magazine, in her Dior suit and court shoes, and her auburn hair swept up into shining rolls in a similar hairstyle to that of the young queen. Give her a cloak and a trident, I think, and she'd make an excellent model for Britannia rallying her troops, Polish or not.

My father was also Polish – a fighter pilot who flew with the RAF during the war, my parents having fled ahead of the German invasion. His plane was shot down over the Channel and he was posthumously awarded a medal for bravery, but that hardly made up for the loss of a husband or father. At the time, I felt as if I'd been hit by his absence harder than Magda, who barely shed a tear, but Mother is hard to read at the best of times, always in control of herself and everything around her.

'Mila!'

I startle. 'Sorry, what?'

'I just said, why don't you take Janey for a walk around the property, or sit with her in the car, till everything has been brought in? You'll just get underfoot otherwise.'

'Let's be explorers!' Janey bounces up and down, energised by this idea.

'I'd be happy to show you some of the footpaths one day,' Jack says.

I give him a stiff nod. 'That's very kind of you, Mr Lord. Maybe when we're properly settled in.'

'Jack, please.'

I can feel Mother watching us and sense that her hostility is aimed more at me than at this stranger. Must she always lap up every drop of male attention?

'Jack,' she says now, cutting in. 'Once all is gathered in, you must stay and eat supper with us. Mila is an excellent cook. I'm sure she can stretch the evening meal to four, and I eat like a bird.' She pats her tiny waist.

'It's Janey's first night in a strange house,' I say softly.

Janey stops bouncing up and down. 'I want Jack to stay. And so does Rabbit, don't you, Rabbit?' Her toy nods floppily.

I manhandle Janey into a red duffel coat she will surely never grow into; in it, she looks more like a troglodyte than a little girl. Thrusting my arms into my own mackintosh, I tie a headscarf under my chin and dig in the Morris's boot for our wellingtons.

'Rabbit's got no wellies!' Janey complains.

'Rabbit doesn't need wellies.'

'Yes, he does, or he'll get his feet wet and die of new-mo-near.'

'Pneumonia. Have you ever seen a rabbit wearing boots?'

'They do when they're exploring.'

'Well, Rabbit is a bit of a weed when it comes to exploring and says he would rather stay warm in your pocket.'

Janey looks crossly at Rabbit, who says nothing. His eye lolls rakishly on its cotton string. 'All right, then, but you're going to have to toughen up,' she admonishes him and I wince – it's one of Magda's sayings.

Off we go, past the barn, up the narrow lane, to the post-box at the top of the hill – a reassuring sign of civilisation. From here we have a good view of the scene below, where Magdalena stands directing traffic. 'Beds first, then mattresses... Leave the longcase clock till last, unless it rains—' Her voice, crystal clear in the still air, has a powerful carrying quality and I am glad to be out of the firing line.

Around the next corner we come upon a stile leading into the woods. Janey tugs my hand. 'Let's go in there!'

I think we can follow the footpath through the woods above the house and, with luck, come out on the other side where the trees give way to furze, and find a way from there down to the gardens. And if not, we can always retrace our steps. It would be good to get a sense of my view from the bedroom window. It will allow us to get our bearings, offer a greater sense of connection.

I climb over the stile – a bit rickety, but not dangerously so – and reach back for Janey, who has already, with intense effort, lifted a foot up onto the first tall riser. The trick is to help her and ensure she doesn't fall without impinging too much on her freedom of movement. Janey is headstrong and takes umbrage easily. But she grabs my hand and fairly flies over the stile. Once we are inside the wood, it feels as if the temperature has fallen by several degrees. Underfoot there is a deep layer of undisturbed mulch, as if from many seasons of leaf-fall, and a pervasive smell of resin and rot. Bracket fungi and galls decorate the fallen trunks, but in the pockets of sunlight that pierce the canopy are little stands of wood anemone and campion. Those school nature walks in Surrey were not entirely wasted, I think, as the names pop into my head.

Janey begins to collect treasures – a stone, a pine cone. Soon the coat pocket not occupied by Rabbit is bulging. We find a big black feather, probably from the wing of a crow.

'Will he be able to fly without it? Shall we find him and give it back?' Janey asks. 'I know if I lost a feather like this I'd be very sad.'

'Let's take it with us and ask any crow we see if it belongs to them, shall we?'

This seems to satisfy her, but after a while, as if she had been bending her mind upon the subject, she says, 'It might be a she. Like the hare.'

The hare. I remembered the almost fluorescent whiteness of its fur, its disconcerting gaze. 'How do you know the hare's a she?'

Janey shrugs. 'I just do.' She skips along for a few paces, then asks, 'Do crows grow lost feathers back?'

'I'm sure they can if someone wishes hard enough for it to happen.'

'Really?' She is agog. The power of it, like being a wizard in a story. 'I will, then.' She closes her eyes and concentrates, her squinched-up face under her too-big hood resembling that of some old wisewoman. 'There. Can I keep the feather now?'

'Unless the crow asks for it back. It would be bad manners to hang on to it then, and crows can send you bad luck.'

'Okey-dokey.'

'You know Granny doesn't like you saying that.'

'You know Granny doesn't like being called Granny.'

We exchange a complicit look.

Further inside the woodland, the trees are more spaced out and the path between less obvious, obscured by the growth of brambles and nettles. 'Don't touch those,' I warn. 'They bite.'

Janey is fascinated by the hairy, serrated leaves. 'How can they bite if they've got no mouths?'

I explain my poetic licence, but the explanation does not impress her. 'So they sting, then,' she says primly, 'and that's why they're called stinging nettles! Silly Mummy.' She is growing up so fast.

In another few minutes the path seems to peter out. When I look up I see that the sky is now tinged with lilac and grey; the sun is beginning to set, and the air has taken on a new chill. A stream runs vigorously between ferns and mossy rocks. 'We'll follow this and go home,' I tell Janey. 'Water always flows downhill.'

Janey frowns. 'No, it doesn't.'

'It does, you know. It always finds a way.'

My daughter shakes her head violently. 'The sea is flat. The sea is *flat*!'

Suddenly, I feel too tired to explain tides and currents and the gravitational pull of the moon. Instead, I capture Janey's hand and try to pull her away.

'Don't want to go that way! Want to go up there!'

She strains against me with remarkable strength.

'Darling, the sun is going down. If we go any further we'll get lost.'

'I want to get lost!'

'Janey!' I give her arm a tug, but she squirms and roars, the warning signs of one of her infamous tantrums, and we tussle. Before we know it, Rabbit has flown out of her pocket and fallen into the stream. She's so bound up in getting her own way that for a long moment she doesn't register my shout about her lost toy, and by the time she realises what's happened, Rabbit has disappeared in the tumbling water.

'Rabbit!' Janey wails and starts to hurtle towards the stream, towing me along with her, slipping and skidding until we find our way barred by a thick stand of wild hydrangea that merges into a bramble thicket, which brings us to a halt.

'Hell.' A wash of exhaustion is sweeping all my strength away.

Janey casts a glance up at me and I expect her to be tear-stained and panicky, but instead, seeing my expression, she says, 'Don't be scared, Mummy. It's a nice wood. It likes us. Rabbit will be safe here, I can feel it.'

I smile at my whimsical child. 'Are you sure?'

Janey nods emphatically. 'Rabbit will be fine.'

We're both tired and confused and I'm longing to leave these woods. 'Can we go home now?' I ask, knowing better than to demand. The light is failing as the sun dips behind the hill. 'We'll come up here again tomorrow and make sure we find Rabbit.'

To my amazement, she agrees. I feel so enervated, I allow Janey to lead me. We forge a path into the deepening gloom where the woods thicken again. I look back over my shoulder to be sure of my bearings and as I do so a green-white light appears in my peripheral vision and in a whoosh envelops then whips past me. An afterimage zigzags crazily, haloing and expanding till I can hardly see anything at all. I close my eyes but it's still there, scintillating in a leaping, jagged horned crescent. My back feels as if it's alight, but not with heat – with cold flame, green-white fire.

'Mummy, Mummy, you're hurting me!'

'I'm sorry, darling.' I readjust my grip. 'Did you see that?'

'See what?'

I shake my head. 'Nothing, darling. I think I've got a migraine coming on.'

'I'll look after you. This way,' Janey says confidently. She hauls me along until a sort of path appears between the trees, and then we are out in the open, in a field bisected by a narrow footpath that leads steeply down to a gap in a hedge, and beyond that the shape of a house. Our house, I realise.

The jagged lights dance and shatter across my vision and my mouth floods with bitter saliva. Turning aside, I throw up violently, my head pounding with light and cascading black stars.

★ ★ ★

I must have lost consciousness, for the next thing I know I'm lying on my back in the cold, and all I can see is an immensity of blackness pinpricked with white – but these, I realise, adjusting my focus, are actual stars, not my visual disturbances. What happened? Why am I out here in the chill night? I put a hand out – wet grass? I dully remember being in a wood, the sound of running water, being towed along...

Terror strikes. Where is Janey? I try to sit upright, too fast; my head swims and nausea rises again. I take deep breaths. It's just a migraine. I get them sometimes when I'm tired or stressed. But where is my daughter? The fear is an echo of the fear I felt this afternoon when Janey was nowhere to be seen, but this time, without Magdalena to bully me into quiescence, it swells into a certainty of catastrophe. Janey lost forever, fallen over a cliff, down a hole in the ground, taken by wild animals, drowned in the sea.

'Janey!' I shout when I can gather enough air to call out, but the sound that emerges is shrill and feeble.

I push myself into a half-slumped, half-kneeling position and look around. Behind me the dark woods loom against a dark sky. An owl hoots eerily but nothing moves. No little red coat, no little blonde head. I take deep breaths to control my fear. Far below, moonlight traces a silver path across the sea and a single silent gull planes across my field of vision, serene and unconcerned by our human drama. Its muted cry drifts through the night air.

But when the sound comes again the hairs on the back of my neck rise. It's not a gull: it's Janey.

'Mummy, Mummy!' And here she is, in her red duffel coat, running uphill towards me with her arms flung wide.

'Oh my God, Janey!'

The tiny figure cannons into me and we merge into a hug of pure relief.

'I brought help!' Janey crows. 'Jack, here she is!'

Looking over my daughter's shoulder, I see a figure looming out of the darkness – a man – the man from the barn, and he scoops me up as easily as if I am myself a child.

'Hold tight,' he says, and I feel the warmth of his body through our clothes.

5

When I open my eyes, I am floating, disembodied, between realms. Above me, strings of light leap and dance. It takes a few seconds to realise these are reflections from sunlight striking the glass of water beside me on the nightstand and not the visual disturbances of my aura migraine. I am in my narrow bed, in the back bedroom of the house.

I piece together the events of the previous day and soothe my rising panic with the memory of losing, then finding, Janey not once but twice. I recall the uncanny sensation that flowed through and past me in the woods, the flashes of light. It seems my migraines are getting worse. Then I remember Jack picking me up, and the momentary sense of safety I felt as he lofted me in his arms. But there is no comfort to be had from that, for hovering in the background, dark and ominous, are the greater events that have landed me here. The weight of shame and responsibility comes crushing down on me again. How foolish I have been. Moving here was an attempt to leave that bad situation far behind, and to keep Janey away from wagging tongues. She's an innocent in all this.

I should feel optimistic, keen for this new challenge. But I don't. Why have I allowed myself to be bullied into sinking every penny gained from Mother's dirty little deal into this broken-down house at the end of the world? I could have bought a little cottage somewhere out of the way; no one would ever have known. Yet here I am in this place called West Penwith. Even the name has a wistful, faraway sound to it, as if it does not describe somewhere in the real world but a location where normal rules no longer apply, a place where you get lost in woods three minutes from your house, and strange animals appear out of nowhere on the road in front of you and cause your normally efficient mother to run the car off the road.

And it is so damned quiet, other than the distant rumble of the sea.

I miss the bustle and traffic of southeast London: the newsagent's on the corner, the bakery opposite, the scruffy park down the road, the smell of diesel fumes and coal fires, the constant noise of people shouting and laughing, the squealing brakes of the omnibus. And I miss Dennis.

With a sigh, I push myself into a sitting position and look across the cavernous room to Janey's bed. It's empty, but the covers are rumpled. My daughter is an early riser, always excited to start a new day. In this, Janey resembles her grandmother. I haul on a dressing gown and stick my feet into yesterday's shoes in order to make it to the bathroom without impaling my soles with splinters from the uncarpeted floorboards. There, I have a desultory wash and wonder how Janey managed so stealthily to slip out of bed and clothe herself without waking me.

Downstairs I find my mother – impeccably turned out

in a navy dress with a brightly patterned silk scarf tossed around her shoulders – sitting with her elbows balanced on the arms of a carver chair, cupping a mug of tea and with her legs stretched out, crossed at the ankle. She is wearing a pair of mid-heeled brogues, the only concession to our rural relocation.

The range door is open and waves of heat waft out of it, making the utilitarian room almost hospitable, and I am taken aback at my mother's hidden skills. Janey is at the table, applying herself to a large bowl of cornflakes. Sugar is scattered across the tabletop and a bottle of fresh milk – half-empty, its top discarded – stands in the middle of the table.

'Better late than never, darling,' Magda says, raising a perfectly pencilled eyebrow. 'Whatever have you got on?'

I've hauled on a mustard-yellow blouse and a pair of baggy twill trousers that I have had to belt, having lost so much weight. 'I thought there would be work to do.' How typical of Mother not even to ask me how I am after my collapse last night, not that it is any surprise. She has never been the most maternal of women and has, to say the least, a brisk attitude to human frailty.

'You're a sight for sore eyes! I hope you're feeling better. I was worried about you.'

Jack Lord's tall frame fills the doorway. He proffers a mug of tea as if he is the host and I the visitor. 'I'm sorry, I don't know how you take it. I've added milk, but no sugar?'

What is he doing here? A shiver of disquiet runs through me. Did he sleep here overnight? And if so, where? I can't believe even my mother would be so shameless. I shoot a look at her, but she is as sleek and self-contained as a pedigree cat. He must have returned early this morning at Magda's request – that would explain the working range, given that she hasn't mastered it yet and no doubt realised I wouldn't be well enough to undertake the task myself.

I take the mug, nodding my thanks and sit down beside my daughter. 'Much better, thank you.' I can't look at him. His presence is too much to deal with this early in the morning. Is it early? I glance at my wristwatch and am shocked to see it is almost ten o'clock. Leaning away from his gaze, I stroke Janey's fringe out of her eyes. 'Did you sleep, sweetheart?'

Janey swallows the last spoonful of cornflakes. 'Yes, Mummy, but Rabbit ran and ran all night and is completely whacked!'

Completely whacked: exactly what Dennis used to say when he returned from one of his week-long trips.

I frown. 'Have you found him, then?'

'No, but I know Rabbit's been having big adventures.'

Looking closer, I see she has mud under her fingernails and a smear of it down one cheek. 'Honestly, Mother, didn't you give Janey a bath before putting her to bed last night?'

'No, darling. It's about time that Janeska learned to take care of herself. Besides, giving children baths was never my forte. I deliberately stepped out of the domestic sphere.' Magdalena rolls her eyes at Jack. 'I'm far too old to be playing nursemaid.'

'Nonsense, Mrs Prusik,' Lord says, gallantly on cue. 'You could never be described as too old for anything.'

'Such flattery,' Magda preens.

I feel nauseated. Her flirting gets worse with each passing year, as if she feels ugly old age pressing in on her. 'You'll be running around after plenty of people if we get this place up and running,' I snap, surprising myself. Goodness, Mila, a bit of backbone.

'*Once*,' corrects Magdalena. 'Once we get the guest house up and running. It's a joint enterprise. And when Janeska is at school it'll be you doing most of the "running around", darling, not me. I shall be *managing*.'

Yes, I think, *that's why I'm here*. To cook and skivvy: the price I pay for being a good little housewife to Dennis and impressing my mother with delicious meals when she came to visit us.

A flicker of unreadable emotion runs across Jack Lord's features. 'You're intending to run a guest house here?'

'Why, yes. The agent told me the house was a most successful guest house before the war, so we are going to get it smartened up again and advertise it as a respite from life in the city, for those who need good clean air and coastal walks.'

He nods thoughtfully. 'I see.'

Magdalena narrows her eyes at him. 'Is that all you have to say? "I see"?'

'It seems a rather large project to take on, that's all.'

'You think we're not up to it?' Magda braces her shoulders, then laughs. 'Well, obviously Mila is a little fragile. She's been through a great deal, but after some sea air and time away from the city I'm sure she'll be right as rain in no time. Won't you, *moj aniołku*?'

My angel. Not my mother's usual style of addressing me; she's trying to make a good impression. 'Yes, of course. I don't know what came over me yesterday. My migraines aren't usually that intense. I was very tired, I suppose, with the stress of the move. But,' – I offer Jack Lord a narrow look – 'as I'm sure you can see for yourself, Mother's capable of anything.'

'I can imagine.' He gives a wry smile, no doubt remembering her fierce bossing of the hapless removals men.

'You said yesterday, Mr Lord, that you did not know anything of the house's history,' Magdalena goes on.

'I didn't quite say that,' he demurs.

'So what do you know?' she presses.

'Just that as a business, it never quite seems to work.'

'Why?' The word slips past my lips.

Lord looks uncomfortable. 'I doubt any of the rumours are reliable, so it's probably best I don't say anything more.'

Magdalena sighs loudly. 'Really, Mr Lord, it's only gossip. I know enough to take it with a pinch of salt. I was rather hoping you might be our eyes and ears down here, help us get to know our neighbours, but I can see I shall have to be more persuasive.' She pouts, then adds, 'Now do tell me about the local church. I realise there won't be much of a Catholic community down here, so I will have to make do with whatever I can find.'

Jack turns his face away. 'To be honest, I don't have much time for church.'

Magda leans back, displeased. 'Well. I expect I shall find out all I need to know one way or another. But thank you so much for bringing the milk and lighting the stove. It was most kind of you.'

He is dismissed; I know that peremptory tone. But Jack stays there, propped against the door jamb, his wide shoulders filling the space as if waiting for something.

Janey breaks the heavy silence as her spoon rattles in her empty bowl. 'I had two bowlfuls of cornflakes!' she announces. 'Granny said I could because I needed to four… four…'

'Fortify yourself,' Magda supplies, pushing herself to her feet. 'Yes, dear, we all have lots of work to do. I am going to drive into town to see the surveyor, and you and Mummy are going to do some cleaning.'

'I have to find Rabbit!'

'Cleaning first, Rabbit later.' Magda wags a finger.

'She's five—'

'It's never too soon to learn how to clean a house.'

Does she have any idea how unpleasant she sounds when she says such outrageous things? 'Janey lost Rabbit last night. I do think we should try to find him before he's ruined,' I say quietly but firmly.

Magda glares at me. 'It's just a stuffed toy. You're not here for a free ride,' she says nastily. So much for the good impression.

Is this how it's going to be? I wonder. Slavery as punishment for my sins, punishment that's extended even to my daughter? We're going to be trapped in this wretched house unless I feel strong enough to march the two and a half miles uphill to the village of Eglosberyan, and even that's hardly a bustling metropolis. Otherwise, it's five miles along the winding lanes to the fishing village of Mousehole, or the best part of eight to Penzance, the nearest town.

Janey leaps from her chair and starts stamping around the room. 'Rabbit! Rabbit! Rabbit! Rabbit!'

I reach a hand to my daughter. 'Come on then, let's go and search for him.' If Mother's going to stop us she'll have to make a scene in front of Jack Lord. But she doesn't say a thing. I expect I will pay for this later.

In the hall, I bundle Janey into her duffel coat and wellies, and together we flee the house, leaving Jack and my mother to their own devices.

After an hour of retracing our steps in the woodland, even splashing our way down the stream, we have to concede defeat. There is no sign of Rabbit at all.

'I'm so sorry, Janey.' I squeeze her hand consolingly, but she is dogged.

'I know Rabbit's here somewhere.'

'Yes, darling, he must be. But we've looked and looked.'

'We haven't looked everywhere. We *have* to find Rabbit.' Her mouth turns down. Rabbit is her special friend – she talks to him incessantly.

I allow her to lead me around the fringes of the stream, right the way back down to the edge of the wood, where the stream passes into a natural culvert. I stare down into the dank darkness of this narrow tunnel. I should have brought a torch, I think, feeling defeated, but Janey is undeterred.

'Rabbit's not in there!' She tugs me onward.

'How do you know?'

'Because Rabbit is surrounded by gold,' she declares.

My strange little girl. 'Perhaps he's washed up among buttercups and dandelions?' I suggest.

Janey gives me an aggrieved look. 'I didn't say *flowers*,' she corrects me.

'Sunlight, then? That's golden.'

She sighs extravagantly.

Sunshine or flowers notwithstanding, we can find no trace of Rabbit and at last we emerge into the top end of the house's grounds, having crashed through bracken and ferns, following the stream, to no avail.

Back home, Janey throws herself face down on her bed and cries and cries. Her sobs rack me as I hold her close and try unsuccessfully to comfort her.

'I thought he loved me!' she wails, and her words strike right to the core of me. 'But he's gone.'

Just like Dennis, I think. *Just like Dennis.*

At the end of the summer of 1948 I was working as a cashier at the bank. Every day a handsome man would come in on some pretext, looking so dashing in his RAF uniform that the other girls would stop whatever they were doing to slick on more lipstick and eye him voraciously, but he ignored them. Instead, he would sweep off his cap, run a hand through his unruly blonde hair and beam at me, only me, with his clear blue eyes. He was a fair bit older than me but I liked that.

His name was Dennis, he told me. He had to ask me four times before I agreed to take a cup of tea with him – for what harm could there be in that? I hadn't been bargaining for him to pick me up outside the bank in a gleaming sports car with its canvas top rolled down, but I'd enjoyed the way the other girls cooed over it, and him. Foolishly, I revelled in their jealousy. Fancy mousy little Mila landing a chap like that! He handed me a silk scarf to protect my hair (I had not at the time questioned how he had come to have such a thing in the car) and, instead of taking me to a local corner house, had driven us out of London, deep into the country lanes of Kent. My initial disquiet was replaced by exhilaration as we flew around the corners and the wind whipped my words of protest away, and by the time we arrived at a charming public house with ivy covering its ancient front, I was laughing at his sheer effrontery, and aroused by the confident way he handled the vehicle.

He said he'd grown up not far from there, in the pretty Kent countryside. He talked about the cars he'd owned and raced, and how he'd spun his BRM off the track at Castle Combe, and won at Gransden and Lulsgate Aerodrome, names that meant nothing to me but sounded wonderfully glamorous. I liked his easy manner and his teasing questioning – did I have a boyfriend, and why not, since I was so pretty? He'd made me both pleased and flustered so that I had to look away, but when I looked up I found him watching me intently.

'You are exceptionally pretty, you know.'

I felt the warmth that rose up into my cheeks. No one had ever said such a thing to me. I knew I was no beauty. My mother – my elegant, stylish mother – was always telling me so. 'You really must do something with your hair, dear. Perhaps go blonde? You'll never get a man looking the way you do.' For a moment I experienced a piercing moment of triumph. *How wrong you were, Mother.*

'I'm not pretty,' I managed limply. 'Don't be silly.'

He reached across the table and took my chin in his hand and my insides rippled with flame.

'Oh, I'm many things, but never silly. In fact, right now, I'm very serious indeed.' And then – in full view of anyone who might be looking – he kissed me.

He made me so nervous that I wasn't able to eat a thing, but I drank three glasses of wine, and this made him laugh.

'Life's too short to be miserable, isn't it? You have to seize the day.' He clinked his glass on mine. 'Bottoms up.'

The war had filled us all with a devil-may-care spirit. We had been close to death for year on year – whether watching bombs fall on our cities or – as Dennis described – seeing the tracer of a Heinkel's ammunition coming straight for him as he piloted his Hurricane over the Hampshire Downs. 'I caught a clear glimpse of the German pilot,' he told me. 'He had pushed his goggles up – I could see his eyes, as light as ice. I pushed my plane into such a sharp dive I thought I was going to black out, and he stayed on my tail the whole time. But in the end it was me who managed to pull out of the dive, but his engine stalled and he smashed right into the hills.'

I gasped. How brave he was. And how warmly he spoke of the Polish pilots he had flown with – their courage and their shared hatred of the Germans who had invaded their country. He had even picked up a phrase or two of Polish from them. When he dropped me back home that first night, he had whispered '*dobranoc*' in my ear. The last time I had heard that word was when my father tucked me into bed. That night I went to bed dreaming of a time when I felt safe and loved. By morning my nostalgia for this lost world had transmuted itself into hot desire for Dennis.

And after that I knew, though I would never have admitted it to my mother, that even had I known Dennis was married with two little boys, I would still have gone to bed with him on our next date, would still have gone on seeing him, would still have moved into our little house in

East Dulwich, would still have had Janey and lived in sin with him, for ever and ever.

I go in to look in at Janey later that evening as she sleeps. Her cheeks are flushed, and when I bend over to tuck the quilt around her, I can see that her eyes are moving rapidly beneath the lids. She makes a little snuffling sound, then her lips draw into a satisfied bow. She is dreaming and I am entranced. My perfect little girl. At least something good came out of my time with Dennis. Something miraculous.

6

For the next few days it rains. Not incessantly, not in downpours, but with sufficient intent to render outdoor activities unenticing. Even the air seems grey. You can't tell where sky and sea diverge; the headland is barely visible – a shadow in a Victorian watercolour. The weather keeps us penned indoors like overwintering cattle, even though it's late July. Confined to the house, Janey has started to teach herself the alphabet. I reward her efforts with the English cakes and biscuits I am teaching myself to bake, ahead of catering for guests when – if – we open next year. We are both good students. I had already mastered madeira cake and fruitcake, now I can also make shortbread and ginger snaps. Meanwhile, Janey has, after Apple, Bird, Caterpillar, Dog and Egg, reached F for Fish.

Magda is thrilled to have had her car fixed. She flutters her eyelashes at Jack as if she is Jean Harlow. 'It's running so smoothly. What clever hands you have, Mr Lord…'

At least this gets her out of the house instead of 'helpfully' overseeing my efforts to organise the kitchen into a workable space and suggesting unfeasible menus for me to practise. ('Lobster thermidor, Mila – that's the sort of dish we should be offering our guests. We want to be a top-drawer establishment – no cottage pie or steak and kidney pie here!') This means, however, that Janey and I are left alone with Jack working on the other side of the kitchen wall, constructing new shelves for the old pantry. The close proximity of a strange man does not appear to bother Janey at all. She keeps running to show Jack her latest drawing. I can hear them talking and laughing as if they have known each other all of Janey's five years. I find myself feeling oddly excluded, fretful – a little jealous, even, before chiding myself at such foolishness. Of course my little girl misses her father and is keen to forge a bond with the nearest available substitute. And as long as I am here to watch over her, she can come to no harm.

I can't quite bring myself to trust so easily. There is something about Jack Lord – so quiet, so capable, so apparently pleasant – that sets me off balance. I sense hidden depths behind those dark eyes, and he is an enigma. I have no idea where he lives, how he spends his time, and he rarely answers a direct question.

As if summoned by my thoughts, Jack puts his head around the door. 'Would you care to take a look at the shelves I've done and see if you need them at the same height on the other side, or if you'd rather I spaced them differently?'

I hang the last saucepan on the new rack he installed yesterday and follow him to the pantry. The tiny room seems too small to contain both of us. I can feel his breath on my neck as he speaks.

'I reckoned you might need catering-sized containers

down here for staples like potatoes and flour and onions and such,' he says, indicating the deep space beneath the bottom shelf. 'I could make big drawers on casters so that you can pull them out easily.'

We agree on this, and on the spacing of the shelves. He measures up the remaining area and makes some notes. His handwriting is small and very clear. He forms his letters slowly, with no flamboyant flourishes, no loops or dashes. He writes the 'a's with a cap on top, the way they are printed in books. The style is not quite cursive, as if he is reining it in, or has to think carefully about each word as he writes it. I wonder if this means that he is not entirely literate, then catch myself in this thought and realise how demeaning it is that I should think him less educated than me because he works with his hands. I remember the painful English lessons I suffered at the Marchant's Hill School to which I was evacuated at the age of eleven with barely any English, a huge hangar of a place where I had been subjected to incessant bullying by both the boys and the girls, little humiliations and sly teasing. I put a brave face on it – you had to if you didn't want to be bullied harder – and learned my new language with grim determination. I shouldn't judge this stranger as cruelly as those children did me.

Jack carries on with his work on the pantry while I finish my inventory in the kitchen, making lists of all the cutlery and crockery and linen we will need to purchase: the glasses and condiment sets, the steak knives and fish knives, egg cups and sugar tongs, individual French butter dishes – the list gets longer and longer, and more arcane. By the time I have got down to fish kettles I fling my pen down in disgust.

Why am I even considering the requirements for poaching a whole salmon when we are months off opening as a guest house and may never even get that far? The upstairs rooms are damp, drab and unfurnished; the roof leaks; the chimney spews smoke into the drawing room – 'Probably jackdaws' nests,' Jack advised us cheerfully – the plumbing complains like a bellicose donkey. In a wind the timbers throughout the house creak as is if we're aboard a ghost ship, and the whole place smells of mildew and mouse droppings. Who would want to come here – to stay for just a week – let alone live here forever?

With my heart in my boots, I go to check on Janey at the table in the dining room where she's working on her alphabet drawings. I pick up her latest sketch. 'This is lovely!' I grin at her. 'But haven't you skipped over a lot of letters?'

She gives me a puzzled look. Every day I feel as if I am falling further in her estimation in one way or another. 'Silly Mummy,' she chides. 'It comes after G for Giraffe!' She flourishes the previous drawing at me – a creature with an impossibly long, bendy neck with its face plunged into a corona of leaves at the top of the tree.

'I thought it was R for Rabbit,' I say, compounding my error.

Janey shakes her head sadly at my hopeless inadequacies. 'I bet Jack will know what it is,' she says, taking the page from me and running off to find him.

Curious, I follow her to the pantry, trying not to look too much like a spy.

'That's really good,' I hear him say. 'You've got the long ears and rangy body just right.'

'Mummy thought it was a rabbit.' Janey's voice is low and condemnatory. 'But I've lost Rabbit.'

'Have you still not found him?'

I can see the back of my daughter's head, the short blonde curls bouncing as she shakes it. 'No. He fell in the stream in the woods, but he's not there any more. He can't have gone far, though, because I can still *feel* him. And the person who lives here tells me he's all right.'

The person who lives here? 'What person, darling?' But her expression has closed up again.

After a while Jack says gently to her, 'When I was your age I used to sense... not voices, exactly, but a presence, in the wild places near where I lived. I think that means, though, that whoever it is will be keeping an eye on Rabbit and making sure no harm comes to him, don't you?'

'Maybe.' Janey seems doubtful.

'I tell you what,' Jack says. 'I've pretty much finished what I can do here today. If it's stopped raining and your mother says it's all right, I'll help you look for Rabbit. How does that sound?'

Janey does a little jump for joy, then she turns and I have to step swiftly back into the kitchen before she catches me snooping.

'Mummy, Mummy, Jack's going to help me look for Rabbit!'

I shoot a glance out of the rain-patterned window. There is a line of silver emerging from beneath the billows of grey cloud and the spatters of raindrops on the glass are no longer coagulating into runnels. I can feel the tug of the outdoors, of fresh air and an escape from confinement. 'All right. Go and put your drawing things away, and get your wellies and coat on, and I'll come with you.'

I gird myself for the excruciation of polite small talk with a stranger that will mean tiptoeing around the dark edges of the real reason we have come all the way down here, the disaster of my marriage, the scandal that trails behind us, my supremely poor judgement, my mother's contempt, Janey's sadness. But, for that last reason, I must commit myself to this ordeal. Rabbit is her dearest companion, the one to whom she confides her thoughts and fears. She sleeps with him tucked under her arm; they share their dreams; she cries into his fur; they have a secret language, secret jokes. They gang up on me. Rabbit helps to keep Janey strong and stable. Somehow, somewhere, we must find him.

Jack meets us out front on the veranda in his battered old waxed jacket and his sturdy boots. Janey has on her favourite red duffel coat and matching wellies. She has done the toggles up unevenly, so I have to undo them and do them up again.

She insists on taking Jack's hand and making me walk on her other side. 'Swing me! Swing me!' she demands, just as she used to do with Dennis and me on Peckham Rye.

Hot fire burns behind my eyes at this memory and I force it away by sheer willpower. I cannot let Jack Lord see me cry, or the questions will be never-ending.

Janey tells Jack in great detail where it was that Rabbit fell into the stream and we walk up the lane to that exact spot in the woods and begin to track back down the valley towards the house. I have already walked this way with Janey in our efforts to find the toy, but the woods feel very different this time, as if they are watchful, aware of our presence. It is not a hostile atmosphere, not menacing, but somehow 'full' – not just with sound and colour, but with life. As we walk deeper in, something shrieks loudly in the trees ahead – an eerie, almost-human scream – and I catch a brief flash of colour, azure blue, before it vanishes again.

'Ow!'

I have squeezed Janey's hand too tightly in my momentary panic.

'It's a jay,' Jack says. 'Just a jay, one of the crow family. Sorry – they do have a very noisy cry. We disturbed it, that's all.'

He points out to us the flowers and plants that we pass – wood anemones, harts tongue ferns, foxgloves, sorrel – and the tracks of woodland animals. 'See, a badger's made that tunnel through the undergrowth. They're big animals.' He shows Janey by spreading his hands wide. 'Perhaps you could draw me one.'

'I've already done B,' says Janey reasonably. 'And anyway I don't know what a badger looks like. Perhaps if we hide up here in the woods at night I could see one and then I could draw him for you!'

'I don't think we'll be doing that,' I say crisply.

Jack laughs. 'It's the sort of thing I used to do as a lad. I made a hide out of branches and ferns and lay in it all night once to watch the hedgehogs in the garden.'

'I know what hedgehogs look like!' Janey crows. 'Mummy read me *Mrs Tiggywinkle* and it had pictures.'

'These hedgehogs were not wearing aprons or dresses, I can tell you,' Jack says with a grin.

'I know *that*. I'm not a *baby*.' She stumps off a little way ahead of us, splashing in and out of the stream, leaving me alone with the disconcerting stranger.

'Did you grow up in the country, then?' I ask Jack as an awkward silence stretches between us.

'Yes,' he says shortly but does not elaborate.

We catch up with Janey where the stream disappears underground. She is on her hands and knees, peering into the dark culvert. 'Rabbit was here,' she pronounces, 'but he's not here any more.'

'Are you sure?' Jack kneels beside her, pushes his jacket sleeve up and plunges his arm down into the water to feel around. 'No Rabbit,' he says after a while. 'But the water is moving quite strongly. If he fell into the stream he'll probably have been carried further down. I know where the stream comes out. Follow me.'

He beats a path through the undergrowth, and Janey and I follow, lifting our legs high over the nettles and brambles and hogweeds. At last we emerge from the woods just above the house and Jack leads us down through the bracken to where the stream runs clear again and we follow it behind the barn and along the furthest margin of our grounds. Still no sign of Rabbit, though Jack checks every step of the way.

'Sorry, darling,' I say to Janey. 'It's not looking very hopeful.'

'He must be here somewhere!' she cries. 'He can't just have disappeared!'

'People disappear all the time,' Jack says quietly.

I look at him, waiting for more, but his expression is closed off, distant. I wonder why he would say such a thing if he has no intention of explaining or softening it.

'Well, Rabbit isn't one for disappearing,' Janey says

crossly. She runs down the grassy bank, calling his name, as if his fake fur ears will prick up somewhere in the shadowy depths of his hiding place and he will find the sudden ability to call out, 'I'm here!'

The stream tumbles down between rocky banks fringed by huge plants Jack says are called 'gunnera', their leaves each as large as an open umbrella. The character of the garden here is lush and tropical, and I say so.

Jack smiles. 'It's pure magic. You can grow just about anything around here if you have the knack. It's where London gets all its early flowers and potatoes, you know.'

He bashes a path for himself among the jungly vegetation to be sure Rabbit hasn't got jammed between the rocks, or got washed up among the tangled root systems, and my mind drifts back to my little house in London with its pocket handkerchief garden and privet hedge. I loved making a nest for my little family, even down to scrubbing the tiled floors, repainting its flaking walls, stocking up the coalhole. I missed our neighbours: the Porters on the left – Jenny and Allan and their three children – and the lovely Jamaican family on our right – Rita and Bobby and the stream of aunties and cousins who came and went, all of whom had come across the ocean from Kingston on the *SS Empire Windrush*. Being a part of a city putting itself back together after the war was exciting, full of promise and potential; having Janey was the stake Dennis and I had laid down in our future. Or at least I thought we had.

'What's the matter, Mummy? Are you sad that we can't find Rabbit? I'm sad too, but you mustn't cry.'

Janey is staring up at me in consternation and when I reach my hand to my cheek, my fingers come away wet.

I dash the tears away and smile at her. 'Sorry, darling. I'm sure we'll find him.'

'I'm less worried about him now,' says my contrary child. 'He says *he'll* find *me* soon. Look, we're close to the sea now. Let's go to the beach!'

Jack comes crashing back down the stream bank, empty-handed. I turn away slightly so that he does not see my tear-blotched face. 'Thanks so much for your help, Mr Lord,' I say formally, adopting Magda's brisk tone when dismissing unwanted company. 'You really have done everything you can, but I think we're going to have to give up the search. I'm going to take Janey down to the beach now.'

He shrugs, unperturbed. 'I'll come with you. I love being close to the sea.'

There seems to be no getting rid of him.

The path takes us down over the low, rudimentary bridge where the stream tumbles to the shore through tangles of tamarisk and a great expanse of white, sea-smoothed stones leading down to the sea. Balancing on the granite boulders takes every ounce of my concentration, but Janey skips across them as if the soles of her feet share a secret understanding with the laws of gravity and equilibrium. I can't recall a time when I ever moved so confidently, with so little fear. Yet despite all my caution through life, I didn't manage to avoid disaster. Perhaps there's a lesson in that.

I walk along the beach with my hands deep in my pockets, keeping my daughter in the corner of my gaze as Janey kneels by a rockpool, examining it with the intense fascination of a neophyte, all thoughts of Rabbit apparently abandoned. Kicking through the dried seaweed, I scatter disembodied crab claws and things that look like dried black seedcases. I pick one up. It's hard and leathery, with spiky corners, odd and alien.

'That's the eggcase of a skate,' Jack tells me. 'We call them mermaid's purses.'

'How curious. Why would mermaids need purses?'

He laughs. 'Who knows? To keep their trophies in? The mermaids down here aren't necessarily the sweet, pretty ones you see in storybooks, but ravenous creatures who sing sailors to their deaths. I'll have to take you to Zennor one day and show you the carving of Morveren the mermaid there. She was drawn to church every Sunday to sing with the choir, and with the power of her voice she enticed handsome young Mathey Trewella away under the sea with her; neither was seen again on dry land. That's the romantic version of the tale, at least. Stories about the spirits of the place down here aren't always so benign.'

I laugh. 'Your mermaids have nothing on the creatures in the tales where I come from.'

As we watch Janey hopping in and out of the lacy surf, laughing her head off as the little waves rush and bubble at her, I tell Jack about *rusalkas* and *mamunas,* the monstrous creatures enshrined in the folklore of Kasina Wielka, the village in southern Poland where I lived with my grandmother and her sister while Mother worked in the city.

'The *rusalkas* tempt men they fancy into a lake and wrap them with weed and drag them into the depths.'

'And then what? Do they have their way with them?'

'They eat them.' I grin.

'And the *mamunas?*'

'The old hags lie in wait for new mothers and steal their

children, putting a changeling in their place. The only way to protect against them is to tie a red string around your child's wrist, or on their pram or clothing.'

'Women, eh?' He raises his brows. 'What savage creatures you are!'

'Not me,' I say, pulling up my sleeve to show him my piece of knotted red string. 'I've always worn it since leaving home.' By 'home' I mean Poland. 'This is the knot Babcia – that's Polish for "granny" – tied for me.'

'When did you come to England?'

'Just before the war broke out. We came to London, but then I was evacuated to Surrey.'

I watch Janey beginning to climb one of the rocks further up the beach and make to get to my feet to stop her.

'She'll be fine,' Jack says. 'It's a soft landing.'

I sit back down, watching my daughter like a hawk.

'Mummy, Mummy!' Janey is standing on top of the big rock, queen of the castle. We wave at one another.

'So, what brought you here from Surrey?' Jack asks. 'Penwith is where all the refugees and misfits wash up. Everyone who comes down here is trying to escape something. What are you escaping from, Mila?'

My inner self wriggles like a skewered butterfly. 'Oh, we didn't live in Surrey. We went back to London after the war, so the city, I suppose,' I say vaguely. 'All the noise and dirt and bustle, you know. But really it was Magda's decision.'

'Does your mother make all your decisions for you?' He gives me a wry look, and I notice how there are caramel flecks in the dark brown of his irises, and more crow's feet around his eyes than I realised.

He makes me so uncomfortable. I look away from him.

'Oh! I can't see Janey.' I shove myself to my feet and go running up the beach to the rock she had climbed upon, but there's no sign of her.

Jack comes thundering past me. We both stare around – at the empty beach, the outcrops of granite, the dark vegetation coming down to the shore.

I shout her name over and over, my voice rising into a wail. There's no reply. Suddenly, Jack starts running towards the sea, flinging off his coat as he goes. I see a scurf of sand fly up where it lands, plumes of water dance into the air as he crashes through the surf, and then he is immersed in the water where I can see a shape in the shallows like the hump of a seal... or a little girl. I let out a hoarse cry. Staggering down to the waterline, I almost trip on something caught in a net of seaweed, lapped by the incoming rivulets, and when I look down, I realise that it is one of my daughter's red wellington boots. Terrified, I retrieve it and hold it close. Jack comes back up with a dark object in his hands.

'Janey?' I wail, but he shakes his head and throws the thing towards me before dragging in another lungful of air and diving beneath the surface again.

I wade into the surf, feeling the retreating waves sucking at my legs as if to take me with them. It is Janey's duffel coat. Moaning, I haul it towards me. It is so heavy that for a wild second I think my daughter must still be inside it – but no, it is just her coat, empty and sodden, the toggles undone and the tartan lining showing.

I howl down into it, the soaking wool muffling the sound. Then I fix my eyes on the patch of water where Jack dived, waiting for him to resurface, and for a long, suspended moment it's as if I can see myself standing on the edge of the tide like a figure from a tragic tale, awaiting the inevitable discovery.

'Mummy, Mummy!'

I turn so fast I almost lose my balance – and there, further up the beach, is a small figure appearing from behind a rock, barefoot and coatless. The relief that overwhelms me is so physical that my knees give way and I sink into the chilly water.

Janey speeds down the strand, her bare feet slapping the wet sand. In one hand she carries the other red wellington, in the other is Rabbit.

Behind her, little footprints fill up with water, then lose their shape and are reabsorbed into the smooth surface tension of the sand.

'Look, look, Mummy! I found Rabbit!' She gives me a hard stare. 'What are you doing, Mummy? You're all wet!'

At this moment, Jack reappears above the surface and Janey crows, 'Look, Jack is swimming in his *clothes*!' This strikes her as so wonderful that she dances into the surf towards him.

My hand shoots out to grab her. 'Oh no you don't!'

Jack wades out of the sea, dripping from head to foot. He sees Janey, and his whole face changes, as if someone has run their hand over it, removing all the wildness. He wades to the shore. 'You gave us a fearful fright,' he says sternly to Janey.

She buries her face against my leg, not used to being told off by strangers.

'It's all right,' I reassure my daughter, hugging her close. 'Look, let's tip the water out of your other welly and you can put it on and we'll get you home and warm.' I take off my coat and wrap her in it.

'You've got to make Rabbit warm and dry as well.' She holds him out to me.

'Where did you find him?' I ask, taking the wet toy from her. I gently squeeze him to wring the water out of his fur.

'The stream comes onto the beach under the little bridge!' She points back that way. 'Rabbit was waiting for me there. And look, Mummy, Rabbit's all better now.'

I turn Rabbit over in my hands. He is certainly cleaner, I think. Then I realise what she means. The tattered ear is neat once more and the eye that was lolling out on a thread now sits securely attached back in his eye-socket. I almost drop him in shock, but Janey takes him back from me and stows him possessively under her arm.

'Rabbit's had a very exciting time, but is glad to be back with me.'

We make our way back to the house, all of us cold and damp and unnerved. Jack puts his jacket around my shoulders when my teeth start chattering, with shock as much as anything else. I'm looking forward to towels and blankets and a change of clothing, but when we reach it, we find it locked. Did I somehow close the door with the latch down? Has Magda returned and locked it against us? There's no sign of the Morris. Janey starts to shiver.

'Look, this is no good,' Jack says. 'We'll all catch our deaths.'

He disappears around the back of the house. A few minutes later, the front door springs open.

'How did you manage that?' asks Janey, as if he's a magician.

He just taps his nose. 'Best not ask.'

Janey grins, restored to her sunny self. I decide not to break the mood by demanding how Jack Lord has just broken into our house.

When Magdalena returns forty minutes later, she finds us all in the drawing room, kneeling around a games board laid out on a low table. At her exclamation, Jack Lord looks up with the dice-tumbler in his hand. He is wearing the fur coat I found in the wardrobe in the back bedroom, since it was the only thing large enough to put him in. His shirt and trousers and jacket are steaming away on the clothes horse by the fire, alongside Janey's socks and duffel coat.

'What in God's name is going on?' Magda demands.

'We're playing Ludo,' says Janey airily. 'Hurry up and roll the dice,' she tells Jack, 'because I'm winning and Granny will make us stop.'

I get to my feet, rather pink in the face. 'Jack's clothes got wet,' I begin to explain.

'I fell in the sea retrieving Janey's coat from the tide,' Jack adds quickly.

We'd decided not to tell Magdalena that it was because we thought Janey was drowning. I'm ashamed to have taken my eyes off my daughter even for a second; Janey knows instinctively that any drama is likely to see her banned from exploring further, and Jack said there was no point worrying Magda when in fact nothing terrible occurred. The decision to omit the details of the incident seems reasonable, but now all three of us feel the weight of our conspiracy as Magda scrutinises us. She has a gift for conferring guilt.

Luckily, she has other things on her mind. 'Mr Hocking is sending a general builder over here tomorrow to assess the work. Stanley Skerritt.'

'Skerritt?' Jack makes a face.

'What's wrong with him?' Magdalena demands.

'Nothing. But…'

'What?'

He bites his lip. 'I probably shouldn't say.'

'You can't just say something like that and then not tell us what you mean,' Magda coaxes.

'I worry he would take advantage of you.'

Magdalena narrows her eyes at him. 'Because we're women?'

'Because you're… not from here.'

'Foreigners?'

'Everyone from east of Camborne is foreign down here.'

'Are you saying he's untrustworthy?' Magda presses.

Jack holds his hands up in surrender. 'Sorry. I shouldn't have said anything. I'm sure he's an excellent builder if Mr Hocking recommended him.' He gets to his feet.

'You look like a bear,' Janey says happily.

He laughs and raises his hands in claws at her with a feigned roar. Janey rushes away from him, squealing. The hem of the coat catches the edge of the table and topples it, Ludo and all. In the midst of the disorder, something flies out of the pocket of the fur coat, a square of folded paper – a receipt, maybe, or a cleaner's ticket. I pick it up off the floor and idly unfold it as Jack and Magdalena right the table and retrieve the game pieces. It's larger than it looks – a piece of blue letter-writing paper, folded in four.

When I read what is written on it, I can't help but give a little cry.

'What is it?' Magda asks.

Wordlessly, I hold it out to her. Two words have been printed in ink in a large, unsteady hand at the top of the sheet.

HELP ME.

'What does it mean?' I ask.

Magdalena scrutinises it. 'It doesn't mean anything. Someone must have been playing a game.'

Jack holds his hand out. 'May I?'

She glares at him, then crunches the paper fiercely in her fist and walks towards the stove.

'No!' Jack cries. 'Don't—'

The ball of paper lets out a flare of bright orange and disintegrates in the flames.

Jack sits down heavily.

'It might have been important!' I cry. 'Evidence, even.'

'Of what?'

'A crime!' Janey offers avidly.

'What nonsense you come out with.' Magda shakes her head at me. 'She has far too much imagination, and you encourage her. Better make sure she doesn't say things like this when she goes to school here or people will think she's simple.'

I put my hands over my daughter's ears, but she squirms away. 'How dare you!' I say sharply to my mother.

'Look, I'm going to go,' Jack says quietly, but he appears pale and drawn, even a little angry. 'I promised I'd do some work for the Lanyons this afternoon.' He pulls the coat tighter around him and retrieves his drying things from the wooden horse, then nods to us, smooths Janey's head and strides out.

It is only some hours later that I realise he has taken the fur coat with him.

7

I settle myself in a chair by the warm range with my hands curled around a cup of tea, savouring the early morning light that slants through the side window, waiting for Janey to come down. The distant sea is a pale golden haze and the lawn laced with sparkling dew. For just a few minutes I feel my mind go quiet and still; then Magdalena appears at the door with a silk scarf carefully arranged over her rollers.

'Make me a cup of coffee and I'll take it back up with me,' she commands.

Obediently, I put my tea aside and go into the kitchen. It has become such a morning routine that I hardly even wonder any more how she ever managed without me. I have cooked and cleaned and laundered and swept and tidied so much over the past couple of weeks I'm beginning to feel like Kopciuszek, or as they call her here, Cinderella. Kopciuszek made wishes that were granted, as I recall, by a tree growing on her mother's grave, though I doubt she ever was tempted to murder her mother and bury her so that she could grow that tree...

I have just handed Magda her mug of black coffee when

a man in paint-spotted overalls and a cap appears outside and raps on the window. Seeing Magdalena in her peignoir, he gives a gap-toothed grin.

'Oh good God, it must be the builders. Do go and see to them, Mila. They may have access to the hall and the reception rooms, but on no account allow them upstairs. I shall require twenty minutes to make myself presentable.' She turns to go, then adds, 'And don't make them tea; I don't want them treating the place like some sort of corner house.'

There are two vans pulled up in the drive, from which a small army of workmen is emerging – at least six of them, not including the fellow who rapped on the window. All I want to do is flee upstairs and hide in the wardrobe. How I miss Dennis. He would know exactly what to say to them, would immediately establish a rapport, crack a joke, clap an arm around the foreman's shoulders and there would be no backchat or slacking.

The grinning cap-wearer appears from around the side of the house and, seeing me on the doorstep, doffs his cap and bows in a courtly fashion. 'Marn, mum,' he says.

I take this to signify, *Good morning, madam* and hold out my hand, which he pumps enthusiastically. We exchange names and after this everything seems a little less daunting. 'My mother is in charge and she'll be down directly, but I'll walk you around the downstairs in the meantime,' I say and he grins broadly.

'Spot on.' Stanley Skerritt takes a long look around the derelict hall, at the damp patches in the outer corner and the fallen plaster, and sucks what remain of his teeth. 'See you got some damp there.'

'Yes. It's worse up there.' I nod towards the upper floor.

He starts to make for the staircase but I catch him by the elbow. 'No, not yet. Do come and take a look at the drawing room and the lounge.'

I lead him into the first of the reception rooms, where he stands with his hands on his hips, looking around. After a while he gives a little whistle. 'It were ansum its day. People always said so.'

'Ansom?' I echo hopelessly.

'Ansum,' he repeats and I realise he means *handsome*.

'Oh. Yes.'

'Poor old dear's gone to wracknruin,' he says, running the words together.

'Yes, it's such a pity.'

He walks to the fireplace and gazes down at the charred hearth and cracked mantel, purses his lips and goes to the long windows, where he taps the frames, then digs a nail into the wood. 'That's all rotten,' he declares cheerfully, striding on. He bends to rub a finger over the mould in the far corner, sniffs deeply. 'Rising damp.'

I laugh. 'May as well knock the whole house down and start again!'

Mr Skerritt stares at me. 'Aye. Well, I might, given the history of this place.'

An icy fingernail runs down my spine. 'Do you know its history, Mr Skerritt?'

'You haven't seen anything hereabouts?' he inquires.

'What sort of thing?'

He shrugs. 'What do I know about White Cove? My family's from Penzance.' And having delivered this baffling pronouncement, he heads for the dining room. By the time

I catch up with him, he is complaining about the state of the back wall and ceiling. 'That's proper nasty.' He gazes upwards, tutting.

I'm framing another question about the history of the house when he says, 'Reckon we should get some ladders up and take a look at the roof.'

'Perhaps you'd like a cup of tea first?' I ask quickly, by way of bribery, despite Mother's express instruction not to.

He havers.

'I think there's some cake...'

Stanley Skerritt removes his cap and scratches the gleaming expanse of his skull. 'Cake, you say?'

I make us both a cup of tea, retrieve what is left of the yellow fruit cake we bought in town and place a slice on a plate before the foreman. He stares down at it, then up at me expectantly.

'Don't you like it? I think there are some biscuits somewhere.'

He grins. 'Down here we eat un with burr.'

'Burr? Oh, butter, right.' I fetch the butter dish and a knife and watch as Mr Skerritt lathers a thick skin across the yellow cake, before dunking a corner in his tea. It's just as well he's eating that first mouthful with his eyes blissfully shut because I cannot help but stare in repulsion.

'So,' I say quickly, 'I gather this has been a guest house before?'

He nods, chewing. 'Oh ar, before the war.'

'Do you know who owned it?'

He looks at the ceiling as if the answer may be written there. 'Local MP and his wife and child, and then the army

70

were billeted here.' He takes a long swallow of tea and practically gargles with it.

I bend my head and suppress a giggle, taking a sip of my own tea to mask the sound. 'What happened? Did you know them?'

He takes another mouthful of buttered cake. 'Did a few jobs for them. Nice couple. Well…' He pauses. 'Nice woman,' he amends. 'Local. Always had a smile for you. Except when she didn't. Always wondered what became of them.'

'What do you mean?'

'The couple disappeared…'

With abysmal timing, Magdalena chooses this moment to appear in the doorway. 'I'm not paying you to sit in here drinking tea and spinning tales!' She fixes Mr Skerritt with her evil eye.

The foreman pushes back his chair so fast that it screeches on the stone floor. Getting to his feet, he bobs his head and hastily swallows the last piece of saffron cake. 'Beg pardon, ma'am.' Jamming his cap over his bald pate, he starts to talk quickly about the damp, and asks if he can take a look upstairs to assess where there might be leaks. 'Then we can set the ladders up and get started.'

'I shan't be paying you till the first of your workmen sets foot on a ladder,' Magdalena declaims regally, dismissing him in her best cut-glass English accent. I notice that she is wearing a perfect replica of one of the suits the young queen wore on her royal tour, in fine navy-blue wool, nipped in at the waist and tight at the knees. All that's missing is a large diamond brooch.

I get up to follow the foreman out, but Magda catches my

arm. 'What did I tell you about not giving the workmen tea? Please don't encourage him in tittle-tattle. We are making a fresh start here and the past is the past.'

'But he said something terrible might have happened to the people who lived here.'

'Terrible things happen to people all the time,' my mother snaps. 'A terrible thing happened to you, or have you forgotten?'

'I don't need to be reminded of it every day or made to feel as if it was my own fault.'

Magdalena regards me dispassionately. 'Well, it was your fault.'

'How could I have known?' The words burst out of me. 'He didn't tell me.'

'Well,' says my loving mother, pursing her mouth, 'if it had been me, I would have guessed.'

'Oh, you would, would you?' Anger is welling up inside me. 'How would you have done that? With some sort of magical intuition?'

'I'd have suspected something was wrong if he didn't come home to *me* every night.'

'He was working.' I close my eyes, remembering. 'He said he was—'

'Your so-called husband was married to another woman. He had another family, two other children. Leaving you with a bas—'

'Don't you dare! Don't you ever call Janeska that.'

'*Syn dziwki!*' Magdalena curses.

'Call me what?'

Janey appears in the doorway, dressed somewhat haphazardly in a pair of tartan trews and an orange shirt with the buttons done up randomly so that one tongue of cloth hangs lower than the other. Her blonde hair sticks up in tufts.

'Nothing, darling. Granny and I were just having a small disagreement.'

Magdalena snorts, bangs her empty coffee mug down on the table, then sweeps out of the room, calling back over her shoulder, 'Since you've wasted milk on the builder, you'd best walk up to the farm to fetch some more while I make sure we'll still have a roof over our heads tonight.'

I watch her go despairingly. Whatever Magda said, no one could possibly have known about Dennis's duplicity, though God knows I have berated myself endlessly for my gullibility. But how was I to know that anyone could lie so smoothly to someone they love? For if nothing else, I'm sure Dennis did love me.

'You look sad, Mummy, what's the matter?' Janey is gazing at me. 'Is it because Rabbit was being rude?'

Her eyes are so like Dennis's – such a limpid blue. Do children inherit a parent's characteristics? Will Janeska also have a propensity for blithe deceit and blind egotism? She has her father's charm and garrulousness, his easy sociability – God knows, she didn't get those traits from me. But maybe each soul comes into the world complete in itself and experience carries out the subtle carving of the final design.

I manage a wobbly smile. 'Sorry, darling. Just remembering sad things.'

'I miss Daddy too,' she says. Janey has a knack for knowing things she should not know.

I sweep her into a fierce embrace. 'Best not think about the past,' I say into the stuck-up tufts of her hair. How I love the smell of her, the warm sweet scent – yesterday's soap and saltwater still faintly discernible.

'Is Daddy not coming to live with us here?'

'No, I'm afraid not, darling. I did explain.'

'But I don't understand. There's lots of room. Granny said it's going to be a guest house. Can't Daddy be a guest?'

'No. No, he can't. Come on,' I say briskly. 'Let's make some breakfast, and then we'll walk up to the farm to buy some milk.'

I disengage myself from my daughter and go to scrutinise our supplies. 'I'm afraid it will have to be porridge.'

'Rabbit doesn't like porridge.'

'I'm afraid Rabbit will have to make do with porridge, or go hungry.'

There is a baleful silence in the adjoining room, then Janey says at last, 'Rabbit will go hungry then.' After a long pause she adds, 'But I suppose I'll have to eat Rabbit's porridge so that it doesn't go to waste.'

After breakfast, and rather more suitably attired, we walk up the lane together, holding hands. Janey informs me that she considered leaving Rabbit behind. 'I told Rabbit to go to bed upstairs,' Janey adds sternly, 'and stay put. But then I remembered the chocolate and I was worried Rabbit would steal it.'

'Is there any chocolate for Rabbit to steal?'

'Oh yes. Fairies brought it yesterday,' Janey replies gnomically. 'So I've brought Rabbit with me after all.' She flourishes him, and I smile, then remember the mysteriously mended eye and my smile fades.

It's a bright, fresh day after the rain with patches of azure showing between the drifting clouds. The tops of the trees twitch and sway in the breeze and little soughing noises flow through them as they are breathing. We pass the lookout spot where Magdalena nearly put the car over the edge and Janey becomes very alert as if she is looking again for the hare that had caused her grandmother to veer off the road, but there is no sign of it. However, at the top of the hill where the lane forks, we do find a dead badger, its fur matted with dried blood, fat flies buzzing around it. Janey is most fascinated and goes down on one knee beside it.

'Don't touch it, darling,' I say.

'It's got worms!' she declares, thrilled, and as I bend to look, I see the mass of white maggots writhing in the wound, and smell the animal's decomposition.

I haul her away. 'It's horrible, Janey.'

'It's not horrible at all, Mummy. It's just dead.'

We have already dealt with the concept of death by dint of the fact that she has lost two hamsters and several goldfish, each of them ceremonially buried in our little garden.

As we walk away, she cranes her neck back until the poor beast is out of sight.

One branch of the lane heads towards the main road, so the other, more rutted, must lead to the farm. I wish I knew the name of the farmer. I should have asked Mr Skerritt. Or Jack.

Except Jack hasn't been back for several days since finishing off the pantry and I find myself wondering where he is and what he's doing. How does he pass his days? He said he likes to do jobs for people, but other than the house at White Cove and the farm, I've seen no other signs of habitation. My heart leaps suddenly at the thought that he currently may be working at the farm.

'Mummy, slow down, I can't keep up!' Janey hauls me back.

'Sorry, darling, was I walking too fast?'

My thoughts circle back to Jack. I recognise something in him. He is a sort of fellow-traveller, someone who, like me, has sustained damage on the road. But I have noticed that many people in this country hide their emotions, give you false smiles that don't touch their eyes.

It was different in the rural village in Poland where I was raised – the women in and out of each other's houses, sharing tasks and gossip, and always with a hug for us children and home-made candies. I recall my Aunt Kamila and Uncle Jan and our cousins and their wives and children and babies. There was so much noise, and singing and laughter and tears and shouting, and always the smell of things cooking – pans of soup and baking bread and little cakes. I felt safe then, surrounded by love. I was only a few years older than Janey is now when my parents brought me to England. How did they know it was the best thing to do, the time to leave? How does anyone know when terrible events are liable to engulf them? Most of the people we knew stayed. I can't think about them. So many died. My parents left practically everything they owned to come here. And then, despite everything, Papa died in the war. It seems so unfair. Is it any wonder that my mother is so brittle, so armoured, so hard to love? She has lost so much, and through no fault of her own. It's probably why she is so hard on me for making such bad decisions.

We pass an abandoned cottage, roofless, its walls

colonised by ivy, and a little further on another tiny house set behind a low wall and a gate on which a dozen iron horseshoes have been tied on with wire, along with strips of weather-faded cloth. This also fascinates Janey, and I have to pull her away when a lace curtain is twitched back and an old woman's face appears.

Now we can see the farmhouse, low and grey, surrounded by a concrete yard and a chaotic mass of rusting machinery. We pass a long byre with a partially caved-in roof where cows low quietly to one another, and Janey wrinkles her nose. 'Poo,' she says succinctly, and I laugh.

'Yes, indeed.'

The whole place has a rundown air, sad and failed. But what do I know of farming? We haven't come to a live in some pretty version of Toytown.

A man with a black-and-white dog catches my eye in a distant field and for a second my pulse quickens, but as he walks on I can see it isn't Jack, but someone shorter, older and stockier. We see no one else till we reach the farmhouse and knock on the door.

There is a long silence and I'm just about to give up when at last the door cracks open.

'Yas?'

No greeting, just the abrupt question.

I explain our errand, taking my purse out of my basket to show the gleam of the coins inside. The person on the other side of the door opens it a little wider. She is small and stout, with a crown of curly ginger-grey hair. She wears a green-and-white gingham apron over a dress that reaches almost to her ankles.

'From downalong, are you?' she asks, indicating the cove.

I nod. 'Yes, we just moved in.'

She purses her mouth and says something unintelligible. Then she reaches out and cups Janey's chin. 'Ansum little chap.'

Janey bridles. 'I'm not a little chap. I'm a *girl*.'

She wears her blonde hair close and short – the curls are growing out after a disastrous experiment with her grandmother's hair dye some weeks back, which left her long locks streaked an odd greenish hue that had to be cut off. The boyish style suits her pretty heart-shaped face though, and she says it makes her feel like Tintin. I have to admit it's a good deal easier to work with than when it was longer and required styling or plaiting, throughout which torture Janey always squirmed and complained.

The woman looks up at me. 'Not sure I'd want to bring up a child of mine down in the valley.'

'Why ever not?'

'T'int a happy place.'

'What do you mean?'

She shrugs. 'Best not talk about unlucky things too much, or you may attract unwanted attention.'

She sounds like Babcia and Aunt Kamila, superstitious to the core. Rural communities have a lot in common, I suppose, cut off from the brisk pragmatism of the cities.

'Well,' I say, trying to sound bright and positive, 'I hope we will change the balance a bit.'

She just gives a derisive little snort. 'Good luck with that.'

I ask her name and she tells me it is Bella Lanyon, and I give her our names in exchange. I have to spell mine for her, and explain its origins.

'Reckoned it were summink foreign,' Bella says darkly. Then she moves aside and widens the door. 'Best come in.'

We follow her through a drab corridor to the kitchen, where a fat slab of pale dough sits on a floured board on the table.

'Making scones,' she says. 'Stay awhile and you can take some with you.'

'That's very kind of you.'

'Hope you've got jam and cream down there for un.'

I admit that we have only butter and honey in the larder and Bella Lanyon clucks her tongue. 'Won't do. Won't do at all. You'll be wanting a jar of our best raspberry – I can let you have it for thruppence ha'penny. Then you'll need some clotted cream – jam on first, mind. That's the Cornish way; do it wrong here and they'll hang you.' She winks, just in case I think she's serious. 'We got fresh eggs too. You'll be wanting some of 'em.'

She rolls the dough out as she talks then cuts rounds into it with a toothed metal cutter, brushes beaten egg over the crowns, and pops them onto a tray in the range. 'Won't take long. I'll get your things while we wait for them to do. Need any bread or potatoes? Got some peas and runner beans, and I daresay Kit can nip out and strangle a chicken for you if you're of a mind to roast un.'

I stare at her in horror, and Janey's eyes are as round as saucers. 'Is that what you do to chickens?' she asks, thrilled. 'Strangle them?'

'Oh yes,' says Bella. 'Just a quick flick of the wrist. It's easier than taking their heads off with a chopper. When they runs around afterwards there's a deal less blood to clear up.'

'Oh my goodness!' I cry. 'I don't think we need to hear all the details.'

'I do,' Janey says. 'I'm very interested indeed.'

The old woman grins at her. 'Got to know these things,' she says. 'Got to know where your food comes from. You'll get on well enough down here if you've got a strong stomach.' She flicks a glance at me. 'But I reckon your ma is going to need a stronger constitution if she'm going to thrive in the valley. It's a hard place to scrape a living.'

'I have a very strong constitution,' Janey echoes, taking great care over the long word. 'I'm strong in lots of ways.'

Bella regards her solemnly. 'That's as well. Womenfolk have much to bear in this life, and in this valley more than most.'

'Well, it's nice to have neighbours,' I say carefully, feeling rather unnerved by this pronouncement.

'Neighbours are all well and good. But people don't often stay.'

'It is remote, I suppose.'

'T'int that.'

She gets up to fetch a pot of jam from the pantry, then gathers some eggs in her big, knuckly hands and arranges these carefully in the basket, before adding a small pot of cream, and then returning for more eggs to make up the dozen. The scent of the cooking scones fills the kitchen and my stomach rumbles.

'What is it about the valley, then?' I press on. 'I imagine it can get cold in winter?'

Weather appears to be a safer topic of conversation. 'It's rare we get too much of a frost down here, though the storms can be fierce.'

'But no snow?'

The old woman laughs. 'No snow, not in my lifetime. Up on the moors maybe, but not down here. Down where you are it's almost tropical.'

'Maybe that's where the hare came from,' Janey offers suddenly. 'The moors? Perhaps it was lost.'

Bella stops what she's doing and fixes her eyes on my daughter. 'A hare? Sure you don't mean a rabbit? Lot of them round here.'

'Oh no,' Janey says. 'It was definitely a hare. I thought it was a rabbit, but Mummy explained that hares have longer ears. And she said that wild rabbits aren't white.'

In an almost slow-motion fall, one of the eggs in Bella Lanyon's cupped hands topples to the floor, where it smashes on the flagstones in an explosion of yellow. I jump to my feet and relieve Bella of the remaining eggs. She's suddenly unsteady on her feet, so I help her to a chair till the colour comes back into her face.

'Are you all right?' I ask.

The farmer's wife lifts troubled eyes to me. 'You've seen her now, and she knows you,' she says cryptically. 'And now she knows, you'll always be in her eye.'

The words haunt me all the way back to the house. *Now she knows, you'll always be in her eye.* What does that mean? And who is *she*? I asked, but Bella revealed nothing more.

I cast my mind back to seeing that apparition in the road, the uncanny sensation of making contact with a wild animal. I had been amazed by the startling whiteness of its coat, which seemed to fluoresce in the still air, but I had not for a moment been scared of it, and neither had Janey. It's true, though, that my daughter is rarely fazed by anything. And what does a child of five know of curses and superstitions?

People everywhere are superstitious. My Aunt Kamila was beset by the arbitrary rules of folk traditions: getting out of bed by placing your right foot on the floor first; never greeting anyone in the doorway but always welcoming them inside before kissing or hugging them; never leaving the house bare-headed.

Magdalena, of course, regards such practices as ridiculous and old-fashioned, suited only to uneducated peasants, which is largely how she views her own family– an odd contradiction, given her Catholic faith.

We walk down a narrow track between tall hedges. Water lies scattered in puddles along its surface after the showers and Janey lets go of my hand to play hopscotch, bouncing and hopping between them, giggling as she misses one and splashes muddy water all over her wellies. A bird chitters a warning call; overhead two crows fly, calling loudly, as if in shouted conversation. The sun is poking shining fingers between the clouds, casting a silver disc on the distant sea. The scene appears so benign and serene that my jittery nerves begin to calm. *Silly Bella Lanyon,* I think. It's probably what happens to you if you spend your whole life in such an isolated place – you see signs everywhere because there's no trace of the modern world running interference with the old ways. Will Mother become equally batty down here? I laugh out loud at the very idea.

Janey runs back to me, Rabbit clutched in her first. 'Are you laughing at me? It's funny, jumping in puddles, isn't it? Why don't you jump in them too?'

I ruffle her hair. 'Because, silly goose, I'm carrying the eggs.'

'Well, put them down then.'

We grin at one another. I put the basket down and together we bounce in and out of the puddles, kicking muddy water at each another till we're breathless and giggling. 'Look at your coat!' Janey crows.

I look down. It is spattered and filthy.

'What will Granny say?' She convulses again.

A little further down the lane there is a granite horse trough with water flowing into it from a little spout, so we stop and I clean us both up with handfuls of leaves until we look less like tramps. 'Better not tell Granny, I think.' I wink at her and she attempts to wink back but cannot confine the movement to a single eyelid. We laugh again.

Then she gives Rabbit – also damp from his clean-up – a violent shake and once more I am reminded of the mysterious mending of his hanging eye.

'Not a word to anyone, do you hear me?' She has the stern tone of her grandmother off to a T and I cannot help but smile.

When we get back, it is to find a confusion of workmen wrangling among themselves. A single ladder leans up against the house, but as far as I can see no one is on the roof and one of their vans is gone, though it didn't pass us on our way down. Even at a distance, it's clear that Magda is in a foul temper. She stands with her arms folded, glaring at Mr Skerritt, who is looking out to sea with the expression of a man who wishes himself somewhere far away.

Janey, always sensitive to atmosphere, makes a face. 'I'm going to play castles with Rabbit.'

'You can play on the lawn, but you're not to go any further than that tree there. Do you see the one I mean?' I bend to her level and point to the crab-apple where the gentle slope of the garden breaks into a steeper angle to make sure she understands what I mean. I will be able to see her clearly as long as she stays on the upper lawn. 'And don't go into the barn.'

She looks disappointed. 'But I like it in the barn. It feels safe in there.'

'Well, it isn't.' There are too many potentially dangerous items in there – old tools and machinery, to say nothing of the ladder up to the rickety hayloft. 'You're never to go in there without an adult.'

'Jack might be in there,' she says hopefully.

I don't have time to argue more with her; Mother is striding towards me. Taking her chance to escape, Janey runs off down the lawn, with Rabbit flailing from her hand.

'What's up?' I ask Magda.

'These people are nothing but cowboys. They have no idea what they're doing, no experience, no expertise at all. And I told them so. I mean, fancy falling off the roof within minutes of going up there! How absurd is that?'

'Oh no. Is the man all right? I saw that one of the vans was gone.'

'A lot of fuss about nothing,' she fumes. 'Just a broken ankle, and entirely his own fault. I'm pretty sure he'd been drinking. Or maybe he was on drugs. He sounded off his head. Now they're all refusing to work, damn them.'

And off she stamps, to give Mr Skerritt some more of her mind, no doubt. I decide to follow and try to get between her and Stanley Skerritt. When Magda is in this sort of temper she can be quite offensive, and I don't imagine it's easy to find replacement builders down here.

She's already haranguing the poor man by the time I catch up with her – and there's Janey, keeping her distance down at the edge of the upper lawn, sitting with Rabbit under the very tree I told her to not go beyond, deliberately testing her boundaries.

'No, of course I'm not going to pay compensation to his family, or to you. He should have been more careful. I can't help it if you employ idiots.' Her accent is becoming more Polish with every sentence.

I step to her side and place a hand on her arm. She shakes it off as if I am an annoying insect, but at least the gesture interrupts her flow, and after a moment she turns on her heel, calling back a threat not to pay him for today at all unless they get on with the job.

'Can you tell me what happened, Mr Skerritt?' I ask quietly as we watch her disappear into the house.

'A ghost pushed Ted off the roof.'

It sounds so ridiculous that I almost laugh out loud. 'Surely not. What really happened?'

'That's what he said and I got no reason to disbelieve un,' he says stubbornly. 'Known him since he was eight or nine. Good lad, never lies, and whatever she says, he ent no drinker.'

'I'm sure the roof is in quite a state,' I say carefully. 'And slippery with moss and stuff.'

'Pushed, is what he said.'

'Could it have been a freak gust of wind?'

He shrugs. 'Mebbe. Trouble is, none of the lads want to go up there now.'

'Did anyone actually see what happened?'

'No, but...'

'Well, then.' I set the basket down and fish my purse out. Out of the zipped pocket where I keep my emergency running-away cash, I draw a folded one-pound note. 'Half of this is for Ted; the other ten shillings for whoever goes up to get the roof repairs done.' That's all my money gone, apart from a sixpenny bit and a few pennies.

Mr Skerritt pockets the note with alacrity, then he turns to the men and yells, 'Jimmy Bones, you're coming up with me!'

A skinny man who looks as if he stopped growing when he hit puberty and then just became wizened steps over to us and, together, he and Stan Skerritt walk back towards the house, harness up and gingerly make their way up the ladder and onto the roof, where they secure ropes around the chimney and pad carefully around, examining damage and necessary repairs.

I walk down the lawn to collect Janey and Rabbit, and we take our purchases from the farm to the kitchen and put them away. Janey is munching on one of Bella's scones when Magda comes in, her brow uncreased now as if nothing has happened.

'I knew a good talking to would get them back to work,' she declares unrepentantly.

8

After that first accident the works carry on for some weeks without any great incident, interrupted only by autumn storms, which drive the workmen indoors. The roof has been repaired, the chimneys repointed, the gutters replaced, the whole exterior repainted in gleaming white, the woodwork in black; the brass door furnishings gleam. The house at White Cove is smart and watertight. The interior, however, is a different matter. A fight breaks out one day between a couple of the workmen, and someone kicks a tin of paint over in the hall and it takes Jack Lord – who's proved himself a very handy problem-solver, fitting in alongside Mr Skerritt's rather less than meticulous labourers – hours, a gallon of paint thinner and a wire brush to get it out of all the cracks between the flagstones. And there's an odd atmosphere, as if we are being watched, and sometimes little things go missing. You put down a book in the evening on the table beside the reading lamp in the drawing room before going to bed, and the next morning you find the book, minus its bookmark, tucked behind the longcase clock in the hall. And then one day the book goes missing altogether, which is extremely annoying when you're keen to find out what happened between Lady St Columb and her French pirate. I even had the temerity to ask Mother if she'd moved it, which of course gave her the chance to sniff at my choice of reading matter. 'Really, dear, if you didn't waste your time on such trivial novels perhaps you wouldn't have filled your head with romantic dreams and fallen for such an unsuitable man.'

I'd say we have a mischievous ghost in the house, especially after Stan Skerritt's outlandish claim, but small items of food have gone missing from the kitchen too, and whoever heard of a ghost that ate Rich Tea biscuits? Perhaps the workmen are pilfering, though it feels mean to suspect them of this, especially since they turn up with their pasties and chunks of hevva cake, and I have no proof at all. From time to time, though, I do have the odd feeling of a presence in the house other than my family and the workmen; a sense of being watched and known. It is both disturbing and comforting. I don't know what it is. It is probably nothing.

'Mummy?'

Janey has appeared at the door, looking forlorn. 'What is it, darling?'

'I can't find my drawing things.'

I smile at her. 'I probably tidied them away. Come on, let's go look for them.'

She skips up the stairs ahead of me, into the now-partitioned bedroom. The workmen have erected a thin wall between us, with a door that opens into my larger part of the room. The plaster is still drying out; when it dries Janey has decided she would like to paint it herself. I am in two minds about this. It should be her space, but I know if the decoration doesn't come up to Magda's high standards there will be trouble, even though no one else will see inside. For the time being I have said to Janey, 'We'll see,' – the eternal parental phrase for buying time and hoping that your offspring will forget. But one job we must do is to scrape off the old wallpaper. It's peeling and faded. I don't mind it in my room, but Janey deserves better.

I go to her wardrobe, the little white one she had in her room in our London house, where it fitted prettily into its surroundings. Here, it looks tiny and dwarfed beneath the tall ceiling, the height of the room only emphasised by the proportional narrowness of the space. On top, there is a cardboard box full of bits and pieces we have yet to find a place for. When the carpenter has finished in the kitchen, I am hoping to nab him to put up shelves in here so that Janey can put her books and toys on them to help make the room her own.

Hefting the box down onto the floor, we sift through the contents: jigsaws and ragbooks, her old Noddy books, her plastic tea set, crayons and some sketchbooks, little ringbound notebooks, a teddy and two dollies that have been neglected ever since Rabbit entered her life, a smart set of doll's clothes Magda once gave her for a dolly she buried in the garden to keep the dead hamsters company...

'Here you are.' I gather handfuls of pencils and crayons and put them back in their tin box and hand them to her. When I pick up one of the sketchbooks, a piece of paper falls out of it. I see the first words on it before Janey grabs it out of my hand and folds it up till it's tiny and my heart contracts. I miss him too.

'That's mine!' she declares fiercely, stowing it in her pocket. 'It's private.'

'Sorry, darling,' I say. I try for a bright tone. 'Have you got what you need?'

She grabs up the sketchbook and crayons and nods. 'Go away now.'

'Charming.'

At the doorway, I turn and watch her for a moment as she rootles through the tin, selects a pencil and pops it into her mouth as she considers what she's going to draw. I have to refrain from telling her off about chewing the pencil, remembering how Dennis had laughed at me when I thought the lead in pencils was poisonous. 'It's just graphite, darling,' he'd told me. 'In olden times they thought graphite was lead, but it isn't – it's quite harmless. Don't fuss.'

Don't fuss: his favourite phrase. Perhaps if I'd fussed a little more, I'd have discovered the truth about our marriage and been able to do something about it before Mother bulldozed through our lives.

There are a hundred and one things on my list of things to be done around the house – second coats to be given to skirting boards, curtains to be hemmed, floors polished, windows cleaned – but the idea of any of these dull tasks feels oppressive. Making a silent pact with the universe, I promise to reapply myself to the list this afternoon. I need to get out of the house for a while, just for half an hour while Janey is drawing and Magda is napping. After that, I'll come back refreshed and ready to get on.

It's a crisp October day, a bit on the chilly side, made more so by a north-easterly wind that's cutting in across the sea, straight into our cove. The prevailing wind here is from the south-west and is thus less bitter. I draw my coat tight around me and secure my headscarf by crossing the ends under my chin and tying them at the back. It's the way I used to wear a scarf when out driving with Dennis before we had Janey. I feel a little hard lump in my throat at this unwanted memory, and stride out as if I can somehow leave it behind.

I have come to appreciate the garden we have here, even though it's on a slope. It has so many hidden corners, so much luxuriant variety, so many unexpected gifts and vistas. Poking around in the little time I've had to myself I've discovered, in addition to the little greenhouse I searched on the first day here, cold frames swallowed by brambles and bracken, terracotta flowerpots that are miraculously sending colourful dahlias shooting up out of their covering weeds, even a small orchard where apples are burgeoning. Someone must once have really loved and tended this place, for, when cutting back the worst of the undergrowth, Jack and I came upon gooseberry and blackcurrant bushes, this year's crop either stolen by birds or withered on the stems. Next year, I tell myself now, we shall make jam.

The thought stops me in mid-stride. Next year. I have not let myself think about any sort of future for so long that this is an alien concept to me, and yet here I am already planning for a distant summer. That is some sort of progress. Maybe Mother was right about the need for a fresh start.

I take the narrow path that leads down to the ancient clapper bridge. Here, there is always birdsong, though I have yet to distinguish between the different types in the way that Jack can. 'That's a blackbird,' he will say confidently as a stream of notes pours into the air, or 'That's a wren,' as some unseen being trills with loud eloquence in the bushes. I find myself smiling as I part the rampant, feathery-fronded tree-ferns, the tamarisk and massive gunnera that border the stream. Each name he offers me, each little piece of information, adds to the connection I am making with my new home, strengthening my fragile sense of ownership.

As I step out into the open where the path unfolds onto the boulder beach, I stop and take in the view. Patches of the sea are a vivid turquoise today, the streaks sandwiched between layers of darker blue. Where the sun strikes down between the clouds, it lays a disc of shimmering silver upon the surface of the sea out near the horizon, and each curling wave top is shot through with light. Gulls plane overhead, slipping silently sideways as if they have found highways in the air that do all the work for them. I have discovered, during these past few weeks, that I can find a sort of peace by walking down onto the beach and letting my mind drift with the birds and the clouds. I have never thought of myself as an outdoorsy sort of person, so this has come as a revelation. And as much as I love walking with Janey, it is sometimes a relief to be without chatter or responsibility.

So today I decide to explore a little further than I usually would. The tide is out and it looks as if I may even be able to round the headland and see what's there, a foray I have expressly forbidden to my daughter.

The rocks are still wet and slippery, the waves having only recently withdrawn, but I have become more used to balancing on them now, and it takes no time at all to reach the point of the headland. I traverse eastwards climbing up, then down, walking a little on the wet sand, then over the next ridge, and soon I find myself on the edge of a tiny beach framed by tall cliffs of granite and compacted earth. There is no sign of habitation here at all; the woods come right down to the beach, making a deep, dark and rather forbidding backdrop to the pretty scene.

I mooch along the shoreline for a while, picking up some curios to add to Janey's collection – a smooth white oval I now know to be a cuttlefish bone, long razorfish shells, and a perfectly rounded piece of sea glass a shade lighter than those patches of turquoise out in the depths. Then, checking the state of the tide, I decide to err on the side of caution and make my way back.

I am just nearing the headland when I see there is a narrow sea cave that I had somehow failed to spot on my way over from our beach. Using my hands to steady myself on the rough granite, I climb up onto the wave-cut platform and peer inside. It's completely dark in there – the sort of darkness you rarely encounter – and when I step inside, it feels as cold as stepping into a refrigerator.

I shiver and turn to step out again. And that's when a glint of light catches my eye. Some scintilla of sunlight has found what must be a shard of glass or some other reflective object on a rocky shelf to the side of the cave's mouth. I can't see what it is from where I am, so I press my hands against the clammy rock and move until my nose is level with a little natural shelf in the granite.

Up out of the way of all tides, someone has placed a collection of objects. I take them down one by one to examine them in the light.

The first is a deep blue velvet shoe with a slim high heel, bearing a decorative silver bow. Lines of salt have bloomed in the nap, leaving faint tidemarks. I stare at it wonderingly. With a nervous laugh I brush my fingers along the instep as if caressing a small animal, then replace the shoe on the shelf of rock.

The second object comes easily into my grasp. Smooth and almost warm to the touch, it is a small box of tarnished silver, hinged along one side, with little curlicues of decoration along the edges. When I thumb it open, it smells of nicotine, but is otherwise empty. I feel sure I've seen one just like this before.

The third object is an exquisite bottle with an ornate stopper and a tiny amount of golden liquid still visible in the bottom. When I remove the stopper a powerful wave of scent engulfs me – woody and citrus and musky all at once, so much more sophisticated and probably far more expensive than the perfume Dennis used to buy for me, and yet it smells familiar. I cannot help but give in to the temptation to dab a little behind my ears and upon my wrists.

The fragrance of it accompanies me all the way home like a protective cloud.

'What is that smell?' Magdalena wrinkles her nose.

'What smell?'

My mother approaches, sniffing. 'Have you been in my room?' she accuses.

I bridle. 'Of course not.'

'Then perhaps you found another fancy man.'

I can feel myself reddening. 'What on earth are you talking about?' Then I remember the perfume.

'That's *L'Heure Bleue*,' Magda pronounces. 'I'd know it anywhere. Who's been giving you expensive perfume?'

'It was the last drop in an old bottle,' I say. I do not want to admit to finding the strange treasure trove in the cave, so I just stare back at her, as unblinking as a cat. 'You don't know everything about me,' I say, finding an unexpected degree of resistance inside me. 'I have nice things too.'

My mother arches an eyebrow. 'Well, it doesn't suit you, it's far too sophisticated. You should stick to Yardley.'

I press my lips together firmly to prevent further retort and go upstairs to check again on Janey. When I got back from my walk and changed my clothes, I had stuck my head around her door, to find her head down, so absorbed that I didn't want to disturb her, and crept away again. But surely she'll be wanting something to eat now; my own stomach is rumbling.

I run lightly upstairs and call her name as I enter my bedroom. After a long delay her blonde head emerges from the door between us. 'I'm busy,' she declares, as high-handed as an empress.

'Aren't you going to show me what you've drawn?'

'I don't think so.'

This is a surprise. Janey loves to show off her drawings, and accompanies each of them with long, complicated stories that explain each stroke and shape: '... and that's the cat that hid in the tree and waited till all the family had gone to bed and then crept in down the chimney and ate all the cakes...' She's not by nature a secretive child, nor a sullen one.

'All right,' I say. 'If you don't want to. I just thought because you've been drawing all this time you must have produced something very special.'

'I have.' She is emphatic and full of pride.

I wait for her to show me her work of art, but she just looks at me. I'm the one to blink first. 'Never mind, then. I just thought you might be hungry by now.'

Janey thinks about this for a while. 'Rabbit's feeling a bit peckish, so perhaps we'll come down for a sandwich.'

'What sort of sandwich would Rabbit like?'

There follows a brief one-sided conflab.

'Rabbit would like crab paste with white bread,' she says after a while. 'And lots of butter!'

'Are you sure about that? Last time you had crab you didn't like it.'

'It's not for me!' she says indignantly. 'It's for Rabbit. Really, Mummy, sometimes I think you don't listen to a word I say.'

I have slipped up and spoiled the game, and here is my daughter upbraiding me in just the same exasperated and contemptuous tone her grandmother reserves for me. A wave of annoyance runs through me.

'Come on, put your drawing things away and we'll get some lunch. Hurry now.'

For a moment she looks as if she may answer me back again, but instead she just gives a theatrical sigh and turns to tidy her pencils and crayons away.

I move closer to the door so that I can see over her head. Page after page has been torn from her sketchbook and strewn across the floor in a messy, obsessive way, which is very unlike my careful, methodical child. I wonder if she has been frustrated while trying hard to capture something more challenging than usual, but when I move to place her pencils back in the tin, I see that each scrap of paper bears the same design – a long, wavy line, executed in a single elegant flourish, with a tall V at one end. It's graphic and powerful as a symbol, but entirely cryptic. How strange... The idea makes me smile, even as she gathers all the pages into a single pile and stashes them under her bed.

Then she picks up Rabbit and we go down to lunch.

In the kitchen, Magda is stamping around, bad-temperedly moving objects and banging them back down.

'Where is my silver cigarette case?' she accuses. 'I left it right here on the counter.' The sharp October sun illuminates the emptiness of the spot where her lacquered fingernail is tapping.

'Perhaps you took it upstairs with you,' I offer helpfully, 'and forgot to bring it down?'

'I *never* smoke in my bedroom.'

'That wasn't quite what I said.'

She looks around, impatient for a cigarette. Then she turns on Janey. 'Where did you put it?'

'Why on earth would you think Janey might have seen it?' I feel a small fury begin to flare. 'She's not a thief.'

But Magda is worked up now, impermeable to logic or the niceties of family life. Her heels strike the slate floor so hard I half expect sparks to fly and am visited by a fleeting memory of being seven years old, my mother storming around the house and me cowering behind the settee, terrified of her temper, sure it is because of something I've done, in dread of her finding me.

My grandmother never raised her voice to me; I wasn't used to such violence of atmosphere. But my daughter is not the mouse that I was.

'What have you lost, Granny? I will help you find it.'

'Don't call me that!' Magda, out of control without her nicotine hit, lashes out as Janey comes towards her, and slaps her across the head, knocking her off balance. Janey stumbles, slips and falls, striking her head on the wall as she goes down.

I fly to my daughter's side, put an arm around her and sit her upright. There is a nasty bruise already flowering on one side of her face and her eyes are open wide in shock. 'Oh my God, Janey! Darling, are you all right?'

Janey does not look at me. She is staring at her grandmother with eyes that are almost black. Is the darkness I see there hatred? Or anger? Or has the impact caused her pupils to dilate? Horrible possibilities flood my mind. I pull her towards me to break the intense connection between them. 'Janey! Janey! Does it hurt? Can you see me?' What is it they do with suspected concussion? I hold three fingers in front of her face. 'Can you count my fingers, darling?'

She pushes me away and gets to her feet. 'I'm going to tell about this,' she declares, retrieving Rabbit from where he went flying. 'Then you just wait and see what happens.'

And she's off and running, back into the hall. We hear the front door slam so hard the entire house seems to reverberate.

I get to my feet. Magda, in her heels, is taller than me, but I feel as if I am towering over her. 'There is nothing so low as to hit a child!' I am surprised at how cool and clear my voice is. 'Nothing. You are an evil woman. You should never have been a mother. You have no natural feelings at all. It's no wonder that I was brought up by my grandmother, is it? It's because you used to hit me, isn't it?'

Magda is taken aback, her usual poise scattered. 'I didn't mean to hit her,' she says. 'It just... happened.'

'Nothing just happens.' I glare at her, though I cannot muster a tenth of Janey's intensity. 'You hit my daughter, just as you used to hit me! She's hurt and bruised, and who knows how much harm that will have done her – and not just physically.'

Any contrition is long gone. She even dares to laugh. 'Don't give me that nonsense. I'm going to her room, and if I find my cigarette case there that little tap will be the least of it.'

I tear after her. I do not want her going through Janey's things. My daughter is a collector of oddities: pebbles, pine cones, feathers, conkers, shells, driftwood, old coins, bottle tops, sea glass and other treasures she's come by from combing the tidewrack and woods. To the untrained eye they may appear to be a jumble of rubbish, but Janey spends hours rearranging them, deep in conversation with Rabbit, or herself. I always respect her privacy.

Magda has no such compunction – she's already rummaging.

'Stop it! Stop! She hasn't taken your bloody cigarette case!' But as I say it, I remember the object I found earlier in the sea cave, beside the perfume and the shoe. It was a silver cigarette case. But was it Mother's? And if it was, who could have put it there? My heart twists with confusion.

Magda makes a yelping sound and turns to me triumphantly. 'Not a thief, eh? Then how does she come to have this?' She drops an object into the palm of my hand: a long silver earring with three shining stones dangling from a silver post that look, even to my inexperienced eye, very much like diamonds.

I stare at it, bewildered. My ears are not pierced, and Magda's taste would never run to anything so flamboyant. 'I can't imagine where she's got this from,' I begin, but Magda is not even listening to me now. She's got a drawer open and is poking around Janey's underthings and socks. Clearly, there is nothing of interest there. She smacks the drawer closed. Now she's on her hands and knees, looking under Janey's bed.

'Wretched little thief,' she's muttering. 'They say bad blood will out, and clearly it has.'

My heart swells with anger. 'Stop it!' I cry. 'You're a monster. Don't you dare say such things about my child!' I grab her by the shoulders and try to wrestle her away but, possessed by fury, she flings me off her and starts to remove items Janey has stashed under her bed.

Out come books, jumpers, some marbles, a Matchbox car, a box of collected natural treasures, and a cloud of dust; nothing precious, no cigarette case. She pulls out the drawings, which scatter as if stirred by some internal wind. Magda picks one up, turns it around, examines it, frowning. She picks up another: the two are identical. So are the rest, all dozen or more of the drawings – a single, flowing line ending in that branching V.

Magda snorts, her mouth downturned. 'I'm not entirely sure your daughter is fully in her right mind.'

I have such a powerful desire to punch her that my knuckles tingle with thwarted intent. Mastering myself, I snatch the sheets of paper out of her hands. 'They're nothing to do with you. Don't you even touch them!' I put the earring on the dresser and apply myself to gathering Janey's drawings into a stack. I am just putting them back when we hear the floorboards behind us creak, and there is Janey, holding Jack Lord by the hand.

'You see,' Janey says to him. 'I told you, didn't I?' Her tone is triumphant; she has dragged him here to act as her witness. 'She's going through my things! My secret things. I knew she would.'

Jack's gaze flicks from the sketches in my hands to Magda, then back to me. His nostrils flare slightly, like a wild animal, but when he speaks his voice is quiet and contained. 'It's not very honourable to go through other people's private things, is it?' he says evenly.

'No,' I readily agree. 'It's not.'

Magda gets to her feet. 'I'm very much afraid that in this case it's perfectly justified, Mr Lord. Janeska, although in many ways a delightful child, appears to have inherited some of her father's more dubious traits, among them lying.'

'I am NOT a liar!' Janey stamps a foot.

'On the contrary, my girl, you stole from me and then you compounded your error by lying about it. I will find it, and then we shall see.' Magda's narrow stare is pale and gimlet.

'It's not fair to accuse a child of theft without evidence,' Jack says. 'Let alone...' His words trail off.

Although his face is impassive, I can feel anger boiling

like a tide between us, a violent, barely contained energy. I have the sense that he could be dangerous. But then he turns his attention back to my daughter and she looks back at him, her upturned face as open and trusting as a flower. My heart clenches. Will she also inherit the worst side of me – my naivete and foolishness?

'Did you take your grandmother's cigarette case?' Jack asks Janey gently.

'No, I already told you so.' My daughter is emphatic.

He smiles at her, then looks to Magda and his expression is stern. 'You see?'

'The case is silver – it's extremely valuable. My late husband gave it to me; it's one of the few items I have left to remind me of him.' Her eyes glint with unshed crocodile tears. I almost admire her brazen ability to summon them.

'Is this it?' Jack proffers an object in his other hand.

Magda grabs it, turns it over, flicks it open. 'Where are my cigarettes?' she demands, looking up.

Jack laughs. 'Clearly there's a phantom roaming the house with a taste for Pall Mall.'

'Bloody builders,' Magda mutters. 'Where exactly did you find it?'

'It was left on one of the side tables in the drawing room, in open view,' Jack says smoothly. 'But there were no cigarettes in it when I found it.'

'So you opened it then?' Magda is indignant.

'Janey said you'd lost your cigarette case; I was just checking that was what it was.'

He sounds so plausible. Perhaps this is the truth, and now that I see Magda's case, I can tell that the one I found on that rock-shelf in the sea cave, alongside the elegant evening shoe and the perfume, is different – more ornate, more tarnished.

'You see, Granny?' Janey's eyes are a deep and chilly blue. 'It wasn't me. I told you so.'

'You did, darling.' Magda is all smiles now.

'I think you should apologise,' I tell her. 'You said unforgivable things to Janey… and worse.'

I do not wish to discuss how she hit Janey, not in front of Jack Lord. He must already think so badly of us.

'I'm sorry,' Magda trills, as if she's made a minor faux pas, or slightly misspoken. She stretches out her fingers to Janey. 'Pax?'

My daughter doesn't forgive that easily. She just stares back at her grandmother and Magda laughs a little self-consciously and pats Janey on the head – a little tap, more of a reminder than a conciliation – and strides out of the room. We hear her footsteps as she goes down the stairs – back to the kitchen, no doubt, where she keeps a spare pack of cigarettes on the top shelf of the condiments cupboard.

We listen to her go, then Janey drops to her knees, chattering to Rabbit as she puts her disarranged things back in their allotted places.

I look over at Jack Lord. 'Where did you find the cigarette case?' I ask.

I can tell he's lost interest in the matter of Magda's cigarette case, for he does not answer me, just crosses the room to the dresser, his gaze fixed on an object there.

'Where did you find this?' He holds up the earring.

Janey looks up. 'Oh, that's mine!' She holds out an imperious hand.

Jack's fingers close around it. 'It isn't yours, Janey,' he

says quietly, then turns and walks straight out without another word.

'Where did you find it?' I ask my daughter when I hear the front door shut down below.

She looks mulish. 'Rabbit found it,' she says when I repeat the question.

'You know you should leave things that aren't yours where you find them.'

'Rabbit gave it to me, saying it was very important and that I look after it.'

'Well, it does look expensive.'

'That's *not* what Rabbit meant!' She is indignant, as if I am being deliberately obtuse.

'What did Rabbit mean?'

She hugs her toy close. 'It's a secret.'

'Have you told Jack your secret?'

I watch her smile into Rabbit's fur and feel a bitter pang of envy.

'Jack is the secret.'

9

Jack doesn't turn up at the house for a couple of days and I can't help but wonder if the incident with Magda and the missing cigarette case has made him keep his distance. But towards the end of the third day, I go out to throw some vegetable peelings on the compost heap, and find him up a ladder on the western side of the house.

'Oh, hello.'

He stares down at me, his face in shadow, and says nothing at all. Then he comes down the ladder, as nimble as a monkey. 'That should see you through the winter,' he says, nodding up at the drainpipe. 'It'd come loose from its fixings, but it's got pretty rusty in places. It'll probably need replacing next year.'

I nod. 'OK. Thanks.' I don't know what more to say, or how to shift to a form of conversation that will bridge the gap between us, and I make to leave.

'Hang on, Mila.' He waits until I turn back. 'I should apologise,' he says quietly. 'I left a bit abruptly. I didn't mean to be rude, but I was angry.'

The sun is falling behind the wooded hill above us,

haloing Jack in red light, the last rays shining right into my eyes. I shield my gaze. 'It's been so busy I've barely had time to give it a thought.' That came out sharper than I meant, but he gives a short chuckle.

'I suppose I deserve that.'

'I can't say I blame you for staying away. It wasn't the most edifying episode.'

'Your mother can be terrifying.'

'She's not very nice sometimes, I have to admit.'

He takes the ladder down and stows it carefully against the wall, then sits on the grassy bank and pats his pockets. 'Cigarette?' he asks, proffering an opened packet.

I decline politely, then surprise myself by sitting beside him.

'Is Janey all right?' he asks after a while, once he's gone through the ritual of finding his box of matches and lighting the cigarette.

'She's a bit absorbed,' I say. 'A little subdued, if I'm honest. I do hope she's not brewing something up. Mr Skerritt's men have been sneezing and coughing all over the house.'

'Sorry to hear that.' He takes a draw on the cigarette and the tip glows briefly red in the falling light. Then, abruptly, he stubs it out. 'Filthy habit. I don't even much like it. Took it up during the war – something to give me a bit a comfort in a quiet moment.'

I pick up the packet. Not Pall Malls like Mother's, I note. '*Whatever the pleasure—*'

'*—Player's complete it,*' he finishes for me.

I think of the magazine advertisement with the young couple sitting companionably together on a fallen log, much as we are sitting on this bank, the man smoking, the woman – with her wavy hair that looks so like mine – looking away from him. I smile to myself, amused by the comparison.

'Where were you posted during the war?' I ask after a while.

'Oh, here and there. I enrolled in the Derbyshire Yeomanry to start with.'

I am surprised. 'You don't much sound as if you're from Derbyshire.'

'I'm not… I just ended up with them. I was in North Africa for a while as part of the 7th Armoured Division, then got drafted into the Armoured Corps to see to the tanks. Saw some action in Algiers and Tunis, and then on the Italian front.'

He looks down at the hands that are so good with engines, with spanners and screwdrivers, as well as paintbrushes and pliers and saws, and I wonder what he is recalling. Hand-to-hand fighting? Shooting Germans? Tanks being blown up? Comrades getting killed or maimed?

He surprises me by saying, 'I loved the desert, you know. You'd think it was the opposite of being in this lush green place. But it was peaceful, and really beautiful, when you got used to the barrenness. That sounds contradictory, finding peace in the middle of a war, but when the fighting stopped I experienced this extraordinary sense of stillness. I would walk out into the wilderness just to… to commune with it, I suppose you could say. This wild, bare land largely untouched by humans, unchanging, sufficient unto itself. It didn't need us at all. It just… was. And it knew itself. I could feel that.'

'Except that all you soldiers were changing it – churning

up the sand with your tanks, blowing it up with your ammunition, bleeding into the ground.'

He gives me a wry smile. 'I know. But all that was transient. And at night it seemed so irrelevant. I would lie out there with my back against the ancient ground, in this great expanse of nothing under a wide black sky full of stars, thinking how tiny and insignificant I was, as small as the rocks – no, smaller, like the grains of sand.

'We don't last long on this Earth,' he adds into the silence that follows as I take this in. 'Human beings. Not in the great scheme of things. We live a little while, we share our time with the other living things, and then when we go, the landscape continues without us, as if we never existed.'

'That's a bit depressing,' I say.

'I think it's comforting, that continuation, being part of the cycle of life. Individually, we don't matter much. It makes your own particular woes that bit smaller and less important.'

I stare out over the sea, in itself another sort of desert. 'It's hard to think that way when you're a parent,' I reply at last. 'I may not be very important, but Janey is everything.'

At that, he turns to me and his eyes are so dark. 'Yes, you're right. She is the future.'

We sit quietly for a time, watching the waves roll into the grey shore as the light fades.

'When I came back from the war, I couldn't stand the company of other people,' Jack says at last. 'The things we do to one another, the violence, the cruelty. All I wanted was to lose myself in nature. When I was demobbed, I walked all the way down here, from Oxfordshire to Cornwall.'

'But that's—'

'Over two hundred miles.' He grins at my astonishment.

'That's quite a feat. How long did it take you?'

'It wasn't a single long walk. I worked my passage, so to speak – stopped in villages and at farms, helped to gather in harvests, mended tractors and cars, did odd jobs here and there. People were so happy that the war had ended, they were really kind – let me into their houses, gave me a place to sleep, sent me off with spare clothes, mended socks, freshly baked bread. It restored some of my faith in the goodness of the human heart. Certainly, I was a lot less traumatised by the time I got down here than when I started out. Even sleeping in fields and in woods was fine – you become attuned to the rhythms and sounds of the natural world, and it put physical space between me and the war. There's nothing quite as nice as being woken by the chittering of goldfinches, or a singing contest between a pair of wrens, to feel sunlight filtered by green leaves falling across your skin. Less good when it poured with rain and your boots wore your feet to blisters, though! My favourite memory is of sitting in a copse just outside Fernham and looking over at the White Horse of Uffington carved into the chalk of the hills opposite. It's huge – a good hundred yards long. You can see it for miles. They think it was made by primitive folk who worshipped a goddess, but I don't think they were primitive at all – that's a pretty arrogant judgment from people who just waged a worldwide war that killed millions. Those ancient people had incredible vision and determination. They were channelling a force of nature with which they had a powerful connection, and I think we've lost that connection in this busy, chaotic world.

I carried that image in my mind. It struck some sort of chord inside me.'

He slides a glance towards me.

'Sorry, I'm blathering away. You probably think I'm a bit touched.'

I shake my head. 'Not at all. It sounds quite... magical. I've never really had the chance to make that sort of connection with England, with nature here.'

He laughs. 'Well, you're in Cornwall now – it's another country. And there's nowhere the ancient lies closer to the surface. There are paths here that have been trodden for so long that they've sunken down and down like a trench through time, the trees above meeting like an embrace. When you walk them, you can imagine you're walking in the footsteps of people from thousands of years ago, that time is folded back on itself. There's an old green lane, or hollow way, up the hill from here.' He waves a hand towards the wood that looms like a black shadow behind the house. 'I go up there sometimes on a hot day. You can feel the pulse of the Earth there beating up through your feet, while up above in the hawthorns and holm oaks flocks of long-tailed tits flit and call. I'll take you up there one day.'

I feel shy as he looks my way, this man who has opened his soul to me. 'I'd like that. Thank you for telling me all this. You bring the place to life. Perhaps I'll learn to look at my new home through fresh eyes.'

There's a sudden rap on glass, and I turn to see my mother's face, pale and forbidding, at the window.

'I'd better go and see what she wants,' I say, pushing myself to my feet.

'You're not her servant, Mila.'

'Try telling her that.'

I can feel his eyes on me as I walk along the veranda towards the front door, till I disappear from his view.

10

Everything outside is so grey today. Rags of clouds are being driven by a stiff easterly across the dull sky; choppy waves are rolling into the cove to break in bursts of foam on the grey beach stones. The trees have lost their autumn leaves and even the russet bracken on the headland has turned a defeated brown in this flat, wintry light. We have to keep the lights on all day, despite Magda's mutterings about the electricity bill, but the men can't see to paint without them. It's the end of November and I am at my wits' end trying to manage everything on my own. My fears about the workmen's coughs and sniffles has been borne out. Mother was struck down by a cold last week and has taken to her bed and I have been running up and down the stairs with cups of tea and coffee and glasses of hot whisky and honey, boiling a chicken carcass for soup, doing my best to keep Janey occupied and out of mischief, all the while chivvying the workmen along in their myriad tasks – not easy given all the mishaps and minor accidents that keep occurring.

So far, we've had Jimmy Bones fall off a ladder; part of

the newly installed gutter fell and struck one of the younger men on the back as he was mixing concrete, badly bruising his shoulder; and Mr Skerritt is hobbling around after treading on a rusty nail that had steadfastly wedged itself between the floorboards in the dingy upstairs hall. Andy Hoskins, the decorator, walked out on the job halfway through redoing one of the guest bedrooms and wouldn't tell anyone why, then the two men hired to finish the work failed to appear, and Stan Skerritt had to complete the work himself, with much muttering and complaint. Meanwhile, Mother is constantly demanding progress reports and blames me for each and every one of these incidents. She is – quite madly in my opinion – determined to have everything finished before New Year so that she can throw a huge party to which she has already invited a number of notable locals. I simply cannot imagine anything worse.

Someone sneezes loudly in the next room and the sound echoes up into the ceiling. It doesn't sound like one of the workmen who have been laying a carpet in there, and indeed, when I put my head around the door it is to find the drawing room deserted except for a disconsolate-looking Janey, with Rabbit tucked under her arm. Her face is flushed. As soon as she sees me she sneezes again, with such force that her eyes water.

I lay my hand on her forehead: it is burning. We have a thermometer somewhere, probably in the bathroom cabinet, but I can already tell she's running a high temperature.

'And my throat hurts.'

This alarms me. Janey never complains. 'Darling, I think you should be in bed.'

'There are strange noises up there.'

'You don't need to worry about them – it's just the decorators hard at work on the room next to yours. I promise they won't come in and disturb you. I'll tuck you up in bed with a comic, shall I? And bring you some medicine.'

'They keep whispering.'

'If they're whispering, how can you hear them?' I ask reasonably.

'Rabbit can hear them.'

I grin. 'So what are they saying, then, sweetheart?'

'They say this place is cursed.'

My grin fades. 'I'm sure that's not what they said. Rabbit must have misheard.'

'Rabbit has excellent ears.'

'I know Rabbit has excellent ears.' I reach a hand to brush the toy's soft ears, the once-tattered one looking if not flawless now, then neat and mended. 'But perhaps he didn't really understand what they were talking about and got it wrong.'

She shakes her head and says vehemently, 'Rabbit is always right. And he's not a "he".'

I am taken aback. 'What do you mean, he's not a he? Rabbit's always been a he. That's why he wears a waistcoat.'

'Silly Mummy, rabbits don't wear waistcoats. Anyway, can't ladies wear waistcoats?'

I concede that this is possible and feel myself being drawn into a logical morass. 'All right,' I say at last. 'I'll call Rabbit "she" from now on, shall I?'

She nods, satisfied to have won this point. 'Rabbit knows everything. She says you should talk to the men in the room.'

I sigh. 'I will. But only once you're in bed. Deal?'

'All right.' Which takes me by surprise since Janey never willingly goes to bed – she hates to miss out on anything.

After tucking her in with Rabbit, I put my head around the door to the guest room and find it entirely empty – not a trace of the workmen or even their tools. Ah well, I tried to carry out my half of the bargain. I go to the bathroom and search through the contents of the wall cabinet, and amid a collection of plasters and ointments, friar's balsam, milk of magnesia, Alka Seltzer and Magda's headache pills, dig out the thermometer and a box of junior aspirin. When I open the latter, though, I find it is empty.

Back in her room, Janey opens her mouth wide to allow me to insert the thermometer. I can see that her tonsils are raw and red and there are ulcers above the back of her tongue. Poor little love. I remove the instrument and interrogate the mercury. It is 101 degrees. That can't be right, surely? I shake the thermometer. 'Let's try that again, darling, shall we?' I ask, trying to keep the panic out of my voice.

This time the reading is 99. Even so, I consult my copy of *The Common Sense Book of Baby and Child Care* I bought when I first fell pregnant and felt overwhelmed by the idea of being responsible for a small life, even though Dennis was so relaxed about the whole idea of child-rearing. And in retrospect, no wonder; he'd already raised two.

Dr Spock is at least fairly reassuring on the matter of Janey's symptoms. Children's temperatures can run hotter than adults', apparently. It is best to keep a weather eye on them and only call the doctor out if it hits 104. Dose them up and keep them comfortable. Honey and lemon is mentioned. Of course, we have no lemon. It'll have to be orange squash for now. Is there any actual orange or Vitamin C in orange squash? I run downstairs and run the tap to make up a tall glass of water with some of the coloured syrup in it and the liquid glows like a London sodium lamp in the low winter light. Then I make Magda a cup of coffee as a bribe for keeping an eye on Janey while I walk up to the village to buy medicine and ask for contact details for a doctor. I can't believe we haven't signed up with the local practice yet.

I stick my head around Mother's door and find her propped up in bed reading an old copy of *Vogue*. In lipstick and a frilled peignoir she looks far more glamorous than any patient has a right to. I put the coffee down.

'Is there anything you need from the village? Janey's got your cold and is running a temperature so I'm going to fetch her some junior aspirin.'

She considers this. 'A magazine from some time this century might be nice. And another bottle of whisky, if there's anywhere to buy such a thing in Eglosberyan. Not Bells, though.'

I make a mental note.

'Can you keep an eye on Janey? I've tucked her up in bed.'

She waves me away with a limp hand. 'I daresay we'll survive without you for an hour or two.'

I make to leave, then turn back. 'Oh, and you should know that Rabbit is a she now. Janey is very firm on the matter.'

Magda arches an eyebrow. 'How very… bohemian.'

Deciding against wellington boots for my foray into the village, I put on a stout pair of low-heeled lace-ups and my gabardine mackintosh, belted tightly, and wind a red woollen scarf around my neck. Then on impulse I dig out an old tweed cap that used to belong to Dennis. As I turn it in my hands, looking for the label that denotes the back in preparation for putting it on, I catch the scent of his Brylcreem and for a moment I just stand there, holding it to my face, trying not to cry.

I check on Janey one more time and I'm glad to see she's asleep, with Rabbit clutched against her cheek. I run a hand gently over her forehead, smoothing away the silky hair. Beneath my fingers, her skin is hot and damp. 'I'll be back soon,' I whisper as her eyelids twitch. 'I'll bring back something to make you feel better.'

Armed with my basket, handbag and umbrella, I feel laden down even without the shopping, but there is no help for it. How I wish I could drive, I think, seeing the Morris sitting unused outside, next to the builders' vans. For a moment I wonder about bribing Stan Skerritt or one of his men to give me a lift into Eglosberyan, but I know that if Magda discovers I've distracted them from their designated tasks for the mere purpose of making my sick child more comfortable there will be hell to pay.

The track up out of the cove is the steepest part of the walk and by the time I've reached the lookout point I'm already hot and panting with the effort despite the chill in the air. From here I gaze down on the house. It looks so picturesque, bordered by the trees and the verdant garden, with a spiral of smoke from the main chimney wisping away into the sky. Imagine if green fields rolled away beyond the garden, I think, rather than the huge, grey, hostile ocean. Then I might feel more welcome here. There is something terrible about the sea, with its inexorable tides, its rumblings and crashings, the way it casts broken things up upon the shore as if slyly to demonstrate its power.

Turning my back on it, I carry on up the hill until, just past the turning for the farm, I see there is another lane forking off to the west. There is, of course, no signpost. Even if signposts had not been removed during the war to bamboozle any invader, the locals do not need them, and who else would be in such an out-of-the-way place? But recalling that the village is further west than White Cove I decide to explore the left-hand lane this time – it may be more direct.

Within a short space of time the track has narrowed and a line of weeds marks the centre of the rough tarmac, where wheels never pass over it. Before too long the tarmac runs out as well, as if somebody simply gave up an impossible task. Another couple of hundred yards on the track passes between two great granite pillars. Do they mark this as a private road? Am I now trespassing?

A blackbird gives a piercing warning call, and a band of sparrows bursts out of the undergrowth as I walk on where the road becomes more thickly wooded, their wings clattering around me like firecrackers. Rooks caw harshly overhead. The only human presence in their realm, I have disturbed them all. I stand there for a moment and hear nothing else at all, not even the sea – just birds and the soft shooshing of wind in the treetops. No cars, no voices. I could be anywhere, at any time in the world's history, and I remember Jack's words about the old hollow way, which must surely be close here.

A spot of rain hits my cheek and I stride out, trying to

make speed. The track seems interminable and the woods around me feel denser with each step. The wind high up in the almost leafless branches is louder now, but indistinct, like a conversation from which I am excluded. The track widens suddenly and when I turn the next bend I can see a house ahead of me. It has two gables and a half-timbered façade, stacks of tall chimneys on a steeply canted roof. The stonework is covered in ivy through which the small leaded panes of many windows can be glimpsed, glinting darkly. The garden is choked with brambles and thorns. It resembles a house in a fairy tale by the brothers Grimm: beautiful but sinister, a throwback from a lost world.

Rain begins to patter down. I can hear it catching the remaining leaves high up in the trees and it's rattling down like hail. I fumble with the umbrella – last used in a loud and smoggy London street many long months ago – and push its wide black canopy up against the tensile strength of its springy wire cage, so unused to the contraption that I manage to catch my thumb in it in my haste, drawing blood.

'Ow! Bloody hell!'

I suck the blood from my thumb as the rain beats down and down, then angle the umbrella into the wind and follow the track as it winds on past the house.

Before long, I can see where the way ahead gets lighter and the trees give way to what must be a junction at the top of the rise, so I plough on, my empty basket bumping against my leg, my arm aching from holding the umbrella up against the wind, leaving the old manor house behind me.

The shower exerts its worst efforts at around the point at

which I reach the junction with what appears to be, if not the main road, then at least an actual road as opposed to a track, and in a gap in the hedge I can see the village about a mile further on above a series of gently sloping, stonewalled fields.

Rain has washed soil out of the hedges along the next stretch of road, leaving it patched with muddy puddles. I can judge the intensity of the downpour by the way the raindrops shatter the surface and how high they bounce off the tarmac. A horn blares abruptly.

'Want a lift?'

A woman shouts out of the rolled-down window of what looks to be an ex-army Land Rover.

'Yes, please!'

She opens the passenger door with a creak and I fight with the umbrella until it gives in and allows itself to be furled and hurl myself inside the vehicle and sit there dripping with my basket on my knees.

'Thank you so much. I think you've just saved me from drowning.'

She grins at me. 'Going into Eglosberyan?'

'Yes.' As if there's anywhere else to go around here.

'I'm Josie,' she says, stamping on the accelerator, and the Land Rover launches forward like an old steam engine, all rattly pistons and chuffing noises.

'Mila,' I say. 'Mila Prusik.'

'Goodness, that's exotic for these parts,' she laughs. 'Are you visiting?'

'We've just bought the house down at White Cove.'

She slings the vehicle around a corner without braking and I think she's gone very quiet because she's concentrating on the road, but then she says, 'Rather you than me.' Her gaze is fixed on the road ahead and her mouth is set. She is in her late twenties or early thirties, I reckon, a bit older than me. Her hair is a tangle of chestnut curls and her face is sunburned, with a pale fan of crow's feet angling out from the corner of her left eye, and laughter lines incising her cheek. She looks as if she might be good fun, when she's in a better mood.

'It's quite a project,' I admit. 'The roof's fixed now so at least it's not leaking any more, and my mother's got a small army engaged in redecorating. She's determined to have it ready for New Year's Eve.'

Josie slides me a glance. She doesn't look half so friendly now. 'Ready for what?'

'Well, guests in the spring – though I think she's being over optimistic – but she wants to hold some sort of housewarming party at New Year's Eve, welcome neighbours and get to know the locals. You must come!'

Without letting a beat of thought pass she says, 'No, thanks.' She changes down through the gears with a clatter. 'It's not a place for welcoming parties.'

'That seems a bit harsh,' I say, affronted. 'We've spent ages making it beautiful again. What do you mean?'

'You can't just gloss over the past with fancy wallpaper and new paint.'

'But no one will tell me about the past. Did something happen at the house? There is a strange atmosphere sometimes—'

The church looms up ahead, its massive granite walls and square tower hugely out of scale for a place of village worship.

Josie pulls the Land Rover in with a screech of brakes to the side of the road and turns to me. 'You can't just buy happiness, you know, with your London money.' And she reaches across me and pulls a lever so that the door swings open. 'This valley doesn't welcome outsiders. Why do you think the house was so cheap? You should get out while you can and go back where you came from. You're not wanted here.'

I feel as if she has punched me. I scramble out of the car, desperate to get away from more of her violent words, and as soon as I do she slams the door closed and puts the car in gear. I watch the Land Rover chug past the church and feel as if my heart has been replaced by a ball of lead.

Not wanted. The phrase ricochets around my head. I've felt not wanted all my life – by my mother, my country, by Dennis…

I remember, woundingly, what Magda yelled at me when the whole Dennis affair erupted. 'I never wanted children. I mean, look at you: a disgrace, a disaster. Costing me everything!'

As soon as she had been able to, my mother had abandoned me into the care of my grandmother Zofia, and her sister, my Aunt Kamila, on the pretext of going back to her job in Krakow. When you're a small child you don't realise that this is an unusual arrangement, that to have two elderly women raising you instead of your own parents is not the accepted order of things. But in the village school at Kasina Wielka the other children teased me and said I was being raised by witches. They pretended to cross themselves when I came near, fled in mock-terror from me, called me Vila rather than Mila, like the evil water spirit who blinded men and drowned them in lakes. This only lasted for a year or so, but the damage was already done.

Being an only child does turn you into a strange little person, I think, living in a world filtered through your own unadulterated imagination. When I was Janey's age I ran wild in the little woods and fields, making up stories about *russalkas* and goblins, stories that were bloodthirsty and violent and had deep roots in the folk memory of the region. I wasn't unhappy, not in the least. I loved school lessons, was even quite good at games – especially running – had a few friends with whom I played from time to time, and Zofia and Kamila were kind to me, even indulgent. But I swore that when I grew up I would keep my own children close and make them feel loved. I would defend them with my life. I would kill anyone who threatened them.

Children, yes. I always wanted more than one. Not that Janey isn't incomparably precious to me – she is the light and soul of my life – but when I see her talking to Rabbit, my heart contracts. She should have brothers and sisters. Well, she does have – half-brothers and -sisters: Dennis's other family. Although, of course, I have never mentioned them to her... And now she is sick, and we are cast away in this grim valley where we are regarded as outsiders. I slump down on a bench beside the churchyard wall and try to compose myself.

I I

'What's up, my robin?'

I jump as someone touches my shoulder and find an elderly woman in a mac and headscarf regarding me with beady black eyes.

'You a relative of Dolly Tregenza, then?'

I must look bewildered, for she indicates a newly dug grave in the churchyard behind me.

'Oh! No, sorry.'

Uninvited, she sits down on the bench beside me with an *oomph* of expelled breath. 'Wet old day. Make me want to weep too, November days like this. My poor old joints play up something awful.'

'Oh, I am sorry.'

She wags a finger. 'No need, maid, I'm used to my aches and pains – they're like old friends. Now, dry your eyes, my robin, and tell me what's up.'

'It's just rain,' I start, but she gives me a sharp look.

'I know the difference between rain and tears.' She digs in her handbag and passes me a handkerchief. It is daintily trimmed with lace – handworked – and initialled with a looping L.

I take it from her with thanks and rather than ruin it by blowing my nose in it, sniff mightily and dab at my tears, then hand it back to her.

'Take it,' she says, folding my fingers over it. 'I've got others at home and I don't suppose I'll need one betwixt here and there.'

Her generosity makes my eyes well again. I master myself with effort. 'Sorry. Someone was just frightfully rude to me, and we're new here and my daughter is sick, and it just felt like too much all at once.'

She taps me on the knee.

'I know who you are. You bought the house at White Cove, yes?' When I nod, she leans in closer. 'Don't listen to the nonsense they say about it. Scratch the history of any house, you'll find it as bad, if not worse. People die in houses all the time, don't they?'

'Someone died in our house?'

''Tis the nature of homes. People live in them, people die in them.'

'Who? Who died?'

'Look behind thee, bird. This whole churchyard is full of folk who lived and died here. My whole family is in there – my mam, my da, my gramma and all. It's the way of the world. I'll be in there soon myself.' She says this matter-of-factly, and does not seem unnerved by the prospect.

'I hope not for a good long time,' I say politely.

'Who knows what the White Lady has in store for

us?' Said in exactly the way my grandmother might have issued a platitude about the Lord moving in mysterious ways.

'The White Lady?' I ask.

'Now then, Lowena Vingoe, don't go filling this young lady's head with your pagan nonsense.'

The speaker is a tall, red-haired man with striking aquiline features and piercing eyes, wearing a tweed suit and carrying a loaf of bread in a brown paper bag.

'*Keep your tongue from evil and your lips from telling lies.* Psalm 34:13,' he intones piously.

Mrs Vingoe huffs to her feet, kneecaps cracking audibly. 'Geddalong with ee, Vicar. It's all tales and scoldin', ent it, the Bible?' She assumes a martial air, hands on hips. 'Now you tell me what you goin' to do about Hepzibah's grave. It'll flood again given all this rain, I'm tellin' thee now. You keep saying all in good time, but it's twenty years she'm been stuck there with that stream runnin' through, threatening to wash her away.'

The vicar gives an exaggerated sigh. 'My dear lady, you know we are doing everything we can to safeguard your mother's resting place.'

Lowena Vingoe fixes him with a poisonous look, then turns to me. 'Don't worry about your little maid. The Lady keeps her eye on the children of the valley.' Then she shuffles off without even a backward look.

The man watches her go, his eyes narrowed. Then he holds out a hand to me. 'Casworan Martin,' he says. 'I'm honoured to be vicar of this parish.'

It's a bit much that people think our names are foreign-sounding, I think as I shake his hand. He notes my quizzical expression and adds, 'My mother was a Cornish romantic, but I don't think of myself as Cornish at all. I was raised and educated in Cambridge.'

His chest puffs up as he says this, as if it is somehow more laudable than being raised and educated down here. I introduce myself and he looks thoughtful.

'The house at White Cove?'

'Yes.'

'Oh, the parties we had there before the war.' His eyes appear misty with nostalgia.

'Perhaps you'd like to come to the party my mother is planning to throw to welcome in the new year.'

'My, my, works must be progressing apace!' He beams at me, energised by the invitation.

No doubt Mr Skerritt and his workers are keeping the community abreast of every tiny detail. Gathering my courage, I ask, 'Do you know much about the history of the house, then, Reverend Martin?'

'More than most. Come and take a cup of tea at the vicarage.'

'I can't stop now,' I say, though his eyes are boring into me. 'My daughter is unwell and I must buy her some medicine—'

He takes me by the elbow, which seems very forward for a man of the cloth.

'Plenty of time for that, the shops don't shut for hours.'

'I really must get Janey some aspirin – she's running a temperature.' I try to pull away, but his grip is firm.

'We will surely have some aspirin at the vicarage. Come. I would be falling down on my responsibilities were I not to offer a welcome to a new member of my flock.'

His gaze is unblinking and I suddenly feel guilty. Mother has been to church here twice; I haven't been at all. I allow him to lead me through the graveyard, telling myself it will only be a short detour.

The churchyard is picturesquely overgrown, many of the oldest stones almost illegible from erosion and the embrace of lichen. None of those ostentatious tombs you get in London cemeteries, pompous with statuary – Victorian angels and crosses – declaring the temporal importance of the inhabitants buried in the six feet of earth beneath them. I like the modesty of this place, the recurring names and small family plots. Laitie, Vingoe and Humphrys, Harvey, Paynter, Prowse and Hutchens.

At the entrance of the church, I see there is an impressive porch featuring an old sundial. The figures of stylised men and horses and running dogs have been carved around and above the numbers on the plaque, and at the base a phrase is inscribed in Latin: *Lepus currere paulo.*

I'll have to look that up, I think, having never paid much attention to Latin at school.

Craning my neck to look up at the church tower, I feel dwarfed and insignificant, which I suppose is the whole point of religious buildings.

'It seems an extremely large church for a small village,' I say, almost to myself, for the vicar hasn't paused, as used to its magnificence as any good servant to the grand house in which they toil.

'Oh, my church has a very long history,' he says without stopping, and I have to trot to catch him up. 'It dates all the way back to the Dark Ages. The pagan Cornish rose here against the Anglo-Saxons and there was a great battle nearby as the Christians asserted their power over this wild, lost realm. The church was constructed here as a symbol of the king's power, to remind the survivors that they had been well beaten and would now have to bend the knee to him and to Christ.'

On the other side of the churchyard wall, we reach a long, whitewashed cottage with a neat front garden spiky with pruned rose bushes. Inside, the ceilings are low and beamed, and it's quite dark. The vicar goes around lighting lamps and bids me take a seat beside the fireplace, where flickers of flame show through the sooted-up windows of a small stove. I put my palms out to it, though I'm not that cold, and find that it's hardly giving out any heat at all. I can hear him in the corridor, talking to someone, and wonder if he is married.

Leaning back in my chair, I look out of the window. In summer, the great church tower must cast its shadow over the vicarage all day long. How gloomy. It's so grey out there now – except for one small splash of colour: bright flowers that look as if they've been left by the roadside, as if they are memorialising an accident, or been dropped there by mistake.

'Maisie is making us a pot of tea and is fetching some aspirin for your little girl,' the vicar says, coming back into the room. He opens the door of the stove and gives the fire a fierce poke so that the flames leap up and a great gout of heat puffs out into the room. Then he closes the door, replaces the poker, fiddles with a regulator on the back of the stove and settles himself in the other armchair facing me so that he is silhouetted against the window. Even with the lamps on I can hardly make out his features except for the reflected flames flickering in his eyes.

'So,' he says, his gaze on me intense. 'Ask your questions, Mila Prusik.'

For a moment I cannot find the words; I find his unblinking attention uncomfortable, invasive. 'I'd love to know a bit more about the history of the area, and White Cove in particular,' I say at last.

The vicar leans back in his chair and crosses his feet neatly at the ankles, as if settling in for a long tale.

'Is this the first time you've lived in Cornwall?'

I nod. 'Yes, we came down from London.'

'You may find people a little hard to understand to begin with. The accent can be somewhat impenetrable to outsiders and locals can be suspicious of strangers, especially anyone they regard as foreign.'

'My father flew with the RAF,' I say, sounding even to my own ears defensive. 'He was shot down over the Channel by the Luftwaffe.'

'A brave man, no doubt. I'll be sure to mention that to anyone who asks about you. But don't worry, my dear, the people here are, for the most part, good souls. They can just take a little while to warm to newcomers, which I'm sure is the case in many places in the world.'

'Mrs Lanyon at the farm has been very kind.'

'She has?' He sounds surprised. 'She can be a strange one. The old ways run deep in this part of the county. It's a place full of ancient mysteries and a great deal of superstition. We are a long way from anywhere down here. Some of the people have long memories for the old folk traditions. Imagine, they say at certain times of the year the village pump produces blood rather than water! I do my best to counter their nonsense with good common sense.' He laughs modestly.

'Do you happen to know when the house at White Cove was built?' I ask.

'Oh, the foundations will be very ancient. There are settlements down here that date back to the Stone Age and beyond. Over at Carn Euny there are the ruins of an entire village from Neolithic times; there were Iron Age forts and Celtic remains and Romano-British settlements. It was once a very rich and thriving area, trading tin and minerals with merchants from all over the world.'

He looks up as someone comes into the room. 'Oh, Maisie, lovely.' He pulls the small table into the space between us, and the dumpy young woman slams the tea tray down so hard that the cups rattle in their saucers.

'There ent no saffron cake, and we're out of aspirin,' she says brusquely, and stumps out again.

My heart sinks. I want to go straight to the chemist, but now that the tea has arrived it would be rude.

The vicar sighs. 'It will have to be bourbon biscuits then.' He gets up and fetches a small wooden biscuit barrel from a larger table by the wall, which is covered in piles of paper.

He makes me take two bourbons, though I'm not overly fond of them, and we sip our tea in silence for a while. Then he says, 'There was always strife in this county. Cornish folk are obstinate and combative and they have a strong sense of identity. They've never taken well to having rules or customs imposed on them, whether those be secular or religious, and they fight ferociously for their beliefs. Having said that, in large part they were welcoming to the early saints – you'll find wells and chapels all over Cornwall dedicated to the first Christian missionaries here, though they say the Celtic crosses you'll find everywhere bore pagan symbols before Christianity came. All those stonemasons, chiselling away a wicked past!' He gives a satisfied little smile, as if he himself gave the order for the work.

'But there have always been dissident elements who refused to bow to change. Family has fought family over the right to worship in Latin or plain English, let alone Cornish. During the fifteenth and sixteenth centuries the Cornish rose against the Crown, though during the Civil War the great families stood with the king and fought for him with ferocity. Then Bishop Trelawney raised rebellion in the seventeenth century, and they tried him for sedition. People still sing *The Song of the Western Men* to remember him; Cornish memory runs as deep as the veins of tin, but unlike tin it is never exhausted.' He pauses for emphasis. 'It doesn't pay to get into dispute with folk here.'

I wonder if he is referring to Mother and her treatment of the workers. There have been a number of fallings-out between them over the past weeks, and I'm quite sure word must have got around. 'I try very hard not to get into dispute with anyone,' I say lightly.

'The history of Eglosberyan revolves around my church.' I note the possessive pronoun. 'It was constructed in the ninth century by King Athelstan following his great triumph – a symbol of Christian power over those who until then had worshipped all manner of spirits of place and pagan deities. He established a monastery here and placed the area in the protection of one of his lords – and he built a great house in the valley – a mile or so above your house.'

I frown. My knowledge of architecture is sketchy, but even I could see that the apparently abandoned house I passed was nowhere near a thousand years old.

'There's no trace of the old manor house now,' he goes on, as if reading my thoughts. 'It was reconstructed a number of times, but you would have passed the grounds in which the new manor was built on your way up.'

I admit that I had actually trespassed and seen the house. 'It didn't look very "new". It looked abandoned, as if no one has lived there for years.'

He purses his lips. 'It's not abandoned,' he says shortly, but doesn't elaborate. 'Your house,' he goes on, 'was built sometime in the medieval period, but on top of a much older structure.'

'Was it?' I shiver. 'It doesn't look that old.'

'All houses undergo changes. I believe part of it was burned down in the eighteenth century and rebuilt then, and there have been a number of extensions and changes before and since that time.'

'And the last owners? Who had the place when you went to parties there?'

'Ah.' He sighs. 'Such a lovely couple they were – Jory Prideaux and his wife Agnes, and their delightful little boy, William. Jory was the local Conservative MP, a splendid chap, and she came from a very good local family.' He goes quiet, reminiscing. 'It once played host to T. E. Lawrence, Augustus John, to Albert Einstein and the first Marquis of Marconi, but it fell into disrepair. The house was ruined when the Prideaux took it on, back in the thirties, but they made it quite splendid. All the best people came to stay there – politicians and actors, business people in need of some fresh air. I was but a callow young man then, but they were wonderfully hospitable to me.

'And then they had to go away, very suddenly, just before the war.'

'But they never returned?'

'No. I regret to say he was killed – so many were lost, as you know.' He makes a sorrowful face. 'During the war the army were billeted there, and they left it in a rather poor state, I believe.'

'And there's been no one living there since?' I prompt.

'A young couple from Exeter took it on and tried to restore it, but that didn't work out either.'

'Mrs… ah… Vingoe? The elderly lady who was sitting with me outside the church – she said someone had died there. And she mentioned a "white lady". Mrs Lanyon said something along those lines too. Is the white lady a local ghost or something? I've experienced a… a sort of presence in the house and in the woods nearby…' I tail off, feeling rather foolish, but the vicar sits up very straight.

'A presence, you say?'

I shrug. 'Sorry, it sounds a bit mad.'

His hands clasp each other so tightly that the knuckles whiten. 'Don't listen to addled gossip,' he says with something approaching violence. 'We live in a *modern* world now. The war is behind us, the future ahead, and you should focus on that and not go digging around in the past, or who knows what you'll unearth. Get on with renovating your house and bringing up your daughter in the correct way.'

The way he says this sounds sly and knowing, and unbearably patriarchal. I shoot to my feet, suddenly furious. 'Thank you for your hospitality, Vicar. Now I must go and get Janey some aspirin.'

Outside the vicarage, my eye is caught by the splash of colour I'd spotted from inside: a bunch of bright flowers laid against the wall of the churchyard. Not flowers bought from a shop, but wildflowers wrapped in delicate fronds of fern and bound with a red ribbon. This detail piques my interest and, almost without thought, my fingers find the knotted red string bracelet I wear around my left wrist to keep evil spirits at bay.

Red – like blood. Blood, the stuff of life. And death.

Is there a similar superstition here, I wonder? Or is the red ribbon just what came to hand?

I move the flowers gently to one side and see there is a sort of granite marker stone behind them, its edges softened by age and rosetted with golden lichen. It bears no inscription that I can make out, just a familiar wavy line. I run my fingers over it, and a tiny electric shock buzzes up my arm, making me yelp and pull my hand away. Hastily, I move the flowers back in place, being careful not to touch the stone again and walk quickly away to the shops. At the little post office I hand over my savings book, saying that I would like to draw out some money from my account. The woman behind the counter regards me, and then the book, with rather more scrutiny than this simple task requires.

'Where you from?' she asks bluntly.

'We live at White Cove.'

'I know thaaat, don' I?' She draws the vowel out in the local fashion. 'I mean, what sort of name is Proo-sick?'

'It's Polish.'

Her sharp eyes narrow further. 'Not German, then?'

'Not German.'

She gives a little shrug, stamps the book, signs it, and very slowly counts out five pounds in notes and change. I tuck my little fortune away – not much left now – hoping not to have to bribe Mr Skerritt again any time soon. When I lift my head, she is still watching me.

'Have you seen anything… odd… yet, down there?' Her tone is half fearful, half avid.

'No,' I say shortly, not inviting further discussion. 'Nothing odd at all.'

She seems disappointed. 'Ah well. You will.'

I bang the door as I leave.

At the newsagent's the snazziest magazine I can find for my mother is a rather dingy-looking publication called *Women and Beauty*, which at least looks a little less domestic than *Woman's Realm* or *Home Chat*.

In the grocer's no one says anything unwelcoming, but it's clear they sell no alcohol, and when I ask for lemons, the girl laughs at me.

'Are lemons that hard to come by?' In East Dulwich, they were piled up in the market, though you couldn't get citrus fruit for love nor money during the war.

'You ent in London now!'

This is said in such a crowing manner that I feel myself go hot, then cold. I pay for my purchases and beat a hasty retreat. I am so rattled that I walk halfway back to the lane to White Cove before realising I've forgotten the most important thing of all: medicine for Janey. Swearing quietly, I head back toward the shops, head down and furious, only to find a *CLOSED* sign on the chemist's door.

'What? No!' I bang on the glass, in the vain hope someone's just put the light out and is still within earshot. 'Hello?'

No one comes. I scrutinise the door for the reopening time, but there's nothing to indicate whether they've just gone to lunch or it's closed for the day.

I can feel a howl of frustration building inside me.

12

'Can I help, *keresik*?'

A tall woman is regarding me with her head on one side, the light catching her long silver earrings. She smiles and I see that her eyes are lined with kohl and she's wearing scarlet lipstick. She looks exotically out of place in this grey village.

'You don't happen to know when the chemist will be open again, do you?' I could not sound more cut-glass English if I tried: Mother's training. When we arrived from Poland, she was determined that we should be more English than the English. Morning after morning she tortured me with elocution lessons until she had scrubbed out my European lilt and made my diction as clipped and nasal as the voices we heard on the radio. At home, she called me Mila, but in public it was always Mildred, which I hated. Once, I had the temerity to correct her in front of neighbours. She upbraided me in icy tones, but as soon as the front door had closed, she gave me such a clout that I'd almost passed out. My ears rang for days. Even now when I am stressed, I will hear that wild tidal sound and see jagged lights and remember the hurt – not the physical pain, not any more, but the shock of being attacked by a parent who seemed to hate me. I have never forgotten, or forgiven, her for it. I wonder if she even recalls it. Did the impact bruise her knuckles, I wonder? While I was slumped against the wainscoting, gasping, did she raise them to her lips to lick away the pain? Once more, I remember the sickening sight of Janey crumpled on the floor, and the livid mark left on her face.

Why have I allowed myself to be bullied into accompanying Magda on this mad dash to the ends of the earth? Why did I not just stand my ground and stay with Dennis, no matter what? I have deprived my child of her father and put her in danger.

The woman is speaking, something about a funeral.

'Sorry?' I focus on her handsome face, trying to make sense of the end of the sentence.

'They've gone over the border, into Devon, for a family funeral.'

Is it all death and funerals, here? 'So, they won't be open again today?'

'Not till the day after tomorrow, I think.'

Oh no. 'My little girl is ill,' I tell her. 'She's got a temperature and I'm worried it'll turn into a fever, so I wanted some aspirin to try to bring it down. And lemon too, to add to the honey for her throat...' I can't form any more words, and I must look pathetic, for she takes my hand. Her skin is smooth and warm, and I feel another buzz run through me, not unlike the sensation I experienced when touching the marker stone.

'Come with me,' she says. 'You don't want to be giving your child aspirin, it won't do her any good, but I can help.'

'I was going to see if I could find a doctor...'

She laughs. 'Well, there is Dr Tregenza if you're really desperate, but he's better at burying folk than curing them!' And without letting go of my hand, she bears me off with her.

When we pass the church, she makes an odd gesture with her free hand. I think it may be a V-sign, like Churchill's victory sign, or is it the other way around, the way that is rude?

We take the lane that runs north and uphill from the village, in the opposite direction to White Cove, and even though I feel mildly alarmed, I go like a lamb.

Her name is Keziah and she was born near here, down in Mousehole, of a fishing family. She lives at a farmworker's cottage a couple of hundred yards outside the village, set back from the road and walled around with ivy-covered granite. Geraniums flame in the pots by the door, even in November; on the gatepost, a black cat sits watching us with unblinking golden eyes, the winter light colouring the ends of its fur a deep russet. When it sees Keziah, it arches its back, gets languidly to its feet and stretches first its front and then its back legs as if it's been waiting some time for her return. When she bends to unlatch the gate, it bumps its head against her in greeting.

The little front garden is full of plants, most in leaf, some in full flower, and as we walk between them to the front door of the cottage waves of fragrance come to me through the air – lavender and basil, thyme and honeysuckle. 'How on earth do you keep them all going at this time of year?' I ask, perplexed, waving a hand to take in the sweet profusion. Our little garden in East Dulwich had become a muddy wasteland in November, populated only by nettles, tufts of self-sown grass and stubborn ground elder. I'd never had a knack for gardening – Dennis and I had even discussed paving it over so that Janey could pedal her little Triang tractor around it. Another possible future that has fled away into darkness.

'Green fingers.' Keziah waggles her long, thin, brown fingers at me. 'And a very sheltered spot. The bees love it here and the flowers love the bees and we love them both. Everything exists in balance and it is our duty to keep it that way. Now come with me and I'll get you that lemon, and anything else you need.'

I wonder who 'we' might be. She wears no wedding ring, I've noticed, though I suppose some people don't. I cannot help glancing at my left hand and seeing the slightly paler indentation left by the absence of my own. Then I follow her through the front door, which is so low I have to duck my head to avoid the lintel, into the interior of the cottage. In the hallway the air is so aromatic that my head swims and for a long moment I stand still, breathing deeply.

Keziah smiles. 'Good. Keep doing that. It will help you to relax.'

'You're very kind.'

Her laugh is short and sharp. 'No, I'm not.'

We move down the corridor, and I cannot help but peer nosily through each doorway we pass: first, a sitting room filled with light, its beams whitewashed and its wall filled with paintings, then a book-lined snug in which a fire burns merrily in the grate behind an ornate metal guard, and finally a kitchen in which jars and bottles are arrayed on a range of shelves – bottled fruit, pickled vegetables, jams and marmalades and unidentifiable liquids. The windowsills brim with tender plants; there are even some tomatoes still ripening. Beyond lies a paradise. Keziah opens the back door and out we go into a green space replete with bowers and pots filled with herbs, walled on two sides with the local granite and on another with red-berried shrubs I think may be hawthorn.

Tucked into a corner between the cottage and the wall is a greenhouse so small that only Keziah may enter. In she goes; I watch her run her hands over the leaves of her plants and move her lips as if talking encouragingly to them and cannot help but smile. If someone caressed me like that, with words and touches full of love, I'm sure I'd flourish too. She comes out a moment later with two bright lemons in her hands. 'For you.'

I am astounded. 'You grow lemons?' An absurd thing to say, since she's hardly magicked them out of the air.

'Of course. Ari's grandmother gave them to us, to bless our union.'

Ah, so she is married, then, and to a Harry.

'We have oranges too, most years, though we had so many last year that I'm letting them rest this season.' She tucks the lemons into my bag as if they are beloved children being put to bed. 'Come and see the rest of my domain.'

She takes my hand again and this time it seems quite normal and leads me down a snaking path of shattered slates, pointing out rhubarb, espaliered apples and pears, fennel, comfrey – 'good for arthritis', lavender – 'for anxiety', lemon balm – 'for a merry heart'.

'I could do with some of that,' I say with a rueful laugh.

Keziah stops and turns her lambent gaze upon me. 'Are you sad, Mila?'

'Sometimes.'

'I think that may be an understatement,' she says gently, and returns to her tour of the herb garden.

'Are you some sort of doctor?' I ask after a while.

'Say that to the Reverend Martin and he'll have you excommunicated! I like to help people, using the old ways, the wisdom we've always had, the remedies that have always been used around here. Cornwall has the perfect climate for growing all the plants I need. Look!' She reaches up into the branches of a glossy-leafed tree and with a twist of the wrist brings down a fruit I don't recognise. 'Go on, take it.'

I hesitate, but she catches my hand and closes my fingers around the fruit. It is apple-sized, red and subtly segmented, with a starlike excrescence on the top like a tiny crown. It feels plush and full in my hand, heavy with goodness.

'A pomegranate,' she says. 'The original fruit. The one Eve gave to Adam.'

'I thought that was an apple.'

'So many things are lost in translation. Go on, take it – it's full of sweet, sweet goodness.'

Back in the kitchen she decants some dark liquid from one of the jars into a small bottle and hands it to me. 'Two spoonfuls every four hours will bring her temperature down and help to ease the rest of her symptoms.'

I sniff the bottle while she rummages for a cork for it. It smells both sweet and pungent, but I can't place the scents.

'It's a tincture of peppermint and elderflower – that's what gives it such a rich colour – and the yarrow will help against fever, and a few other bits and bobs. You can add some honey if it's too bitter for her, and that will help too. I have honey if you need some. I don't take much from our hives, but I have a little store.'

I assure her that we have honey; I'm already feeling overwhelmed by her generosity. I reach into my bag for my purse. 'Let me give you something—'

'Absolutely not!' She is stern. 'I am here to help, not to profit. The Lady channels her bounty where she will.'

A ripple of disquiet runs through me. 'The lady?' I echo.

'Why yes, *keresik*. This is her realm.'

There comes the sound of the front door opening and closing, and a rush of wind and noise rolls through the house. Into the kitchen bustles a short, round woman with great billows of wiry black hair escaping from a woollen tam-o'-shanter. She is carrying a bulging potato sack and wearing an enormous multi-coloured cardigan that is unravelling in places so that threads trail and holes show the dusty black dress she wears beneath it. The tattered edge of a red petticoat dips beneath the hem of her dress and on her feet she wears short yellow rubber boots covered in mud. She looks like a mad fairy godmother.

'Oh, hello, I had no idea we had company! How joyous to meet you. You must be one of the ladies from White Cove? I've just come from the farm and Bella said she'd met you. Sit down, sit down, we must celebrate the arrival of another sister in the village!'

'Sister?' I ask faintly.

'Why, yes!' The newcomer empties her purchases out of the potato sack: bread, butter, eggs, milk – and a shining white animal skull. 'Silly me, I didn't take a basket with me. Wasn't meaning to buy food when I went out. Billy told me about this beauty he'd unearthed,' – she strokes the skull – 'so I fairly ran down to fetch it, and I couldn't find Billy, so I went to look for him at Bella's, and of course there he was, getting marrow bones for the dog.' She turns to Keziah, her eyes shining. 'I can't wait to have a good old go at it. Isn't it the most beautiful thing? Horses are such special animals... and so are hares.' She beams at me. 'Bella said you'd been blessed by a visitation. Though,' she pauses, 'that's not exactly how she phrased it.'

Keziah laughs. 'Calm down, you'll overwhelm poor Mila.' She turns to me. 'This is Ari – Ariadne, my beloved.'

I lay my hands on the back of one of the wooden chairs at the nearby table to steady myself. There is too much charged energy in such a small space; my skin is alive with it, and suddenly I feel that I must go home at once. 'My daughter is unwell,' I say, too quietly, and have to repeat it. 'I must go.'

Keziah lays a hand on my shoulder. 'Be calm, Mila. All is well. And your daughter will be fine – it is just a passing sickness. She is watching over you; you are in her eye.'

The same phrase Bella Lanyon used, I think. 'Who is this white lady? Is she a ghost, an apparition, or what?'

Ariadne laughs. 'She's no ghost. She is in everything. She *is* everything. She watches over us.'

I frown. 'I thought God did that.'

Keziah smiles. 'You've been spending too much time with the Reverend Martin!' I can't disagree with this, but Ariadne's statement is equally unsettling. 'I don't understand.'

'You will, *keresik*. Some things cannot be explained in words. You will have to feel her in your head and heart.' Keziah touches her own.

This has all become too philosophical for me, and I have more pressing matters to attend to. 'You've been very kind, but I must get back to my daughter.'

Keziah and Ariadne exchange a look, and in it is both love and conspiracy, and something else – a sort of triumph?

Ariadne takes off her woolly hat and lays it on the skull. 'I think it rather suits him,' she says, cocking her head to examine the effect.

'You won't paint him like that though, will you, my lover?'

Ariadne laughs. 'No. Not at all.'

So, she's a painter. That explains a bit, I suppose. Artists can be very eccentric. There were two jolly, handsome young men living at the end of our street in East Dulwich who went to the Camberwell School. I thought then – naively, because I suppose I am naive – that they were just rooming together, to halve the rent, but since then I have wondered.

'Well then,' says Ariadne, who has completely taken over. 'We shall walk you to the door.' And she slips her hand beneath my elbow and guides me out of the kitchen. 'But you have to promise you will come back to see us again. I'd like to have you sit for me. For a painting!' She grins, showing gappy white teeth, in case I have other ideas. 'And if you don't, we shall be forced to come and find you!'

I fairly run back through the village and down the twisting lanes to White Cove, my bags of shopping and gifts and my umbrella bumping against my legs.

'Let Janey be all right,' I pray fervently to an unseen power, unsettled by all the strange encounters I have had today: Josie, who told me we were not wanted here; Lowena Vingoe with her talk of graves and white ladies; Casworan Martin, the creepy vicar; and now Keziah and Ariadne. This place certainly seems to attract eccentrics, I think. Of them all it is the Reverend Martin who has most unnerved me. There is something about him that set my senses on edge, though he was perfectly proper and hospitable.

I was brought up Catholic by my very traditionally religious grandmother and aunt, starting each day with a prayer and Bible verses, going to mass every Sunday, treading carefully beneath the attentions of a vengeful God who saw my every deed and heard my every word. I lived in trepidation of doing or saying the wrong thing and being punished for it. But then with war approaching, my parents had reappeared one day and carried me off with them to England where, Magda informed me fiercely, the people were not very religious and where I should cast off all those outdated practices in order to fit in. And yet she wears that gold cross around her neck every day and has been to Sunday services in Casworan Martin's church. My mother is a woman of many contradictions.

As for me, I don't know what I believe. The early terrors of hell and confession have passed with time, but I still sense the presence of something greater than myself – in the air, in the woods, in the sea. Is that presence God? The bearded tyrant of the Old Testament? The crucified young man of the New? The Holy Spirit that is everywhere around us, or all three in concord? There is a comfort to be had in the idea of a greater power watching over us, I think, one who may intercede with fate on our behalf, alter the path of events, if we beg them hard enough, gather us in to glory when we end. Certainly, the idea that we are here to weather life's tides all alone is a bleak one indeed. And it's hard to shake off those customs with which we are ingrained. But I cannot help but feel alienated by the idea of God being male: the concept seems so narrow and exclusive. I cannot think that a male god could empathise with much of what I feel, of who I am: how could he comprehend the panic a mother feels at her child's sickness? Maybe this White Lady is just a different aspect of godhead, one remembered and honoured by the women, one who offers nurture and comfort, and has – because she is female – been pushed aside? It's just too strange to make sense of, and my head feels scrambled.

Janey is sitting up in bed when I get back, her cheeks flushed and her eyes too bright in her hot face. I take her temperature again, and it's still hovering around the 100 mark. I find myself wishing, despite everything Keziah said about him, that I'd taken down Dr Tregenza's number. I could call the operator and ask to be put through. This is, I decide, what I will do if Janey gets any worse. But I will give her a dose of the herbal mixture first, though it feels like magical thinking to expect something brewed up in a local kitchen to be efficacious.

I unstopper the bottle, and at once recoil at the smell, which is pungent. I anticipate that persuading Janey to swallow it may be a struggle – she's a fussy eater at the best of times and has very set ideas about what is and is not palatable. But when I offer her the first spoonful, she takes it – miraculously – without complaint, and closes her eyes as if concentrating on the taste.

After a while, she says, 'Rabbit would like some medicine too.'

Together we pretend to dose Rabbit, and then Janey takes her second spoonful and snuggles down into the bedclothes.

'I'm going to have a sleep now,' she declares.

'Are you sure? Shall I read you a story first?'

Janey shakes her head vehemently. 'No, I already have a story in my head. If you tell me another it'll get in the way.'

This is a new one. 'Will you tell me your story?'

She considers this for a moment. 'Maybe. But not now. I have to understand it first.'

'All right,' I say brightly and brush her damp hair off her face. 'Tell me the story when you're feeling better.'

I go into Magda's room to give her the magazine and whisky – neither of which fully meet her expectations – and endure her complaints before she decides that her appetite has somewhat returned and that she's well enough to eat something. After some discussion regarding supplies we settle on shepherd's pie and boiled carrots.

I have just got the pie under the grill to brown and am peeling the carrots when out of the corner of my eye I see a shadow pass the kitchen window, and then I hear the creak of the back door opening. Gripping the peeler so tightly that my knuckles show white, I wait, weapon at the ready.

'Are you going to peel me to death?'

'What are you doing here?'

By way of an answer, Jack shakes his wet hair out of his eyes, shrugs off his jacket and hangs it in front of the range to dry, as if he owns the place.

'That smells good,' he says conversationally, nodding towards the grill, and when I don't say anything, adds, 'I gather you've been into the village.'

Nothing is private in this place. 'I walked up to fetch Janey some medicine. She's got Mother's cold.'

'Yes, I heard Janey wasn't well. I came to see how she was.'

'She's sleeping now. She seems a bit better.'

'You know, you can put that peeler down now.'

I look down at my hand, then put the potato peeler on the work surface. 'Sorry, it's been a rather strange day. A strange week, in fact. I've... we've missed you. There's so much work to do and we've been short on decorators and carpenters all week.' I tell him about the various mishaps and no-shows.

'You have to get used to that sort of thing down here,' he says after a while. 'It can be hard to pin people down, particularly coming up to Christmas. The weather's not conducive to travel and they don't much like working in this valley.'

'Why ever not? Our money's as good as anyone else's, isn't it? You'd think they'd want to earn a little extra at Christmastime.'

'It gets dark early at this time of the year. They don't want to be here after dark.'

'Why, though? Are they afraid of something here?'

He shoots me a look. 'They are a superstitious lot. And the valley can be a bit... oppressive.'

'Bella Lanyon said that women have much to bear in this valley. What did she mean by that?'

Jack looks uncomfortable. 'She's had a tough life, poor old bird. The farm's been failing for ages. They barely scrape a living.'

'*We're* hardly going to scrape a living unless we can get

the house done up.' My voice rises on a note of despair. 'What is the matter with people down here? Some of them are so unwelcoming. One woman said we should leave, and Reverend Martin gave me a lecture about the area that made it sound as if I'd arrived in a land of savages. Though he did appear very keen on coming to Mother's party...'

Jack's expression becomes shadowed.

'I have to say, I didn't much take to him,' I go on quickly. 'He seemed rather pompous, and overly proud of "his" church, as if he were a sort of feudal lord.'

'Did he take you into the church?'

I shake my head. 'No, we just walked through the churchyard to get to his house.'

'You went into his house?'

'I think he was trying to welcome me to the parish, and he promised me some aspirin, though they didn't have any, it turned out.'

Jack makes a derisive sound at this and I'm not sure what he's objecting to – that I met the vicar, that he invited me in, or that there was no aspirin.

'Next time, I'll drive you into the village,' he says. 'And I'll show you round the church. It's full of strange things.'

'What sort of things?'

'You'll see.'

'You don't have a car, though.'

'The local garage got a copy of the keys to Magda's made for me.'

'Does she know that?'

'It was her idea.'

I find the thought of Jack and Magda cosily making such

arrangements disturbing. 'I'd rather get driving lessons,' I say at last.

'The lanes around here are pretty quiet at this time of year. Maybe I could teach you—'

'Teach her what?'

Magda glides into view, pale and fragile from her malady but with lipstick and powder carefully reapplied and her peignoir floating behind her, like a glamorous ghost.

'I told Jack I wanted to learn to drive, and he offered to teach me.'

'You? Drive? I don't think so, and especially not in my car!' she trills, as if the very idea is absurd. 'Mila's completely impractical and uncoordinated. She'd put the Morris in a hedge in an instant and kill you both!'

'She strikes me as being a lot more capable than you think she is,' Jack says, and I feel a wave of warm gratitude for his defence of me.

Magda makes a face and Jack says quickly, 'Because she's your daughter, and you're evidently extremely capable.'

Magda simpers and rearranges her posture to make the most of her lean figure and neat bosom. I can hardly believe what I'm seeing. What strange game is this they're playing?

'Well…' Magda smiles at Jack coquettishly. 'Maybe once we have the house ready for our party guests…'

'I can help with some of the finishing,' he offers. 'The painting and decorating, at least. I daresay I'm a fair bit cheaper and more reliable than Mr Skerritt's boys.'

'And a good deal more personable!'

And so they are the best of friends again and a deal is struck to get the work done, and Jack stays to supper.

After we've eaten, I go upstairs to check on Janey and

find her asleep, cradling Rabbit. When I bend to kiss her forehead, I find it is dry and cooler than it was a couple of hours ago. It appears that Keziah's magic potion is working. Relief pours out of me in a great sigh.

'Mummy?' she murmurs, her eyelids flicking open.

'Yes, darling?'

'Did I hear Jack?'

'Yes, he came and ate with us.'

'Good.' She closes her eyes again, satisfied.

13

Jack and Magda have motored into Penzance for painting supplies and to buy a stepladder so that Jack can finish the ceilings.

'How are they going to get that in the car?' Janey asks, when I tell her this.

'I have no idea.'

'Perhaps it will go through the back window and into Granny's seat and she'll have to go in the boot!'

'Or on the roof!' Which makes her giggle.

It's a few days after my expedition to the village and whatever was in Keziah's medicine – the elderflower and yarrow potion – really appears to have been efficacious, bringing down Janey's temperature almost immediately, soothing her sore throat and disappearing the little ulcers. She seems to have got away without even a cough, though Magda is still hacking, and refuses to try any of the remedies I brought home except for the lemon, which she has added into her evening 'doses' of whisky and honey. 'I can't be doing with all that mumbo-jumbo,' she'd reiterated. 'If it gets worse, I'll call Dr Tregenza.'

I'd stared at her in disbelief. 'You had his number all this time and didn't think to give it to me when your granddaughter was so ill?'

She had waved a hand at me – a go-away gesture. 'Children are always getting ill. They throw these things off in a couple of days. I don't know why you were in such a panic.'

I wanted to remind her that she had not been there any of the times I had got sick – with seasonal colds, with tonsillitis, and once with a bad case of scarlatina that swept through the village. It was my grandmother and aunt who worked to keep my fever down and soothe the fiery rashes on my skin with cold flannels. There was no penicillin to be had, there was such an epidemic, so they would pray over me, and once brought the local priest in to bolster their efforts. When I awoke and found him standing over me, I was convinced he had come to give me the last rites, and burst out of the swaddling bedclothes and ran outside crying, and would not come in till he had gone. I do wonder if my aversion to the Reverend Martin may not be some echo of this childhood terror.

While they are out, I decide I will have a go at stripping the wallpaper in my bedroom, which I find increasingly depressing by the day. Once it's off, or at least in a sufficiently ragged state, Magda won't be able to forbid me to 'waste my time' on redecorating my private space. Well, that's my reasoning at least. Since no one else ever enters my room, she can't see the importance of tackling it now. 'It's not as if anyone else is likely to see it, is it?' Because of course, now I am imprisoned, as a kind of nun.

So, armed with a kitchen knife, a scraper and a bucket

of soapy water, I attack the wall opposite my bed, the one I look at last thing at night and every morning when I wake up. The pattern is of blowsy old roses, the colours faded with time and over-exposure to light from whatever prettiness it once boasted to its present drab greys and depressing mauves. Where damp has got in, the paper has bubbled and blown, so that the walls of my room appear soft, uneven and untrustworthy. Who knows what they harbour? My plan is to strip it all back, make good any damage underneath and paint it a clean, pale yellow – a colour that promises sunshine and spring warmth. It might even cheer me up. To that effect, I have slipped Jack some money to buy me paint in a suitable shade, making sure first of all that he understands exactly what I mean.

'Butter yellow?'

'Lighter than that.'

'Cream?'

'With a touch more colour to it.'

'Mummy means like primroses,' Janey supplied, out of sight in her adjoining room.

Jack and I exchanged surprised glances. 'Yes,' we say simultaneously.

There was a contented silence on the other side of the wall.

The first section of wallpaper, once soaked, lifts along its edges and starts to come away in a single satisfying length as I pull its bottom edge away from the skirting board. I shift my grip and pull a few more inches at a time, maintaining the same tension on each side until the top section finally gives up its close association with the wall and cascades down over my head.

This is going to be easy! I think triumphantly, disentangling myself. Determined to be neat in my task, I roll up the discarded sheet and set about the next length. There are a couple more stubborn patches where more glue has been applied around the window frame, but soon I have an almost bare wall. There are a few marks and some remnants of glue, but a good scrub should take care of those.

I drag my bed out and set about the wall behind it, but whoever applied the wallpaper paste in this section seems to have done so with a heavy hand and I am forced to use the scraper. The scraps of paper that come away after a lot of soaking and chivvying are thicker and smaller than the full lengths I removed from the opposite wall and by the time I have cleared two-thirds of it I am sweating and swearing quietly to myself and wishing I had never started. The air is full of dust and fragments of paper; they coat my bed, the floorboards and me. Belatedly, I realise Janey has emerged to watch me and I have to curb the tenor of my mutterings.

'Best go back into your room, darling, and close the door, or it'll make you cough.'

Remarkably, she does as she is told.

I get a good grip on the bottom of a frayed length and gently tug it away from the wall, balancing strength and tension till it unpeels all the way to the ceiling, leaving just a few obdurate bits of old paper but a lot of marks, especially near the base. I work away for another hour, keeping my ears pricked for the return of Mother and Jack all the while, but it seems they are taking their sweet time.

Eventually, I clear the debris into a heap. Some of the paper will be useful as firelighters, but all the dust and bits need to be swept up and Hoovered. I run downstairs to fetch dustpan and brush, a refuse sack and the Constellation from the cupboard in the corridor between the pantry and the hall, and struggle back upstairs with the heavy round body of the vacuum cleaner banging against my legs, and its grey, corrugated hose draped over my shoulder like an elephant's trunk. I set about the task with determination, the noise and vibrations of the vacuum cleaner making my teeth rattle. There. I stand back and survey the scene.

Now I can see there's a strange pattern running around both walls, about a foot from the top of the skirting board. Surely too high to be scuff marks, even from the movement of furniture? I investigate the marks under the window: an uneven series of wavy lines, some with an angled V-shape to the right extremity, made with what appears to be dark pencil. I walk around the room, following the lines, and it is as if they leap and undulate, till I feel as if my head is spinning. I have seen this pattern before. On Janey's drawings, and somewhere else...

My heart begins to bang with a sense of the uncanny.

I put my head around the door of my daughter's room, thinking that maybe she has peeled back the wallpaper in her room and found these odd markings and copied them in her sketches. But she is not there. And her wallpaper is intact. I push away the crawling sensation that assails me as a result of this eerie connection and go to look for her.

I check the bathroom along the corridor, Magda's room, the guest bedrooms. I call Janey's name, and the syllables echo in the high ceilings, but I receive no reply. She is nowhere downstairs, and there's no sign of her anywhere outside, either. Out there, hail is rattling down out of an iron-grey sky. I can't imagine she'd choose to be out in this weather. Now I'm beginning to feel anxious. Janey has a knack for going missing; she leads a parallel life to me and Mother, as if following a thread that's invisible to the rest of us. I make my way, running head down, hunched against the hail, into the barn, but it's dark and cold and the ladder that leads up to the hayloft is laid on its side along the wall.

Back in the house once more, I return upstairs. I check under Janey's bed in case she's playing a game with me; I check under my own bed, even though it's pulled out into the middle of the room. It's while I'm down on my hands and knees that I hear the noises – a sort of distant scrabbling. I freeze, listening, trying to pinpoint the sound. It's as if it's coming from the corner of the room. But there's only the fitted wardrobe in the corner, where I found the fur coat.

Crossing the room, I find the wardrobe door slightly ajar, as if someone else has been in here and opened it. I listen hard, barely breathing. The scrabbling noises have stopped, as if whatever was making them has become aware that I'm listening.

With a swift, galvanic heave, I throw the wardrobe door wide, and as I do so I hear the noise again, a scuff on stone, but muffled and further away, below and to my right. How very odd. I push my clothes aside and lay my hand questingly on the back of the wardrobe... and it moves.

I gasp and jump back, my heart skittering at this wrongness like a stone skipped across waves. Removing my clothes from the rail, I hurl them onto the bed and return to the wardrobe, feeling a stir of air like chilly fingers across my forehead as I crane forward to examine what appears to be its false back. Gingerly, I press my hand against it and it swings away from me into dark air. I can sense rather than see space behind it, sense rather than see a void above and below.

'Janey?' I call, and my voice quavers into this blackness, echoing in all directions so that the sound multiplies and splits into many voices and whispers. I reach into the blackness with the primeval fear of what may lie in darkness – the biting teeth, the clutching claws, the crawling peril of insects and spiders…

My fingers meet rough stone about eighteen inches into the void. If I move my hand up, I find something that juts out – and the same if I reach down. A staircase hidden in the wall? Why would you need such a secret thing in a house of this size? It's hardly so grand that it requires servants' passages. It's the sort of thing you come across only in fairy tales. And ghost stories.

I remember Casworan Martin's words about the house – *it's older than it looks* – and shudder.

But I remember the scrabbling noise and the sound of a footstep on stone. What if someone has got in and taken my daughter? What if she's trapped somewhere in this liminal space between walls and floors, in the hands of some deviant?

'Janey?' I call, and my voice sounds small and feeble as it disappears into the darkness.

I run to fetch a torch and play its beam into the void behind the wardrobe.

It *is* a staircase. It doesn't go straight up or straight down, so I don't get a clear view, but curves and disappears into darkness a few feet below. Gathering my courage, I step into the dark space, balancing on one of the narrow stairs, and at once feel overwhelmed by claustrophobia. I hate small spaces, being enclosed and unable to move. As a child I had nightmares of being buried alive, of waking in a coffin weighed down by earth and stone, breaking my fingernails trying to claw out. Night after night I would wake up screaming from the same dream. This may have been after a boy at school told me this very thing had happened to an old widow buried in the local churchyard and how her sister had dreamed she heard the widow's voice calling on her to dig her free. They had apparently rounded up half the village to disinter the widow and upon opening the coffin had found her revived but gone out of her mind with terror. No doubt it was an apocryphal tale, but it haunted me.

Down below, there is a dragging, grating sound and cold air comes arrowing up the staircase, raising the ends of my hair.

'Janey?' I swing the torch beam around the corner of the narrow stairs and inch my way down, my free hand flat on the clammy stone, the safety of the known house distanced by each step.

The staircase winds around another angle and steepens. I can feel the edge of the step on the ball of my foot, it is so narrow. I play the light down past my feet and see another three steps below, and then below that the beginning of what appears to be a wider space, delineated by a vertical glow of grey light to one side.

More dragging. The grey line widens and light spills in. I clatter down the remaining steps, push aside a swinging shutter, and jar my foot on flat ground. The area smells of ash and mildew, pine resin… and coal. I swing the torch around and see that I am surrounded by brooms and buckets, sacks of coal and stacks of logs. Light spills through a small door that now stands ajar, and when I push it open it gives onto the passageway behind the house. I have only ever seen the coalhole from the outside when coming to refill the scuttle and to collect the logs Jack brings here; to come upon it down these secret stairs is disorientating.

Outside in the low afternoon light, I find Janey in the passageway, her face and hands and Rabbit all smutty with coal dust.

I grab her to me, at once furious and utterly relieved. 'Whatever did you think you were doing? Didn't you hear me calling you?'

'I was exploring. Explorers never answer their mothers when they're on an expedition.'

I hold my daughter away from me. 'Janeska, if I call you, no matter what you are doing, you must reply. Do you hear me? It's important. I was scared to death that something had happened to you.'

'I'm fine. Silly Mummy.'

'Maybe I am, but I am still your mummy and you must do what I tell you.' I regard her solemn little face all smudged with coal dust and grime. 'How on earth could you see where you were going? You could have fallen!'

She shrugs. 'Rabbit has very good eyes.'

For some reason this enrages me. 'Rabbit is a stuffed toy! Rabbit cannot see. You could've fallen down the stairs and banged your head and died and we would never have found you!'

Janey's eyes become round at this thought. Then she says, very matter-of-factly, 'But you would, because I'd have started to smell bad – like the dead badger with the worms.'

How very macabre. 'That's not the point. You must not explore without me, do you understand?'

'But you're always busy, Mummy.'

This is true. I have been running everywhere at Magda's beck and call. It occurs to me, shamefully, that in the past month Janey and I have not been on a single 'expedition', or even for a walk further than the little bridge, or the edge of the woods. 'I promise I will make time for us to have a proper expedition,' I tell her. 'But first we must get you cleaned up before Granny comes back.' I pause. 'And I think it's probably best not to mention this to her right now.' I can imagine the lecture we will get: Janey for exploring where she should not, me for not keeping her under control.

'We should *lie* to her?' Janey's lips curl into a bow of sheer delight.

'Not a lie, exactly. Just best not to mention it.'

'Can I tell Jack?'

'No, I don't think that's a good idea at all.' I'm not sure why I say this. 'I will tell them about it at the right time.'

'What is the right time?'

'It's something grown-ups know about and children come to learn.' The sort of infuriating pronouncement I've inherited from my aunt and grandmother.

By the time Jack and Magda return from the shops with their purchases, Janey has been bathed and had her hair washed, with just a little less screaming than usual, and is installed in the drawing room with a teddy-bear jigsaw I meant to save till Christmas. Rabbit is hanging by his – I mean, her – ears from a peg at the end of the mantelpiece, steaming gently. I have only had time to wash my own face and hands and brush the worst of the dust and cobwebs out of my hair.

Magda at once exclaims over the use of her new coffee table as a jigsaw board and Jack and I exchange a look; she appears to have returned in a thoroughly bad mood.

'Did you manage to get everything you wanted?' I ask.

To this, my mother purses her lips and declares she's going to make herself a 'decent cup of coffee', implying such a thing was not to be found in the wasteland that is Penzance.

When she's gone, I look over at Jack. 'What happened?'

He makes a face. 'We met the mayor's wife over curtain fabrics in Alfred Smith's and Magda gushed about how happy she was they'd be coming to her New Year's Eve party.'

I know what's coming next. 'She said they're very sorry, but they won't be able to make it?'

'Words to that effect.'

'Oh dear.' It's not that I care who comes to the wretched party, only that I know how furious Magdalena will be if she feels snubbed.

'She's been in a foul temper ever since. I'm afraid I didn't manage to get your paint, either.'

My turn to be disappointed.

Jack holds up his hands before I can say anything more. 'They'll deliver it next week and I'll help you get the room painted as soon as they do.'

So, I must live with the strange markings for a week.

After coffee and two cigarettes, which make her cough and hack, Magda appears restored to better humour. I make tea for Jack and me, and orange squash for Janey, and we all have some of the saffron cake bought from the bakery, eaten plain rather than accompanied by Mr Skerritt's preferred slabs of butter.

'This reminds me of my mother's *babka*,' Magda reminisces, and I raise an eyebrow. My grandmother's baking skills left a lot to be desired. It was Aunt Kamila who baked *szarlotka* and *racuchy* and poppy seed cake. I have the sense that accurate memory is not the point of this conversation, and I am right.

'Did your mother bake saffron cake, Jack?'

'It's a Cornish speciality,' Jack says noncommittally, and I can't tell whether this means, '*Of course not, she wasn't Cornish*,' or '*Obviously*.'

'Do tell me about her.' Magda crosses her slim legs out in front of her, the better for us all to admire her neat ankles, silk-stockinged calves and smartly shod feet.

Jack fidgets. He leans over the coffee table. 'Look,' he says to Janey, 'here's a corner piece. I always find it's best to start with the corners. Then you can find all the edge pieces and make a frame and work inwards.'

Janey is unimpressed by this advice. Greedy for instant gratification, she's concentrating on the biggest teddy bear and has already assembled one of his large round ears, his shiny eyes and nose and part of his bowtie.

'I don't remember much about my mother,' Jack says at last, keeping his gaze fixed on the jumble of jigsaw pieces. 'I lost her when I was quite young.'

To give her credit, Magdalena looks stricken. 'I'm so sorry, I had no idea. You poor boy.'

She tries to engage Jack on the subject of his mother,

but he applies himself to the puzzle, and soon he and Janey are making good progress, Jack focusing on the brown background, leaving all the brightly coloured bits to Janey. I watch as they bend their heads together, laughing, Janey exclaiming in triumph whenever she manages to fit two pieces together, Jack quietly disengaging the ones that have been wrongly forced together.

My mind strays back to the hidden staircase. I remember how the torchlight played on the back wall of the void behind the wardrobe, the sense of the darkness flowering above it, which must, I think, issue up into the attic space. I have only briefly examined the attic – just once via the cascading ladder that pulls down onto the top landing between the first two guest bedrooms. I had gone up to the top of the ladder and shone the torch around in a desultory manner – enough to see that it was empty – and had been relieved by that. I was worried there might be detritus left by previous owners, the usual items stowed away for a possible future that never came, or worse: strange chests and boxes containing who knew what horrors.

I watch the jigsaw progress for another few minutes until I can bear it no longer. I will just pop up and satisfy my curiosity, I think, and I push myself to my feet, making a bathroom excuse.

Back in my room, I close the door then cross to the wardrobe, click on the torch and step into the hole behind the false back, this time with far less trepidation, since I know now what lies below, and I have a good idea what lies above. I tell myself that this excursion is just to make sure I have checked the final part of the staircase so that I can stop thinking about it. It's an interesting historical feature in an old house, that's all. Probably somewhere they hid priests or seditious plotters during periods of persecution. I hadn't paid that much attention to English history at school; Magda was thrilled by it, and with the perverse instinct of the teenaged, I had therefore veered away. Besides, the idea of learning some other country's history bored me. I was Polish and had been dragged from my country and brought to this new world and dumped at a boarding school where I had no friends and everyone made fun of my accent and my shyness; why should I bother learning anything about the place that turned out such horrid people? And yet, some of it must have stuck. Facts are reassuring, pegs to hang uncertainty on. Once the thought had struck me, I was sure this was why the hidden staircase must have been constructed. What was it the vicar had said? That there was always strife in the county. That the Cornish are obstinate and combative and fought ferociously for their beliefs. I can feel the pieces slotting into place as neatly as Janey's jigsaw puzzle.

Up I go. It is so much easier going up than down, and, I remind myself, when the sense of space beneath me becomes unnerving, I can always unhook the loft ladder and descend onto the landing if I don't fancy negotiating these precipitous stairs on the way back down.

Comforted by this thought, I reach the final steps and emerge into open space. I manoeuvre my arms up and over the square opening and steady myself, then play the torch beam around. I have not, in fact, come out into the attic – at least, not the area I'm familiar with. It is more like entering a small monastic cell, which perhaps tallies with the idea of the priest hole. It appears that a wall has been constructed between this part and the rest of the cavernous attic, making a narrow room. There is even a small window on the sloping side, currently limned by deep red sunset light, which must be the roof at the back of the house. I push myself up through the opening and find that I can stand upright in this new space.

I move away from the hole and at once knock something over. It makes a hell of a racket and instinctively I reach out and grab it before it falls down the hole and thence down the stairs. When I set it upright again, I see that it is a battery-powered lantern. I turn it on and suddenly the whole space is flooded with golden light.

My eye is drawn to an object lying against the wall.

It appears to be a corpse.

It is not, in fact, a corpse.

On closer inspection, I find that the long, body-sized shape is a khaki sleeping bag – the 'head' a small round cushion that's being used as a pillow. Someone has been camping here, maybe even living here. A suspicion buzzes around my head as I take in the methylated spirits stove, canteen of water, jar of coffee, packet of tea, Rich Tea biscuits, candles, pile of neatly folded clothing, a rucksack and what appears to be a pair of Army-issue boots. And some books.

I pick the top one up and angle it towards the lantern. It's a copy of Howard Spring's *A Sunset Touch* – the novel Magda bought a couple of weeks ago from the bookshop in Penzance, and which promptly went missing, and below that my *Frenchman's Creek*. Also in the piles are a little volume entitled *West Penwith: Flora and Fauna*,

R. M. Ballantyne's *The Gorilla Hunters*, J. Meade Falkner's *Moonfleet*, and J. R. R. Tolkien's *The Hobbit*. At the bottom of the pile is a battered copy of *Treasure Island*. I read some of the Swallows and Amazons novels years ago but could not find sufficient connection with them. I have never read *Treasure Island*. I pick it up, curious, and am just opening the cover when I hear a tell-tale scuff on the stairs. My heart stops. There is nowhere to hide, and neither the book not the rubber-covered torch is much of a weapon.

A head appears through the opening and I open my mouth to scream. The book falls from my hand and butterflies itself on the floor.

The figure flows up into the attic with such speed that I barely have time even to yelp before a hand has been clamped over my mouth and Jack is there in front of me, his eyes dark pools in his pale face and the lantern light making a halo of his hair.

'I'm going to take my hand away. Please don't scream.'

He removes his hand, watching me warily, and my knees give way. I sit down hard on the makeshift bed, my heart stuttering.

Jack holds his hands out, palms towards me as if in surrender. 'I'm sorry. I didn't mean to scare you.'

'Well, you did! I don't know what gives you the right to go sneaking around inside our house, right above my sleeping daughter!'

Jack hangs his head. 'Look, I know. It was wrong of me. And I'm sorry.' His expression is anguished. 'I'll move my things and get out of your way – as you can see, I don't have much.'

He starts to gather his belongings into the rucksack. I

retrieve *Treasure Island* from the floor. It has fallen open to the flyleaf. I catch sight of childish writing, blocky and unsteady – *THIS BOOK IS THE PROPERTY OF WILLIAM PRID* – before Jack takes it from me and sets it aside. He passes *A Sunset Touch* and *Frenchman's Creek* to me. 'I only borrowed these. The rest were left by the previous owners.'

The writing bothers me. I'm sure I've seen those unsteady capitals before…

'You've been living up here?' I ask.

'Sometimes,' he admits.

'Why?'

'To be brutally honest with you, I don't really have anywhere else to go. Well, I do, but it's awkward.'

'How long have you been here?'

'Here? In the attic? Only recently. Before you bought the house, I was living in it – and then when you moved in, I camped wherever I could.'

'But why?'

He shrugs. 'This valley is special.'

I want to say it doesn't seem very special to me – a dark, dank cleft running down to the grey sea, no cheer, no warmth, no beauty – but I find I can't, because there is something about the area leading to White Cove: it casts a spell. 'Well, the house is ours now. You can't stay here. I mean… you just can't.' I watch as he rolls up the sleeping bag.

'I really didn't mean to frighten you,' Jack says as he finishes tying it up. 'Or poor Ted, who fell off the roof. I didn't push him, though. I was just shuttering the window to stop him looking in and he was so surprised when he glimpsed me that he lost his footing. Then I think he couldn't admit that it was his own fault and had to make up a story about being pushed by a ghost.'

'Well, I suppose that's one small mystery solved.' Also, the missing biscuits and the books and the strange noises in the night. I think about the items in the cave too: the shoe, the perfume and the cigarette case. Is Jack just a small-time thief? If so, he's not doing very well out of it. But this doesn't seem right, either, based on what I know of him thus far. I don't think he's dishonest and yet there's something I can't quite piece together.

'Where will you go?' I ask.

'Please don't concern yourself. I've had to look after myself my whole adult life. I daresay I'll survive a while longer.'

His tone is odd: defensive, but also angry, as if I am in the wrong for turfing him out of *our* house. He has to go, of course he does, and yet at the same time, I don't want him to. In a strange way his presence here seems right, protective, correcting an emotional balance in the house, providing a kind of buffer between me and my mother. Everything works better when Jack is here. The atmosphere is less tense. He makes Magda laugh and Janey loves him. But it's more than that. I'm beginning to see him as a part of my world, yet I don't really know why. He is like a jigsaw puzzle with pieces missing – not lost, but deliberately hidden away.

'Why don't I ask Mother if you can stay in one of the guest rooms?' I suggest after a while.

'I don't need your charity,' he says unfairly. I have hurt his pride.

'It wasn't meant as charity,' I say, but he doesn't answer me. We make our way back down the steps and while I emerge into my room through the back of the wardrobe, he carries on down the narrow staircase to the coalhole, his rucksack rustling against the wall. I hear his steps fading to silence and feel the strangest little catch in my heart. Where will he go? I peer out of the window and see that it has started to rain, the drops shivering the leaves on the nearest trees.

14

Jack is less communicative when he returns to work the next day, to the extent of Magda exclaiming, 'I can see you've got out of bed the wrong side!' when he fails to indulge her teasing, and I cannot help but feel guilty at her choice of words – guilty for turfing him out of his secret attic room. Goodness knows where he slept, and I daren't ask him, for fear of hearing he half froze to death in a hedge. Certainly, he is wearing the same clothes he wore yesterday and doesn't appear to have shaved. It was a really cold night last night, wet too, and I heard the wind soughing through the trees as I tossed and turned, unable to sleep for wondering where he had gone. He doesn't seem actively hostile towards me, though, and when I bring him a cup of coffee halfway through the morning, he thanks me with a brief smile, before getting on with his tasks.

He works quickly and quietly, achieving more in a couple of days than Mr Skerritt's decorators in over a week. The hall gleams with its new paint, the mossy greens bringing out the tones in the flagstone floor and the warmth of the wooden furniture. Magda has even installed a couple of tall indoor palm trees in shining brass pots on either side of the door into the drawing room. They look like magnificent sentries. The drawing room itself glows with glorious colour. I have to admit that my style-conscious mother has an eye for just the right fabrics and textures to bring such a cavernous room to life and make it feel homely and welcoming. Huge canvases of semi-abstract landscapes in gilt frames adorn two of the walls; there are antique brass candlesticks on the mantelpiece, velvet cushions on the sofas and chairs, a big Persian rug covering the floor like a sumptuous indoor garden. The tall skirting boards make a smart border and the intricate stucco ceiling with its Jacobean strapwork is spotlessly white. From the central rose hangs a crystal chandelier that must have cost more than the whole decorating budget; spending money well is Magdalena's forte.

It is all so much more than I could ever have expected, or wished for. I feel as if I am living in a sort of palace, and yet, surprisingly, I don't feel out of place.

Janey and I gather pine cones in the woods and paint them gold to add to the display. We have spotted where holly grows too, complete with bright bursts of red berries, and we plan to gather some before Christmas.

'Can I pick out a tree?' Janey begs. 'We'll need a really big one!'

I explain that the woods don't belong to us and we can't just march in and cut down trees.

Janey tilts her head. 'Rabbit says we can take just one,' she informs me solemnly. 'As long as we honour it, and her.'

I smile. She does come out with some odd things. 'We'll see.'

Later, I report this little exchange to Jack, with whom I have re-established a degree of our earlier rapport. He looks at me curiously. 'Does she often say things like this?'

I consider his question. 'I think she uses Rabbit as a sort of alter ego to give weight to the things she says. Rabbit is more than just an imaginary friend – he, or rather she, has become like a little god whose pronouncements can't be questioned.'

He nods noncommittally. 'I saw her drawings…'

'She's good, isn't she?' I respond enthusiastically, proud of my daughter. 'She can really capture a line, a shape. Did you see the one she did of a seagull last week? It was excellent. I doubt I could manage anything half so good myself.'

'I meant the ones she was doing in her room that day Magda was looking for her cigarette case.'

I go quiet, remembering that awful day and hoping he won't mention Janey's bruised face. 'Oh, those. Yes. They were a bit strange and obsessive!' I laugh nervously. 'Perhaps she was really trying hard to capture the perfect line she could see in her head, over and over.'

'I think that's exactly what she was doing. It's funny, though – I used to do the same thing.'

'You did? As a child?'

He nods. 'Sometimes a pattern gets stuck in your mind and you have to keep drawing it to get it out, or to get it right. I don't know which.' He looks away, smiling, maybe reminiscing. 'Perhaps that's what made me an engineer in the end, that eye for detail, that determination to get it right.'

'Certainly makes you an excellent decorator. Magda can't stop cooing over the quality of your work.'

'I like to put the extra effort in. This place deserves it, after being neglected for so long.'

'I'm sure you'll get lots of work out of it – if you want it – after everyone's come to the party and seen how beautiful you've helped us make the house.'

His expression becomes shuttered and he doesn't say any more but takes himself off to deal with a loose stair-rod Magda asked him to attend to earlier.

I go back upstairs and check in on Janey, who is having her afternoon nap. The paint for my bedroom was delivered this morning and I have liberated a roller and a paint pan from the decorating supplies downstairs. I think that tomorrow, if I work quickly, I will be able to get a first coat at least on one of the walls before I am missed and redeployed to other duties. I have already covered over the disturbing marks and lines around the bottom of the walls with a layer of masking undercoat, but even though I can't see them, I can still feel them running and leaping as I lie on the edge of sleep. And it occurs to me now in a sudden jolt that those shapes are similar to the inscribed line I found hidden behind the bright flowers, carved into the stone outside the churchyard. This makes no sense: Janey hasn't seen that inscription, and she drew her sketches before I peeled off the wallpaper in my room.

I dismiss the connection as pure coincidence before it can gain traction. But later that afternoon, when Magda asks Jack if he could possibly take the car up to the village to fetch supplies, I catch him at the front door and beg a lift. There is something I want to look at again, just to put this mad idea to rest. I have stolen one of Janey's drawings while she sleeps and folded it inside my pocket.

Inside the Morris, Jack turns to me. 'Are you sure it's safe to leave her with your mother?' He holds my gaze until I colour.

We have never spoken about that day – not about the bruise on Janey's face, nor the sea cave, the cigarette case, nor the earring. It's all bound together in a knot of guilt and shame that neither of us is willing to unravel, not now, at any rate; the world feels too fragile.

'Yes,' I say briskly, refusing to tug on the loose end of the string. 'She'll be fine. Anyway, we'll be back in no time.'

He says no more to this but revs up the engine in readiness for the steep climb up the drive to the top of the hill. As we round the first bend, I see a red vehicle at the top. A post office van. Jack drives up to the turning spot, where the postman flags us down.

I wind down my window. 'Hello, is there a problem?'

The postman shuffles together a small stack of envelopes and comes across the road to me. 'Not a problem as such, miss, but...' He holds the envelopes out to me. 'I... I'm not sure what to do with these. They've got no stamps on them, you see. Or a full address. I've been leaving them in the box till I had a chance to see you and, well, here you are.'

I stare at him uncomprehendingly, then at the uppermost letter, which is addressed to:

Daddy
Our House
London.

My heart clenches. *Oh*. Poor Janey. All this time. By the look of the pile, weeks and weeks – maybe ever since we moved in.

'I didn't know what to do,' the postman says sympathetically. 'I wasn't sure whether I should bring them back to the house or not... I didn't want to embarrass anyone.'

I give him a grateful smile. 'That was kind of you. I'll take them, shall I?'

He hesitates. 'Technically, once they're posted they're the responsibility of the Royal Mail...' he starts.

'But they're not technically posted if there's no stamp on them, and no address,' Jack says gently, and the two men come to a complicit agreement.

The postman hands me the stack of letters and I put them quickly away in my bag before he can change his mind.

Once they're out of sight, I can see him relax. 'How are you finding it out here?' he asks. 'Quite remote, isn't it? I hope you've settled in down there... despite... everything.'

What does he mean by 'everything'? I muster my composure. 'Well, the house is coming along nicely, and the views are... spectacular.'

He grins, relieved. 'Ar, they are that. Well,' – he tips his cap to me – 'must be getting on and finishing the round. They say there's snow coming in.'

'Do they?'

'Sometime tonight, mebbe. Though it's rare for it to stick in the valley. I'm sure you'll be all right.'

'Thank you,' I say warmly. 'It was kind of you to do this. Take care.'

We drive the rest of the way to the village in silence as my thoughts churn. My poor little girl, missing her father all this time so much that she's been writing and writing to him. How sad must she be that he has never written back? How lost and abandoned? I can feel myself welling up again. Should I give her the address and some stamps so that she can send her letters to him? Or would that just be prolonging the agony? I can't imagine what Magda would say – or do – if she were to find out we were still in touch with Dennis.

I find myself imagining his handwriting on an envelope dropped onto the doormat in the hall, invading the pristine new space – or worse, him standing there, having driven down from London to fetch us back. For a moment my heart lifts at this fantasy, but it is only for a fleeting instant, immediately replaced by dread. Would I want Dennis to reappear in my life, knowing what I know now? If you'd asked me this question only a few weeks ago I might well have leaped at the chance to return to my old life, but now? I don't think I would. I miss our little house that I had made as pretty as I could, but now I am beginning to remember the arguments we had when I asked for a little more money, for a rug, for better curtains, to get a carpenter in to repair the rotten window frames. How Dennis always pleaded poverty and the difficulties of his job. How he always explained away his absences by making himself a victim of an overbearing manager or a demanding company policy. How I had to eke out meals for Janey and myself when we ran out of what little housekeeping money Dennis would give me, with his grudging 'all I can afford'. How sometimes I went hungry so that Janey had enough to eat, or a pair of shoes that fitted her. How our Jamaican neighbours would bring spicy stews or children's cast-offs to the door and I saw the pity in their eyes. And all the time Dennis was maintaining a four-bedroomed family house in Chiswick, a sports car and private school education for his eldest son. My cheeks flame with renewed fury.

How many other inconvenient truths have I buried, I wonder, as the Eglosberyan church tower comes into view. How many lies have I told myself as I wrapped a comfort blanket around my spirit in much the same way as Janey has breathed life and personality into Rabbit? And suddenly, I am fully and deeply ashamed. I have not committed myself to our new start. I have not thrown myself into remaking our future as I should. The house at White Cove is mine now, and it is – or soon will be – beautiful and welcoming and a very good business. And I will learn to drive and not feel trapped here, and Janey will go to school, and we will make a good life for ourselves. And I will be a better mother, and I will stop being so afraid of everything.

Jack pulls the car in on the lane behind the church, the one that leads down to Keziah's cottage. I can't help but gaze down the road, straining my eyes to catch a glimpse of her, or of her odd companion Ari, but there's no one in sight.

'Come on,' Jack says. 'Let's get the shopping out of the way and then I'll show you the church.'

We walk down the road through the village and purchase our supplies in the grocer's and then head back towards the car. 'There's something I want to look at before we go into the church,' I say and quicken my pace as Jack goes to put the shopping in the boot.

I hold the shape of the leaping lines that were hidden under my wallpaper in my mind while I take the piece of folded paper – one of Janey's obsessive drawings – out of my pocket as I approach the back wall of the churchyard. The little stone is not hard to find, for someone has replaced the flowers I saw last time with a bright posy of pink briar roses, blue borage and sprigs of unseasonal honeysuckle. I bend and brush the flowers out of the way so that I can view the carving. I hold the drawing up beside it. They are all but identical – a fluid, rounded line, topped at the right-hand end by a tilted V-shape.

My heart stops, then thunders, and little dark stars dance in my vision. What the hell does it mean?

I meet Jack at the steps into the churchyard, and he regards me curiously. 'Are you all right?'

I show him Janey's sketch. His expression appears unreadable, but unless I'm mistaken he's masking a degree of shock.

'What does it mean?' I press on. 'I found the same pattern under the wallpaper in my room. That pattern she's been drawing over and over. I knew it reminded me of something. I just checked – there's the same design on the old stone outside the churchyard.'

His eyebrows shoot up. 'Really?'

I take him over to the marker stone and watch as he moves the flowers aside and gazes at the odd abstract line that matches so closely my daughter's sketch. When he looks back up, he looks energised, lit up in some way.

'That's extraordinary.'

'But how could Janey have come across it? She's never seen this stone.'

'I never had till today, either.' He looks thoughtful, distracted; then he glances up into the darkening sky. 'Come on,' he says, taking me by the arm.

We pass beneath the sundial on the porch and into the cool, obscure interior of the church. Once inside, Jack drops my hand. I stop and stare upwards, awed by the yawning space overhead. 'It's enormous!'

Jack laughs. 'You can tell that from the outside, surely?'

'Well, yes, of course. It's just, well, it's like a small cathedral.' It is not, obviously, anywhere near as large as the only two cathedrals I have set foot inside – the Katedra Wawelska in Krakow – where Stanislaus the Martyr, the patron saint of Poland, is buried, his tomb surrounded by gleaming gold pillars and presided over by praying angels, where I used to go every month or so with my grandmother and aunt to light candles for the dead and dying – and Westminster Abbey with my parents just before my father joined the RAF. In comparison, this church would be unremarkable if sited in a town – but here, in the middle of a small Cornish village, it seems ludicrously oversized, out of proportion to the tiny population it serves. And there is a sense of real magnificence to Eglosberyan church. Someone must have invested a vast sum of money in the building of this place.

'*Eglos* is the Cornish word for "church",' Jack says. 'There are all sorts of Cornish towns and villages with *eglos* in their names.'

'What about the berry bit?'

He shrugs. 'Probably the name of a long-ago saint.'

We walk around the shrouded space in silence for a while, taking in the scent of wax, wood polish, cold stone and candles; the stained-glass windows and carved plaster knights and ladies lying prone and praying for all time.

'This place is mentioned in the Domesday Book,' Jack

says, coming to stand beside me as I gaze up at the carved screens over the chancel. And when I look blank, he adds, 'I keep forgetting you're a foreigner! That was the census book made by William of Normandy when he conquered England in the eleventh century to take stock of all the lands and wealth he'd won. But it was constructed long before that.'

'That it was!' declares a loud voice, and we both jump.

Turning, we find Ariadne, the eccentric artist who lives with Keziah. She is carrying an armful of holly, its red berries glowing bright in the gloomy air.

'I thought I spied you,' she says brightly. 'I don't often come in here.' She inclines her head towards me and says in a stage whisper, 'I'm not welcome.'

'Surely churches are open to all?'

'Not according to the vicar.' She makes a face. 'Not that I care. This place just memorialises bloodshed and atrocity.'

'Well, that's certainly one way of looking at Christianity!' I declare gaily, though my insides briefly shrivel at the thought of how my Catholic family would cross themselves in horror at such a pronouncement.

Ariadne gives me her toothy grin. 'Actually, it's a perfect opportunity for me to right the balance a little.' She lays down her bundle of holly on a nearby pew and brings out a heavy velvet bag, fastened with a tasselled drawstring, fiddles it open, digs around and brings out a pebble which she places beneath the pew.

Jack and I exchange a glance.

She pops another stone beneath the pew to the right of the aisle and then steps over the red cord that ropes off the sanctuary.

I feel my throat tighten. Whatever is she doing? It feels like a form of trespass, of sacrilege, disturbing and transgressive.

Jack draws me away. 'Look at the craftsmanship in these scenes!' He directs my eye to the intricate rood screens, the carvings picked out in rich red and blue, green and gold: streams of medieval huntsmen racing across the arches on their stylised mounts, depicted in exuberant, lively detail – the dogs bounding alongside, their prey vanishing into the bosky woodland branches and leaves that form the edges of the screen. I remember there is a hunting scene on the front porch too, all around the sundial.

Ariadne reappears, looking well pleased with herself. She takes my hand and presses two of her pebbles into it. 'Because you're one of her own,' she says cryptically as she closes my fingers over them. 'And one of ours now, too. And don't forget to come and see us. In fact, come now, because Keziah will never forgive me if I say I've seen you and not brought you back for tea.'

'I can't come now.' I smile to lessen the abruptness of this refusal. 'We have to get back.'

'Nonsense!' She loops an arm through mine and turns to Jack. 'You'll carry the holly for me, won't you, my lover?'

Jack bows. 'Nothing would give me greater pleasure, my lady.' He turns to me. 'We'll be quick,' he promises. 'You can't say no to Ariadne and Keziah – they'll put a curse on you if you do.'

Ariadne punches him gently on the arm in a surprising gesture of affection and familiarity. I had thought Jack a solitary, friendless man and I find myself smiling. Keziah and Ariadne are unusual women, but their generosity is undeniable, and Janey trusts Jack. Perhaps there is a life to be made here, with a circle of friends to support us and joy to be found, after all.

Jack leads the way up the aisle with his arms full of holly, and Ariadne and I follow on behind, Ariadne stopping occasionally to drop one of her pebbles beneath a pew.

'What did you mean about righting the balance?' I ask curiously.

'The world is all about balance: you can't have too much of one thing without losing too much of another. The power of the masculine must be offset by the power of the feminine; death must be offset by life; hate, by love; order by a little chaos—'

Jack has come to such a sudden standstill that we almost cannon into him. There is a figure in front of him, silhouetted by the light from the open door.

'You!'

The figure comes forward. It is Casworan Martin. He is glaring, his fine features contorted into something approaching disgust as he stares past Jack at Ariadne.

'I thought I forbade you ever to enter my church again!'

'Now, now, Vicar,' she mocks him. By the arm crooked through mine I can feel that her muscles are tensed, as if she is preparing to spring on him like a great cat, ready to rip out his throat, and when I look at her, she is baring her teeth, though it takes me a moment to realise it is in a grin, albeit a fierce one.

'This is a house of God!' he roars, stabbing a finger at her. 'I'm surprised the Lord has not smitten you down!'

Ariadne chuckles. She unthreads herself from me and throws her arms wide. 'Come on then, God,' she challenges. 'Give me a good smiting!'

Jack is watching the vicar and I am surprised to see something close to hatred in his eyes, but after a tense moment all he does is turn to Ariadne and me. 'Come on,' he says. 'Let's get out of this monument to death.' And he shoulders past the vicar, deliberately grazing him with the prickly bundle of holly, and steps out into the light.

I scurry to catch up with him, avoiding the Reverend Martin's gaze, but unfortunately not his attention.

'You cannot run with the hounds and with the hare!' he informs me gravely. 'You are keeping company with some ungodly folk, Mila Prusik. Be careful of your almighty soul. I am always here if you need someone to talk to, to instruct you in the ways of the righteous.'

Once outside in the churchyard, Ariadne bursts out laughing. 'Ridiculous man! Hares and hounds, indeed. How dare he?' She makes a gesture towards the church, two-fingered, rude.

I am, I have to admit, just a little scandalised, but even so I follow her and Jack down the lane to Keziah's cottage gladly, leaving the overlarge church and its field of gravestones behind me.

'Jack,' I catch up to him. 'What did you mean, exactly, by a *monument to death*?'

He looks a little abashed. 'Sorry about that. I lost my temper. I didn't mean to upset you – I know you're probably Catholic.'

I assure him that I am not affronted. 'I just want to understand what you meant.'

It is Ariadne who replies. 'Do you know why this church is here, and why it's so huge, so overbearing?'

I tell her what I remember of the historical sermon the Reverend Martin delivered to me.

'Yes, this place marks the last stand of the ancient Cornish,' she tells me. 'They rose in rebellion and in defence of the land and their ancestors and were massacred here by the forces of militant Christianity, who were determined to destroy all vestige of local custom and worship.'

Jack takes up the story. 'King Athelstan sent his army to crush their insurrection. The Cornish fought bravely but they were vastly outnumbered. No mercy was shown, no prisoners were taken. One by one they were murdered, and those taken captive were executed till all the streams that come off the moors from here down through the valley and out to the sea ran red with Cornish blood!'

'That's why the old name of this bit,' – she sweeps a hand wide towards empty farmland – 'is Gwel Ruth. The Red Field. To this day the family who own this farm won't plough up the field – too many dead souls, too many bones. They say it's cursed and nothing good will grow there. Even animals pastured on it don't thrive. And see here—' She indicates a stone marker all but buried in the hedge.

'A Celtic cross?' I venture.

'Look on the other side,' she tells me.

I step into the hedge and carefully part the brambles swarming over the granite, then look back at Ariadne, puzzled. 'I don't see anything unusual?'

She comes to stand beside me. 'Look harder.'

It's shadowed and obscured by the vegetation, but as I stare I can make out the trace of what looks like a head, primitive and crude, two holes for eyes and a short, straight line for a mouth. I touch the stone with my fingers to feel the indentations. Faint wiggly lines radiating out from the head towards the edges of the marker must be long hair.

'Is it a woman?'

Ariadne smiles. 'There are lots of them around here, mostly defaced, with Christian crosses carved into them to mask what stood here before: waymarkers delineating her realm. We live in a special, sacred place, infused with the blood of the Cornish.'

Jack gives her a warning look, and she grins.

'Well, it was over a thousand years ago and those tales are too grim, so let's go and have some tea and a slice of my beloved's honeycake and put the darkness away from us!'

At the cottage we are greeted by a waft of warm air and the scent of baking, and find Keziah in the kitchen with flour on her hands and on her nose. Ariadne brushes the latter smudge off with a finger and then kisses her roundly right in front of us, without the slightest embarrassment, and suddenly I yearn to have someone in my life whom I could so fearlessly love with passion and honesty. I had loved Dennis like that once, but now I look back on it, I realise that our relationship was always hidden from view, even our wedding carried out at the registry office – 'We don't need all that fuss!' – attended only by Magda and my friend Daphne, and two friends of Dennis's whom I had never seen again. He had never encouraged visitors to the house, not even installed a telephone, and Daphne had faded out of my life as soon as I became pregnant with Janey, because Dennis disapproved of her bright lipsticks and cutting sense of humour. If only I had seen the way he had isolated me was deliberately controlling; at the time I thought he wanted only me. Yet again, I cringe at my naivete.

I suddenly become aware of Jack's eyes on me, watching me watch the two women exchange caresses, and I cannot help but blush.

We all sit around the table drinking spiced tea and eating the honeycake Keziah takes from the oven, timed so perfectly it is as if our visit was pre-arranged. There is much laughter and teasing. Keziah fetches some darned socks for Jack. 'I'm going to teach you how to wield a darning needle yourself. I've never known anyone go through clothes the way you do!'

So, Keziah and Ariadne appear to have been washing and mending Jack's clothes while he has been sleeping in our roof space, frightening workmen and making the joists creak at night. A couple of months ago such bizarre behaviour would have horrified me, but now it just seems a bit eccentric. I feel far more at ease in the company of these warm, joyful people than I could ever have imagined possible. I look around the kitchen with its shelves of pots and bottles, the sprays of herbs hanging drying from a rack, at the tiles decorated in a riot of colours, depicting flowers and birds, fruits and beasts, all apparently hand-painted, each one different. How Janey would love this, I think, and then feel a stab of guilt.

'We should go,' I say quietly to Jack. 'I need to get back to Janey.'

He nods and downs the dregs of his third cup of tea. 'Of course.' He pushes his chair back and the screech of the legs on the stone floor scratches a hole in the convivial atmosphere.

Keziah leans across the table and takes my hands between her own. 'You must bring your daughter to meet us; she will be much beloved.'

There is a beat of silence and then she adds, 'Your mother too, of course.'

I must have let my reaction to this last invitation show for she adds, 'Your mother is a sad and disappointed woman. She is afraid of failure, of ageing, of loneliness. But she will see the light if she stays here long enough and lets the White Cove work upon her.'

I have no idea what she means. 'I didn't know you'd met my mother.'

The two women exchange a sly look. 'We've known many women like Magdalena. Take her swimming at the next full moon and you will see her change.'

I laugh. 'It's December!' I cannot imagine my mother ever going swimming.

'Maybe a walk through the woods along the red stream will suffice. Anywhere the moonlight shines on water, so the goddess may enter her soul.'

I laugh. 'She doesn't even own a single pair of flat shoes!' Just a pair of mid-heeled, handmade brogues which probably cost a small fortune.

'Come on,' says Jack. 'Before they get you stripping off to dance around the Merry Maidens stone circle!'

Ariadne punches him on the arm again. 'Rude man! I shall remember that the next time you bring us a shirt that needs mending.' She beams at him. 'I don't really mean that. We love him, don't we, Keziah? He is one of our own.'

'Yes,' Keziah agrees. 'Right in the eye of the hare.'

Ariadne and Keziah walk us up the corridor towards the front door, stopping at the entrance to a book-lined room. 'Just a moment.'

I follow them inside. On the wall to the side of the door, where you would not see it unless invited into the room, is a painting of a huge white hare against a gilded background, like a saint in a medieval icon – like the figures on either side of the sarcophagus of Stanilaus the Martyr. Beneath it is a shelf full of candles, pebbles, bones and pots of feathers and bits of wood. It has all the appearance of a shrine, or one of Janey's collections.

'There she is,' Keziah breathes, resting her chin on her partner's shoulder. 'Isn't she beautiful?'

The hare's great dark eyes gaze out at me dolefully.

'She looks as if she's in pain,' I say quietly. I do not know why I say this.

Keziah and Ariadne exchange a glance. 'Oh yes,' Keziah breathes. 'She knows.'

'Knows what?'

'The way of the world. The hurt men do.'

'Why a hare, though?' I ask. 'Is there something special about hares?'

Ariadne takes my hand. 'My dear, remember what the vicar said? You're running with the hare now, not the hounds.'

'I don't understand.'

'You will, my darling.'

'Is it to do with,' – I look from her to Keziah – 'women…

being with women?' I feel embarrassed even as I say it, prurient even. I can feel the blood flushing my cheeks, but Ariadne just throws back her head and laughs.

'In a way!'

I can't bring myself to seek further clarification for fear of wading into quicksand, and by the time Ariadne and Keziah have finished chuckling, all I want to do is escape.

As I turn to leave, my eye falls upon a vase full of flowers upon the little semi-circular table near the window: a bright posy of pink briar roses, blue borage and sprigs of unseasonal honeysuckle. Just like the flowers outside the church.

Jack and I walk back to the car in silence. I feel mortified by what feels to me to have been a faux pas. I also feel thoroughly confused. The moon is starting to rise far away over the fields, out over the sea, depositing a pale glisk of silver on the horizon. I check my watch: it is well past Janey's teatime. 'I must get back.'

'It'll only take a few minutes to get home. Don't fret,' Jack says. I can feel his smile in the darkening air.

'Sorry. I do find it hard to relax, especially with Ariadne and Keziah. I do like them, though...'

'I know they're unusual. They're both brilliant women in their way. Keziah was a forces nurse during the war, believe it or not. She gave it up and came back to Cornwall and threw herself into gardening and beekeeping and making herbal remedies. It's her way of making up for the horrors she's seen.'

'Righting the balance?'

'Yes, exactly. And Ariadne is a very successful artist. Her paintings sell for thousands all over the world.'

I am shocked. Then I remember the hare, the lambency of its eyes, the glow of its fur, each filament delineated with extraordinary care, how it appeared ready to leap into the room. It is a striking piece of art, but I wouldn't have expected it to be the sort of painting art collectors would pay a small fortune for.

'Her work is usually rather more abstract – she specialises in landscape and nudes. She has a great sensitivity to shape and form. In fact, I've never seen her paint anything quite so detailed as the hare before.' He sounds thoughtful.

'She asked me to sit for her!'

'You should. You'll be famous.'

'I don't think I want a crowd of strangers staring at my naked body.'

'No one would know it was you.'

'I'd know.'

'So would I.'

In the moonlight his teeth flash white as he grins.

'How would you know?' I ask, suddenly suspicious. 'Did you spy on me from up in the attic?'

'I would never do that!' His tone is vehement, shocked. 'What must you think of me even to say such a thing?'

'You can't really blame me, can you? I mean, it's not very normal to stow away in someone else's attic, is it?'

'Stowaway – like on the ship. I rather like the sound of that. I suppose that's what I was doing, if you want to put it like that.' He sighs. 'There's a lot you don't know about me, Mila. A lot I'm not ready to tell you yet, but I'm not a bad man, I swear. And I will prove it to you.' He is fervent.

'You don't need to prove anything to me,' I say perplexed.

He looks over my head, out towards the sea. 'Look, this is what I was waiting for. Orion has risen. Can you see?' He points into the darkening sky. 'There's his belt – three bright stars in a line.'

'I know that one. He's the hunter, isn't he? From Greek legend?'

'Yes, and there are his hounds – Big Dog and Little Dog – but can you see the collection of stars near his feet?'

I squint. There are so many little clusters of stars scattered across this sector of the night sky, but nothing seems to make a clear shape. And then suddenly I see it. An undulation of stars, ending in a forked wedge. 'Oh!' I yelp.

'You've seen it,' he says, satisfied. 'That's the top line of Lepus. The Hare.'

'Oh! It looks to be the same shape as the engraving on the stone and Janey's sketches.' A thought strikes me. 'I wonder if she saw it in the encyclopaedia?'

Jack's face is in shadow as he turns to me and I cannot read his expression at all. I think he might be about to agree with me, to reassure me, to bring some much-needed clarity to my tumbling thoughts, but what he actually does just complicates everything even more.

15

I flicker into consciousness the next morning out of a dream in which I am on a cliff, then falling; I am a bird, swooping beneath dawn-tinged clouds, then plummeting; I am caressed by the sea, then sinking. I am in Jack's arms, and he is kissing me and my knees are folding…

Jack kissed me. That wasn't a dream; that happened.

I jolt to awareness that the whole shape of the world has changed between the world before that kiss last night and the world after, and I have no idea whether it is for the better or the worse. I close my eyes and let the remembered sensations wash over me. The smell of him: musk and soap and paint and turps and the sweetness of Keziah's honeycake. His tongue probing inside my mouth. His arms crushing me against him so hard I felt my spine flex to the point of discomfort, and yet I had not wanted to pull away. If anything, I had wanted to melt into him, to dissolve into his body.

I have never felt desire for any man other than Dennis. No one else had even ever kissed me till he came along. I had known little of love, and nothing at all about sex, since

Magdalena had never told me anything other than to keep my legs closed and my clothes on – advice that had rocketed out of my head like a lit firework as soon as Dennis kissed me. I may be older now, but am I any wiser?

I find myself wondering whether Keziah put something in my tea yesterday – some sort of love potion, something to break down my inhibitions and propel me into Jack's arms. I know from the efficacy of her treatment for Janey that she is a mistress of herbs. But is it possible to change people's emotions with them? And if so, why would she do such a thing? I can see that the two of them are fond of Jack, and I think they're even becoming fond of me, and some people just can't help themselves from matchmaking, but who believes in magic and love potions? We're not living in a fairy tale.

Besides, haven't I been harbouring a secret yearning for Jack these past months, half-hidden even from myself? There is no doubt that I kissed him back. I can clearly remember the sensation of our hungry mouths colliding and merging, muscular tongues, hard enamel, the delicious taste of him.

I also remember breaking away from his embrace, getting into the car and refusing to say a word as he drove us back down the winding lanes, and how he caught my arm before we entered the house, how I had pulled away, saying vehemently, 'No. No! I can't do this!' My feelings were jumbled up. I was excited, but afraid. Confused and unnerved. How could I trust my feelings for Jack when my feelings for Dennis had landed me in such a mess?

And so I had bolted inside to my daughter, whom I had found in the kitchen, ploughing her way through a heaped plate of baked beans that were piled up over slices of white toast, and at once picked a fight with my mother. 'You've given her an entire can! That's far too much for a child! You'll make her sick!'

And of course, Magda rose to the bait and complained that I was back late, which was true, and I countered that we were buying her whisky and cigarettes, which was also – partly – true, and in the heat of this battle I managed to put aside that just-made memory of what Jack and I had done.

As I am dressing, a further thought occurs to me. What if he kissed me to stop me asking more about the hare stuff? It seems an unworthy thought, but my mind returns to it periodically like a tongue probing a new gap between teeth, testing the rawness, the unfamiliar space, feeling for the tip of new growth.

Jack and I avoid being alone with one another for the next few days. I do not know what to say to him. I feel ashamed somehow. Of the kiss? Or how I ran from him? I don't know how to feel, and it seems neither does he, for he won't look at me or talk to me about anything except the most practical tasks. I have humiliated him, I think. He is a proud man, a damaged man, and I ran from him. I am not proud of this, but I can't think straight. Besides, there is the bustle of Christmas to prepare for, and then the wretched party.

On the Friday before Christmas Jack sticks his head around the kitchen door and asks if we want to choose a tree from the conifer woods further up the valley.

'I want to go!' Janey roars. 'I want to choose it!'

I can see there will be tantrums if she is prevented from

exercising what she has come to see as her right. She has chattered on about the tree so much: the exact height and shape of it, where it should go – in the far corner of the drawing room, so the lights can be seen shining through the French windows by anyone arriving at the house. She has very definite views for a five-year-old. But she cannot go alone with Jack so I find myself in the passenger seat as we take the Morris up the hill.

As we pass the postbox, I recall the stack of letters the postman gave to me that I have, out of respect for Janey's privacy, thus far left unopened, tied in a bundle in my chest of drawers. I think how my little girl must have run up the steep drive, secretive and determined, to deposit her letters one by one. I think how disappointed she must be never to have received a response. Even St Nikolas replied to her. The previous year, camped in Magda's pristine and unwelcoming flat – having been prised out of our house in East Dulwich after the awful showdown with Dennis – she had spent a full day drawing all the things she would like from St Nikolas: a pony, a cat, a house, a cake and Daddy (all stick-arms and -legs and a big round head). The night before last Christmas, I had devoted myself to writing back to Janey in Santa's own large, bold hand, explaining how hard it was to fit a pony on a fast-flying sleigh; that he was afraid the cat jumped out and ran away (because you know how cats are), that there would be cake, of course, and that although Daddy couldn't be there on the day with her, he was sending her all his love and lots of chocolate. I drew snowflakes around the letter and made a North Pole stamp which I stuck on the envelope and added Rudolph's muddy hoofprint. And I'd left the envelope – addressed to

Janeska Prusik rather than Dunlop (Dennis's surname), Ealing, London – under the Christmas tree (acquired after a long, hard fight with Magda, who didn't want pine needles on her carpet) on top of her gifts. No wonder, then, that she thought such an inadequate address would reach its recipient.

When we left the Dulwich house, I told Janey that her father was going away travelling, and that was why we were going to stay with Magda: a cowardly excuse. At times afterwards, I even toyed with the idea of telling Janey that Dennis had died, but stopped myself just in time before offering up such a devastating lie. Magda, frustrated at my inability to 'come out with it', wanted to tell Janey 'the truth' about Dennis, but I forbade it. How can you make such a young child understand the complex, grubby world of adults? How to tell her that her daddy has another family and that he chose them over us? How to tell her any of what went on without poisoning her memories of Dennis forever? But perhaps now that we are established in our new home it is a better time to talk to her about what has happened. Is she strong enough to take it? Will she understand any of it at all? She seems happy enough, but sometimes she hides her feelings, and I have found her crying in her sleep. I have kept hoping that time will erase Dennis from her memories, render him insubstantial and colourless till at last all thoughts of him fade away, but that is just my wishful thinking. I see from the way she is with Jack that she is missing having a father figure around, but, as I listen to the pair of them chattering away about the difference between magpies and crows and rooks and jackdaws, I realise I cannot remember Janey ever having any such interaction with her father, and that feels quite telling.

We drive up the valley till Jack turns off near the old manor house. The sight of it makes Janey alert and excited. 'It's just like a castle in a story! Do you think a princess is sleeping inside it, under a spell?'

I have been reading fairy tales to her. She was particularly taken by the idea of the Sleeping Beauty, enchanted by the bad fairy, whom she immediately identified as Magda. I had to disguise my laugh as a coughing fit till Janey had asked solicitously, 'Are you all right, Mummy? Shall I get you some of Keziah's medicine?'

I turn around now and grin at her, remembering my own reaction to seeing the house. 'It does look enchanted, doesn't it? All those bushes and brambles.'

Janey and I both crane our necks as Jack drives past without slowing down and brings the car eventually to a halt by a copse of trees. He gets out and shoulders his spade, then opens the door for Janey, and she hops out and takes him by the hand, which surprises me. A fiercely independent child, she usually balks at being held by anyone, preferring to exercise her freedom.

Jack navigates the indistinct pathway through the woods with the ease of a man to whom this place is as familiar as his own garden. I turn around at one point to see where we have come from and see only a jumble of trees and undergrowth, cut through by faint animal highways made by badgers and foxes and whatever other wildlife inhabit these woods, and I shiver. Without Jack I would be well and truly lost.

I quicken my pace to catch up to him and Janey until

we emerge into a clearing. Jack points out a small conifer. Janey shakes her head. He indicates another, larger one. She considers it for a long moment from different angles, then nods vigorously.

Jack turns to me. 'Do you think this one is the right height?'

'If you stand closer to it, I can get a better idea of scale,' I suggest.

Jack steps over to the tree. He is not as tall as Dennis, who was an imposing six foot two, but even so the tree is a good foot taller. Within the context of the forest it looks small, but I try to imagine it back home in the drawing room. Would its top graze the ceiling once it's in a pot? But Janey's mind is made up.

'I want this one!' She presses herself in as if to hug the tree but it's too spiny and resistant, so instead she hugs Jack. And they stand there together, frozen in time, Jack in his olive-green waxed jacket and black wellies, Janey in her holly-berry-red duffel coat, the conifer embracing them both, and for the oddest few seconds I feel locked out of the scene, an outsider in a way I have not felt since I first set foot in the evacuation school in Surrey, tongue-tied and barely able to speak English. Then the moment passes and it's just Jack and Janey laughing at something they've seen.

'It looks perfect,' I say, and Jack sets to digging a wide circumference around its base. 'Wouldn't it be easier just to cut it down?' I ask. There is already sweat beading on his forehead.

'Of course. But the easiest way isn't always the best way.'

'We're going to keep it alive!' Janey announces. 'We're

going to have a live tree in our house and I'm going to give it a drink every day while it's living with us.'

This seems fanciful, but I smile and straighten her bobble cap. 'That sounds lovely,' I say.

'Then it can come back here where it belongs and we won't be stealing it from the Lady, just borrowing it.'

I frown. 'What lady?' I think at once of the abandoned-looking house. Are we trespassing on some old lady's grounds here, digging out one of her trees?

Janey takes Rabbit out of her pocket and has an intense whispered conversation with him. She looks up at me, her eyes limpid and guileless. 'She's everywhere here, can't you feel her?' She hugs me.

I remember what Ariadne said. She's in everything. She is everything. Who is this 'she'? Why does my daughter sense her presence when I do not?

Janey's hand digs in my pocket and brings me back to the moment. She holds up what she has found there: one of the little stones Ariadne took out of her velvet pouch in the church and gave to me, like the ones she placed in the sanctuary and under the pews in her weird little ritual. Gold ink catches the low winter light and I realise that a familiar symbol is painted on it: the sign of the leaping scribbles in my room, on Janey's sketches, on the engraved stone, in the stars...

For a moment a jagged white light gathers at the edges of my vision and I feel slightly faint. Not a migraine, please, not now. I shake my head and force myself back to the moment and the visual distortion wavers and disperses. 'Yes, darling, you can have that.'

'It's not for me.' Janey lays her lips on the pebble as if

dispensing benediction, then skips over to where Jack is working at extricating the conifer's roots. When at last he eases the tree out of the pit he has dug and encourages its root-ball into a hessian sack, Janey places the pebble inside the hole left behind. 'It's a promise,' she explains gnomically.

Between us, Jack and I – well, mainly Jack – carry the tree along the woodland trail back to the car, with Janey dancing along in front of us as if she has memorised the route. All the way, I sense we are being watched, feel an itch of a gaze between my shoulder blades, and then inside my head as if words want to be spoken. The sensation is unnerving: I feel my neck and arms rise in goose flesh. For no particular reason I remember the white light that whizzed through the trees on that first foray Janey and I made into the woods behind the house and as soon as I think this, the white light is crackling like white fire along the edges of my vision again. I know that if I give into it I will have one of my migraines, maybe even fall down and lose consciousness as I did so embarrassingly on that first night. Gritting my teeth, I concentrate on getting back to the car, and once again, within a few moments, it abates.

The Morris looks absurd with the tree strapped to its roof, overhanging at either end. Jack drives very, very slowly back down the hill. We pass the spot where Janey saw the hare and Mother nearly put the car over the edge, and I hold my breath as we negotiate the hairpin bend, fearing that the weight of the tree may shift and send us plunging over the edge, but we make it down the final stretch to White Cove without incident.

Safely back at the house, I regard the root-ball in alarm. 'That's never going to fit in a bucket!'

'Don't worry about that.' Jack jogs up to the barn and returns with a wide half-barrel balanced on his shoulder. Twenty minutes later the tree is standing sentinel outside the house, a guard from the natural world against all comers.

Jack stands back, wiping his hands on his trousers. 'It's a strange custom, not bringing it in till Christmas Eve, but I suppose it's a useful transition for the tree. It can get used to its new pot in this sheltered place outside before we take it in to a different environment.' He turns to Janey. 'You will water it every day, won't you?'

She nods vigorously, as if she has just acquired a pet, then runs inside.

Jack touches my arm to detain me as I make to follow her. 'I have something for you.' Reaching into his jacket pocket he brings out a little book and hands it to me. *West Penwith: Flora and Fauna*. 'I thought it might help you to feel more at home if you know the names of the things that live and grow here.' Then he leans towards me and pecks me briefly on the cheek, before striding off, leaving me to turn the little book over in my hands. I open it up, and see that the flyleaf is missing, which has weakened the integrity of the binding. Still, it's a lovely little book, full of black and white photos of wildflowers, trees, butterflies and animals. I flick through it at random and find a listing for mistletoe.

Cornish: 'ughelvar'
A partial parasite that can be found on a number of different host-plants like sycamore, ash and hawthorn. Only the female plants bear the famous white berries. Because mistletoe blossomed even during a frozen winter, the Celts came to see the plant as a sacred fertility

symbol, the administration of which could restore vivacity to both animals and humans.

I can see this is going to be a fascinating source of lore and information. On a whim, I check the index for 'hare'.

Cornish: 'skovarnek'

One of the wildest of our native wild animals, the hare has long been associated with Eostre, the shape-shifter and goddess associated with the moon, and also with Aphrodite and Eros, because of their high libido, or with Artemis, the goddess of wild places. The Greeks celebrated hares in their art and their stories, and with a constellation: Lepus, the Hare, which runs immediately to the south of Orion the Hunter.

And beneath this is drawn an undulating line ending in a V.

The next day the four of us drive into Penzance to fetch decorations for the tree and the house, provisions for Christmas, and for the party. I can hardly believe the latter is only ten days away. There have not so far been many formal acceptances but, as Magda says, it's probably not the way things are done down here where everyone knows everyone else and it's just that we don't see the invitees every day, so they've not had the chance to say if they're coming or not. This does make it rather hard, however, to plan in terms of quantities of food and drink, and even glassware and crockery. To be sure we are prepared, Magda rampages around the only two shops in town that sell household goods, tutting over the quality and the prices, and eventually we come away with a heavy box of plates and one of champagne and hi-ball glasses.

She leaves orders with the startled landlord at the Admiral Benbow for a crate of champagne to be delivered on Christmas Eve, and at the grocer's we buy bags of dried fruit and apples. At the fish shop, the fishmonger taps his nose when she comes in and waits till the rest of the customers are safely out of earshot. 'I've never been asked for carp before,' he says. 'And I did say, didn't I, that it might not be possible to honour your order, Mrs Prusik, since you're not supposed to take them home if you catch them here, but…' He slips into the backroom and comes out with a carefully wrapped parcel which he lifts over the counter to me. It is cold and chunky with ice. 'My son Alfred knows a man who knows a man. But you're not to say where he came from, all right?'

Magda turns the full beam of her smile upon him. 'Mr Harvey, you have saved our first Christmas here.'

In the shop that sells everything on Causewayhead, Janey and I have a lovely time selecting Christmas decorations while Magda and Jack carry the carp and other purchases back to the car. We buy fairy lights, glue and coloured paper with which to make paper chains, and balls of ruched crêpe to hang in swags around the walls, armfuls of tinsel, and little orbs of blown glass to hang on the tree. We find a set of tiny wooden soldiers in bright red jackets with strings threaded through the tops of their caps, and dancing milkmaids in yellow and white, and red candles for the candelabra.

We did not bring our Christmas decorations down from London. I did not have the heart for it. The three Christmases that Dennis and I spent together were the happiest of my life, even if they were not done in the traditional Polish way I remembered from my childhood, and even if he did rush off after lunch to see 'an old friend on his own', which at the time I had thought so charitable and generous. I know better now where he went. Heaven knows what excuse he gave his actual wife as to where he was on Christmas Eve night.

Stop it, Mila!

When I catch myself in loops of thought about Dennis and my previous life I try to cut them off as fast as I can. There is no point in dwelling on the past. Except, it niggles at me. I had bad judgment when it came to Dennis and now I may be making a similar mistake about Jack, about whom I know so little.

But look at how he is with Janey, my treacherous brain reminds me. *See how she trusts him.*

Janey is five, I retort, and there is no answer to that.

We are on our way back to the car when someone calls my name. It is the Reverend Martin, a trilby on his head and his dog collar muffled by a grey wool scarf. His breath puffs out into the air like smoke as he crosses towards us and my heart sinks.

'Would you like some help with your parcels, Mila?'

Instinctively, I start to refuse – but already I am losing my grip on one of the bags, so reluctantly I accept his offer. 'We're parked just up at the top of the road.'

Janey stubbornly refuses to hand over her bagful of decorations, and instead pulls her bobble cap down with her free hand, then comes around the other side of me to keep her distance from him.

We make polite small talk about the weather and other uncontroversial things as we walk up Causewayhead to where Mother and Jack sit waiting for us in the Morris. At the sight of Casworan Martin, Magda slips out of the car, brushes down her skirt and gives him a radiant smile.

'So kind of you to give my daughter a hand, Vicar,' she simpers.

The vicar doffs his hat in a courtly fashion. 'Not at all, Mrs Prusik. It's what I'm here to do.'

'In Penzance?' She looks from him to me, as if we have been hiding some secret assignation from her.

'On Earth.'

Magda laughs heartily. *It's not that funny,* I think.

I notice that Jack has not exited the vehicle to greet the Reverend Martin. I stow our purchases away, and Janey crawls into the back seat with Jack. They sit there, glowering out at the vicar and Magda, who are laughing together, with almost identical expressions.

'I'm so delighted you'll be attending our little New Year soirée,' Magda is saying as I return dutifully to her side.

'I wouldn't miss it for the world. Of course,' – he wags a finger – 'I shall have to remain entirely sober!'

Magdalena laughs heartily at this. 'I am sure we can make up some delicious virgin cocktails for you, Casworan.'

Oh, so it's Casworan now. A shudder runs through my sternum.

'I hope that you and your delightful family will be joining us for the Christmas Eve midnight service,' the vicar says smoothly.

'I'm afraid I shall have to stay at home – my daughter is only five,' I say quickly.

The vicar tears his avid black regard away from Magdalena, who clearly bewitches him. 'Of course, of course. Still, I hope you will start coming to our regular services. And there is a marvellous Sunday school for the children. It will be good for her to make friends of the right sort,' he says, his eyes darting to the car.

'I have to tell you, Vicar, that I suffered a severe loss of faith when I lost my beloved Tomacsz during the war,' Magda says, drawing his attention back to her. 'Though I have been trying hard to regain it.'

'Have you really tried, Magdalena?' The vicar's voice has taken on a low, sonorous quality, like the tolling of a bell.

I watch my mother blush. Actually blush.

'It is so hard for a woman alone in the world.'

The Reverend Martin takes her gloved hand in his and captures it with his other hand. 'It would be the greatest honour if you would allow me to help you find your way back to God,' he declares. 'I will place myself entirely at your disposal, my dear lady, and we will talk and pray together until the light shines into your world again.'

'I really must get home,' I say quietly to Mother. 'I'm not feeling very well.'

I am expecting an angry reaction, but maybe because of the presence of the man of God, she simply pats me on the cheek. 'Poor Mila, so fragile. We must get her home, but I will come to see you, Reverend Martin, if I may?'

'Come for tea at the vicarage.' He beams. 'I will make sure we are alone so that you may bare... your soul to me in utmost confidence and privacy.'

She makes to pull away, but he does not let go. 'Magdalena,' he muses. 'From Mary Magdalene, the apostle of the apostles. She was, we are told, very beautiful, so you are well named.' He leans over her hand as if he will kiss it. 'Perhaps you too contain devils within you which should be driven out. It is a gift invested in me by the Father, the Son and the Holy Spirit – the ability to drive out demons.'

Magda laughs, as if this is all mere flirtation. Is he flirting with her? If so, it is the creepiest attempt at seduction I can imagine.

'I have heard from many people over the years that they believe an unclean spirit inhabits your abode, and although it is not a regular activity for one in my position, I would also be more than happy to perform a ceremony of deliverance there.' He is almost whispering now, his words tumbling out in a hiss. 'Indeed, it is my duty to perform this cleansing before you open your doors to the wider world. I cannot tell you how superstitious the locals are.'

Magdalena appears taken aback by this strange turn in the conversation. It looks as if she would like to reclaim her hand, but Casworan Martin is gripping it still. 'Well, personally I give little credence to such things as ghosts and curses.'

'It might be a good step towards establishing yourself in this community, Magdalena Prusik.'

I can see that if she is to fit in with the locals, she must first win over people like the vicar.

The Reverend Martin looks at his watch. 'I could come with you now,' he tells her. 'We can go via the church and I will fetch what I need for the deliverance. There is no time like the present.'

Magda starts to make an excuse, but really, what can she say? We are about to set off for home and have nothing else planned, and of course my personal discomfort counts for nothing at all.

'Well, of course, you are most welcome...' She is wavering.

I look to the car, where Jack is still gazing out of the back window, his face a mask of dislike. Janey has her head bent over something – no doubt the comic we bought her at the newsagent's.

'It might be a bit of a squeeze,' I start, and Magdalena and the vicar both turn to regard me, and I realise that by saying this I have just made matters worse.

'Nonsense,' says Magda. 'You can easily fit in the back with Jack and Janeska, and the Reverend Martin will ride up front with me.'

I watch triumph steal across the vicar's aquiline features like a dark curtain; then, as if I have imagined it, a gentle smile replaces it.

The drive back is achieved in relative silence, for Magda is concentrating on the road and Jack is staring out of the window. Even so, I can feel the hostility boiling off him in a wave. When we stop in Eglosberyan, the vicar fairly runs into his church, so keen is he to complete his mission.

'Drive off without him,' Jack urges, and I almost cheer.

'Yes, do,' I add. 'I'm really not feeling very well.'

Showing no sympathy for my condition, Magda rounds on us as if we are naughty children. 'I shall do no such thing. It would be the height of rudeness.'

'Well, I will take my leave of you here,' Jack says, leaning across me to open the car door.

'Don't you dare! Whatever will the vicar think?' Magda is appalled.

'I don't give a fig for what that man thinks,' Jack retorts.

The delay caused by this small contretemps is too short to provide Jack with escape, for the vicar is jogging back towards us, fabric draped over his arm and a leather case in his hand.

'Fuck!' says Jack furiously. He folds his arms and glares ahead while Janey's eyes go wide at his use of this forbidden word.

As Magda drives us back down the winding lanes, the Reverend Martin thumbs through his prayer book in search of the correct litany. Jack stares out of the side window, his expression thunderous. Through the gap between the front seats Janey's eyes bore unblinkingly into the back of the vicar's head and at one point he reaches up a hand and touches his hair, as if he can feel the heat of her regard.

When we turn the corner at the viewing point at the top of the lane that leads steeply down to the house, sunlight shoots blindingly white across our path, and Magda is forced to employ the sun shield, and, oddly, the vicar groans as if physically struck. Despite this, we make it back down to the house without further incident.

When we have all disembarked from the Morris, and Mother has headed into the house with her precious carp and the Reverend Martin, Jack takes me by the elbow. 'Be careful of him, please,' he says.

'He's a man of God. I'm sure he won't do us harm.'

'No god would welcome that one into his fold.'

'Rabbit doesn't like him,' Janey confirms, taking Jack by the hand. 'But she says he's nothing. Less than nothing: a void.'

We look at her in surprise. Does Janey even know the meaning of the word *void*?

'I'm sure Rabbit is very wise,' I choke out at last.

'Yes,' says Janey. 'She is.'

Jack helps us to carry our purchases to the front door, but refuses to come in. 'I won't set foot inside while he's here.'

'He told me he'd been inside the house before. To parties before the war.'

Jack's face is like stone.

'Why does he think the house needs exorcising?' I press.

'What does exorcising mean?' asks Janey.

Jack and I exchange a glance. 'It's a ceremony to make bad things go away,' I say at last.

'There aren't any bad things here,' she says firmly. 'Except him.'

Jack takes hold of my arms. 'Just don't listen to anything other people say. And whatever you do don't listen to *him*. I don't know what his game is, but I don't trust him an inch.'

'Mother seems to like him.'

'Your mother is a woman much in need of male attention,' Jack says sharply. 'But you should warn her off Casworan Martin. Just look after yourself and Janey, that's all I ask.'

And with that he turns and strides away.

Janey hangs back as I start to take the bags and boxes into the hall, and when I try to usher her inside she pulls back, fierce and strong.

'I don't want to.'

The light is beginning to go out of the sky and the sun is painting the clouds at the end of the bay with apricots and rose. 'You can't stay out here, it'll be dark soon.' She resists my attempts to haul her, leaning back and digging her heels in. 'Come on, Janey. Granny will be furious.'

'Don't care.' She stamps her feet on the stone of the veranda.

'It's getting cold out here.' I have to resort to pure bribery. 'If you come in now you can have some of that chocolate cake we bought.'

She considers this offer for a moment. 'Still no.'

I close my eyes. I really can't cope with one of her meltdowns now. 'I tell you what,' I say at last, 'we'll make an angel for the top of the tree just like they do in Poland.'

That makes her perk up. 'Can we make wings for it? And a crown?'

'We'll try!'

I run up to the barn and gather a few handfuls of the old straw that lies strewn there. Can I even remember how to make a straw angel after all these years? I recall Babcia scattering straw beneath the table at Christmas, and by the door – a magical barrier to keep bad spirits out. A primitive, ancient tradition... much like the one the vicar is about to pursue. I laugh to myself, feeling somewhat fortified.

I sit Janey down in a corner of the drawing room and gather up the shopping that needs to be put away. I can hear voices as I approach the kitchen. It sounds as if the discussion of the 'exorcism' has turned into a cosy chat over a cup of tea. I hover out of sight, eavesdropping, and hear the Reverend Martin say, '...a lot of unhappiness here, poor troubled souls. Of course, the stories are probably nothing more than gossip and superstition. Still, a little ritual of deliverance won't do any harm, and we'll be able to spread the word that the house has been blessed, which may allay some fears in the village.'

'What sort of stories?' I hear Magda ask.

'Oh, the usual sort of thing. Unhappy women disappointed with their lives, unable to settle here, driven to distraction, vanishing without trace.'

'How awful,' Magda says. 'But maybe they were already troubled when they moved down here and found the remoteness didn't suit them, and they simply went away, and the rest was the sort of nonsense people make up.'

'Well, of course, dear lady, you are very perceptive. People disappear all the time, and if they haven't mixed in with the community – well, folk love to spin a tale, don't they?'

I step into the kitchen. 'I thought the couple who lived in this house when you came to parties here were a Tory MP and his wife,' I say, putting the shopping down on the table. 'That's hardly not mixing in, is it?'

I see irritation in the man's eyes; he was enjoying holding forth with Mother, who is sitting with her legs crossed at the knee, the better to show off her shapely calves.

'Oh, I'm sure there was no great mystery there. They just upped and left for London. He had work to do there for the government, no doubt very hush-hush. He had a fair bit to do with the Atlantic Cable at Porthcurno, just down the coast, you know?'

Magda looks questioning.

'There's a cable that runs beneath the sea from here all the way to France, Spain, Gibraltar and Newfoundland for telegraphic purposes – an extremely important communications system. They established a defence system along the beaches here – pillboxes and anti-aircraft guns, even a flame barrage. Two hundred miners dug tunnels to house all the equipment – that's when the army requisitioned this house. I was honoured to be present when Lady Wilshaw presided over the opening of the facility.'

'How fascinating,' my mother says, but I can tell she's annoyed that I have intruded on their intimate conversation and pushed it into such mundane realms, though I'm sure the mention of aristocracy and MPs will have thrilled her.

I move into the kitchen to put the food away and fetch Janey her promised chocolate cake and orange squash, but by the time I make my way past them with my propitiatory gifts in my hands, they are onto the arrangements for the ritual.

'Let us pray together and then we will walk through the house with the cross and the holy water and perform the litany.'

'Do you really think it's necessary?' Mother is asking again, but her expression is avid – this is theatre; this is drama. There is a hole in her social world into which the vicar's dark words have flooded.

I scuttle from the room before I can be drawn into this charade.

Janey and I have managed to make a rudimentary straw doll for the top of the tree by the time Magda and the Reverend Martin emerge in solemn procession from the kitchen. He is dressed in a white alb with a dramatic black chasuble draped over it and holds a large crucifix and a vial of what must be holy water, which all seems rather fancy for an Anglican vicar. I cannot help but wonder, rather unchristianly, whether he has a dressing-up box in his church, but Magda looks as if she is loving the whole proceeding. She follows in his wake bearing a silver chalice which is certainly not ours, and with one of our best white linen cloths draped over her arm, like a medieval handmaiden.

My daughter and I stop what we are doing and stare. Then Janey bursts out laughing, and the peal flies out across the long room and up into the carved cornices.

Magda looks as if she would like to reach out and strangle her granddaughter. The priest's pale face flushes, a purplish tide creeping from his neck to his cheekbones, as if someone is filling him up with Ribena. His pale eyes fix on Janey with cold loathing. Then, slowly, he raises the crucifix and holds it out between them as if it is a weapon and Janey – a child of five – his enemy.

I take my daughter by the hand. 'Come on, let's go upstairs and I'll read you a story,' I say, giving her hand a tug. But Janey stands firm. I pull a little harder.

'No!'

I recognise that tone. From which of us did she inherit this obdurate nature? Surely not from me; I've rarely dug my heels in about anything. And yet, a small inner voice reminds me, *You defied your mother in marrying Dennis, don't you remember?*

'Do what your mother tells you, Janeska!' Magda cries now, her voice simmering with rage. She is in a hitting mood, I can tell; just as well a man of God is present.

'Shan't.' Janey pulls free of me. 'Go away,' she tells the vicar. She takes Rabbit out of her pocket and holds him – or rather, her – up in front of her with one hand, and in the other the straw angel, in a curious mirror image of the Reverend Martin with his cross and holy water. The scene is so ridiculous I want to laugh out loud. Flourishing the stuffed toy and the doll, she takes a step towards the vicar. 'The house doesn't want you here. *She* doesn't want you here.'

Something changes in Casworan Martin's demeanour. His face seems to drain of colour, and unless I am mistaken, the hand holding the cross begins to tremble. He takes a step backwards.

'If this little girl won't do as she's told she should be disciplined,' he says quietly. 'Spare the rod and spoil the child.'

Magdalena smiles back at him, and it is not a nice smile. 'Thank you, Vicar. It's what I keep telling my daughter. She is spoiling Janeska by indulging her wild fantasies, and see what is the result: a rude, obstinate beast! The child does indeed need to be disciplined.' And she puts down the chalice with exaggerated care on the brand-new, shining sideboard and crosses the room towards us as if she is going to take the suggested chastisement into her own hands.

I step in front of Janey. 'Don't you dare.'

'Do not make a scene in front of the Reverend Martin,' she says, her jaw rigid.

'If you think not making a scene is more important than treating your granddaughter with love and care, then I pity you,' I tell her fiercely. I feel as if a cold white fire has been lit inside me and that if provoked it will roar out and incinerate everything in its path. 'You are not responsible for disciplining my daughter.' I poke a finger at her to emphasise the words. 'I know what you mean by *discipline* – you mean physical violence. It's why they took me away from you: because you hit me. How old was I – two, maybe three – when you knocked me across our sitting room in Kracow and I lost my front teeth? And younger than that when you struck me so hard that you broke my arm.'

Memories are beginning to tumble out of me now, as if the fire inside me has burned down the barricades in my brain that were holding them back.

'I had bruises all over me when I arrived in Kasina Wielka. I remember Grandma Zofia and Aunt Kamila dabbing me with ointment and whispering together. I remember when you came to take me with you to England they wept and begged you to leave me with them. I have no idea why you didn't leave me in Poland – you never wanted me. You sent me off to boarding school as soon as you possibly could, even though I couldn't speak the language here and didn't have a friend in the world. You haven't got a maternal bone in your body.'

Her eyes have become slits. 'Because we would never have been prioritised for entry into England if we hadn't had you with us,' she hisses. 'It's as simple as that.'

The brutal honesty of this statement strikes with a dull impact that doesn't even hurt, not now, all these decades later, because I think I have always, in my subconscious, known it to be true. It makes horrible, inevitable sense. I feel my shoulders drop, my spine straighten and my head clear as if I have been freed from a crushing guilt I never knew I carried: believing I had done something to make her dislike me, that I was insufficient, too flawed to love. Whereas the insufficiency is Magda's alone.

'Oh yes, of course. I am your passport to clean starts in different places.' I sweep my hand wide to take in our grand drawing room. 'And see, the pattern has repeated itself, and here we are.' I feel power flowing into me. The power feels like a greenish-white light, coming at me from all angles, both inside and out, filling me up with warm, calm confidence. It is the power I have sensed in the woods, by the sea; it is the spark of electricity that ran up my arm from the stone outside the churchyard wall.

I turn my attention upon the priest. 'It's ironic, really, that you came here to exorcise demons, because I think you may have succeeded rather better than you expected. Please pack up your ridiculous costume and paraphernalia and leave us alone. This is my house, and when all is said and done, I prefer it left as it is, demons, ghosts and all.'

Janey presses herself against my leg in companionable solidarity and I feel the cold fire flowing from her as well, as if we are sharing the white energy. Together we regard Casworan Martin, who after a long beat of silence lowers his crucifix and turns to Magda.

'I will not stay where I'm not wanted,' he says, his voice cracked with fury. 'You may call upon me at the vicarage, Magdalena, if you feel the need for ministry.' He turns back to me. 'As for you, I can see you are a lost soul.' He retrieves the silver chalice, then stalks towards the kitchen, there to divest himself of his robes and put away his demon-ridding kit.

I turn to Janey. 'Shall we make some wings for your angel now?'

The grin she returns to me is gleeful.

Later, I look in on my daughter, who is tucked up in bed with Rabbit. The pair of them lie nose to nose on the pillow, toy and child, as sweet and peaceful an image as you could ever conjure after such an unsettling day.

Magda, meanwhile, has retired to her room, pleading a headache, which is as close to a climb-down as I'm ever likely to witness. Somewhere inside me there's a niggle of anxiety about how we will all three go on living here together after the revelation of such damaging truths, but I push it aside. It is hardly a shocking discovery that my mother never really loved or wanted me, for she has demonstrated this every day since I was small, even if to have it spelled out in such brutal fashion would, you might imagine, crush me. Oddly, though, I feel freed by her declaration. There was a time when I'd have tried to worm my way back into her affections, to grovel in apology, to attempt to win her approval by enslaving myself to her comfort, but knowing there are really no affections to win back means I can stop thinking about our relationship in these terms. I feel not diminished by the uncovering of the cruel truth, but curiously empowered. Now it's just me and Janey, and I must be strong and resilient to protect and provide for my child. She will, I vow, never feel unloved or unwanted. She shall be confident and happy in a way I was never allowed to be.

Later, I eat an omelette with toast and butter, more of a breakfast than a supper, but that in itself seems apt on such a topsy-turvy day, then take myself off to sit in the drawing room by the light of the fire, my hands cupped around a mug of hot chocolate, and feel a deep peace settle over me. I know the worst now, have rolled with the blow and accepted the hurt, and the festering poison has been drawn out into the open where it will gradually evaporate.

I sense that the house feels this too. It is as if it is satisfied with this turn of events and I feel as if I sit held safe within its wide embrace, the soft warm silence it contains, and the far-off shushing of the waves rolling in onto the beach no longer fills me with dread and loneliness but provides a soothing background noise that calms my racing thoughts.

No matter what Casworan Martin may say, I do not feel like a lost soul, not damned at all, but blessed. I have been seen and accepted, maybe for the first time in my life, and found that my soul has joined with something larger and finer than the vicar's narrow, proscriptive view of the world, though I cannot explain by what or whom.

Well, we shall see.

16

The rest of the week is taken up in preparations for Christmas and for the New Year party. I have decided to make an effort in this, for all our sakes, and it seems Magda is also being conciliatory (as far as she is able), for during this time she is extra nice to Janey and to me, does not pick fights or make snippy criticisms, or try to parent my child in an inappropriate manner. I even find her Hoovering one day, and fail to mask my astonishment, because she catches my look and raises her eyebrows. I bite back the sarcastic remark that is dying to escape me and continue with my own tasks as if the world has not changed shape at all.

Magda is no cook, which I have always known. In Poland, if other people had not made our meals, we would have starved, so the task of preparing food falls to me. The day before Christmas Eve I make *kutia* – a sort of rice pudding with dried fruits, honey, nuts and poppy seed; *makowiec* – poppy seed rolls – which fill the whole downstairs with their fragrant, yeasty smell; and *kompot z suszu*, made by boiling up apple slices with dried fruit and cloves and cinnamon, and soon the whole house is redolent with the aromas of Christmas. Janey haunts the kitchen to steal scraps and to play with the apple peel.

Magda comes in, cigarette in hand, and surveys the bubbling compote. She dips a spoon in and blows on it, before tasting it thoughtfully. 'Well done,' she says at last, and goes out again, leaving Janey and me staring at one another in amazement.

I set about making the *uzska* – the little dumplings we will eat with the beetroot soup – and then put the mixture in the Frigidaire so there will be less to do tomorrow. There, the carp stares out lugubriously at me, and I stare lugubriously back. The fishmonger did at least gut the beast, but otherwise left it whole, at Mother's command. I can't imagine how she thinks I know how to cook such a thing. I dread preparing this part of the Christmas Eve feast. Dennis didn't much like fish of any sort, let alone some illicitly caught, ugly monster from the depths of some unknown lake or reservoir, so I have little experience of such things. When I walk up to the village to find a small gift and card for Janey from Dennis, I will ask advice from Keziah, who has promised me one of her famous honeycakes.

I'm just about to go and find Mother to ask her to keep an eye on Janey when I hear the crunch of tyres on the gravel outside. Running to the front door, I find that a red van has pulled up, and the postman is struggling under the weight and bulk of a huge cardboard box.

Like magic, Janey appears at my side. With the glorious narcissism of being five years old, she asks, 'Is that for me?'

I ruffle her hair. 'I think it's for all of us,' I say,

remembering Magda fretting that the order had yet to arrive for 'the few little luxuries' we couldn't get hold of locally, which she'd tasked her friend Theresa with acquiring. Judging by the size of the box, it looks as if 'the few' turned into quite a collection, and even I, who am quite frugal by nature as well as by necessity, feel a frisson of excitement.

Janey, though, is agog. 'Is it from Daddy?'

My heart becomes a falling stone. I remember, guiltily, the stack of letters stashed in my drawer upstairs, the ones the postman gave back to me, addressed to Dennis in Janey's childish writing.

'Darling, I don't think so.'

How swiftly a child goes from exhilaration to despair. Her eyes begin to well up. 'He hates us, doesn't he?'

Now the stone has become a piercing dart. I throw my arms around my daughter and smother her in an embrace. I wish so hard I could make up for the loss of her old life and the love of her banished father. 'Oh, sweetheart, no. Of course he doesn't. Daddy will always love you.'

'Then why isn't he here?'

'It's very hard to explain, darling.'

'No, it isn't. It isn't hard AT ALL.'

She pulls away from me and flees up the stairs. I hear the door to her room slam with a shudder that runs through the frame of the house.

Love is love: the heart clarifies everything right down to its finest essence, this much I know. But now that Janey has made me think about Dennis, I do wonder why he hasn't sent her a gift, or at least a card. He has our address here, though Magda was loath to pass it on.

'Just cut him out of your life as if he doesn't exist!' my mother had scolded.

'That's simply not possible; he's Janey's father.' I had tried to be patient but she had become incandescent.

'Of course you can! Women do it all the time. He hurt you, he lied to you, he destroyed your life! You're a fool, Mila. When will you understand that you cannot be free unless you cut the cord that binds you to him? He's just a dead weight, dragging you down!'

At the time I had burst into tears and shut myself in my room in much the same way Janey has now.

'I can't believe you have to make twelve different dishes for your Christmas meal!' Keziah leans forward, amazed. 'Ariadne and I just do a roast chicken, with herbs and winter vegetables, just like any normal Sunday.'

'Don't forget my special pudding!' Ariadne says in mock outrage.

'What's special about it?' I ask, thinking it must be a secret family recipe or a strange local custom.

But Keziah points to the bottle of brandy on the counter. 'It has about half of that either in it or on it!'

'Oh!'

'Then we have a jolly good sleep in the afternoon,' says Ariadne. She nudges Keziah and they grin at each other. 'Though sometimes we don't sleep at all.' She smiles like a satisfied cat.

Their delight in one another is infectious and I laugh too and cannot help but feel a little jealous of their easy affection and teasing banter.

'We eat our meal in the evening on Christmas Eve,' I tell them. 'We don't eat all day and then we have to wait until the first star shows in the sky before we tuck in.'

Ariadne looks appalled. 'What, nothing at all?'

I shake my head. 'Not a thing.'

'Poor Janey.'

'And you're roasting a carp?' Keziah shakes her head.

'It's traditional.'

'So are turkeys, but...'

'I know. Mother was determined to mark our first Christmas here in "style".'

'Well, I can't say I've ever cooked a carp, but I don't think it'll be too hard. How large is it?'

I show her with my hands, and she bursts out laughing.

'Oh heavens, a monster!' Seeing my dismay, she goes on quickly, 'Why don't you serve it on a bed of caramelised onions, with plenty of lemon slices? I'd roast it for just under an hour.' She gives me more detailed instructions which I jot down in my notebook, feeling an immense sense of relief to have expert advice that makes the dish sound at least palatable. Keziah fetches me a couple of lemons from her cold store, and some herbs from the windowsill, and packs the honeycake she promised me into the bottom of my basket. I am just about to take my leave when Ariadne comes at me with a great bunch of greenery.

'Mistletoe! You can't celebrate your first Cornish Christmas without mistletoe!'

I recognise it immediately from the little book Jack gave me – a bunch of bright green sprigs bearing pairs of fleshy leaves and masses of translucent white berries. Holding it up above our heads, Ariadne hooks me against her bosom with her free arm so hard that I can barely breathe and plants a huge kiss on my cheek that would have landed on my mouth had I not turned my head so quickly. She smells of marzipan and spice from the Christmas cake we've just eaten.

'Your first Yuletide here, and many more to come!'

I extricate myself, a little embarrassed. 'I must go. I have to buy Janey a couple of things.'

'We have something for her. I hope it will fit her.' Keziah slips out of the room and returns with an armful of pale blue silk. She shakes it out in front of me. It is a dress made for a fairy princess, with a high bodice and a froth of net underskirt making it bell out like an exotic flower.

I laugh. 'Well, that certainly makes my gifts to her look rather paltry.'

Keziah's face falls. 'We didn't mean to outdo you. I hope you know we would never want to do anything like that. I had some of the silk left over and—'

I touch her arm, overwhelmed by gratitude. 'It's beautiful. Janey will love it.'

'We have something for you too.' Ariadne produces a small parcel wrapped in brown paper, tied with an extravagant scarlet ribbon.

'But I haven't brought you anything!' I am mortified.

'Friendship isn't weighed out in things,' Ariadne chides, clucking her tongue.

The net underskirt is tamed and the silk dress folded into a cotton bag Keziah lends me so that I can sneak it into the house without sharp little eyes fixing upon it. Then I run down to the village shops and buy Janey two Ladybird books, some sweets and the sort of nondescript card Dennis favours.

I am struggling down the lanes with all my bags when I hear a car coming from behind me, so I step into the hedge to let it pass. But instead, it pulls up alongside me and I see it is a battered Land Rover. In it is Josie, who was so curt with me on my first visit to the village all those months ago.

'You look well laden.'

This is a friendlier opening than I was expecting. I nod and grin. 'A bit.'

Josie reaches over and swings the passenger door open. 'Go on, get in. I'll take you to the top of your lane.' She pauses. 'I suppose I ought to apologise for last time. I was feeling rather out of sorts, and I think I may have been rude. Had some bad news.' She doesn't elaborate.

'Thanks,' I say, stowing the bags in the footwell and getting in. 'You were... a little hostile.'

She shoots me a rueful smile. 'I know. Sorry. It's just... well, when they said London people had bought the house at White Cove I probably had the wrong idea about you – rolling in money, coming down here to swan around, lording it over the locals and all that.'

I nod. 'Yes, we're not *that* sort of London people, not by a long chalk.'

'No, I gather.'

'Oh.' My mind spins. I wonder what she's heard and from whom. 'Where do you live?' I ask as the rattly old vehicle rumbles down the lane.

'The big house.'

'The one in the trees? That looks...' I stop before the word 'abandoned' comes out. '... like something out of a fairy tale?'

She snorts and accelerates forcefully out of a bend.

'Maybe, if you mean one of the nasty old tales. Yes. It's been in the family for yonks, but it's huge and falling apart.'

'Are you living there on your own?'

Now the look she shoots me is unreadable. 'Sometimes.'

We drive in silence for a while and then suddenly she says, 'Would you like to come in and have a look at it?' And when I hesitate, she adds quickly, 'You might as well, it's on the way.'

Not the most gracious invitation, but I find myself accepting – after all, it is only a short detour, and I can't deny my curiosity. *Which killed the cat*, a small voice in the back of my head tells me helpfully.

On the way down the hill Josie turns the Land Rover in through an entrance between the stone pillars I spied all those weeks back, that were then all but swallowed by the surrounding vegetation but stand proud now that the hedges have died back for winter. She drives fast along a narrow, bumpy track hemmed between tall, leafless trees. Despite the season and lack of canopy, the track seems dark and forbidding and misgivings begin to crowd in on me. My instinct tells me to ask her to turn around and drop me back on the road, but my tongue feels glued to my mouth by the awful British politeness I have acquired.

At last we round the final corner and I see the house from an unfamiliar angle, recognisable only by the towering chimneys and steep gables. When Josie parks in a courtyard tucked around the side of the house, I understand why I have never seen signs of life here – I came upon the house only from the other side, where the brambles and thorns have so encroached as to make the front door all but inaccessible. On the courtyard side, the house is austere and workmanlike, not in the least romantic. I cannot help but feel a small pang of disappointment at the puncturing of my fairy tale fantasy.

As if she has intercepted my thoughts, Josie says, 'It was a very grand old house once – the local manor house. There's been a house on this site for well over a thousand years. But of course, none of that original building remains – well, not to see, anyway. It's been destroyed and rebuilt, destroyed and rebuilt, down the ages.'

'How was it destroyed?'

'Don't you know about the history of the valley?'

'Not very much.' I tell her what I've gleaned so far: the stand of the Cornish against the forces of King Athelstan, the river running red with blood, the construction of the great church in Eglosberyan.

She utters a dry chuckle. 'That's not nearly the half of it. This place has been the locus of all manner of dramas, wars and rebellions, tragedies and triumphs. It's like the history of Cornwall encapsulated a single building. Come on.' She jumps out, bangs the car door shut and beckons me to follow her.

A minute later, I stand in the hallway, gazing around. If I had thought our house was gloomy when I first saw it, the atmosphere in this place is far more oppressive. It engulfs you at once with a watchful, brooding presence, amplified by the rows of dark portraits hanging on the walls, all eyes turned upon me.

'It's not very welcoming, I admit.' Josie waves a hand at the portraits. 'The Laitie family goes back to the sixteenth century. You can see where I got my radiant beauty from,' she says wryly, pointing at the painting at the foot of the staircase, a study of a dark, rat-faced man with mean eyes. 'That's Sir Francis Laitie, who sailed with John Hawkins – drowned when his slave ship foundered in the Atlantic storms of 1567. Probably serves him right, but the money he left behind paid for the rebuilding of most of what you see here. There are a couple of his daughters.' She indicates a portrait of two elderly women dressed in Puritan garb – dark robes with plain white collars and caps. 'They never married – hardly a surprise, given the look of them – and after they died the place fell into disrepair, though there are a few treasures.' She touches the dark wood panelling. 'This apparently came from the wreck of a Spanish galleon. Parts of the house got burned during the Civil War when the locals took sides and some Royalists holed up in it, and then it was rebuilt and extended by some distant relative who appeared to reclaim it.' Her mouth quirks. 'They call him the "dark horse" of the family – but by that they don't mean he was bad, but the colour of his skin – he came back from the Carolinas, where the Laities had founded a dynasty by breeding with their slaves. No one seems to know what happened to him – he just appears to have vanished – but he had progeny, and I suppose that's where my colouring comes from. Mummy always said we had a touch of the tar brush.'

I raise my eyebrows at that, but she just dips a shoulder and walks on.

'And your mother...?' I start.

Josie holds up a hand. 'Our family all seem to die early. Nothing thrives in this valley. People say it's an unlucky place. But I remember when I was growing up here it was full of sunlight and bluebells and laughter and I felt loved and protected, watched over if you like. Now, not so much. Everything goes through cycles, I reckon: good times, bad times. It just seems to be more pronounced here. They used to call this place Nansahwerek – the *Sorrowful Valley*.'

I digest this unsettling pronouncement as she walks me through the hall, past a cloakroom where workaday waxed jackets hang beside what appears to be a fur coat, and into a long, vaulted room where a fire smoulders resentfully, trapped in the deep hearth behind a wrought-iron screen. An armchair has been drawn up to it to make the most of the heat and a small table piled with books and a mug of half-drunk tea is set to one side of it. Apart from this cosy nook, the rest of the room is sparsely furnished and looks barely inhabited. A Victorian patriarch rules the wall to the far end and Josie walks over to him. 'Grandfather,' she says, making a face. 'Awful man. Drove two wives to despair and ruin, and drank himself to death. Then his three sons fought among themselves for control of the house and the lands when he died. The estate got broken up, and they lost what was left of their money when the tin mines failed. White Cove was on one parcel of the land.'

'Oh.' It's strange to think of our house and gardens belonging to the owners of the grand, lost house in the woods.

'That's why it's hard for me to see it sold,' she goes on, 'and why I was rude to you. Sorry about that. I was on my way into Penzance, summoned by the bank manager to discuss the woeful state of my bank account.' She spreads her hands. 'Places like this suck money out of you. As you can see, I've sold off most of the contents just to keep it going. I'll probably have to let the King Charles chair go next. It's probably our greatest treasure, but I can't see how I can hold on to it the way things stand. Incredible to think a king once sat upon a chair I sit and read in,' she muses, then falls quiet.

'I'm really sorry. I know what it's like, to be reduced in life.'

She looks at me quizzically. 'You? I heard no expense has been spared in doing up the house down at White Cove, that it's all looking very smart and luxurious.' There's a bitter tone to this.

'You're welcome to come and have a look,' I say. She's offered me a lot more information than I've given back. 'My mother is terribly good at interiors and is determined to "get it right" – that is to say, she wants, I suppose, to honour the feel of the house, to make the refurbishments sympathetic.'

'Blood red walls and shrieks in the night then, eh?' Josie says, and when I look appalled, she laughs. 'Sorry, not everyone shares my sense of humour.'

I shrug. 'I didn't mean to be oversensitive. This house move came at the cost of everything I thought I had.'

Her dark eyebrows shoot up. 'Go on?'

I find I'm not ready to talk more about my circumstances yet, so I shake my head. 'I made a bit of a mess of my life and now I'm trying to rebuild it.'

She nods slowly. 'We all bear our burdens. Sorry if I jumped to conclusions.'

She leads me into a small, dismal kitchen that appears to have been installed about fifty years ago and now looks mean and shabby, then through the original kitchen, stone-floored and stone cold, followed by a dining hall with faded frescos on the walls and hammerbeams across the ceiling which make me gasp. 'It's like a museum!' But it also smells of mildew and mould, much as our house did before it was forced into the twentieth century, and it has that same sense of fullness as opposed to emptiness, as if ghost-furniture and the trappings of life are lurking just out of sight behind a cheap theatre backdrop.

Josie does not offer to show me the upper floor. 'It's worse up there.'

'How do you mean, *worse*?'

She wrinkles her nose. 'As damp as anything. The roof needs doing; no way can I afford that, so I've just had to let it go. It'll probably all fall down around my ears one of these days.'

I wonder why she's bothered to invite me in... a sort of peace offering? For sympathy? To make me feel guilty that our London money has brought our house back to life when this greater, more historical treasure has been left to rot? As she walks me back to the Land Rover, I say, 'I'm afraid we... ah... borrowed one of your trees for Christmas,' because how much worse would it be not to acknowledge this if she saw the Morris pulling away under its unwieldy load?

She nods. 'I told Jack it was fine.'

So she does know Jack. My mind circles back to that comment of hers when I asked if she lives here alone. *Sometimes.*

'It was very good of you,' I say stiffly, but she just shrugs and gets into the car.

On the way back down the lanes I think of her holed up in this echoing husk of a house over the holidays, so as we come within sight of White Cove, I say impulsively, 'You should come down to see us on Christmas Day, have some tea and cake.'

Josie gives me a hooded look. 'Thanks, but no. I don't "do" Christmas.'

I laugh. 'Like Keziah and Ariadne.'

She bridles. 'No, not like them. Not like them at all.' She sounds fierce and I realise I have been naive – of course there are all sorts of currents and undercurrents flowing around established communities like this.

'Well, if you change your mind, just turn up.'

She nods curtly, then leans across and opens my door from the inside and waits impassively as I extricate my basket and parcels. 'Careful with that mistletoe,' she says. 'It's dangerous stuff.'

'I was told it brings peace and good luck—' I begin, but she has driven off.

After hanging the mistletoe up in the hall and putting away the cake and my purchases, I slip upstairs while Janey is occupied in hosting an intense tea party in the drawing room between Rabbit and two small dollies that rarely see the light of day, to wrap and hide her gifts. I open the top drawer of my dresser where I keep all those miscellaneous bits and pieces that never find a proper home to fetch the sticky tape – and there are Janey's letters. I pick up the little stack and sit on the bed, gazing down at them. I should not open them. Warring thoughts churn through my mind. It's an invasion of privacy. But my daughter is only five and she has no one but me to look out for her welfare. I already know her state of mind: she is missing her father and trying to stay in contact with him. I don't even need to open the letters to know this.

I'm afraid curiosity wins out. Some of the letters are not sealed into the envelopes she must have quietly filched from the bureau downstairs but consist simply of folded pages from her sketchpad and somehow it seems like less of an intrusion to open these.

One simply reads *Dear Daddy* in wobbly letters, beneath which blooms a big flower rendered in yellow crayon, her name, and lots of kisses. Another shows four stick figures standing in front of this house, the double-width front door and the French windows remarkably accurately delineated; Janey is quite the little prodigy. She buried herself in comics from the time Dennis and I split up, and with little help from me taught herself to read in a matter of weeks, and then to write first her own name, then a scattering of other words. Some of her drawings are accompanied by stories, not all of them in recognisable English, but stories nonetheless. I gaze at the figures. Magda's red hair makes her identification easy; Janey has also given her a long nose and a pair of very high heels. By contrast, the figure that must be me appears to be wearing wellington boots and her brown hair is flying in the wind. Janey holds Rabbit, easily distinguishable by his long white ears. For a moment I think the male figure must be Dennis but with dark hair. But everyone else's hair is accurately rendered and Janey is a stickler for detail. The third figure is clearly meant to be Jack, and he is holding Janey's hand on one side and mine on the other. Magda stands alone, a little way off, so that the ordering of the figures goes Magda, me, Jack, Janey... and Rabbit. How odd, I think, that she is holding Jack's hand rather than mine. And yet the three of us appear to be a unit, and Janey is smiling a huge red smile. I stare at the image for a long time, feeling my emotions tumble over one another. This does not seem to be a letter crying out to Daddy for help or love, and yet how can I forget her tears and her anger, and sense of betrayal?

I unfold another. This one contains only a drawing of Rabbit, looking much whiter and cleaner than he… she… usually appears, and wearing a small golden crown, and, oddly, long red hair. There is just a single word beneath the image: *Berviana*, or *Bevianu*. How strange. She must have made it up, perhaps as the start of one of her more imaginative stories.

Emboldened now, I tear open one of the envelopes. The sheet of paper inside has a raw edge from being ripped out of a spiralbound notebook. It contains a simple undulating line ending in an inverted V. I open another: the same image. And the next, and the next. The symbol inscribed on the walls upstairs, and on the memorial stone outside the church. The symbol of the constellation of the hare in the stars. On one sheet there is a single symbol, on another three of them; on the last sheet – I count them – fifteen. And on one of them she has written in capital letters: *MY SECRET*.

This page trembles as my emotions flow into my fingers. I fold the 'letters' up and slide them back into their envelopes, then into the pile. Whatever would Dennis have made of these had they reached him?

He'd think she was mad, says the little voice in my head.

17

That night I wake in a sweat, disoriented and confused. I do not know whether I am in a house in Dulwich or Cornwall, or somewhere outside, in the woods. A pulse beats deep and heavy between my legs, and there's a vague ache low in my abdomen. Has my period started during the night? I reach for the bedside light and turn it on, but there is no stain on the sheet, and when I put my fingers to myself I find them slick only with a clear glisten of secretion. Images return to me in indistinct tatters – my hands tangled in Dennis's hair as his tongue probes me, but then the hair had become thick and dark, not fair. And Dennis never did this to me, even as foreplay, and suddenly, shamefully, I realise that when my nocturnal lover had lifted his face from between my legs with mischief in his eyes it had been Jack gazing up at me – and not even Jack in his familiar form: this Jack had long ears protruding from his head, like Bottom in *A Midsummer Night's Dream*. And yet he was no ass in my dream, but some other wilder creature. I feel myself blush from the roots of my hair to my toenails and turn off the light again to shroud myself in darkness. Again, though, my treacherous mind returns to the dream, and to that time when Jack kissed me beneath the stars. And now I can't help myself. My fingers find their way back to the secret valley of my own body and I arch my back in the darkness and give myself up to a few brief minutes of pleasure.

'Mummy, Mummy! It's Christmas Eve!'

I wake with a start, and there is light streaming into the room – the sort of deep, bright light that you never get in December at an early hour. I have clearly overslept, and there is so much to do.

Janey's head is level with mine and she is grinning from ear to ear like a little imp. 'Come on, Mummy, it's late! Even Granny's up!'

She is fully dressed and appears to have combed her hair. I push myself upright and rub my face.

'You said Jack's name. In your sleep.'

My heart thuds. How long has she been sitting here, watching me? 'What?'

'You said, "Jack, oh, Jack."'

'I'm sure I didn't.' I am mortified.

'Rabbit heard it too, didn't you, Rabbit?'

The toy nods its floppy ears in assent.

'I'm sure you and Rabbit misheard,' I say primly, swinging my legs out of bed.

'Rabbit hears everything and you're always saying I have ears like a bat.'

I turn my head to hide the tell-tale flush in my face. She's five, what does she understand of such things? 'Go and wash and get ready for breakfast.'

Janey giggles. 'Silly Mummy, it's Christmas Eve and you said we won't eat anything today till supper.'

Of course I had. I groan. Food is a wonderful way of distracting small children and without such a lure I feel out of ideas. Then I remember. 'Go and get your coat on – we'll go up into the woods to find a *podłázniczka* to hang in the dining room.'

'What's a podlaz...?'

I forget sometimes that Janey hasn't been brought up with these ancient Polish traditions, or with the language. I gave both up when I married Dennis, trying to make myself a perfect English wife, without realising he already had one, and that in me he was probably seeking something different.

'It's a branch we bring in on Christmas Eve to hang over the table to bring luck for the following year,' I tell her, and she takes this in thoughtfully.

My grandmother and Aunt Kamila used to bring in a great bough of spruce every Christmas and the whole cottage would be filled with the sharp, resinous scent of it, cutting through all the sweet and spice and fish smells of their cooking. They would hang it over the little table in the kitchen where we ate our meals and we would decorate it with ribbons and fragments of cloth cut from old clothes, with pieces of lace and skeins of wool, and thinking of that reminds me of all those bits of faded cloth tied to the gates on the way up the farm lanes. People are always seeking protective talismans against the random dangers of the world, aren't they? I look down at the knotted red string around my wrist, and smile.

Underneath the *podłázniczka* we'd sing carols and the old songs known only to the villagers that told of dark forests and savage beasts and death and rebirth, of sins and redemption, hunting and salvation. It was, I suppose, our way of reconciling the wild world on our doorstep with our human way of life, and the origins of both songs and custom probably went much further back than Christianity, roots driven deep into the rich, dark earth of the forest. That's what *podłázniczka* means – *the edge of the forest* – and it strikes me now that it's particularly pertinent to us here at White Cove, where the woods come right down to our gardens, and where the cool depths of the woods enshrine an uncanny presence.

As I cut through the drawing room to fetch the handsaw from the utility room, I come upon Mother sitting in a pool of light, eyes half-closed in a sort of bliss, a cigarette poised halfway to her lips. Has she sneakily coloured her hair? It flares more scarlet than usual in the morning sun – but when she hears me and tilts her head out of the light, I see it is its usual colour after all.

'Where are you off to?' she asks, taking in my baggy corduroys, jumper and mackintosh.

'Just up into the woods for a while to get a *podłázniczka* for the dining room.'

She clucks her tongue. 'Such an archaic custom. It'll drop pine needles all over the food!'

But already she has lost interest in the subject, her attention bent on reigniting the cigarette, which has gone out.

Janey and I make our way up the steep little lane and then turn left into the woods and climb over the stile, and this time Janey has no need of my help; she has grown up so much in these months in Cornwall. In moments, we are engulfed by the cool woods, the soft rot of the season underfoot, the loamy smell mushroomy and sensual, reminding me of my dreams. I drag my thoughts away.

My daughter dances from tree to tree along the narrow track, inspecting, touching, whispering to them, 'Not you, not you, not you.'

We reach the stream. At this time of year it is bordered by huge feathery ferns and the wide, heart-shaped leaves of the plant known locally as winter heliotrope that the little book Jack gave me calls, more prosaically, butterbur. When the light strikes the water, you can see the pebbles lying in the streambed speckled with crystal and feldspar. 'Don't drink the water,' Keziah had told me. 'It carries arsenic.'

'Handy if you want to murder someone,' I'd joked.

I think of what I've been told about it running red with Cornish blood in the aftermath of that thousand-years-ago battle. *All the way to the sea.* I shiver. Running red through the woods, a crimson snake amid the green, down past our house, through our gardens, out onto the boulder-strewn beach. Was it still red by the time it debouched there? Was the sea stained rust and pink, the way it goes brown after heavy rain, when mud and sediment is carried into the waves?

It is clear now. Perhaps it has forgotten.

'Look, Mummy! This one is perfect!'

With shock, I realise that Janey is on the other side of the stream. How has she got there without my seeing? What sort of inattentive, irresponsible parent am I? Splashing through the stream, I join her quickly. 'Don't go running off like that, it's dangerous.'

She just laughs and pulls me with her into the trees. 'This one!'

The fir she has selected has a low-hanging branch thick with needles, extended like an arm, making the tree look unbalanced. The secondary twigs are all longer on the downward side: it will hang perfectly from the beam in the dining room. I take the handsaw out of my rucksack and while Janey pats the tree and says thank you, I cut the bough away.

Now there is sap on my hands, sticky and pungent: tree-blood. I wash the blade of the saw and my hands in the stream, feeling that I have carried out an act of violence. We carry the branch home with us, crows cawing overhead.

The air in the house is thick with smoke when we return – acrid cigarette smoke mingling with the sweeter smell of the apple logs Jack brought for us. Magda has arranged a small pile of wrapped gifts to the side of the hearth. We will open them this evening after our Christmas supper.

While Janey is washing, I take out the card I bought her from Dennis and stare at it. I just can't do it. I can't perpetrate the falsehood. And yet I can't bear to see her sad and disappointed, this first Christmas in our new house. In the end, I put the card away, and take the wrapped gifts down to add to the collection by the fire. Janey comes into the drawing room and her eyes rove greedily over the brightly wrapped parcels. She knows she's not allowed to touch them, but it doesn't stop her investigating every single one using Rabbit as her proxy.

'Come and give me some help in the kitchen,' I say brightly to distract her.

'Will that fish be there?' She has developed a horror of the carp, having been surprised by its mournful face staring out at her when she went to get a pot of jam from the Frigidaire.

'It's safely wrapped up in tinfoil now, ready to roast,' I promise her.

She wrinkles her nose. 'I don't want to eat that ugly thing.'

I can't say I blame her. 'You can eat around it and just have a mouthful, for luck.'

'Yuck,' she says. 'Can't I have some cake now?' She looks down at her stomach, then back at me pleadingly and, on cue, it starts to rumble. 'My tummy is empty.'

'The whole point of not eating till the evening is to make us grateful for the food we have then, and for the world that feeds us.'

'And to give thanks to God in his greatness for providing for us.' Magda has appeared at the door, looking more immaculate than ever. She has arranged her hair in great bouncy curled waves, using her largest foam rollers and the Wella setting lotion she loves so much; its sharp chemical scent stings my nose.

'Rabbit says God isn't a man!' says Janey.

I suck my breath in. The look on my mother's face is priceless. 'Of course God is a man, you little heathen!' She transfers her scandalised gaze to me. 'I blame you, and Dennis, for this.'

I lay my hand on Janey's head. 'Run along into the kitchen and I'll come in and give you some cake in a minute.' I give her a gentle push and follow her to the door, which I close firmly behind her. Then I round on my mother.

'Please don't ram your religion down my daughter's throat.'

'*My* religion?'

'I'd rather leave it up to Janey what she chooses to believe when she's old enough to choose for herself.'

'I suppose you think you're very modern, very progressive.' Magda's mouth contorts into a sneer and I see she has lipstick on the edges of her teeth, as red as blood, as if she has been savaging something, or someone, upstairs in her lair.

'I'll be damned if I'll let you spoil her childhood the way you spoiled mine.'

We glare at one another. My eyes feel hot, for once not with tears. Then Magda laughs. 'What a ridiculous conversation, especially today of all days.'

The rest of the day is somewhat strained, but we try to make the best of it. With ill grace, Magda helps me to haul the Christmas tree into the drawing room, and Janey and I spend a happy hour dressing it with tinsel and lights, hanging the glass baubles and the little soldiers and milkmaids from its boughs and the straw angel on the treetop. I hang the *podłázniczka* up in the dining room, and it doesn't drop a single needle. As twilight falls, Janey runs in and out of the house, scrutinising the sky for a sight of the first star which means we can sit down to our Christmas supper. The clouds are thick tonight; even the moon is visible only by an eldritch glow.

Magda and I have just removed the carp from the oven when Janey comes running in, followed by a tall figure.

'Jack!' I cannot help the grin that stretches across my face. Our eyes lock over Janey's head.

Magda at once removes herself from the drudgery of

kitchen work and embraces him warmly. 'Come in, come in! Mila, fetch Jack a glass.'

'You can sit in Rabbit's place,' Janey declares magnanimously and leads him to where Rabbit sits at the head of the table.

'Goodness,' says Jack. 'I *am* honoured. It looks as if Rabbit is in charge tonight.'

'Rabbit is always in charge.'

Janey has decked Rabbit out in a red dress, complete with a crown of tinsel and feathers and holly, and a sceptre of mistletoe.

Jack bows deeply to Rabbit. 'Forgive me, ma'am.' He hands the toy reverently to Janey, who tucks it into place beside her.

'That's a very smart dress Rabbit has on,' says Magda, obviously trying to make an effort.

'Oh yes,' Janey says. 'It's a special dress. She chose it because it was this time of year when she was killed and so were lots of other people and she lay down in the stream and was covered in their blood – so that's why it's red – and then she turned into Rabbit, so that the Lady could use her to talk to me. They called her a saint, but she was just a girl, she says, and anyway saints are just a link between us and the div— Oh, I don't know. It's just what Rabbit told me.'

'The divine?' Jack supplies.

My mother and I exchange perplexed looks.

'Really, darling, you and Rabbit have the most violent imaginations.' I try to make light of what my daughter has just said, but my mind is racing. 'Can you please stop thinking about such unpleasant things, especially on Christmas Eve?'

'Okey-dokey.'

'Don't say that, it's common.' Magda raps the table.

Janey just looks her grandmother up and down with scorn. 'You can sit down now,' she tells Magda imperiously.

Magda purses her lips, no doubt biting back what she'd like to say if Jack were not here. 'Right then, I'm serving drinks.' She flourishes a bottle of vodka. 'Will you join me in a traditional toast, Jack, dear?' She's already had a couple, almost neat; I can't imagine what state she's going to be in for midnight mass at this rate, let alone how she's going to get there.

Jack takes a glass from the dresser and allows Magda to drop ice cubes into it, followed by a large measure of vodka and a dash of tonic water.

'No lime, I'm afraid, but we do have a miraculous lemon.'

'One of Keziah's?'

I nod.

Janey has Lucozade – a special treat. It gleams in her glass like liquid sodium light. We all raise our glasses.

'*Na zdrowie!*' Magda declares. 'To health!'

'*Za nas!* To us!' I raise my glass.

'To three beautiful women!' Jack says.

Janey giggles and I colour. Magda preens; being called beautiful is no more than her due.

After this the evening flies by, and even Janey eats a little of the carp, which is remarkably delicious. We set its scales carefully to one side and after the meal I wash them and press one into my mother's hand, give one to Janey, one to Rabbit (which Janey at once incorporates into the crown) and one to Jack, who regards it curiously.

'It's for luck, and love, in the year to come,' I tell him.

'And wealth!' cried Magda, raising her glass.

'To luck,' I grin, and raise my glass.

'To love,' Jack replies, catching my eye.

'Presents now?' Janey asks hopefully.

I glance at the mountain of dirty dishes.

'They can wait,' Jack says. 'Enjoy yourself a little. After that feast, I reckon you've earned it.'

And so we all pile into the drawing room, where the fairy lights are twinkling on the tree and the fire is poked to roaring life. Janey flings herself down beside the heap of gifts as if they are all hers to give and receive.

I give Mother a smart casket of Elizabeth Arden cosmetics. Jack gives her an elegant silver cigarette holder he found in an antiques shop in Penzance. Magda has given me a copy of *What Shall I Cook Today? 124 Thriftful, Helpful, Tested Recipes*. My mouth twists in a wry grin. 'Thank you, Mother.'

Janey is less than impressed with her Noddy books. 'They're a bit babyish for me now,' she pronounces. She is much more excited by Jack's gift to her: a wigwam made of bamboo poles and cotton printed with running bison, and she has to be dissuaded from running outside to put it up immediately, but is soon distracted by Keziah and Ariadne's blue silk dress. She prances around the drawing room with it pressed against her, yelling in a highly unladylike fashion, 'I'm a princess! I'm a princess!'

I unwrap the pair's gift to me with some trepidation, for fear of likely impropriety, but it turns out to be an exquisite little painting of our house at White Cove, seen from high above, nestling in its dark valley, with the grey sea lapping the shore below it.

Magda coos over it. 'That will look lovely in the hall!'

'It's going in my room,' I tell her firmly.

Jack does not appear to have a gift for me, and I try not to feel disappointed as I hand him the wrapped scarf I have knitted for him over the past couple of weeks out of the wool unravelled from an old cashmere sweater that had come badly out of a war with London clothes moths. He runs his hands over it wonderingly and holds it to his cheek. I wonder if he can smell me on it, even though I washed the wool in Lux flakes.

'No one's ever knitted me anything since I was a small child.'

I wait for him to say more. He never speaks of his childhood, but this appears to be as much of a revelation as he's prepared to make.

Magda gives him a bottle of good whisky, and I recognise it as the one I bought her last week as an early partial Christmas present – she has just surreptitiously removed the tag, not wanting to be overshadowed by my more personal gift. 'You can leave it here and we can share it,' she tells him, which doesn't make it much of a gift at all.

Janey has made Jack one of her special works of art. It is rather like an advent calendar, the design being a large white house that looks very much like the house at White Cove, with windows and doors that open onto little pictures behind. I marvel over her precocious skills as he admires it effusively, shedding glitter whenever he opens a door or window, much to Magda's exasperation. Behind one window there is a flower, behind another a tree, behind the next a piece of shiny chocolate wrapper, a drawing of a cake, a seal, and three tiny figures: a brown-haired woman, a blonde man and a child. Janey giggles when he opens this one and pokes my leg.

Magda cranes her neck. 'Where am I?' she asks crossly.

'You've gone to church,' Janey says primly, and I realise she must have been working on her card this afternoon after her grandmother and I argued, and that she must have been eavesdropping.

The last window reveals Rabbit in all her regal glory – crown, ears and all.

'I shall treasure this,' Jack tells her, and smooths a palm across it to close all the little windows. It comes away silvered with glitter.

'Oh dear,' I say. 'You're going to be finding bits of glitter for weeks.'

'It's not glitter,' Janey says. 'It's magic.'

'Ah, magic. Of course. In that case I shall have to be extremely careful of it.' Jack grins at her.

Janey nods solemnly. 'You should.' She pauses. 'Didn't you get Mummy a present?'

'Darling, that's not very polite. No one *has* to give presents.'

'I almost forgot!' Jack leaps to his feet. 'Come on, Mila. Your present is outside. It's too big to bring in.'

'Don't tell me, you've got me an elephant!'

Janey claps her hands delightedly. 'A giraffe! A rhinoce— rhinocerosses. A tiger!'

'Now, now,' I chide her. 'Don't get too carried away – you won't sleep. You should really go to bed—'

But she's already out of the door with Jack and into the hall. Magda looks back at me. 'Well, come along, then. I suppose we'd better see what ridiculous thing he's got you.' She seems most put out.

Out on the veranda we find Jack and Janey standing each side of a shining bicycle with a big red bow tied to its handlebars.

I burst out into astonished laughter.

'This is too much! Thank you, Jack.' I am hugely touched, and astonished by his generosity.

'It's not new,' Jack says defensively. 'But it's in good working order. I've given it a new chain and recalibrated the gears, and the lights and brakes work now. I'm afraid it's not a lady's bike, but I hope it'll do if you wear trousers.'

Magda's laugh is sneering. 'She'll never get it up these hills.'

This just serves to make me grimly determined. *I bloody well will,* I think. *Even if it kills me.*

'There's a little seat you can add to the back.' Jack points out a bundle by his feet. 'For taking Janey to school.'

This amuses her greatly. 'If I get really fat, poor Mummy will huff and puff.' She mimes a huge stomach, puffing out her cheeks.

'You'll have to eat a lot more carp, then,' I say, and she makes a face. 'Come on, Fatty, off to bed with you,' I tell her. 'If it's not raining tomorrow, we'll try the bike out.'

After some persuasion, Janey gathers her new treasures and we go upstairs. I read her a story from her book of fairy tales and tuck her up with Rabbit. She's fast asleep even before I finish *The Princess and the Pea*, so clearly she is not, whatever she claims, of overly sensitive royal blood. I turn off the light, close her door quietly and slip back into my room. Ariadne's painting lies on the chair where I have placed it. I pick it up and let my eyes rove over the clever brushstrokes. How economic she is with the simplicity of the shapes of hill and headland, arc of beach and sweep of sea. It takes perhaps five minutes of examination before I spot the hare: tiny, tucked into a fold in the woods, its presence given away by a pair of pricked white ears. I run my fingers over it and smile.

I walk out into the corridor and am just about to descend the staircase when I hear something below. I crane over the banister, to see two heads bent together at an intimate angle. I gasp, realising what I'm seeing, and, alerted to my presence, Jack and Magda spring apart like magnets repelling one another. They stare up at me in a sort of tragi-comic pairing – Magda's crimson lipstick all smeared like a clown's smile, Jack's mouth dragged down in an expression of woe. As he gestures towards the mistletoe hanging above them, Magda catches him by the lapels of his dinner jacket and kisses him again, deliberately, possessively, until Jack pushes her away with a sort of violence, and she starts laughing in great, wild shrieks.

I cannot bear to be part of this pantomime. Running back to my room, I shut the door and put my back to it, heart thudding. Then I lie down on my bed, limbs rigid, blood beating in my ears like an awful internal sea, till at last I hear the car's engine start up and it revs away up the lane. Mother going to the midnight service in Eglosberyan. I wonder if she had the gall to take Jack with her, despite his loathing for the priest, but I am too angry and miserable to find out. I pull the bedclothes over my head and swear into my pillow.

So much for my dream of a new start, for thinking that

kiss with Jack beneath the stars meant anything at all.

I fantasise about packing Janey's and my things and heading back to London. I still have a key to the Dulwich house somewhere, don't I?

You fool, my inner voice tells me. That place is long gone to some other couple. Dennis sold it. It was Mother's bargain with him: the proceeds from the sale in return for our silence, for not telling his 'real' wife, or the authorities. He would be ruined if it all came out. He'd lose his job, his marriage, his children, probably his liberty: bigamy is a criminal offence. And anyway, I am a different woman now, though no wiser, it seems.

I swear some more, savagely, silently. *Damn them,* I think. I must not let this horrible new setback hurt me or Janey. I will bloody well push through it. I will stay strong. I have to make our new start work, to make Janey's world safe. And so, I decide, I will work around Mother. I will act as if she does not exist.

I am too het up to sleep so after a long while I decide to go downstairs to make myself a cup of cocoa, which I intend to fortify with a considerable measure of whisky.

The lights are all still on downstairs. I place the fireguard in front of the smouldering embers, turn off the Christmas tree lights at the socket, and am about to head for the kitchen when my heart clutches suddenly. Is there someone moving around in there? I pick up the poker, slip across the room to the door. Did Magda not go to church after all? Or is there an intruder? I flatten myself against the wall and push the door open with my toe till I have a view into the kitchen through the archway, where an aproned figure is standing at the sink.

'Jack!'

He turns around, sleeves rolled up, suds to the elbows, scouring pad in one hand, saucepan in the other. We stare at one another wordlessly, and then we both gabble at the same time, cancelling out any chance of communication. I stop. He stops. He puts the pan down and looks at the poker.

'Go on, then,' he says. 'I'm sure you think I deserve it.'

'Don't you?'

'She kissed me.'

'What, she's so strong you couldn't fend her off?'

He flushes. 'I thought it was just going to be a polite Christmas peck under the mistletoe.'

'Mother doesn't do polite pecks.'

'Mila, I didn't want to kiss her, not like that. It's you I care about. You and Janey.'

'You're only saying that because I caught you with Magda,' I return hotly, and I see how it wounds him, and for a moment I revel in being the one who inflicts pain, rather than the one who receives it.

'Do you really think so badly of me?'

'Honestly? I don't know anything about you. You're a bit of a mystery, aren't you, Jack? You won't talk about your past, you don't appear to have a home, you hid yourself in our attic! But this isn't just about you and me. There's something not right here. There's something rotten between me and my mother, and somehow you've got caught in the middle of it. I need to sort that out. I can't cope with more confusion in my life. I need everything to be clean and clear. Not just for myself, but for Janey. She deserves the very best life I can give her. A steady, safe, dependable life.' I enunciate those last words as if there is a full stop between each one. Then I stop and draw in a deep breath. This is the most I've ever said to Jack in one go. It must be the alcohol. Or the fury. Probably both.

Jack takes off the apron slowly, folds it, lays it aside. He looks hollowed out. 'I'm so sorry, Mila. But I understand. I'm trying to repair my own life too. Really trying. The trouble is it's hard to build on ground with no foundations. I can't remember much of my life before the war. It's as if I've blotted it out. Every time I feel I'm getting close to what I've lost, it feels as if I'm standing on the edge of a deep, dark pit that's trying to draw me in. I'm really afraid I may just jump. Being with you and Janey... it shines light into that pit, makes it feel less deep, less dangerous, more like something that can be dealt with. But it's my problem to deal with, not yours, and it's not fair to drag you in too. You have enough on your own plate, and I don't want to make more trouble for you.'

We gaze at one another. Then the grandfather clock in the hall gives out a low chime.

'Happy Christmas, Mila,' Jack says.

He brushes past me as he leaves.

18

For other families, Christmas Day is the special holiday, the one they look forward to for months, building up to the special roast lunch, glorious excess, the whole family gathered. For us, the celebrations are over with. I feel hollowed out and oddly dislocated from the rest of the world, knowing that everyone else around here is joyously absorbed while we find ourselves in the bleak aftermath of a disastrous evening.

Mother is avoiding me, as well she might. I suspect she has a shocking hangover, apart from any sense of shame. Even Janey seems more subdued than usual. She keeps looking around, then running outside and coming back in looking disappointed. In the end I ask her, 'What's the matter?'

'I can't find Jack. I wanted to show him something.'

I give an inward sigh. 'Jack's not going to be here for a while.'

Her eyes flash. 'Why not?'

How to explain the tides of emotion, the twining serpents of trust and distrust to a child of her age? I reach out and brush her hair off her forehead. It's getting long – I should give it a trim, but Janey is like a skittish horse whenever I try, tossing her head, backing away. 'It's complicated, darling.'

'No, it isn't! I want him here.' Her jaw is set, her lips compressed. For a disconcerting moment she looks disturbingly like her grandmother.

'I'm afraid the entire world doesn't revolve around what you want.' God, how I hated it when Magda used to say this sort of thing to me. I am turning into a horrible parent. 'What I mean, darling, is that he has other things to do, other places to be right now.'

She folds her arms. 'He belongs here.' She stamps her foot.

'What is it you wanted to show him?' I ask, trying to distract her from the rising tantrum.

'You wouldn't be interested,' she tells me petulantly.

'I promise I would.'

I watch as her expression becomes calculating. At last, she says, 'Will you take me out on the bicycle if I show it to you?'

If that's what it takes, I think, and we strike a bargain.

'Put your boots on,' she instructs, peremptory.

I do as I am told.

Her dark mood passes quickly as her sense of mission takes over and she leads me down the lawn, through the pampas grass and bamboo, the carcasses of the summer gunnera, down to where ferns and ivies grow in profusion by the side of the stream that leads down under the stone bridge to the sea. Just before we reach the bridge, Janey parts the vegetation and disappears from view. A little hand reaches back for me. 'This way, Mummy.'

I want to scold her for the solo explorations that have

led her here beyond my prohibition, beside the gurgling waters of the stream, but the moment feels magical, as if we are stepping out of time, and I don't want to spoil it. I beat back the nettles to which Janey seems immune, and follow her into the shady depths. For a long moment I can see nothing much except leaves and bramble runners. Then my eyes adjust to the gloom and as Janey pulls the undergrowth away, I see there is an archway of granite beneath which is a little rounded wall, upon which my daughter is leaning, gazing down. I crowd in beside her and place my hands on the little wall. The stone is cold and clammy with damp beneath my palms. It seems to vibrate into my arm bones, though more prosaically, that is probably just the beating of my own pulse, which is faster than usual, excited by this new discovery. Inside the semicircular wall is a cool, black space of what appears to be absolute nothingness.

'What do you think it is, Mummy?'

'I think it's a well, darling.'

'What's a well?'

'It's where people used to go to get their water.'

Janey's forehead wrinkles. 'But there's water all around here.'

Of course, she is right – there is running water in the stream and the great waves of the sea shooshing into the beach. 'Perhaps there were times when the stream ran dry,' I suggest.

'How would they get the water out?' She leans further, and I have to pull her back. The opening is too small even for Janey to fall into, I think, but you can never be too careful.

'By lowering a little bucket on a rope and then pulling it back up again, full of water.'

She takes this in thoughtfully. 'Didn't they have taps?'

Such a logical child, despite her wild side. I laugh. 'No, darling, taps are really quite modern inventions.'

'I think this well is very old,' she pronounces. 'And look, it has a lady guarding it.'

My spine prickles. 'What lady?'

'Here.' She takes my hand and guides it across the back wall, in the shadow beneath the arch.

My fingers feel grooves and indentations: two holes and a straight line. The hairs start to rise – one by one – on the back of my neck. I reach out with my free hand, push the cloaking ferns away and light falls full on the granite. There is a face carved into the stone beneath the arch. It is the same face Ariadne showed me on the back of the Celtic cross in the hedge in Eglosberyan: two eyes; a straight, slashed line for the mouth; the radiating hair. It is primitive but powerful. This one, though, has the addition of two lines pointing straight up out of the circle denoting the head, like horns. Or ears...

My heartbeat thunders. What does it mean? Why does everything seem to come back to the same image, or some version of it? The discovery feels momentous and world-shattering, and yet at the same time intimate, personal. I draw a deep breath.

'Thank you for showing me this,' I say. 'It's absolutely extraordinary.'

I run my hand over it again, my skin tingling, caressing the stone, making a silent goodbye. Our very own well, bearing the image of... whoever this being may be. I must tell Keziah and Ariadne, I think; I must tell Jack.

Janey beams. 'Now let's go on the bike!'

A few minutes later we are back at the house, fixing the child seat onto the frame directly behind my own. 'I'm just going to ride it around here on the flat for a bit,' I tell her, 'to get the hang of it again. Then we'll wheel it up to the top of the lane and go from there. Okay?'

She nods slowly, as if making a great concession. 'I could ride my tractor, if you don't think you're strong enough.'

I laugh, though I'm stung. 'I'm quite sure I'll manage.'

I get on the bike, get off the bike, adjust the height of the saddle, get back on again, squeeze the brakes. Then I pedal it gently around the parking area, the gravel crunching under its wheels. It's been years since I rode a bike – and that was a heavy great bone-rattler at school that clanked and bucked every time you changed gear, but after a few minutes I am grinning. This bike handles so silkily in comparison to that old monster, I feel as if I have grown wheels. I roll it over to where Janey waits impatiently and help her up into the little seat. 'Hold on to me, all right?'

Off we go, around the garden paths, Janey giggling and clutching at my waist when we hit a bump or take a corner. 'Whee!'

I bring it to a halt at the bottom of our lane. Could I pedal it up, with Janey on the back? The idea of losing control with her on the bike is awful, so in the end we get off and push it up to the postbox corner. The incline is far less evil from here to the top of the hill. There is a moment, just a moment, when I stand on the pedals and push for all I'm worth thinking, *I'm not going to be up to this*. There is too much resistance, the bicycle is too heavy, too unwieldy for my puny muscles to move uphill. But then, inch by inch, it gets easier. The wheels crank around a full rotation, then another, and more quickly another – and suddenly we are moving smoothly along, the hedges flowing by like rivers of green, the trees waving us on our way, even the crows overhead shouting encouragement. I can feel Janey's hands on my waist, holding tight. I can hear her laughing in my ear – golden, joyous – and I think, *I can do this. We will get there. Together. We will we remake our world.*

'You look like hoydens!'

Magda regards us disapprovingly from where she sits in her armchair, legs crossed, ringed with blue smoke. The ashtray on the table beside her is already half full of lipstick-covered butts.

Oblivious to her grandmother's mood, Janey dances over to her, gleeful. 'We've been all the way to St Levan! Mummy is really good at bicycling, and we flew back down the hill like birds!'

I had been, I must admit, terrified of that last downward sweep back to White Cove, terrified that the brakes would fail, that we would miss the bend where we first saw the white hare and plunge over the edge to our deaths, but it was as if I felt a steadying hand on my back, on the bike, all the way down, even as we freewheeled the final section with the wind in our hair and the winter sun in our eyes.

We were both giggling uncontrollably by the time we dismounted, and Janey had flung her arms around me. 'That was the best fun ever, Mummy. Let's do it every day!'

I regard my mother now, hunched and sallow, her skin unhealthy-looking, her eyes dull, the make-up she has so expertly applied looking tawdry and false, a mask painted on a corpse.

'It's a lovely morning out there. You should go for a walk – it would do you good,' I tell her.

She gives me baleful look. 'In these shoes?'

I see she is wearing her highest heels, her silkiest stockings, and I realise why.

'Jack's gone,' I say shortly. 'He's not coming back.' I look over at Janey, her mouth has opened in an O of disappointment. 'Not today, or for a few days at least.' I return my attention to Mother. 'I hope you confessed your sins last night,' I say pointedly.

She looks uncomfortable. 'I didn't get as far as the church.'

'What do you mean?'

Magda fiddles with lighting another cigarette. 'I had a bit of an... incident with the car.'

Alarmed, I ask, 'Did you crash? Are you all right?' It strikes me that this may be why she is looking so ill, but she shakes her head impatiently, waves a hand.

'It was nothing. I thought I saw something strange, so I pulled the car in. And then I... fell asleep.'

'What did you see?'

She takes a long draw on the cigarette. 'I really have no idea.'

19

It is Boxing Day, another day closer to Magda's grand opening party on New Year's Eve when we will see in 1955, now less than a week away. RSVPs arrived in the post in ones and twos before Christmas, some enclosed in a festive card; I daresay there will be a torrent of them as soon as the post comes through again. Already I have lost count of the replies, though I'm sure Mother knows the exact number by heart.

There is, because of the party, a tacit truce between us. The kiss has not been mentioned; Jack has not been mentioned. Magda is, I can tell, making a great effort to be nice to me. The new cynical side of me ascribes this effort to the fact that she depends on me so completely to produce the canapés for the party. So when I suggest that she accompanies me and Janey on a walk through the woods and lanes that afternoon, she amazes me by agreeing and even goes so far as to change into a pair of flat shoes, a tweed skirt and jacket. I have never seen my mother wear trousers; she regards them as 'mannish'.

Janey makes the most of having two adults accompany her. She swings from our hands, she gabbles her stories about all the animals and plants we pass. 'Look, that's a *nettle*. Don't touch it, it bites!'

I love that she thinks that Magda has never seen a nettle before. I hide a smile.

'Those black birds up there are rooks. They have white beaks and they live in a *rookery*.' This is a new word for her, and she is inordinately proud to have a chance to use it in educating her grandmother. 'Can you hear them all talking to each other? They always sound as if they're having an argument, like you and Mummy.'

My mother and I catch each other's eye; she looks away first.

It is a beautiful winter's day – the sort of day when the light angling through the trees feels as clear and sharp as a struck bell. Sound carries for miles on such a day – from the top of the hill you can even hear the sea far, far below, rolling into the wide crescent of the boulder beach. Here and there the gorse has burst into explosions of rich yellow flowers which give off a faint scent of coconut, a promise of a distant spring now that the year has turned its corner. Janey collects feathers: a black-and-white one – from a magpie, or a seagull – and one that is tawny-striped, and tucks them away in her bag with Rabbit, who is still adorned in her crown as if making a royal progress to survey her domain.

From up here, the house looks tiny and insignificant amid the natural vista of thorn and furze, trees and ferns and lawns that run down towards the sea. From this perspective we humans are tiny and unimportant in the grand scheme of the valley. It will always be here, this geological feature, this cleft in the landscape, channelling water from the moors down to the rolling sea. The trees will go on growing, then falling and decaying and nourishing the new saplings that grow in their place; the woodland creatures will make their homes in the banks and trunks and branches, and among the roots, which burrow down with the worms and centipedes and fungi; the birds will fly over the treetops and call and pair and mate and raise young – and we, we are just a part of this everlasting cycle, living and dying and becoming part of the earth, the air and the water that make up this landscape. I think all these thoughts in fleeting moments in the quiet space between Janey's stories and the tap of Magda's soles on the track, where the strip of grass down the middle now grows shorter and browner and narrower than it did when we first arrived, and a sense of peace settles over me. What do parties and arguments and refurbishments matter in this great wheel of life? All we can do, I think, is be happy and good to one another and keep whatever small part of the world on which we live and tread safe for the next generation, and those to come.

We turn off the tarmacked track and into a little greenway that runs along the contour of the hill towards Eglosberyan. It is sunken between its fringed hazel hedges, the bottom trodden hard and smooth by the passage of feet on their way to market or to church for century upon century. The branches that curl overhead are only sparsely leafed at this time of year. In late spring and summer it must be a cool, lovely, tranquil space that lives up to its name, and I remember Jack describing such a path, and calling it a 'hollow way'. Even now, in the bleak midwinter, it is full of birdsong, though the greenery is provided only by holly and ivy.

I find the words and music of the hymn flowing through my head and I'm all but transported back to carol services at the Surrey boarding school, with the teachers lined up on the dais and Miss Richardson thumping at the piano in front of us, and the boys on the left-hand side of the assembly hall tunelessly blaring out the words while Margaret Dean and Julie Barber surreptitiously kick me in the back of the knee, trying to tumble me over. I look back over my shoulder. Janey is showing Magda a plant growing by the side of the sunken path. Their heads are bent together and I think how forgiving and confident my daughter is, despite everything. I'm sure we can work this out. Once the house is full of guests, Magda will be in her element, socialising, laughing, flirting, holding court, overseeing her domain. And Janey will go to the village school and make new friends there. And I...? I will... I will do my damnedest to make a go of it all.

And so my mind circles back to Jack. *I care about you*, he had said. I have tried not to think about those words in the thirty-six or so hours since he uttered them, but they have been there constantly in the darkness of my mind, like shining treasures in a cave, waiting for me to examine them again and wonder what they truly mean, and every time I think about them, it is as if I am wrapped in a soft blanket. Someone cares about me. Someone with no familial connection or duty, who had no need to utter such a momentous statement. I find myself smiling, walking a little faster, then laughing aloud into the bosky air.

As if they approve of my thoughts, the unseen birds

chirrup and trill. A robin, blackbirds, rooks, a wren. I pick them out absentmindedly as some other part of me recalls Jack's mouth on mine as we stood by the car under the stars.

There is a moment when the whole scene falls quiet, as if all life is suspended. The birds all stop singing at the same time. There is the eerie sense of being in some liminal space between worlds, neither of my own time, nor any other. And then with a clatter of wings the rooks burst out of the trees, cawing raucously, the blackbirds shriek alarm calls, and there is suddenly a cacophony of hoofbeats and barking and howling and shouting and screams. The ground trembles beneath the soles of my feet; even the air seems to tremble with the violence of the noise.

Something streaks towards and then past me, too fast to see what it is, trailing an impression of orange fire, and when I look behind me I see a melee of horses and dogs milling around and I cannot make my mind understand what I am seeing. Where all was peaceful now all is chaos. Men shouting, horses stamping and circling, pressed into the sides of the narrow greenway, into the branches and brambles, dogs baying, their breath clouding the chilly air.

I start running towards this chaos by instinct. Where is Janey? Where is my mother? I can't see either of them in the churn of legs and the tangle of hounds. I can hear my own voice entering the hubbub – a shrill wail amid the baying and stamping and shouting.

And then something else streams past me, heading *towards* the huntsmen. I *feel* it pass as much as see it: a sensation of biting cold that flows through my calves and ankles as if I've been caught in a tiny, localised snowstorm. White flickers at the edges of my vision, leaving zigzagging afterimages. The tone of the cries ahead of me alters in a way that makes my spine shiver. The sound is uncanny. My heart stutters, as if cold fire has flowed through me and has now engulfed the scene of chaos up ahead, muffling it with its elemental power, pushing it out of the immediate physical world of a Boxing Day hunt into some realm of limbo into which a wild hunt has erupted. I have a weird sense that this scene has been played out innumerable times, in many different periods of time, between different dramatis personae, each enacting their allotted roles.

The chaos changes, breaks apart, thins out and springs into focus again, very much in the here and now. I begin to make out individual shapes – men on horseback, moving back up the greenway, the hounds' baying turning to an eerie, perplexed whine. I take in the dogs' odd demeanour, ears flat to their skulls, tails down, circling nervously, teeth bared in a snarl. One by one, the horsemen turn and run except for one dark horse which rears up, whinnying wildly before casting off its rider and following the rest, dragging the man screaming behind it.

How did I ever get so far from my mother and daughter? I try desperately to accelerate but it feels as if I'm trying to run through some viscous substance, or as if unseen hands are holding me back. By the time I reach the place where the hunt milled about, the dogs and horses have all gone, leaving churned-up ground in their wake. All is quiet. I can see my mother kneeling in the undergrowth by the side of the greenway, her eyes huge and round. Beside her...

My heart lurches. 'Oh God, Janey!'

My little girl lies tumbled in a heap. Her eyes are closed, her skin is pale as paper. I begin to tremble so hard I can barely manage to keep the pads of my finger still on the pulse point at the angle of her neck and jaw.

I cannot find a pulse.

Oh God, I cannot find a pulse.

'Janey! Janey, please, please, wake up, darling.' My fingers press deeper and there it is – the faintest flicker of the blood beating through her, barely there, as if her life is ebbing away beneath my touch.

I gather her to me. How could this happen? We were just out for a Boxing Day walk. It was peaceful, happy – Janey and Magda becoming friends again, my mother making the rare gesture of accompanying us on a walk. And now this. What to do? I don't know what to do. We are in the middle of nowhere, more than a mile from White Cove and the car, and yet another mile into the village.

'Help!' I scream into the arch of the greenway and the word comes out as a croak, feeble, inaudible, the cry in a nightmare in which you cannot move, cannot shout. I stare at my mother with hollow eyes, feeling empty, helpless. She looks drained, terrified; tears are pouring down her cheeks and I realise she thinks Janey is dead.

'She's not dead,' I manage to utter. *Not yet.*

That galvanises her. 'I'll run home for the car.' She turns to look back the way we have come. 'It can't be that hard to find the way.'

I'm trying to think, trying to herd my scattering thoughts, trying to keep panic at bay. 'No,' I say at last. 'Josie's.'

Terror makes me strong. I pick Janey up and cradle her and start to run down the greenway, hardly able to see over her head to where I am placing my feet but somehow, miraculously, not falling. I can hear Magda behind me, panting to keep up but I can't think about her, not right now.

'Where are we going?' she wails between breaths, but I do not answer. I must save every scrap of my energy to keep running. What if this isn't the right way? What if we get there and there's no one in? Stupid, panicky thoughts thunder through my head. I tell my gibbering brain to shut up, shut up. I glance down. Did Janey's eyelids just flicker? I bend my head towards her. 'Darling, hold on, hold on. We'll get you help.'

Suddenly we are out of the hollow lane and into a wider track. I stop for a moment to orientate myself. Downhill, sea; uphill, Eglosberyan. I take a breath and follow the track straight on through nettles and brambles to either side until at last – there! A chimney shows above the trees.

My chest is tight with effort, my lungs and arms burning. 'Nearly there!' I whisper to Janey. 'Hold on, darling.'

Another burst of effort and the manor house comes into sight as the track comes out onto the road. Two minutes later, my boots are hammering up the tangled path to the front door and I am yelling, 'Josie! Josie!'

There is no sign of life. The windows are dark, the door remains shut. Oh God, oh God! I flee around the side of the house to the rear courtyard where Josie took me in on my brief visit – and there is the Land Rover, muddy and battered. I have never been so glad to see anything in all my life. I shout Josie's name again and again, and suddenly she is there in front of me, framed by the big old riveted wooden door.

Immediately she takes in the situation. 'Come in, quick, this way.'

'Do you have a phone?' I puff. 'To call the doctor?'

'No phone, sorry. I'm such a hermit. Plus, broke. What happened?'

Tears are spilling out of me now – a combination of the relief of having got here, and disappointment that there is no phone. Janey twists in my arms and her face contorts, but her eyes do not open and she makes no sound. I know that expression though: pain. My little girl is in pain.

'Can you drive us to the doctor?'

'Of course! Wait here. Let me get my car keys.'

Magda and I stand in the hallway and I see my mother gazing around in wonderment, taking in the beams, the exposed timbers in the walls, the rough plaster, the framed portraits. 'What is this place?'

'I can't talk about this now,' I say.

'Look, she moved!' Magda bends over Janey. 'Janeska! Janeska!' She reaches for the small limp hand, chafes it between her own, raises it to her lips. 'Thank God.' Her eyes meet mine. 'I thought we'd lost her.'

'We may still. Who knows how injured she is? Did you see what happened?' I ask, and my voice is trembling.

My mother shakes her head. 'It was all so fast. One minute we were just walking along and she was chattering about the plants she recognised, the next the hunt was upon us, and it was chaos. Janey got knocked down and the hounds seemed to go for her, and then the men tried to pull them away, and then, I don't know…'

Josie is back, wellies on, struggling into her waxed jacket, car keys in one flailing hand. Once outside, Magda crawls into the back of the Land Rover without a word of complaint about the state or smell of it, and I climb into the front with Janey in my arms. Josie drives with her usual speed and surety but takes the corners with greater care than usual. We are just approaching the junction to the village when we see ahead of us a small army of men and horses and hounds.

'The fucking hunt!' Josie says with impressive viciousness.

'I think,' Magda says, 'maybe one of their horses kicked her. I'm not sure exactly what happened. Or those dogs...'

Her words trail away. I can hear the horror of the recalled moment hanging in the air between us.

'Did they bite her? The dogs?'

'I... I don't think so. I don't know...'

I am already feverishly pulling at Janey's clothing, touching her arms, her legs, her torso. My hand comes away clean, no blood on my fingers and again Janey twists in my arms, her mouth opening a silent scream, her hands in fists, as if she is reliving the incident, fighting off the dogs.

I can see the huntsmen now, individually unrecognisable in their jackets and caps. They press themselves and their mounts into the gateway as we approach, since Josie is giving no sign that she is going to slow down for them, and then there is a scramble bordering on panic because she changes down gear and accelerates, leaning on the horn. One of the horses rears up; others prance and pivot as if they're engaged in some ancient savage dance. One man falls into the hedge and I feel a swift moment of satisfaction as we pass. Josie winds down her window and roars, 'Bastards!'

And then we are in the lane leading up to the centre of the village, the church tower looming over us. She passes the church at speed, going around the circular graveyard with a screech of tyres. We pass the spot where Jack kissed me, and then she pulls the Land Rover in at the side of the road and I stare out in confusion. 'Does the doctor live next door to Keziah and Ariadne?'

She suppresses a snort of laughter. 'Just get out. Come on, quick! Whatever else she is, Keziah's a lot more use than any doctor around here.'

She's already running towards the cottage shouting their names, and there is a dark frizzy head at the door, and then both Keziah and Ariadne are running towards us, arms outstretched.

'What happened?' Ariadne cries.

'Never mind that now.' Keziah is all business. 'Follow me.'

Half an hour later, Janey is tucked up in a little bed that Ariadne has made up in the room presided over by the painting of the crowned hare. She has been examined minutely by Keziah, soothed with ointments, wrapped in a white linen shirt. Colour has come back into her cheeks, but she still hasn't opened her eyes, or made any sound. But she does seem more peaceful than when she was twisting in my arms, giving her silent rictus scream. Nothing broken, not even the skin, but she may have taken a blow to the head, though Keziah tells me the skull is undamaged.

'Shouldn't we take her to hospital, just to check, or call Dr Tregenza?'

'It's a long way to a hospital with those facilities. As for Dudley Tregenza… honestly, I wouldn't trust him with a dog. Sometimes when the body has suffered a shock it needs to absorb it and deal with it. I think the best thing is for her to lie quietly for a while and we will keep a close watch on her.' She runs her hand across Janey's cheek and forehead and I recall how Jack said she had been a nurse. 'Her pulse is stronger. We will let her sleep. Light the candles, Ariadne, and we'll say a prayer for her.'

Magda and I exchange a glance. I bow my head as Magda whispers the words of the Lord's Prayer and Ariadne goes to the little shrine and lights the candles and incense there.

Josie coughs, discreetly. 'I'm just going outside for a cigarette, if you don't mind.'

Magda, prayer finished, pushes herself to her feet. 'You wouldn't happen to have a spare cigarette, would you?' And so an unlikely alliance is forged.

Keziah and Ariadne join hands and then reach out to me. 'Come,' Ariadne says, 'we'll form a circle of protection around your daughter. Three women; there is nothing stronger in all the world than three women joined in a single purpose.'

I hesitate, but what harm can it do?

White Lady who illuminates the Earth with your light
Who nourishes the seeds of the Earth with your heat
Who blesses the water we live by and the food that we
    eat
Who channels the forces of life and death
Who watches over us with her triple faces
And who chooses to run in the guise of a hare

We call upon your grace in our time of need
To strengthen the life-force in this child, who is one of
*   your own.*
Be with us now and always, O Wild One
And we will ever honour you in this world
In the hollow places
And in the world to come.

20

Janey sleeps on. The women come and go calmly and unfussily, bringing me sugared tea and fortifying cake. The day draws down to darkness and still Janey does not wake. I watch her eyeballs jagging beneath their light coverlets of skin, and sometimes her feet twitch as if, like a dreaming dog, she's trying to run. When I need to go to the bathroom, Magda takes my place at her side. She is grey-faced, haunted.

'It's my fault, I should have heard them coming. It should have been me they struck, if anyone. I could have pushed her to safety.'

She says versions of this over and over until Keziah takes her hand. 'It wasn't your fault. You didn't run her down, did you? Those men, those... hunters. All they do is bring destruction and mayhem.'

'The dogs were out of control. They just went for her, as if she was their prey.'

'I think the fox they were chasing ran past me,' I say, remembering. 'Something did. And then—' I recall the weird flow of cold air, the sense of whiteness, and shake my head. What I cannot make sense of is best left unsaid.

Keziah, Ariadne and Josie make their way to the kitchen, telling us they're going to prepare food, and leave Magda and me quiet with Janey. My mother's face is tense with guilt and anxiety, the deep creases making her appear older than her usual carefully presented self. *Three women*, I think. *Three generations of women. The strongest structure in the world.*

'It really wasn't your fault, Mother,' I say, but it comes hard; I have been silently blaming her for hours. 'There was nothing you could do.'

She raises her eyes to me. 'I haven't been the best of mothers,' she says, so quietly I might almost have imagined it.

Does she mean grandmothers? I frown, but she continues.

'I never wanted children. Never even thought about being a wife or mother. Life was too full of other possibilities. I had a good job, had just been promoted and we all went out to celebrate. It was such a fun evening. I was twenty-four, happy, successful, wearing a divine Schiaparelli copy in scarlet crepe, heels to match, a little leopard-print scarf...' She falls silent, remembering, her mouth drawn down. 'I thought a lot of myself, laughing, all the men's eyes on me.' She gives a bitter little laugh. 'I flirted with him, but I flirted with everyone – it was how I showed my power...'

Magda looks to the ceiling and the candlelight smooths away the webs of fine lines and wrinkles that show her true age. I can imagine her at twenty-four, shining with hope and expectation, elegant in her dress and scarf and high heels, her auburn hair gleaming under the lights of the city's bars, throwing her head back and laughing at the young men vying to impress her.

'He said he just wanted to see me safely home. And he did. But when we got there he kissed me, and I pushed him away and that made him angry. He forced the door open, and then he forced me.'

Comprehension dawns. 'He raped you?'

The words hang in the incense. After a long pause Magda nods.

The horror of it settles over me like a shroud. My mother – my proud, strong, difficult mother, raped. 'I'm so sorry, Mama.' I haven't called her that since I was small. 'What a terrible thing to have happened to you.' Tears prick my eyes.

She will not look at me. 'I could not believe that I had fallen pregnant. Just once, so fast, both of us so drunk. I thought in the weeks that followed that I was just unwell, suffering from shock, but soon there was no denying it. I asked around, discreetly; you had to be secretive about such a thing. To get pregnant was bad enough, but abortion? In Poland?' She shakes her head. 'People knew of a doctor here or there by rumour – someone's cousin, a friend of a friend, who had gone to them. They were fine, it was expensive but the baby was gone; look at them now happily married to a husband they'd never have caught otherwise. But then there were other stories, darker stories: women who had bled to death, had died of infection, who paid over a small fortune and been fiddled with by the doctor and still remained pregnant. Some of those I asked were appalled at the very idea I'd want to get rid of the baby. "He should marry you!" they cried. "We'll make him marry you! You can't kill a child, that's a sin." They were dreaming of weddings strewn with roses, of the traditional unveiling, the solemn sanctity of the marriage bed, raising a great brood of children.' She sighs and looks back at me and her gaze is distant. 'That was *never* my dream. I had just been promoted to the role of office manager. I was organised, thorough, meticulous, indispensable, powerful. Another promotion would soon be within my grasp. I knew it, and how I wanted it. I had planned so minutely how I would change our systems, run things more efficiently, save money, introduce new methods, rearrange the office to make better use of the space and the light – those were the thoughts that occupied me. Not all the mess and pain and fuss and chaos of raising a child. Let alone doing so on my own, a social pariah, pointed at and gossiped about, a scandalous woman on the road to damnation.'

'So that's why I was raised in Kasina Wielka? By Babcia and Aunt Kamila?' Something doesn't quite fit. 'But Daddy did marry you. You wouldn't have needed to be pointed at and gossiped about.'

She looks directly at me now, her eyes a chilly blue. 'You think it was your father who raped me?'

I feel ashamed now, as well as confused. 'Well, no.' It's true, I cannot imagine my father ever carrying out such a violent, despicable misdeed. He was such a gentle man, full of self-deprecating humour.

'Tomascz wasn't capable of raping anyone. He was far too… *fastidious*.' The way she says the word is derisive, contemptuous. 'He married me for both our sakes, out of convention.'

The errant puzzle piece is falling into place and I begin to feel bereft. I am an unwanted child, the product of rape. I have over the years come to terms with the fact that I never really had a mother who loved me; now it seems I am to lose the man I thought of as my father as well.

Magdalena presses her lips together as if shutting in any further words on the subject. Then she glances back down at Janey, pale but peaceful, as beautiful and delicate as a Renaissance angel.

'Tomascz was a friend. We came to an… agreement which worked for both of us. We would marry, I would have the child, my mother and her sister would raise it, while we went about our lives separately even though – most of the time – we slept beneath the same roof.'

I am shocked. 'What, you both… went with other people? He had other women, and you had other men?'

Magda's lips curve; she is truly amused. 'Oh, Mila, how naive you are.' She laughs. 'We both had other men, darling. Your "father" was a homosexual. He had many lovers – was well known for it in our circles. But if you wanted to get on in the business world it did not do to have scandal attached to you, so my pregnancy and need for a husband coincided with his need for the semblance of respectability, and so we married and I gave birth to you.'

This is a lot to take in. At last I ask, 'Then who was my father?'

'Why do you need to know? He just put a seed in me by force and I never saw him again. I can't even remember his name now.'

I do not believe this, and say so. For a long time she says nothing and I think this secret will go to the grave with her. But then her head comes up and she looks me in the face. 'He was Hungarian. I could not even pronounce his name. He was dark, clever, a poet, but they also said he'd killed a man, and that was why he was in Krakow. I thought that was...' She pauses, weighing her words. '... alluring. It's why I let him kiss me. What an idiot I was, to think that kissing a murderer was exciting, a daring – almost romantic – thing to do.' She shakes her head. 'Well, there you have it. There must've been something in that tea Keziah gave me, some sort of truth drug, for I've never told that to another living soul. And now I daresay you will hate and despise me even more. Your own mother nothing more than a slut and a fool, as well as a terrible parent, interfering in your life, breaking up your relationship with Dennis. It was bigamy, to be sure, but I should have left the decision of whether to stay with him or not to you. To be honest with you, Mila, I simply could not bear to see you happy after the mess I made of my own life.'

I stare at her. I have indeed blamed and hated her for destroying what I had thought was my marriage. She was cruel, and seemed to revel in the destruction of my little world. I was so damaged by the break-up, by Dennis's craven abandonment of me and Janey, with barely a goodbye. I remember him emptying the contents of his pockets and wallet into Magda's hands – 'Here, take it, take it all, but don't tell Angela!' Striking his cowardly deal with my mother: the proceeds of selling the Dulwich house in return for our silence and disappearance – 'As far away as possible!'

Which is worse? I wonder now. To be raped by a near-stranger, or betrayed by the man you married and had a child with? We have both suffered so much. And suffering does not always make you a nicer person. In my mother's case it made her cold and vengeful, as if by punishing me she could recoup a little of the power she lost over her life. I should feel boiling anger at this – with Magda, with the man who forced himself upon her, with the world. I should scream, and howl, and weep buckets – but I can't. I feel emptied out. The terror at almost losing Janey has drained me of all other emotion.

We sit in silence for a long time; eventually a little compassion flows back into one of the empty chambers of my heart. I think about what my mother has been through: rape, a marriage of convenience, a child she never wanted, fleeing the country of her birth ahead of war, being widowed there. What a bitter story she has lived, and all the time I must have been a walking reminder of everything she lost. It explains so much.

I reach across the little bed and take her hand. It feels cold and bony in my grasp. 'I'm glad you told me. It was brave of you.'

She withdraws her hand. 'I don't think it is brave. But if we are to try to make a new start, I must clear away the dead wood. I cannot make up for the past, but I will try to do better in the future, with you and with Janeska.'

'That's all anyone can ask.'

I see her face twist as a new thought strikes her. 'I suppose while we're clearing the air I ought to…' She grimaces. 'I ought to apologise. To you. For kissing Jack. I was rather… inebriated. But that's just an excuse. I shouldn't have done it. I knew you were becoming close, and I was jealous, so I sprang upon him. He had no idea what was happening until it was too late. There, I've said it. I'm just a bitter old woman who craves the admiration of young men.'

There are livid spots over her cheekbones, though the rest of her face is deathly pale, all the blood drawn away to those two pools of crimson. It strikes me that this confession has been, in a curious way, the hardest of all for her to make.

'Thank you. Yes, it was wrong, and it hurt me deeply. You must apologise to Jack too.'

She looks away from me, her flush deepening. 'Oh Lord,' she says. 'What an almighty mess.'

'It is. But we can clear it up. Make a new beginning.'

Magda gives me a weak smile. 'A new beginning. I suppose so. We must try. I *will* try.'

'So will I.'

On cue, the other women return, bearing trays of food, and a carafe of some bright purple liquid surrounded by tiny glasses.

'My best sloe gin.' Ariadne grins, pouring measures for us all. She waits till we each have a glass in hand then raises her own. 'To Janey. To health.'

We all drink. The gin is sweet and potent. Magda's eyes water, but even so she insists on a second toast, in Polish, and we all take refills. Josie hesitates over hers then downs it in a single gulp. 'What the hell? The Land Rover knows the way home.'

Keziah hands out bowls of soup while Josie slathers butter onto slabs of homemade bread, and we balance the hot bowls on our knees. The spicy lentil soup is thick and garlicky, and utterly delicious. I hadn't even known I was hungry till my spoon scrapes the bottom of the china.

I am just reaching for a second slice of bread when Janey

stirs, emitting a small groan. I put my bowl down on the floor and stroke her face but although her eyelids flicker she does not waken. I am just tucking her hand carefully back beneath the covers when I feel something brush my skin. I look down. In her fist she is grasping something white. Gently, I pry her fingers apart. A tiny tuft of white fur lies in her palm, but as soon as I try to take it, her fist closes tight again.

It can't be, can it? *Don't be absurd*, I scold myself. I remember the hounds, their patchwork of brown and black and white. Dog hair, then.

Keziah runs her checks once more, pressing her fingers to Janey's neck and skull, taking her pulse. 'No swelling, and no temperature. It's just a matter of time before she wakes up.'

Magda yawns hugely, and seeing this, Josie says, 'I can drop you home if you like – or you could have a bed at mine if you'd prefer not to be on your own. It's a bit ramshackle, but there's the room with the four-poster—'

My mother is already accepting the offer before the sentence can be completed. Her eyes gleam; how can she resist, even amid all the drama, an invitation to spend a night under the roof of the grand old manor house? It represents everything she aspires to – aristocracy, status, wealth – even if the house is run down, its owners' stock long fallen.

'Go on,' I say. 'There's nothing you can do here, and you've had quite a shock as well. I'll stay here with Janey.'

'I'll run you back in the morning,' Josie says, 'to see how she's getting on.'

When they've gone, the atmosphere feels more peaceful. I think of all the roiling emotions my mother carries within her. Is it any wonder she's been a terrible mother, an insufficient grandmother, and a bitter, insecure woman in such need of male attention? All those deep-buried reasons for her anger, her bitterness, her jealousy. Gaining a degree of understanding of what has made her the way she is has made me feel very sorry for her, prompted some fellow-feeling in me. Although I can never forgive her for hitting my child, I have forgiven her, I think, for hitting and abandoning me. Perhaps now that she has spoken out she will have a better chance of controlling her temper, or at least being aware of its true source.

Keziah and Ariadne are in the middle of a gentle squabble as to who is going to stay up with me keeping vigil over Janey (they are both determined to do so while at the same time accepting the logic that three of us staying awake and being exhausted tomorrow is excessive and makes no sense) when there is a loud knock at the front door, and then a voice calls, 'It's me!' and Jack comes barrelling down the corridor and sticks his head in through the doorway.

He fills the doorframe as much with the electric storm of energy he gives off as with his physical presence, a man invading an all-female space.

'I heard what happened – at least, I heard a garbled version of it, down at the Lanyon farm. It was all they could talk about. "Bleddy hunt," Bella said. "They know they ent allowed on our land." They said there'd been some sort of accident, but no one seemed clear on who was hurt or how. I went down to White Cove and saw Magda's car there but no lights on, and no one answered the door, so I ran back up the lane again, and down the greenway, since that's where Bella said it had happened, and then I went on to Josie's and there was no one there either – she passed me in the Land Rover as I was coming up the hill and nearly ran me over. She didn't even stop!'

'I'm afraid she was probably a little drunk,' Keziah says apologetically, and she and Ariadne move apart so that now he has a view of Janey lying in her makeshift bed.

'Oh God.' He crosses the room in two strides and throws himself down on his knees beside her, then looks up at me, stricken. 'They hurt Janey?'

'The dogs knocked her down, and maybe she was kicked by one of the horses,' I say unhappily. 'It was chaos. It all happened so fast. Whatever they were chasing went flying past me and the lane was so narrow there was nowhere for us to get out of their way.'

Jack's face is taut with anger. 'One of the huntsmen got dragged by his horse, I gather. Broke his leg. Bloody well serves him right. And I'm delighted to say the vicar took a tumble too.'

'The vicar rode with the hunt?'

'Oh, there's nothing Casworan Martin likes better than to persecute the innocent,' Ariadne says. 'Especially if a little bloodshed is involved. Plus, joining the hunt means he gets to hobnob with all the so-called great and good of the area – the judge, two magistrates, the head of the local police, various town councillors, rich businessmen playing at being country squires. They pretend it's all about upholding tradition and keeping "vermin" in check, but really they just love the chance to prance around in their hunting pinks, showing off their horses and enacting a bit of cruelty upon the local wildlife for good measure.'

'I hate them,' Jack says savagely. 'They're barbarians.

Not a one of them fought in the war – they all begged off, manned a desk. If they had they'd be a lot less willing to inflict pain on another living being.' He gazes unhappily at Janey. 'Oh, I forgot!' He digs in his pocket and brings out a little patchwork bag with a pair of long ears protruding from it. 'I found this in the greenway. A moonbeam was shining right on it through the trees or I'd have missed it. I'm afraid it's in a bit of a mess.'

I take the bag from him and extract Rabbit. The toy is streaked with mud and dried blood and one of its ears is nearly detached.

Keziah reaches out a hand. 'Here – I'll give it a gentle clean. I don't want Janey upset by the state of her beloved companion when she comes to.'

Jack watches her leave the room, then returns his attention to me, his eyes burning. 'If anything happens to Janey, Mila, I swear I'll kill them.' The anger is contained, but the tone is quietly murderous.

There is a dark side to Jack, something I can't pin down. But here he is, a welcome visitor in Keziah and Ariadne's house, and Ariadne is at this very moment plying him with sloe gin. I cannot believe these good people would welcome a dangerous man into their midst.

Keziah comes back in some time later bearing Rabbit, who now looks very clean and bare without her crown or trappings. Her fur is sparkling white, and her ear has been neatly sewn back in place. I remember how pristine Rabbit looked after Janey lost him in the stream and then found him, perfectly remade…

'I think,' I say quietly, 'this isn't the first time you've done this.'

She looks puzzled by this, then holds Rabbit out to me. 'I've dried it as best I can.'

How long before Janey gets too old for her little companion? I wonder. When she makes friends at school next year will she discard her? I realise I am thinking about the future, a future in which Janey is alive and well and making friends. Am I deluded? Is she going to survive this trauma? I look tremulously back at Keziah and her large dark eyes meet mine.

'Rabbit is very important,' she says softly. 'Go on, give Janey her friend. I believe it may help.'

I take the toy – still slightly damp from its wash – and tuck it in beside my child so that they lie nose to nose – white skin, white fur, white linen, white blanket, all gilded with the gold of the flickering candles, wreathed about by incense and hopeful breaths and prayers, with the haloed hare gazing down over us all.

And Janey stirs. At first imperceptibly, then her arm comes out from beneath the covers and encircles Rabbit, pulling the toy in to her body. I see her nose twitch, like a little cat's, questing after the scent of her beloved companion, and then she sneezes.

Shocked, we all laugh.

'I don't think she likes my lavender soap,' Keziah remarks drily.

Janey's eyes open wide.

I take in a great breath. Now is when we will know, truly and inexorably, how she is. For a long drawn-out moment I am suspended between hope and dread, fearing for the imminent revelation, and then she says, 'Mummy?'

All the air whooshes out of me and I feel almost dizzy.

'Janey, darling, I'm here. We're all here – Keziah and Ariadne and Jack and me. We've been waiting for you to wake up. Are you all right? Does your head hurt? Does anything else hurt?'

The words tumble out and over themselves in a torrent and I see my child's forehead wrinkle into a frown, the questions and sensations all too much to process at once.

'Shhh,' says Keziah, beaming. 'Give her time.'

Janey lies there, blinking, frowning, maybe remembering. Then she says, 'Rabbit's lost her crown.'

Janey sits up. She eats some soup. She chatters away as if nothing has happened. She beams at Jack and pushes me away when she's fed up with being hugged. Keziah leaves the candles burning and Janey goes peacefully back to sleep, and I am so relieved that she seems largely unharmed that I burst into tears and am dragged into the kitchen for a cup of tea.

At last, Keziah takes Ariadne by the hand. 'Come on, let's leave these two to keep an eye on the patient.' And when Ariadne demurs, Keziah bundles her physically out of the room. Over her shoulder she says, 'Just check on her a couple of times. I'm sure people as sensible as you two can sort out a system. There's a pile of bedding on the sofa in the front room. Help yourselves to cushions.'

Ariadne turns to grin at Jack. 'Don't do anything I wouldn't do.' Which makes him snort.

'Are you all right?' Jack whispers after a while as we watch my daughter sleeping peacefully.

'It wasn't me who got knocked down by the hunt.'

'I know that, but it must have been a terrible shock for you.'

He reaches over and strokes a strand of hair away from my eyes, a gesture that speaks more than words of care and tenderness. For once, I do not move away or reject his touch. Instead, I hold his palm to my cheek, feeling the electricity of skin-to-skin contact, and we stay like this, aware of one another, sharing a long moment of connection, of intimacy.

'I couldn't bear to have anything happen to you or Janey. You both mean a great deal to me.' His voice is husky with emotion.

I pull back a little so that I can see his face, but I keep hold of his hand. I can feel his pulse beating steadily against my palm. His eyes are darkly intense.

'Mila, I'm so sorry about Christmas Eve, I would give anything for it not to have happened—'

I interrupt him. 'It's all right, Mother explained... about a lot of things. She's mortified about ambushing you like that under the mistletoe. As well she might be. And I think I understand better now what made her do it. I don't attach any blame to you.'

Some of the tension appears to run out of him.

'I've told her she's got to apologise to you.'

He laughs. 'God, Mila, please, no. I don't need an apology. I can't think of anything that would be more excruciating. Can we just forget it ever happened and try to pick things up where we left off? It was such a lovely day up to that point. I felt like part of a proper family again, for the first time in... I don't know how long.'

'We can try. I'd like to.'

Beside us, Janey stirs, emitting a little satisfied expulsion of air, like a tiny burp after a good meal. There is the ghost of a smile on her lips. Is she asleep? Or is she listening to us?

'She looks a lot better,' I say quietly, stifling a huge yawn. 'But I'm still worried about her. She could take a turn for the worse during the night.'

'Stay here,' he says.

He is back in a few minutes. 'Come on,' he says. 'You need to sleep. You're exhausted.'

'I can't leave her.'

'I'll watch her while you sleep for a couple of hours. Then I'll wake you up, OK?'

I hesitate. The next yawn nearly breaks the hinge of my jaw. 'You promise you'll wake me at once if her condition changes in any way?'

Jack touches his chest. 'On my life.'

He takes me by the hand and leads me down the corridor where he has made up a cosy nest on the floor of the front room before the glowing fire, its coals slumbering behind their fretwork screen. Pulling me to him, he kisses me gently on the lips. 'Goodnight, Mila Prusik. Sleep well.' And then he is gone.

It must be tiredness that makes my knees give way, though I tingle from head to foot. I fall asleep in moments, vaguely remembering the smell of him – tobacco and soap – and the feel of his arms around me. I sleep so soundly that I do not wake up until light is pouring in through the little window and there is a padding pressure on my chest. My eyes come open all in a rush, and there is a small black head butting against me, fishy breath in my face, a cool, damp nose against my own.

'Oh!' I remove the cat, which is mightily disgruntled and

drags half the bedclothes with her claws hooked into them as I shift her.

I sit up, horrified that I appear to have slept through the night without once checking on my daughter. She could have died and I would not even have known. I hurl myself to my feet.

Janey has not, of course, died in the night. She is sitting up playing some game with Jack which involves a layering of hands and a lot of smacking, which does not seem to me a particularly suitable game to play with an invalid. Not that Janey looks much like an invalid today. On the contrary, she is glowing with energetic health. Rabbit sits in attendance, arrayed in a crown of winter flowers adorned with the feathers from Janey's bag. She looks like a cross between a warrior and some sort of fertility goddess.

'Why didn't you wake me?' I cry to Jack.

As he raises his eyes to mine, Janey takes advantage of the distraction to administer a sharp slap, and giggles naughtily.

'You needed to sleep. And as you can see, she's doing fine.' Jack looks exhausted.

'You've sat up with her all night!' I feel guilty.

He shrugs. 'It was my pleasure. You'd had quite a shock. And I have to say Janey seems much recovered. We've been up since dawn, haven't we, Your Highness?'

'I've had breakfast,' Janey declares smugly. 'Jack makes very good porridge.'

'You don't even like porridge,' I say accusingly.

'I do when Jack makes it.'

'Contrary little madam.'

A short time later, Keziah and Ariadne appear and soon the house smells of fresh coffee and toast and sausages and eggs, and Janey insists on getting up and dressed and sitting around the table in the kitchen with all of us grown-ups, and this is where Magda and Josie find us an hour later, when a second breakfast of tea and cake and dates is laid out and the atmosphere is so convivial it feels like a party, over which Janey and Rabbit preside.

At last, into a lull, Janey asks Ariadne, 'Did you ask her to let you paint her?'

Ariadne beams at her. 'Who, darling?'

'The White Hare.'

Everyone stops talking.

'Do you mean, did I ask her permission?'

'No, I mean, did she come to you, so you could paint her?'

Ariadne places her elbows on the table and rests her chin in her hands as she gazes at Janey. 'I sense her every so often. But mainly when I am walking in the woods in the valley,' she says softly. 'I have never actually seen her.'

'Oh.' Janey seems taken aback. 'I've seen her lots of times. Mummy's seen her too, haven't you, Mummy?'

'Well...' I laugh nervously. 'We did see a big white rabbit the day we arrived, which I suppose might have been a hare. But really it was only there for a moment. So it could've been a trick of the light.'

'I saw the hare.' Magda's voice is low and emphatic. 'I nearly crashed the car. I felt it in my mind too – not a voice, but a feeling.' She stares around at us, defiant. 'You probably think I am mad.'

Keziah puts a hand on Magda's shoulder. 'Not at all. I think you are blessed.'

'I saw her on Christmas Eve too, when I was driving

up to midnight mass. She stopped the car; I was driving so wildly I might well have crashed. But there was a white light in the lane and I slowed down, and I sensed her there, right in the middle of the road, telling me to go home. And I felt her presence again, that same sensation in my head, yesterday,' Magda mumbles, looking down at her hands.

I stare at her. I cannot quite believe that my brisk, no-nonsense mother, who is so scathing about the superstitions of Kasina Wielka, could just have come out with this.

Then Josie pushes her chair back so that the feet scrape on the floor, and starts noisily to clear the plates.

'She saved me!' Janey crows, oblivious to Josie's discomfort. 'The White Hare. She came flying up the track and knocked me down before the horse could hit me. Everything became very slow. She was making me sleep even as she chased the dogs off, and at the same time I saw her chasing them, and how they ran away. They were afraid of her!'

I remember seeing the hounds backing away, their expressions of fear – the snarling, the flat ears, and how they ran, whining. I remember the sensation of cold fire that flowed past me. But even so, something in me rebels. This is all too strange, magical hares that even my mother can see, that Keziah and Ariadne revere. I get to my feet. 'Time to go home, I think.' I look over to Josie, who grins.

'Can't say I blame you – this conversation has taken rather an odd turn!' She shakes a finger at Keziah. 'I don't know what you put in that tea!'

Magda and Janey are safely installed in the back of the Land Rover and Keziah and Ariadne fill bags with treats for us – mince pies and sloe gin, a loaf of bread – and pack them in beside Magda. I hang back, waiting to be able to get in, and Jack pulls me aside.

'Remember what I said, Mila, about picking up where we left off?' His gaze burns into me until I feel lightheaded.

'I've got to go!' I smile into his eyes, then quickly get into the car before I do something terrible, like kissing him.

As the Land Rover pulls away, it feels as if my heart is threaded on a string attached to Jack Lord. It pulls tight, attenuates, but never breaks even as the Land Rover roars and we speed back down the hill to White Cove.

21

The rain is hammering down so hard that it sounds more like hail than water hitting the windows. Between the rivulets I can see the grey haze of sea and sky, fused somewhere along an invisible horizon. There has been no let-up in an hour or more. You can hardly imagine the clouds can hold so much rain; the downpour seems infinite, unstoppable. It is New Year's Eve, and the days that have run up to this point since Boxing Day seem to have passed in a blink.

'What wretched weather for a party,' Magda says, appearing at my side. 'People won't want to come out in this.'

Glasses are lined up on the sideboards in the drawing room: elegant, gleaming stands of them reflecting the candlelight. Mother's friend Theresa came good on her promise to send Polish luxuries from London. I have spent a happy day making *cebularz lubelski* – little flatbreads packed with poppy seeds and topped with caramelised onion or with slivers of roasted venison and cranberries; pickled mushrooms and smoked cheese; blinis with salmon and jewels of roe; and sugared *kalisz* wafers. I really hope people do turn up after all the effort we've made.

'Perhaps they'll want to come even more,' I say to soothe her nerves. 'What better way to brighten such a grim evening than to come to a smart cocktail party in your best togs?'

Magda makes a face and pats her hair. I can smell the expensive setting lotion she has used to fix her auburn waves in place.

'You look spectacular,' I tell her.

She gives a little smile, as if such an extravagant compliment is no more than her due, but I can tell she is pleased. She runs her hands down the black satin dress that skims her cinched-in waist and narrow hips. The strands of pearls and exquisite clip-on earrings lend an opalescent nacre to her smooth, pale skin. She looks as if she's just stepped out of the pages of the January 1955 edition of *Vogue*, and I tell her so, which makes her laugh. She holds me at arm's length and looks me up and down. 'I suppose you'll do.'

'High praise indeed!' My outfit is hardly *Vogue* standard, it must be said, but I like it even so. The blues and greys in the soft wool of my dress remind me of the sea in summer and go with my eyes.

'But just one more thing.' She hands me a small box expertly wrapped in black-and-white paper with a sparkling ribbon and watches as I open it. 'You said you'd finished the bottle, so I thought you might like a new one.'

It is a bottle of *L'Heure Bleue*, just like the one I'd found in the cave all that time ago, but pristine, and full of its fragrant amber liquid. I loosen the ornate glass stopper and dab some on my wrists and behind my ears. Magda inhales, and nods approvingly. 'It suits you.'

A peace offering. 'Thank you.'

'Mmm, Mummy, you smell nice!' Janey comes skipping in, wearing the blue silk dress belled out by the netting underskirt that Keziah and Ariadne gave her for Christmas.

'Tonight Rabbit's letting me be Princess Berianu,' she declares.

'That's a very fancy name.' I grin. 'Where did you come upon that one? In one of your storybooks?'

She shakes her head. 'I just know it.'

And suddenly I remember her drawing of Rabbit with a crown and long red hair, and the strange word written beneath. Berianu, not Beviana. One of her imaginative creations, then; my funny, clever little girl.

I take the perfume upstairs and brush my hair. In the mirror, a very different woman looks back at me: confident, attractive. Grown up. I smile at her and she smiles back. 'Not bad, Mila,' I tell myself. 'Not bad at all.'

As the light begins to fade, Magda uncorks the first bottle of champagne and pours two glasses. We clink them – a truce. 'To the future,' she says.

'The future,' I echo.

Half an hour later we hear the low note of a vehicle changing down gear and the squeal of brakes on the final bend of the lane, followed by tyres crunching across the gravel. Our first guests: Farmer Lanyon and his wife Bella and their son Kit, with Keziah and Ariadne sitting in the back of the truck like posh scarecrows, under a vast umbrella. They leap out and smother us all with kisses and

Keziah presses a large jar of honey into Magda's hands. 'Sweetness for our sweet new friends!'

Keziah looks particularly impressive in a long white dress resplendent with silver necklaces and amulets; her dark hair is bound up with ribbons and she wears a large white hellebore tucked behind one ear. She looks like the ancient spirit of winter. Ariadne has chosen dark green velvet draped in swags around her capacious figure, long ruby-red earrings and a pair of scarlet boots – like the manifestation of Yuletide. Beside them, Robert and Bella Lanyon look earthy and sensible, though I can see the farmer has wound a striking scarf in gold and black, the Cornish colours, around his neck.

As Mother ushers them quickly inside out of the rain, Ariadne manoeuvres me under the mistletoe and delivers a huge smack of a kiss right on my lips. 'Got you this time!' she declares gleefully. 'Lovely girl.'

A procession of headlights now streams down the hill; it seems the rain hasn't put people off after all. One by one the cars pull up and their occupants scurry into the house under umbrellas, or with coats held overhead. Dr Tregenza and his quiet wife, and a couple of town councillors – which should slake Mother's desire for acceptance into our new community. There are some ladies from the Women's Institute, who look around with beady eyes, taking in the gleaming paintwork, the potted ferns, the waxed floor tiles. One of them catches me watching her and gives me a wink. 'Proper job.' She grins and heads at once for the drinks.

Next come a local writer and her husband, two artists from Lamorna, and a couple of pretty girls who immediately fall upon Kit Lanyon and start flirting outrageously with him. The poor lad is pink in the cheeks and looks desperate to escape their attentions. I meet my mother's eye over the heads of our guests. She looks triumphant, revelling in her glory. She smiles at me and I hold her gaze steadily. *We have an understanding now*, this looks says. *We can work with it*. She gives a little nod.

The doorbell rings and I run to open the door and there is Stanley Skerritt and his wife, a large woman arrayed in bright purple. I encountered our builder before Christmas and invited him on the spur of the moment before regretting my impulse, knowing Magda's snobbishness when it comes to social hierarchies. They stand, dripping a bit, in the hall, gazing around at the transformation, but Magda is in an expansive mood and they are at once whisked away on a tour of the downstairs refurbishments, champagne flutes in hand.

'I was sure this place were a goner,' says Mrs Skerritt as they pass me, 'given its history and all. You've worked wonders on un.'

More people arrive and every time I open the door I find myself looking for Jack, keen for him to see me in my best clothes and make-up, instead of my usual workaday togs. Surely he will come? But there is no sign of him, not even when I stare out into the wet darkness up the winding lane.

I walk among our guests with platters of canapés, sometimes explaining what they are, and though I half expect people to turn their noses up, everyone seems happy to give our foreign food a try and appears surprised by how tasty the little treats are.

'It's like going on a trip without leaving the valley!'

Robert Lanyon declares. He raises his glass. 'Here's to some luck for all of us here. It's about time the tide turned.'

'May your cows grow fat and fruitful, and your potatoes grow large and fair!' I toast, which makes him snort his champagne.

'May the Lady be kind to us, for once,' Bella says darkly.

The room is so full now that the music on the radiogram is drowned out, so I cross the room to turn it off. I'm just reaching for a glass of champagne – only my second in over two hours – when someone tugs at my skirt. 'Mummy, Mummy, come quickly!' Janey's eyes are huge and round.

'What is it, darling?'

'It's Jack,' she says in an urgent whisper.

I crane my neck, but I can't see him. Her tugging becomes insistent.

'Outside. With the nasty man.'

'The nasty man?'

'The one in the black dress.'

Casworan Martin.

We thread our way through the party guests, trying not to draw attention to ourselves, and pass through the dripping coats and stacks of wet umbrellas in the hall. I wrench open the front door. Outside, between the rain-wet cars, two figures appear at first sight to be dancing, a clumsy waltz in which both are trying to lead. Then I realise they are not dancing.

'They're fighting!' Janey declares, thrilled.

I close the door quickly behind me. No one must see this.

'Hey!' I call, hoping to shame them into stopping, but they are so intent on the struggle and the rain is coming down so hard that they don't hear me.

Jack swings a fist, but the vicar sways backwards like a flower in a high wind. Jack closes on him and Martin raises an arm and brings his vast furled black umbrella down on Jack's head like a club. Blood spurts, but Jack just shakes his head like an enraged bull and grabs for the man's coat. The Reverend Martin twists away from him, surprisingly nimble for an older man, and I think he's going to escape, but Jack catches hold of the end of his long, red woolly scarf and yanks so hard that his opponent almost loses his footing. When the vicar swipes at him with the umbrella again, he wrests it out of his hands and throws it one-handed like a javelin out into the darkness.

Martin takes his opportunity to spin away, unwinding the scarf and lengthening the link between them, till it catches tight around his throat and he comes to an abrupt halt, choking.

'You vicious bastard! It was you – I saw you! I saw what you did. You tried to kill her!' Jack roars. Hand over hand he pulls the scarf towards him, reeling Casworan Martin in like a flailing fish.

The vicar is thrashing an arm, mouthing inaudible words, trying to free himself from the strangling scarf. Even through the streaming rain, in the limited illumination given off by the porch lights, I can see that his face is turning puce. I realise the fight must be about the hunt riding Janey down, and for a moment I feel my swelling rage as well and want nothing more than to see Jack bash the hell out of this horrible, pompous, destructive man, but then I think about Magda and her party and how embarrassing this could be, the local vicar about to get strangled to death on our very doorstep.

'Jack!' I shout again. 'Let him go!'

This time it seems that my voice carries, for Jack's head comes up like a scenting dog, searching for me. Gifted this moment of distraction, the vicar seizes the opportunity to spin and ram his skull into Jack's face, making crunching contact with his already-broken nose. Jack howls, lets go of the scarf and flies backwards, fetching up against the Lanyons' truck with a crash.

Shooting a look of loathing at me and Janey as we stand in the shelter of the veranda, Casworan Martin staggers between the parked cars and makes a lumpen, lopsided run for the lane, his scarf trailing behind him like a tail.

'Stay here,' I warn Janey, and then I run out into the rain to Jack, where he sits dazed, the blood running in pink trails from his nostrils.

Getting an arm around his waist, I use my shoulder to lever him upright. He does nothing, and I redouble my efforts until at last, as I exert all my force, he scrabbles to get his feet under him, and we stagger towards the house. As we approach the veranda, he veers aside, shaking his head, staring up into the darkness of the winding lane that leads up the hill towards Eglosberyan. In the rain-shattered illumination of the porch lights I see how droplets of blood spin out into the night like twinkling red stars.

With more strength than I know I possess, I push him up against one of the veranda pillars. 'Stop, Jack. Just stop. You can't go anywhere in the state you're in – and you definitely can't go after Casworan Martin. Look at me.'

He swings his head slowly towards me. His hair is plastered to his skull and his eyes are unfocused, mad-looking. For a moment he seems like a stranger, a wild and dangerous stranger.

'Jack? Jack!' I shake his shoulder with increasing panic.

He doesn't respond, doesn't even seem to recognise me. Janey runs over and grabs his hand, calling his name. For a long moment he stands swaying and blinking, then he looks down at her and stares dazedly.

'You've got to come inside.' She tugs at his hand, not towards the front door but towards the side of the house, and I understand her intent – to take him into the scullery, through the back alley. 'Come on, Jack, this way.'

'Yes, come on, Jack. No one will see you.' Or me – I must look a state too; my hair is dripping, carefully applied make-up surely long gone, my woollen dress sticking to my underwear, wet to the skin.

He shuffles his feet, his movements slow and ponderous. It is like trying to propel a reanimated corpse; he seems to have lost all understanding of how to use his limbs. Janey pulls him on one side, and I hold him up on the other and we make painfully slow progress towards the back alley. Did the vicar really hit him so hard? He must at least have suffered a concussion.

Together, we manage to get him through the back door and into the scullery where I sit him down and pat his face carefully dry with a tea towel. Still, his nose gushes blood and soon half the white tea towel is scarlet and sodden. 'Tip your head back,' I tell him, but he just sits there like a stone, head bowed.

'Go and fetch Keziah,' I tell Janey. 'But don't say why. No one else must know, okay?'

'Not even Ari?'

'Just go, quickly.'

She gives Jack an assessing look, then pulls Rabbit out of her bag and sits the toy, pale blue dress, crown and all, on his lap. 'Rabbit will look after him till I get back,' she explains, and off she goes.

I kneel beside Jack and take his hand in mine but it lies in my grasp like a cold, dead thing. 'Can you hear me? Please, Jack, say something.'

He makes no sign of having heard me. A choking sob rises in my throat and I swallow it down. 'Oh God. I'm so sorry, Jack. Please be all right, please come back to me.' I hate the pleading tone of my own voice. It sounds wheedling and hollow in the tiled confines of the scullery. I raise his limp hand to my lips. 'Jack. I love you.'

If I am expecting these words to work some small magic, I am to be disappointed. The only sound is his laboured breathing and the drip of the blood from his nose onto the stone floor, where a small glistening pool is spreading as if his very life is leaking out of him drop by drop.

I hear footsteps. Janey appears, dragging Keziah behind her. Keziah takes one look at Jack and goes down on one knee beside him. I watch with awful fascination, as if paralysed in a dream, as her white dress soaks up the pool of blood, the crimson liquid climbing slowly upwards as the fabric absorbs it, like some alien tide.

'Your dress,' I say, belatedly.

She waves a hand, batting away my words. 'Never mind that. What's happened?'

'There was a fight and the vicar hit him. I can't get him to react to anything,' I say quietly. 'It's as if he simply isn't here.'

Keziah waggles her fingers in front of Jack's eyes and peers at him intently, then manually tips his head back and matter-of-factly mops the blood away. 'Go and switch the light off, then on again,' she tells me.

I do as I am told.

'That's a good sign, at least,' she says. 'His pupils are reacting to the light. Right, first things first.' Her fingers play across his nose, his eye-sockets and cheekbones, padding, feeling. At last she says, 'Well, the nose is broken, but nothing else appears to be as far as I can tell.'

I hear a small grating sound as she gently manipulates the bones of Jack's nose back into place. He does not even flinch. I am amazed by Keziah's practicality in the face of this disaster, and say so.

'I've seen far worse than this,' she says quietly.

'You have?'

She shoots a narrow look at me. 'I wasn't always some villager, you know,' she says. 'I served as a nurse during the war, on one of the hospital ships. I saw some pretty grim things, I can tell you. I think Jack may have suffered a shock and has entered a sort of fugue state. Sometimes this is to do with a powerfully triggered memory, or it may just be physical trauma, or both. What happened exactly?'

I relay to her briefly what happened, with Janey interrupting, 'The nasty man hit him so hard he fell down!'

'Certainly hard enough to break his nose,' Keziah says ruefully. 'But I think there's more to it than that. Poor Jack's been through the mill, but he's a toughie. It'd take far more than a fist fight with Casworan Martin to bring this on.' She brushes his hair off his forehead with great tenderness. 'Jack. Jack, you're safe. You're among friends.'

He blinks and for a moment I feel sure there is a flare of recognition in his eyes, but then it is gone again.

I move close to him, so close I can feel his breath on my face. 'Jack, please come back to us. We all love you, Jack.'

'Oh!' says Keziah.

'What?'

'I swear his nose twitched, broken bones and all. When you leaned in close. Are you by any chance wearing perfume?'

I frown. 'Well, yes... I don't usually but...'

'The olfactory sense is the strongest sense we have. Could you go and get it?'

'Yes, but I don't see—'

'Just do it,' she commands.

'I'll get it!' Janey is on her feet, then gone. She re-enters through the back door a few minutes later, with black coal smuts on her party dress.

'Janey! You must never use those stairs, not without me!'

She purses her lips, a very Magda expression. 'You said we had to keep Jack a secret.' She sounds far older than nearly six. She hands the bottle of *L'Heure Bleue* to Keziah, who waves the unstoppered bottle under Jack's nose, which has at last stopped producing its scarlet flow.

We all hold our breath. His eyes go wide and he blinks rapidly. His forehead corrugates. Tears begin to swell and then to roll, one by one, fat and oily, down his cheeks, cutting pale paths through the drying blood.

For a long moment he surveys the room, his frown deepening.

'Jack,' I whisper.

He looks at me uncomprehending, then down at the toy

in his lap. The movement sends carmine drops onto the pale silk of Rabbit's gown – one, two, three. Janey watches with a frown.

With visible effort, Jack wrestles himself back into the present.

'Mila,' he croaks, and then he's gone again, and my heart breaks open.

'Jack, oh, Jack.'

'My name isn't Jack,' he says. 'It's Will.'

I start to say something, but Keziah rests her hand on my shoulder.

Ariadne appears at the door, looking relieved to have found us. Keziah puts a finger to her lips and beckons her in.

'Hello, Will,' she says, turning back to Jack. 'You are home. You are safe here, among friends.'

'Home? Am I?' He looks around, hopeful, questing, then his face crumples. 'Oh. I remember now.'

'Who are you?' I ask him. 'Who are you if not Jack?'

'I'm Will. William Prideaux. That was my name. My mother... My mother is... My mother was Agnes Prideaux.'

Prideaux. My memory shuffles through its card index. *William Prideaux...* I know I've come across that name before....

'My father was Jory Prideaux,' Jack says. 'We lived here at White Cove.'

22

I stare at Jack.

Or rather, at Will. William Prideaux.

I can't think of him as Will; he's Jack to me. I know him as Jack. He *is* Jack.

I feel I'm losing him. I feel as if the world is slipping sideways. 'Jack,' I say, but he stares into space, his dark eyes haunted, unfocused.

Keziah puts a hand on my arm. 'It's all right. Just wait. Let him talk.'

Silence stretches between us, taut as the strands of a cobweb, then Jack takes a long, rasping breath and his gaze comes back to me. 'The valley that runs down to the cove is a very special place. You can feel it, can't you?' he asks, though he does not wait for an answer, and it's hard to know whether he's even seen me or knows who I am. 'Once you've lived in this valley, you'll never be free of it. Its uncanny beauty gets inside you, right into the marrow. It has its own climate, its own peculiar character. In the same way as people can draw you in and repel you at the same time; both beguile and frighten you. When

I was growing up here I felt the valley, the garden, the beach, the coast was all mine – my kingdom, my domain. I hated having to share it with all those people who came to stay in the house; they never appreciated it for what it was. They never embraced the wildness. They never sat quietly in the woods, listening to the stillness, to the birds' calls or the stream navigating its way over roots and boulders, or to the breeze in the leaves, or the sound of things growing. It was so much better when they all went away and I could share my space again with the rabbits and foxes and blackbirds and robins, the grass snakes and goldfinches, the ravens and the basking sharks. And with the white hare.'

'Ooh!' Janey squeaks, but I pull her to me and shush her with a finger to my lips. Even I am finding it hard to not interrupt and ask the questions I am sure we're all desperate to ask, but I know we mustn't break the spell.

'My father wasn't interested in the wildlife,' Jack continues. 'Once he was with me when a black-backed gull drowned a jackdaw in the stream that runs through our garden, under the stone bridge and out onto the beach. The jackdaw squawked and flapped its wings, but the gull was too strong for it. Daddy tried to chase the gull away but it wasn't scared of him at all – it just picked up the body of the jackdaw and hopped further down the beach to eat its eyes, and Daddy shouted at it and called it disgusting. But my mother said Nature is like this – that it can be cruel and savage as well as wild and beautiful. So it was Mummy I went to when I saw the hare. Her eyes went wide and then she grabbed me and hugged me hard and said never to mention it to Daddy. "Always be respectful of the hare," she told me. "If you ever see her, bow your head and say good day, and listen in case she has a message for you. She is the guardian of the valley, but she doesn't usually allow herself to be seen. She will show herself to you only when it suits her, but if you honour her and her land, she will do all she can to protect you."'

He runs his hands over his face and I am struck again by the lividity of his bruises against his pale skin, and feel a powerful urge to reach out and touch him, but he starts to speak again.

'I was a solitary child. I never had many friends here, partly because White Cove is quite a long way from the village. Sometimes I played up at the big house with my cousin Josie, but they sent her away to a special school in Truro. She wasn't here when... when it happened, even though it was Christmas Eve. Poor Josie, left alone at that place...' He drifts to a halt, remembering.

As the silence stretches out, we all look at one another. Janey is agog, drawn into Jack's storytelling, even if she can't grasp the complexities of his words. Keziah leans forward and touches him lightly on the arm. 'Tell us what happened that Christmas Eve, William. Can you remember?'

Jack's frown deepens and the corners of his mouth turn down. 'I used to love Christmas here,' he starts again. 'The tree covered in lights, special wood for the fire to make the house smell nice. Chocolates and nuts and presents... Mummy always gave me books for Christmas. *Treasure Island* was my favourite. I used to go down to the cave around the corner of the headland and pretend to be Ben Gunn, cast away and gone to skin and bones. I kept my small treasures in there – special pebbles and bits of sea glass and shells and feathers and things I found...' His voice trails away.

Ah, I think, *the shoe and the cigarette case and the perfume bottle.*

'The party, Will? Can you remember the party?' Keziah presses.

His expression darkens. 'That bloody...' He glares around defiantly as though looking for someone. '*He* was here. Casworan Martin. He wasn't a vicar then, just a – what do you call a priest in training?'

He looks right at me. 'I... I have no idea,' I say.

'Curate,' Ariadne supplies.

Jack nods. His gaze becomes dreamy again. 'Mummy wore a beautiful dress of deep blue velvet and all her best jewellery. "Got to make a good impression," she said when she came in to brush my hair. "It's important for Daddy now that he's an MP." When she was happy with how I looked, she sent me downstairs to see if Bella needed any help laying out the food and the glasses, so I ran downstairs and it all looked so pretty but Bella said she didn't need any help and she gave me a couple of sausage rolls. I was just going back upstairs with them when I heard Mummy and Daddy arguing, and I stopped and didn't know what to do. They argued a lot. My father had a fearsome temper, and when he got angry, you knew it was best to get out of his way. I heard a cry, and Daddy came out of their room all red in the face. He stared at me on the stairs and I thought he might hit me for taking the sausage rolls even though Bella gave them to me, but he just went past me.

'I went to see if Mummy was all right, but she wasn't. She was sobbing. I said, "Please, Mummy, you'll spoil your beautiful face," and then she turned to me and I saw that her beautiful face was already spoiled because there was a big red mark near her eye. She gave me this wobbly smile, pretending nothing was wrong. "Don't worry about me, darling," she said. "Go on downstairs and I'll be down in a little while when I've finished doing my make-up."

'When I went down, I found that the first guest had arrived: Casworan Martin. He was wearing a long, black dress – at least, that's how I thought of it then; now I'd call it a robe. My father was standing close to him. They were talking intently and when he saw me over my father's shoulder he said something, and stepped away from Daddy. "Here's my little man," my father said, looking all smiley. But I could still see the anger behind his eyes.

'Other guests were starting to arrive, so I went out to look at the cars. People who came to my parents' parties tended to be rich, so their cars were pretty spiffy. There were Morrises and Rileys, and soon a Rolls Royce Silver Phantom which pulled up alongside Daddy's Aston Martin. From my vantage point, out of the rain, at the end of the veranda, I watched a Daimler Double Six come down the lane, followed by an MG Drophead Coupe and a Standard Flying 10.

'I could hear the sound of the party coming out of the French windows as more and more people arrived. Candlelight flickered and voices flowed back and forth in waves. Laughter rose and fell, glasses clinked. I pressed my nose to the window of the drawing room, and my breath fogged the glass.' He pauses, closing his eyes.

'Just like this party,' Janey whispers, and I put a finger to my lips.

'Will you tell us more, Jack?' I ask softly.

He draws a ragged breath, and continues. 'The room was really full. All the women in their gowns, men in black tie and tails, chattering and drinking and swaying to the music from the phonograph. Behind me in the darkness I could hear the black sea roll and rumble. Then it started to rain, absolutely belting it down, so I went in. Mummy was laughing with Mr and Mrs Tonkin and when she put down her nearly empty glass of champagne to fuss with my wet hair, Mr Tonkin immediately went to get her another.

'"Aren't you growing?" Mrs Tonkin said, as if this was something out of the ordinary. "He's a proper little man now," she said to my mother.

'Mummy gave a laugh. "I asked Bella to save you some cake, sweetheart," she said to me as Mr Tonkin came back with more champagne.'

Keziah and I look at one another. 'Bella Lanyon?' I whisper, and she nods.

'Bella gave me a large chunk of chocolate cake,' Jack says. 'I took it up the secret stairs and went up to my room and ate it while reading the *Red Arrows*. I may have dozed, I'm not sure, but hours slipped by and I became aware that it sounded a lot quieter downstairs. I slipped out onto the landing, in time to see Mrs Pritchard. "You must come to dinner," she said, kissing Mummy on both cheeks.

'"That would be lovely," Mummy replied, but I could tell she didn't mean it.

'I saw Daddy turn around and go back into the drawing room and a couple of minutes later come back with his cigarette case in his hand. "Going out for a smoke," he said brusquely and stepped right past my mother before she could say anything.

'I waited for the door to close behind him, then ran down to see her. She didn't see me at first – she was staring into space, and I thought how tired and sad she looked now that she was not holding her smile in place for her guests.

'"Hello, Mummy."

'She focused on me and brightened. "Hello, darling."

'"Is it over?"

'"Yes, darling… I really think it is." And tears started to well up in her eyes.

'"It's all right, Mummy, there will be lots of other parties," I said.

'"Will there, though?" Then she seemed to pull her mask back on and said with a sort of forced gusto, "Did you get some cake? Shall we see if there's any left?"

'In the kitchen Bella was piling up dirty plates and glasses. "I think that's enough for now, Bella," she said. "You can go home – I can't keep you here on Christmas Eve."

'"I haven't quite finished cleaning, ma'am."

'"That's fine, I'll do the rest."

'Mummy was firm, so Bella took off her apron and got her coat. She lives up at the farm so she didn't have too far to go. When she had gone, Mummy looked around at all the dishes and glasses and leftover food and made a face. "Whatever is it all for?"

'"Christmas?" I ventured, and she gave a little laugh that didn't sound very happy. Then she ruffled my hair. "I'm going to go and see where Daddy's got to."

'I followed her into the hall and watched as she put her fur coat on. She opened the front door and stared out into the darkness. All the cars had gone except of course for our Aston Martin. By the porch lights I could see that her lips were very thin and pressed hard together. Then she turned around and said, "You go upstairs and wash and brush your teeth, and I'll come and tuck you in as soon as I come back." She gave me a little push towards the stairs.

'I made it look as if I was doing what I was told, but I waited until she had got down to the end of the lawn, then I followed her, pretending I was Chingachgook from *The Last of the Mohicans*, treading so carefully that not even a deer or a hare would hear me. I got to the pampas grass down near the little bridge and that's when I saw them – all three of them. Mummy stood silhouetted against the sea, the moon making her fur coat shine all silvery, as if she was a ghost. She was staring out into the darkness. At first I couldn't see what she was looking at but then I realised there were two people down on the beach, holding one another. Daddy and someone else in a long black dress, and they were kissing. Mummy started to scream and the two figures broke apart. I heard Daddy shout, "Stop her noise!" and the other person came running up the slope towards her and that's when the moonlight caught him and I realised it was the curate, Casworan Martin.'

'Oh my God!' My hand goes to my mouth. Jack's father and the vicar? I look down at Janey, worried that what she's hearing will frighten her, but her eyes are solemnly trained on Jack.

Jack's hands are balled in his lap now.

'"Run, Mummy!" I shouted, but she just stayed rooted to the ground, and Martin came for her and grabbed at her, catching her by the hair when she pulled away. I saw a tiny star flying through the dark air, and then I realised it was her diamond earring.

Janey gives a great intake of breath. I recall that long, glittering earring she found, which Jack took away with him. Could it be this very one?

'Mummy turned to run and almost knocked me over, and she didn't stop, she just ran on. I don't think she even saw me. And then Daddy was coming, running up from the beach, his face contorted with aggression and he was shouting terrible words, threatening to kill her.

'I'm afraid I hid. I crawled under the little bridge and sat up by the side where the water doesn't reach and hugged my knees to my chest and tried not to make a sound, or even to breathe.

'I heard – and even felt – Daddy's feet go thumping over the bridge, and then the other man's, lighter and slower. But I stayed where I was. When they had gone, it all went quiet for a bit. I could hear the water in the stream and a breeze in the trees, and an owl hooting up in the woods. And then I heard a scream: a high, piercing shriek. I've heard rabbits shriek like that when a buzzard or fox gets them, so that's what I told myself I heard. But I just didn't dare venture out from my hiding place. I stayed there with my teeth chattering and all my muscles trembling with shock and cold. And then this strange feeling of warmth came over me and this pale light – not silvery like the moon, but a sort of warm white light with hints of green, and it smelled... I don't know, this sounds odd given that it was December – but it smelled like spring... and it enveloped me and after a bit I fell asleep.

'When I woke up it was still dark, but there were grey

shades in the blackness, and when I crawled out from under the bridge I saw the edge of the sun come up and all the clouds around it flared orange and pink. And then I remembered what had happened the previous night. I felt as if I had a heavy, cold stone in my chest. I could hardly make my way back towards the house, I felt such dread.

'The first thing I noticed when the house came into sight was that the Aston Martin was gone. The second was that there appeared to be a large animal lying on the lawn. But when I got closer, I realised it wasn't an animal. It was my mother's fur coat. I pulled at it but she wasn't in it. I went into the house. It was strangely quiet inside, as if the house was breathing and listening. I didn't dare call out in case Daddy found me. So I slipped upstairs, trying not to make a sound, and avoiding the stair three steps from the top where the board creaked like an opening coffin.

'I stayed in my room, trying to pretend everything was normal, but listening, questing out with every pore of my body to try to understand what had occurred. I heard and sensed nothing – no one else but me, and the house. At last, I got up enough courage and crept along the landing to my parents' room. The door was open and so were the curtains, and the bed was still made – the white cover untouched and unwrinkled.

'*They must be out somewhere*, I told myself. Maybe they'd gone shopping. But even as I thought this I knew it was absurd: it was Christmas Day.

'I gathered up the plates and glasses and piled them in the kitchen and I swept up the crumbs and bits in the drawing room. Soon, the light started to go out of the sky and then I remembered the fur coat lying out on the grass and I went to fetch it in, in case it rained and got spoiled. And that's when I found her shoe, lying underneath it, and for some reason that shocked me badly. Where would someone go wearing only one shoe? I hung the coat up and I took the shoe into the kitchen to clean it.

'When night fell, the cold stone in my chest felt really heavy. Where could my parents be? And then I began to wonder if the shriek I had heard the previous evening had perhaps not been that of a dying rabbit after all. I began to wonder... but then something stopped me from thinking about that. It felt almost like a physical block, someone pushing me away from a dangerous place, and a quiet voice in my head, saying, *No, no, no, come away*. I sensed that green-tinged light again. It wrapped me and helped me to sleep. And as the days passed I thought about my parents and what might have happened to them less and less.

'After maybe a week I heard a car coming down the track. It was a plain black Austin Ripley, and as it drove down onto the gravel by the barn, I recognised Sergeant Hocking and a younger policeman sitting beside him.

'When I heard them knocking on the front door, I went up the secret stairs into the attic and lay there in the dark, listening to the distant murmur of their voices down below as they walked around the house and eventually came upstairs. When I could tell they were right below me, I held my breath.

'I heard the sergeant say, "And where is the little boy?"

'The cold, heavy stone in my stomach rose up into my throat and choked me, and suddenly I couldn't breathe at all. But they must have gone away because a while later I looked out of the rooflight and saw that the Ripley wasn't there any more.

'I lived in the White Cove house like an animal, scavenging whatever food I could find. I did think about knocking on the door of Josie's house but I was afraid her parents would send me away as they had Josie. So I lived off the tins in the pantry and a sack of potatoes I found in the barn.

'I spent my time reading all my books again, and drawing on the walls of my room. I kept drawing the same thing: a wavy line ending in a V, with an eye. I had no idea why I kept drawing it, but doing so gave me great comfort. Then one day I opened my encyclopaedia onto a map of the constellations, and there it was: Lepus, the Hare, the one that Orion the Hunter chases with his dogs. And somehow I knew it was *her* symbol, representing the feelings I had in the woods, and the voice in my head, and the green-tinged light. And the more of these lines I drew, the more protected I felt. But there were times when I didn't feel her presence, so then I would write notes to the hare, in case words worked better than drawings at reaching her. I wrote *HELP ME* on little squares of paper and put them in special places. Now I wonder whether I thought of her as a she because I missed my mother...'

'Ah, bless you,' breathes Ariadne. She pats him on the arm. 'Of course she was doing her best to protect you. You were one of her own, and an innocent.'

Jack blinks rapidly. 'One day I had a dream in which I was running and running and running with the hare, and we were being chased by monsters, or maybe it was people, or people with hounds, and there was a voice in my head telling me to *Wake up, wake up!* but I couldn't seem to escape the chase. The hunters were nearly upon me and I started screaming as one of them caught me, and I woke up to find a man shaking me and it was the curate.

'"So there you are," he said with great satisfaction. And he called back over his shoulder, "He's up here, the little scamp!" And two other people appeared behind him: a man and a woman. The woman said, with a sort of false niceness, "Now then, young man, you have to come with us."

'The voice in my head whispered, *No no no no*.

'I fought them. I bit and scratched them. I called on the strength of the white hare, but there was nothing she could do. When I called for her, the young priest went all pale around the eyes and caught me by the shoulders and shook me so hard that my teeth rattled and I thought my eyes would fall out. "You little heathen!" he cried. "You're just like your mother!" He turned to the others. "Now you can see what I mean. The boy needs to brought back to the path by good God-fearing folk."

'"But his parents—" began the other man.

'Casworan Martin rounded on him. "The mother is in a lunatic asylum and the father has been called up to London on government business. He signed care of the boy over to me." And then he reached into his pocket and pulled out a piece of folded paper and handed it to the man. Even from a distance I could recognise my father's handwriting. So it was true. They had given me up.'

23

'Oh, Jack.' I can see the strain retelling his past has taken upon him. He looks drained and haggard. And then a tear starts to track down his cheek, followed by another, and another.

'Ah, poor lad,' Keziah says softly, but it is Janey who is the first to hug him, throwing her arms around him and burying her face in his jumper. 'Don't cry, Jack!' she begs, her words muffled by the thick wool. 'You're safe now, away from those horrid people. You're here with us and we all love you.'

She hugs him so tightly that he exhales a huge breath, as if expelling a demon.

I feel a huge upwelling of sympathy and sorrow for the man I see before me, hunched over, his broken nose wadded with bloodstained cotton, his fists clenched in his lap, his cheeks wet with long-dammed tears. I reach over and take one of those fists in both of my hands, and it lies clammy and unmoving in my grasp. I play my thumbs lightly over and over the tight skin in a caress. 'I'm so sorry this happened to you,' I say, and then remember saying these very words to my mother just a few days ago. What a world of hurt we live in and how cruel people can be to one another. How can we balance out the wickedness and horror? I don't know, but we must try. Even the smallest acts of kindness must eventually weigh down the balance on the better side.

His dark eyes seek mine over the top of Janey's head. 'I'm sorry I wasn't able to tell you the whole truth till now. Those memories got buried so deep that I couldn't get at them. All I knew was that I had to come back here, to the house where I was born, where I grew up. I... I should have told you that much, but I was afraid that you and Magda would send me away.'

Before I can say a word, Janey cries out, 'We would never send you away! You belong here.' She comes back to me and takes my arm so that the three of us are connected. 'We are your family now,' she tells him. 'And this is your home.'

It *is* his home, I realise, and all sorts of contradictory thoughts roil through me as the consequences of that spin through my mind. It is probably legally Jack's – Will's – house, if he can prove that he is indeed William Prideaux. I am at one and the same time happy that he is here, sitting in the home where he grew up, and fearful of where this leaves us – Mother, Janey and me. How will Magda react to this news? I can't see her leaving here without a fight. But perhaps we can all stay? But then how would that work? She would never accept charity. And anyway, what has happened to his parents? Might they not just reappear and claim the house? All these questions spiral around my skull in the space of a few seconds, only to be obliterated eventually by pure emotion.

My touch eventually eases Jack's fist to release its

white-knuckled grip upon itself, and at last he darts a look at me – then around at Ariadne and Keziah, down at Janey and Rabbit, and it's as if he's casting off a skin as he shakes his head and his torso, and sits up straighter.

'I'm sorry for spoiling the party.'

The laughter that breaks out of me is involuntary, incredulous. 'What? Don't be ridiculous. As if it mattered! And anyway, you haven't. No one else saw the fight. That's the least important thing here. The least important thing in the world!'

'Well, that's something.' He sounds doubtful.

I can see his jaw set. He's been avoiding thinking about this for so long. At last, he says quietly, 'To be honest, I had such vague recollection of that night and even that faded when I had to deal with my own new reality. The children's home I was sent to upcountry was more like a prison – bars on the windows, locks and bolts on the doors, high walls outside topped with barbed wire. They called us "problem children" and that's how they treated us. They gave us new names for a new start, but really all it meant was that our families didn't want anything to do with us and had cut all ties. That's what they told us, and since none of our families came to claim us, that's what we believed. Who could blame us? When war broke out, I managed to run away and join up. I was underage, just, but no one really cared about that sort of detail. And frankly the idea of getting away from there, of travelling, even of killing people, seemed a lot more attractive to me than staying in that awful place.

'For a long time, I simply erased my past. I wiped the memory of that terrible time out entirely. When my thoughts approached it, they just met a blank area – a sort of hazy green-tinged fog – until tonight, when I saw *him* again, coming through the rain-wet cars, with the party going on and the Christmas lights shining, and it was like stepping back twenty years.'

'The vicar.'

'The vicar.' He spits the word out. 'It's so strange how the mind works. I've been living around here for a couple of years now – in the house while it was empty, in the barn, sometimes in the woods, or up at Josie's.' He pauses. 'Funny, really – Josie didn't even recognise me when I came back here. We hadn't seen each other since we were kids, but I recognised her right away. Perhaps it's about context – there she was on the lane to the big house, exactly where I'd expect to see her, but she'd been told our family moved away to London, and there was some scandal about Mother being in an institution, and she didn't expect to see me ever again. She almost fell over with shock when she realised it was me.'

'But she didn't say anything!' Ariadne says, sounding scandalised that anyone would think to hide secrets from her.

'I made her promise not to. It was freeing… being Jack Lord. Everyone would've been asking questions, they'd stare at me suspiciously, wondering what happened to our family if the name Prideaux was ever mentioned. Anyway, the first time I saw Casworan Martin, even after two decades, he walked past me in the street in Eglosberyan and… I blacked out. My knees just went out from under me, black stars, everything. When I came to myself a few minutes later all I could think was that whoever that man was, I hated him, really hated him. I'd forgotten why until this evening.' He goes silent again.

'The hypocrisy of that fucking man,' Ariadne says furiously. 'It's just sickening. Preaching on at the rest of us! What happened to *Give honour to marriage, and remain faithful to one another. God will surely judge people who are immoral*? Do as I say, not as I do, eh? I always thought he was an odd one, but really he's just a repulsive human being.'

I look at her askance. Of all people, Ariadne's the last one I'd expect to quote from the Bible.

'I can't understand how your parents could have just vanished,' Keziah says after a while. 'I mean, even down here Prideaux isn't a common name. And, well,' – she spreads her hands – 'people gossip like nobody's business.'

'I asked around as much as I could without drawing too much attention to myself,' Jack says. 'Checked parish records, newspapers. Daddy never returned to parliament – I was told there was a by-election for his seat. Rumour was that he'd been given a change of identity and became a spy or something, and someone I met in London told me that he'd been killed during the war behind enemy lines, so maybe that was true. He doesn't seem to have left a will behind, nothing to acknowledge my existence at all.' He makes a face. 'I don't know what happened that night, but it's as if the world is split in two – separating into the time before, and the time after – and nothing has been right ever since.'

'I think we need to confront that frightful man,' Ariadne says, getting to her feet. 'And find out exactly what happened.'

We look up as a figure appears at the door.

'Oh, here you are!' Magda looks radiant and resplendent, a gracefully ageing film star, thoroughly satisfied at the end of her party, which she has been hostessing all this time. She scrutinises our solemn faces, and her gaze settles on Jack. 'Oh my goodness, Jack! Whatever happened to you?'

We look from one to another. Who's going to tell her? I start, and Keziah and Ariadne add their gentle voices to the grim tale.

'Oh, Will, your poor mother.' Magda's face has hardened, her eyes are flinty.

'I have to find out what happened to her.' Jack – Will – looks desperate, as if the newly acquired memories are eating him from the inside.

'I quite understand, but perhaps it's best to wait till tomorrow…' Magda starts, then, furious, adds, 'Oh, listen to me. Of course it can't wait. Where did the wretched vicar go? I never saw him in the party.'

'Last seen scuttling back up the lane,' I offer, and Keziah laughs.

'So much for living up to his name!'

I look at her blankly.

'Casworan is Cornish for "warrior".'

Ariadne guffaws at this irony and we all start to laugh.

'I'll get my car keys,' Magda says. 'Are you all right to drive?' she asks Will, staring at his broken nose and bruised eyes.

'I most certainly am.'

'Me too!' Janey squeals. 'I want to come too.'

'Oh no you don't,' I say firmly. 'You need to go to bed. It's miles past your bedtime.'

Her eyes flare. 'I am not going to bed, and you can't make me.'

'Now, then, madam—'

'I don't think we can all fit in your grandmother's little car,' Keziah says diplomatically.

'That's all right, because Josie is here,' Janey announces. 'Rabbit heard her Land Rover arrive.'

'Oh yes,' Magda says, 'I forgot. She came looking for you,' she says to Will. 'She was worried about you getting back to the manor house in this weather.'

'That's sorted then,' says Keziah. 'We'll go with Josie. If we all go to see the vicar mob-handed he won't be able to wriggle out of answering your questions. I'll explain everything to Josie as we go.'

'She knows most of it,' Will says quietly. 'Just not the last bit.'

'Oh.' Magda looks most put out.

'I think,' I say reluctantly, 'that I'd better stay here with Janey.' It would be highly irresponsible to go haring off into the night with a five-year-old. Then I catch the word in my head, and shiver.

'We need to be there, Mummy,' Janey says with grim determination. 'Jack needs us.'

'Honestly, darling, I'm sure he doesn't. He's got Keziah and Ariadne and Josie and Granny to be with him.'

'He needs us most.' She is adamant, and the worst thing is that I know she is right. Besides, how can I stay here and wait to hear the outcome at second or third hand? I snatch a glance at Jack and find that he is watching me intently, even beseechingly. 'Oh, all right,' I tell her at last. 'Go and get your waterproof and wellies on.'

My daughter grins like a demon, and scampers off.

Magda moves to let Keziah and Ariadne past, then stops Will as he follows. 'I'm so sorry... about what happened... at Christmas,' she says confidentially.

He looks bemused.

'The... ah, kiss,' she says, her cheeks pinkening. 'I was a little bit tipsy and may have overstepped the mark.'

Will grins. 'Oh that. I'd forgotten about it already.'

Which is probably the worst thing he could have said. Magda flees the room.

'You see, Will,' I say to him, 'she didn't apologise when you were "just" the handyman, but now you're the son of a Tory MP...'

He shakes his head. 'I'm no one's son, not any more. And I'd like everyone to call me Jack. I'm used to it now. Will Prideaux is long gone. He lived in an entirely different world and I'm not that abandoned little boy any longer.'

I put my hand on his arm and we stand there quietly for a moment, with no need for words, then move together into the hall to collect Janey and join Madga in the car.

Up through the rain-wet lanes we drive, tailing the winking red brake lights of Josie's car as it speeds up the hill and zooms around the corners. I don't think the Morris has ever been flogged so hard as Jack guns the engine to keep up with the Land Rover.

Everything is quiet except for the sound of the rain, which

batters down relentlessly, making rivulets through which the wheels of the vehicles cut and splash, throwing plumes of muddy water into the tall hedges to either side. We pass the turning to the manor house and I see Mother crane her neck for a glimpse of its Tudor gables and tall chimneys. She's hardly stopped talking about the place ever since spending Boxing Day night there at Josie's invitation. 'It could be glorious,' she told me wistfully, 'if it was restored. All the Jacobean furniture, those wonderful inglenook fireplaces, the orangery, the hammerbeams. If only we were rich, I would—' and she would go off into an enjoyable private reverie as if having refurbished the house at White Cove hasn't satisfied her ambitions.

We emerge out onto the Eglosberyan road and the rain comes down harder than ever and the poor Morris's windscreen wipers are failing to clear the glass – not that that stops Jack from accelerating as his destination comes into view. At last we pull in beside the churchyard wall and look towards the vicarage. There are no lights on there. 'He's gone to bed,' I say, disbelieving.

'Lying low,' growls Jack.

The occupants of the Land Rover pile out. Josie's face is grim, so clearly Keziah and Ariadne have filled her in on the vicar's role in the drama.

I catch Jack by the arm. 'No violence,' I plead. 'Not in front of Janey. She shouldn't even be here.'

'I suggest she stays in the car then,' Jack says shortly, but already Janey is toggling her sou'wester on tight and is climbing out of the back seat.

I take my daughter firmly by the hand. 'You really are impossible,' I tell her.

'I know.' She beams. 'But I need to be here.'

Water is roiling around our feet. You can hear it gurgling and chuntering as it flows swiftly around the stone walls.

'It'll be flooding the churchyard again,' Keziah says.

And that's when we hear it: the sound of metal striking stone – a screech in the darkness, and then a man swearing loudly and horribly. It's coming from the graveyard.

'Back in the car,' I tell Janey, giving her a little push, but she twists away from me with ease and runs after Jack, who is also running – not towards the vicarage but into the churchyard.

Keziah and I exchange anxious glances. The rain is dripping off her dark curls, the flower in her hair is lost, her white dress and shawl are ruined, but she bares her teeth fiercely, looking wolfish. 'Come on,' she says. 'This has been a long time coming.'

Inside the churchyard the moon shines through a sudden gap between the clouds, illuminating a bizarre scene: the priest, his sodden robes plastered to his scrawny body, is trying to divert streams of water that are converging determinedly on a low-lying grave, digging frantically even as the water washes away his efforts.

'That's Hepzibah Vingoe's grave,' says Josie. 'It's always getting flooded.' She pauses. 'I have to say he's taking his duties very seriously to be out in this weather, trying to preserve it.'

Keziah is frowning. 'It seems somewhat out of character.'

'Where is the verger?' asks Ariadne. 'Isn't it his job?'

'Surely it could wait till tomorrow,' says Magda, pulling her hat down tight to her ears.

'There's something odd going on here,' says Jack.

The moon is shining her beams right on the grave site now, limning the vicar in its cold silver light as he digs and swears and kicks, spilling mud and stones back into the upwelling grave. He is fighting a losing battle.

He looks up and catches sight of Jack. 'What do you want?'

'I need to talk to you,' says Jack.

'I know only too well your idea of talking,' the vicar says darkly. 'Can't you see I'm busy?'

'I need to know exactly what happened that night.'

'What night? Oh, hell!' Water gushes up out of the ground and spurts over the Reverend Casworan Martin's shoes, and now Jack can see the top of the coffin in the hole, like a dinghy bobbing at anchor.

'Tell me what happened to my mother!'

'I don't even know who your bloody mother is. Go away, you madman!'

Jack laughs at him then, the rain sheeting down his face as he throws his head back. He looks primal, powerful. A thrill runs through me.

Keziah and Ariadne have appeared on the other side of the graveyard, blocking any escape through the lychgate to the south, and when I look around, I see Magda and Josie standing by the church door, underneath the sundial on the porch, so he can't get in there either.

'I'm William Prideaux!' Jack shouts through the deluge.

The vicar comes to a dead stop, like a clockwork toy that has run out of power. If he could go any paler, I'd swear you could see right through him.

'That's impossible!' Casworan Martin clutches the spade like a weapon. Rain bashes onto his domed forehead, splashes off his pale eyelashes, drips from the end of his nose and chin.

The coffin shivers in its rising pool of muddy water.

'I saw you,' Jack says grimly. 'I saw you and my father together. I saw you hit my mother. I saw you knock her down. I saw how the blow made her earring fly off – that's how hard you hit her. And then you and my father chased her back up through the garden, and I never saw her again. I need to know exactly what happened to her that night.'

The priest stares at him, his mouth agape. 'But you died,' he says at last. 'They told me you died.'

'Will Prideaux died. Jack Lord lives on. As you can see.'

The vicar scans the face of this boy-turned-man. His eyes dart wildly, taking in every detail of him. 'You never did look like your father,' he says at last. 'In fact, your father always said he didn't think you were his.'

'How bloody dare you!' Jack takes another step towards him, his fists balled.

'He said you were a feeble child, always with your head in a book, always going on about birds and toads. Couldn't swim, couldn't even run. Always at your mother's side. And yes, you look just like her, dark as a bloody dago. I see it now. She was never a beauty, was she, Agnes Prideaux? Or should I say Laitie? Yes, that's right. She always thought she was so grand, far too good for Jory, all that heritage, but no money. She was so cold, is it any wonder he looked elsewhere for his pleasure?' Martin is openly sneering now. The rain shearing off his head makes it look as if his whole priestly façade is slipping.

'Have you no shame?' I cry. I can't believe a man of God can behave in this way.

His eyes slide past Jack to take in me and Janey. 'You, and your bastard spawn! Yes, I know your secret. I make it my business to know everything I can about those entering my parish. Second-hand goods, that's what you are.'

I'm having to hold Jack back with all my strength as he surges towards the vicar; I can feel the murderous intent streaming through him like fire. I think had it not been for earlier events and the toll they've taken on him I would have had no chance of preventing him from wresting the spade out of Casworan Martin's hands and beating him to a bloody pulp with it.

'No, Jack! That's what he wants – to provoke you, to make it your fault. You came here for answers, not to kill him.'

I feel tremors of intent running through Jack's frame like electricity as his instinct wrestles with his rationality. At last some of the tension goes out of him and he says, 'Just be straight with me. What happened that night? Where did my parents go? I deserve to know the truth.'

The vicar draws himself up. 'I don't have time to answer your questions now. Can't you see I have God's work to do keeping this poor soul in her grave? If you want to do a good deed, you could help me fill it up again. Then maybe I'll answer your questions.' His tone is wheedling. There is something sly in it, as if a trick is being played.

'Don't,' says Janey suddenly. 'The coffin does not want to be where it is. It's made of pine from my valley, and it *knows*.'

I stare down at my daughter. The voice is hers, but the words are not. She seems to be shining in the moonlight, but maybe that's the silver of the moon gleaming on her yellow oilskin and sou'wester.

The moon's light also falls upon Casworan Martin, and as if terrified of it, he cowers, putting his hand between himself and the celestial.

'She sees me!' he shrieks, and when I look up, I swear I can see the shadow of some long, lithe creature running across the face of the moon.

Janey steps forward, holding Rabbit out in front of her, as if the toy holds some protective power. Rabbit is gleaming too, the silk of her dress pink with Jack's blood and slick with rain. She directs Rabbit towards the grave of Hepzibah Vingoe and the muddy water bubbles and swells like soup that has reached a boil. Another flourish of Rabbit and it upwells in a massive gush.

'What happened here is wrong!' Janey cries, and her voice is not her voice.

Up the coffin comes, like a small boat borne on a tidal surge, and the wave of water rises up to tower over Casworan Martin, then crashes down, making him stagger. The coffin hurls itself out of the maelstrom, and knocks him flat.

For a moment there is a deep stillness, then I become aware of the sound of the rain, battering down, the wind in the far-off trees, and see a barn owl plane silently over the churchyard, white wings spread wide, moon-face watching us with what feels like judgment. Then it is gone.

Jack is standing stock-still, staring – not at the vicar, who lies moaning, sprawled up against a row of headstones, the dislodged coffin pinning him in place, but down into the pit left behind, from which the muddy water has miraculously drained through a deep channel made by the force of its sudden flow. 'Oh my God,' Jack says.

In the compacted earth below the coffin there are glimmers of ivory. As my eyes adjust to the light, I realise what I am seeing. Bones. The delicate lines of a hand, the fingers curled protectively around the lower part of a skull, which is lying on its side. In the crook of darkness between the jaw and the spine something shines brightly – not bone – perhaps glass?

Magda and Josie reach us before Keziah and Ariadne. We all stand around the opened grave, gazing in. Magda crosses herself. Keziah murmurs a prayer. Ariadne puts an arm around Jack, who is trying to say something. Janey cranes over the hole, fascinated, resisting my attempts to hold her back.

'There's my earring!' she cries. 'The one I found. How did it get in there?'

Jack pulls something from his pocket. 'No,' he says quietly. 'I have that one here.' The earring lies glinting on his palm, long and silver with three shining stones dangling from a silver hook. Then his fingers close over it, and he drops to his knees beside the grave. 'Oh, Mama…' And he starts to sob.

24

The police are called. Casworan Martin is taken to hospital to have his injuries checked out before being questioned, though unfortunately there appears to be very little wrong with him other than some fairly significant bruising. Josie drives Jack into Penzance to give a statement. The rest of us repair to Keziah and Ariadne's for towels and dry clothing, hot tea and cake and the very necessary pressure release valve of talk; though it's hard to discuss a possible murder and illicit burial in front of an avid child who refuses to be put to bed.

I do manage to usher Janey upstairs and help her out of her gladrags while the rest chatter below us. Off comes the soaking pale blue dress and frothy net underskirt, off comes Rabbit's blood-stained copy.

'It's nice not being Berianu any more,' she says as I pull a long woolly jumper Keziah has lent us over her head.

'Is it, darling?'

'Yes, it was complicated hearing her voice in my head. She speaks for the White Lady, because the Lady doesn't use words, so she has to use people to say what she needs us to

338

hear. But it's hard to understand sometimes, and sometimes Berianu doesn't have the right words either because she lived a long, long time ago. She was a sort of princess before she became a saint, and she got killed, and the White Lady was very angry about it because Berianu was her servant.'

'Well, that's all very complicated,' I say, perplexed. 'How do you know about Berianu and the White Lady? Did someone tell you – Jack, or Keziah or Ariadne?'

Janey looks offended. 'No. Rabbit told me. But Rabbit's just Rabbit again now. And he's a he again.'

'Oh, all right. Nice to have you back, Rabbit.'

'And I'm just me now.'

'Well, that's a relief.' I give her a hug, then concentrate on drying her hair and chafing some warmth back into her hands, and try not to think too much about the bones in the grave, which seem to have upset me far more than my five-year-old daughter.

When we return downstairs, no one makes much concession to Janey's presence other than some carefully chosen vocabulary, and in the end we just involve her in the discussion.

'But Jack said he saw his mother get up from the curate's attack and keep running,' Ariadne says, blowing on her tea.

'Well, clearly that's not what killed the poor woman,' says Magda. 'Maybe it was Jack's father when he finally caught up with her. Maybe it was something else.'

'Fancy driving off and leaving your child all alone.' This is still the aspect of these awful events I cannot come to terms with. 'Fancy never coming back for him, and signing over his fate to a man like Casworan Martin.'

Keziah shakes her head. 'Something terrible must have happened to make Jory Prideaux disappear like that. He must've killed her, deliberately or not.'

'Deliberately?'

'He could hardly have been able to continue his career if his homosexuality, or even bisexuality, went public. He couldn't afford to have her speak out.'

'But he didn't continue his career, did he? He just vanished.'

'You don't think there's a second body in there?'

I laugh. 'Not even Casworan Martin could have managed that. Perhaps the story Jack was told was true – Prideaux took undercover work and was killed in the war.'

'There must be records somewhere,' Ariadne says.

Magda purses her lips. 'It took a year for me to find out what happened to Tomascz. They just told me that his plane went down and that he was missing, presumed dead. I had no idea what had happened to him all that time. The war has been a smokescreen for all sorts of wretched secrets.'

Janey gazes at her grandmother. 'Poor Granny. You must've been very sad.'

Magda looks surprised by this assertion. Her eyes meet mine. I know the truth of her marriage of convenience now, but it is her secret to keep. She smiles gently at Janey. 'I was, darling, but I'm fine now.'

'Jory Prideaux must have been alive to provide Martin with the paperwork to take on Will's guardianship, since Jack recognised his father's handwriting, though I can't imagine he ever meant for him to consign the boy to that terrible children's home,' Ariadne says.

'Guardianship,' Keziah snorts.

'I wonder what will happen now,' Magda says after a long silence falls. 'About the house.'

We all look at her.

Jack returns to White Cove in the late morning. Magda drove Janey and me home for a second breakfast, and Janey took a nap while we cleared up the place, which looked as if it had been hit by a bomb. It's hard to believe after the strange night we've passed that we've just held a New Year's Eve party.

Hearing the rumbling note of Josie's Land Rover, Janey comes running down the stairs in her pyjamas; Rabbit, in her hand, is naked except for his old waistcoat and his old piece of knotted red string. She runs to the door and opens it in time to see Josie drop Jack off then drive away, waving a hand at us all.

Jack looks strained and peaked, and the bruises around his nose and eye-socket appear even more pronounced, as if someone has smashed blackberries into his face.

'You do look a sight,' Magda says undiplomatically and he gives her a lopsided smile.

'Sorry. Enough to frighten the horses, eh?'

We settle him into one of the big armchairs in front of the fire with a tumbler of whisky while Janey runs upstairs to get dressed.

'Happy New Year!' I say to him, with an ironic grin.

He raises his glass to me. 'Happy New Year, Mila.' He turns to Magda and toasts her too. 'What a bizarre start to it.'

'I'm so very sorry about your mother,' I say quietly.

'We all are,' Magda says firmly.

He tells us about giving his statement, but says the police are being tight-lipped. 'They don't know what to think. I mean, it's not as if they don't have murders and all sorts to deal with down here – there was that chap thrown down a mineshaft by a Mousehole gang last year – but dealing with an historic murder, with a vicar involved, is a bit different even for Cornwall.'

Magda lights a cigarette from the stub of the one in her hand. She has smoked cigarette after cigarette this morning and paced around, fizzing with nervous energy. Now, the pale light filtering through the French windows illuminates the stress in her fine-boned face. She leans forward. 'This probably isn't the best time to ask, but then I don't suppose there is a best time to ask such a thing, but, Jack, what do you mean to do about the house?' She waves her hand wide, taking in the whole of the lovely drawing room, looking stately again after our efforts. I can hear a pleading note in her voice, very unMagdalike, and remember that this is all she has now.

All any of us have.

For a long time, Jack doesn't say anything, and the tension mounts. He takes a swallow of whisky and blinks as the burning liquid slips down his throat. 'I would, if you don't mind, like to live here again.'

Magda's jaw tightens as she prepares herself for the inevitable.

'But I would like you to stay – all of you. You bought the place fair and square. And so did the last people who were here. Under some ancient law of *bona vacantia* it passed into the hands of the Duchy of Cornwall when the army moved out after the war. I don't intend to make any sort of legal challenge, and I'd prefer to maintain my identity of Jack Lord if I can. People around here are used to keeping secrets – Josie, the Lanyons. I know they won't rat me out.'

'But the court case…' I start.

His expression darkens. 'If it ever goes to court. The sergeant told me that the Church is getting involved. I bet they'll do everything they can to hush it up. That's how it works with institutions like that: they'll stifle any whisper of scandal, no matter the moral cost.'

'Surely they can't…' I start uncertainly.

'Oh, they can. But I don't really want it all laid out under the glare of the public spotlight. All the tittle-tattle, my parents' affairs endlessly raked over and speculated about. The papers would have a field day.'

'But the Vingoe family – won't they want to know what's happened to their relative's grave?'

Ariadne says, 'They've been asking for Hepzibah to be moved for ages, but the vicar kept blocking their application. Now we know why. He was always horrible to poor Lowena.'

I remember his cruel words to and about the woman who had comforted me when I sat crying on the bench by the lychgate that day.

Jack shrugs. 'The Vingoes know how things work down here. I'm sure poor old Hepzibah will be properly reinterred.'

Magda goes to put the kettle on and make a pot of tea, and Janey comes and sits on the floor by Jack's feet. He ruffles her hair. 'How is our princess today, and the mighty Rabbit?'

She turns her face up to him like a flower. 'Oh, we're fine.

I'm not a princess any more and Rabbit is just Rabbit. He's very happy to be back, aren't you?' she asks her toy, and he nods his head, his ears flapping as she shakes him back and forth.

'Why didn't Josie come in?' Magda asks, returning with a tea tray.

'Tired,' Jack says succinctly. 'It's been a long night.'

'Of course.'

'And – awful timing – she's got the surveyor coming tomorrow to assess the state of the house. The bank's sending them in. She is very afraid they're going to foreclose on their loans if they judge it to be in too bad a condition.' He makes a face. 'Poor Josie, after all she's done to help me, I wish I could help her. But I haven't got a bean.'

'Would beans help?' Janey pipes up. 'I'm sure we have some beans!'

I grin at her. 'Not that sort of beans, darling. Unfortunately.'

'Does she need magic beans, like in the story?'

'*Jack and the Beanstalk*? I'm sure those would come in very handy.'

Magda looks stricken. 'It's just dreadful to see such a beautiful old house fall into dereliction. Imagine what it must've looked like in its heyday – with its walls bright with tapestries and its gardens full of herbs and flowers. All those grand rooms and that marvellous hall... I never slept so well as in that huge fourposter bed with the curtains drawn around me. It was like being a queen...' She falls silent.

'Will Josie have to leave?' Janey says, horrified. 'It's her home, isn't it, the big house?'

'It's been in the family for hundreds of years,' Jack says

morosely. 'But she'll have to sell it to pay back the loans if the bank calls them in.'

'That would be an absolute tragedy,' Magda says – as if the loss of the great house is worse than what has happened to Jack and his poor mother.

'She needs a pot of gold,' I say, trying to add a note of levity.

'Does she? Is that better than beans?' Janey has become very alert. 'Is it like treasure?'

'Yes, poppet, that's exactly what she needs.'

'Rabbit knows where there's treasure, don't you, Rabbit?' The toy flops its great ears vigorously. 'But you told me not to move anything I found.' She regards me sternly.

'Yes, darling, I did.' How annoyingly literal children can sometimes be. 'Just what sort of treasure has Rabbit found?'

'Come on, I'll show you,' Janey says, scrambling to her feet.

25

Down through the garden she leads us in the pale light of that January afternoon, across the lawn and through the stands of bamboo and the banks of ferns, down towards the sea, till we reach the little stone bridge where the stream gives out onto the boulder beach of the White Cove.

'There,' Janey says, pointing.

'Where?'

With a sinking heart, I wonder if she means the mass of early golden buttercups peppering the squat feet of the bridge – metaphorical gold if ever I saw it. But by way of an answer, Janey takes Jack by the hand and leads him to the shadowed opening beneath the great clapper stone. I can tell he is hesitant to crawl under there; I suppose the last time he did so must have been the night his mother died.

'I should have brought a torch,' he says dubiously.

'You don't need one,' Janey assures him, slipping into the black space. 'Come on!' She reaches a hand back towards him and he takes it. They both disappear.

Magda and I stand on the path, gazing into the enigmatic darkness beneath the huge granite slabs. The sound of the water burbling noisily over the streambed is hypnotic and after a while I fall into a sort of trance. I think how this little bridge must have stood in this place, fording this stream, for well over a thousand years. I imagine all the feet that must have trodden the path between beach and valley in all that time, over and over – to market, on pilgrimage, to the church, to war, imprinting their human journeys upon the landscape, imposing their needs and experiences on the natural world in the way humans have always done ever since our time began.

My daydream is interrupted by a cry, then by Jack exclaiming, 'Good grief!'

Janey responds, 'I told you!'

Seconds later, Jack emerges from the shadows, bent double, walking crablike, his hands full of—

Ariadne dashes – nimble for all her size – along the stream towards Jack and catches his arm to steady him. He looks dazed, as well he might. He lays down his finds on the grassy sward at our feet, and the sunlight pierces their long-concealed mystery: a long string of large, round beads and discs, and two bracelets of twisted metal. The buttery sheen of the metal is evident even through the grubby coating of earth and moss. Gold.

Ariadne kneels and brushes her fingers over the largest pendant of the necklace, gently removing the worst of the dirt to reveal bright enamelwork that looks as if it might have been made yesterday. Then she looks up at us, her mouth a perfect O of astonishment. 'Would you look at that?'

Three tiny hares chase one another in a never-ending circle around the circumference, white upon green.

'The great cycle of life,' Keziah says reverently. 'Fertility, birth, eternity.'

The other beads are of different coloured glass, some engraved with wavy lines, some with dots, and a couple appear to be of stone. Held up to the light, there are flashes of red and purple.

'Amethyst,' Magda says, beguiled.

'And garnet, I think,' says Keziah.

Now Janey plonks down her find too: a rather basic-looking clay pot. But there must be something heavy inside, for it weighs her arms down, and when she puts it on the ground, something hard clinks against the clay. She reaches in and pulls out a filthy handful of mud and vegetation and twigs and spiderwebs, and goodness knows what else. Disturbed, woodlice scurry off into the grass. Within the handful of soil and weeds is a mound of small, irregularly shaped bits of metal. Fascinated, I pick one out and rub the soil off it. It is a coin, rough-edged and tarnished, but evidently a coin nonetheless. I rub at it some more and filth and verdigris comes off on my thumb, leaving it smeared brown and green. I clean my hand on the grass and scrub the disc some more.

We all crane over it, hoping for something as simply identifying as a date or the head of a well-known monarch, but the mystery can't be solved that easily. There is, however, a faint design on one side, and what appears to be a running animal on the other: certainly, something with four sticklike legs and a curved back. A horse? A dog?

But my heart knows what it is: it skips in leaps and stutters with excitement, and a kind of fear. I turn the coin over and rub the first side again. Two tiny indentations, and below those a horizontal slash. More gentle investigation reveals raying squiggles encircling these features. I almost drop the coin in my thrill of shock.

Ariadne takes in my expression. 'What is it?' she asks urgently.

'Come with me,' I say, taking her by the arm and fairly dragging her to the well. There, I push aside the vegetation – sparser now in the depths of winter – so that she can see the carving in the granite of the back wall, and she gives a little cry.

Reaching out, she touches the inscribed face, which is wet with yesterday's rain, still dripping from the overhead ferns. As if in sympathy with the carving, tears begin to run down her own face. 'Oh my,' she says, over and over.

Keziah picks her way between the ferns and brambles and gently pushes her beloved aside to gaze on the well-head. When she has stared at it for long enough to imprint the depiction on her memory, I show her the flipside of the coin.

Everyone else now crowds into the little space, except for Janey, who hangs back. I see her kiss Rabbit's head and button his waistcoat. Her expression is closed, even a little sly.

Jack's dark eyes meet mine over the top of the women's heads as they bend to inspect the well, and he smiles, his face filled with a sort of radiant delight.

By the time we return to the grassy sward by the bridge, after everyone has exclaimed over the ancient face at the well and on the coin, it is to find Janey sitting with the finds, her eyes slitted against the pale sun, as serene and possessive as a dragon with its gold-hoard.

'We ought to report the find,' Ariadne says after we have oohed and ahhed over the artefacts some more. 'It could be really important in what it tells us about the history of the area. Also, I think we have to, legally.'

Magda picks out one of the twisted bracelets and cleans it in the stream until the gold gleams. Then she slips it over her wrist, turning her hand this way and that to admire the effect. 'So beautiful.' All the lines and tensions have gone out of her face, as if it is gold that is the answer to all her needs, and will make her young, lovely, maybe even immortal. At last, she removes the bracelet with a sigh. 'Are you sure we have to report it… all?'

Of course, we can't keep the treasure. We carry our finds back to the house and with trembling hands I dial the operator and ask to be put through to the local police. They know my name and address at once – I gave them a statement after the events in the churchyard, and I can hear the excitement in the voice of the constable as he asks me questions: where did we find the items, how did we come upon them, what does the hoard consist of?

'I'll have to report it to the county coroner,' he tells me. 'But I'd love to have a look at it before it gets taken away. Perhaps I could just pop down and confirm what you've got before I call it in?' There is a pause, and he lowers his voice. 'I really wanted to be an archaeologist,' he almost whispers, 'but don't tell my sergeant.'

The site is excavated: our first guests at the house at White Cove are a team of archaeologists from the University of Exeter, a curator from the British Museum and another from the Royal Cornwall Museum. They fill the house with excited chatter and expert opinions, with sketchbooks and cameras and clutter and empty teacups. A large tent is erected at the bottom of the garden, where the finds are cleaned and minutely examined and catalogued. Jack and Magda and I are in and out on an almost hourly basis, driven by avid curiosity. The only person who seems to have lost interest is Janey, who despite the chill in the air is determinedly occupying her own tent – the wigwam Jack bought her for Christmas.

The archaeologists, working methodically along small parallel trenches, uncover other finds in the vicinity of the bridge and the well: more coins scattered in ones and twos, a knife with a decorative hilt, and another necklace made with glass beads and semi-precious stones, which they believe dates from the early Anglo-Saxon period. Some of the glass derives from the Mediterranean, they think; some is in the Byzantine style, whatever that means.

'It means,' one of the younger archaeologists tells me as we sip coffee together at the entrance to the tent, watching storm clouds pile up on the eastern horizon, 'that whoever lived here was either wealthy enough for traders to come from far away to do business with them, or influential enough to be brought rich gifts.'

A few days later there is a cry of amazement, followed by a lot of shouting and scurrying, and Jack and I run down to the site to find that they have uncovered, near the well, an even more extraordinary object than those Janey found under the bridge. It is an enormous collar of beaten gold, a flattened arc shaped like an exaggerated crescent moon, ending on either side in pointed horns, with space enough between to allow a slim neck to pass through. All over it is engraved with little dints and lines and whorls; someone has spent hours incising these delicate patterns.

'It's a moon-necklace,' the woman from the Royal Cornwall Museum breathes.

The curator from London is determined to use the correct terminology. 'A lunula. The British Museum has one or two from the early Bronze Age.'

It turns out to be made from pure Cornish gold and could be anything up to three thousand years old.

'This is incredibly exciting,' the man from the British Museum tells me at breakfast the following week. 'It's one of the earliest pieces I've seen.'

The woman from the museum in Truro picks up the lunula as if she wants to keep it away from him, and perhaps she does. 'This is a tangible piece of ancient Cornish history,' she says. 'It's crucial that it stays in the county.'

Over the course of the next few days, the two curators have an intensely polite argument about where the lunula should be housed and appear to strike some sort of bargain whereby once the coroner has released the finds, it will remain for the time being at the Royal Cornwall Museum, but be lent out for exhibitions to the British Museum. In return, half of the coins and one of the necklaces will go to the British Museum. All this seems right and proper, but it looks as if we may never see any financial gain from our finds. I suppose that's how it goes and since it is out of our hands, I try to put this aspect of the matter out of my mind and to concentrate on the fascinating details of the artefacts.

A numismatist comes down from London to examine the pot of coins. He takes up daytime residence in the dining room, spreading the coins out on the largest table on top of one of Magda's (no longer white) linen tablecloths, which my mother has gladly sacrificed to the cause. Her interest in history is passionate at the best of times. Surrounded by all these experts and notable finds made on our own property has rendered her almost giddy with excitement.

There are, according to the numismatist, coins in the hoard that date back to the time of the Romans – mainly sesterces, some identifiably from the reigns of Valerian, Claudius II and Victorinus, from the third century AD, which he explains to Magda may well have come from one of their military outposts. 'There was possibly a fort just outside Bodmin, but we believe that their incursion into the county was minimal. Cornwall was a wild, remote place which posed no great threat and so hardly warranted a large expenditure of troops or resources. But there are some tantalising hints that their occupation was more widespread – yours are not the first Roman coins to be found in the county – but of course traders travelled widely and used whatever currency came into their possession.'

The numismatist gets very animated when one of the coins turns out to be even earlier, from the reign of the Emperor Galba, who ruled in AD 68–69. But it's the Iron Age and later coins that truly fascinate him. Most are copper or silver alloy, all patinated green. Some show identifiable designs – chariots, trees, wheat, dogs, horses, crescent moons.

He shakes his head over the coin showing the running beast on one side and the face from our well on the other. 'I've never come across anything like this before,' he admits. 'I think it might even be Celtic. But the local tribes, to my knowledge, didn't mint their own coins.' He scratches his head. 'The head looks female. A queen. Or tribal ruler? That would be most unusual. I wonder if it's Mediterranean, the remnant of some ancient goddess culture? The hare is often associated with Celtic cultures, and then there's all the moon symbology... It's not really my field.'

More experts arrive, including a scholar with a spectacular mane of red corskscrew hair whose specialism appears to be in early religions and mythology. She is thrilled by the face in the back of our well and by the lunula that was found there and takes reel after reel of photographs of the site.

'She's absolutely extraordinary,' she says, brushing her hand across the eyes of the carved face. 'You know, you really should cut the vegetation back from her.'

'To let the dog see the rabbit?' I suggest, before catching myself. 'Oh, that's inappropriate.'

The scholar laughs. 'She's apotropaic. You need to let her do her work.'

I frown.

'Sorry. I'm used to being among academics – so many long words! It just means that she's here to be protective. Her gaze is supposed to ward off bad luck and evil influences.'

'That's good to know. We will cut it all back, as soon as the dig team has gone,' I promise as we walk back up to the house.

'There's an ancient well further up the county – at Whitstone,' she tells me as we go into the dining room. 'It has a face carved into it that's very similar to yours. I believe it was dedicated to the goddess Anu or Rhianu, though when Christianity came along it was subsumed into the new religion and became known as St Anne's Well.'

'That's why Berianu was called that,' Janey says, out

of nowhere. She's sitting quietly at a table behind the numismatist's collection, engrossed in cutting out bits of spare curtain fabric to make clothes for her dolls. 'She served the Goddess.'

'Did she now?' The young woman raises an eyebrow. Then looks at me. 'I think you'd better send this one to study with me when she's older.' She transfers her attention to Janey again. 'I wonder if the saint known as Berianu may have been a later version of that name and that became Christianised, quite literally. That happened a lot. They rewrote history to suit the Christian narrative and would turn a local character into a saint and attach all sorts of moral stories to their name. The village up the hill is Eglosberyan, isn't it? That sounds as if it means Church of St Beriana – maybe a change of grammatical inflection there. But how did you know all this?'

Janey just shrugs. 'She told me.'

'Who told you?' the scholar asks.

But Janey's expression becomes closed and uncommunicative.

'I'm sorry,' I say when Janey avoids further questions by skipping off to play outside with her new Pedigree Pin-up Doll, which appears to have ousted Rabbit in her affections. 'She does come out with some odd things.'

'But she found the treasure?'

I nod. 'The items beneath the bridge, yes.'

'How did she know where to look?'

'Janey's quite the little adventurer,' I say defensively, not much liking the direction this conversation is taking.

'Sometimes it's as if a place talks to you,' the scholar muses. 'Some locations are particularly resonant, especially places with geological structures similar to what you have here. A valley this deep can channel the things that have happened within it so that they create a series of echoes of the history, especially if those events have been traumatic.'

'You think the valley is... haunted?'

She laughs. 'Well, I suppose that's a way of putting it, but not haunted, exactly. It's more that landscape is sensitive to what happens to it, on it, around it, you know. The land is like a body. It carries scars, and it remembers. And down here particularly, the geology reinforces that. The structure of granite is full of crystals – mica and quartz and feldspar, and that can trap energies inside them. And water carries memories too... and water feeds the trees and underground networks of fungi, and the animals and birds.

'Combine all that with a remote location and a population with a strong identity and a long tradition of nonconformity that goes all the way back to a matriarchal culture and you have a potent mix. People here were slow to convert to the new religion; they espoused the old ways. Many of them still do. If not precisely the ancient goddess cultures, then spirits of the wild, spirits of place. This area has an atmosphere, don't you think? It has real depth and richness, a sense of grandeur and power.'

'I have felt a presence here,' I say after a while. 'Not threatening – not to us, anyway – but just a sense of being watched, or maybe watched over.' I shrug. 'A sort of awareness, much larger than we are. Is that what you mean?'

She smiles, rather sadly. 'You are so lucky to live in such a beautiful, ancient place. I'd give my eye teeth...'

'You should come down and stay when we're properly open as a guest house,' I tell her, and she smiles.

'Perhaps I shall. And perhaps your daughter, Jane—'

'Janey. Actually Janeska – we're Polish—'

'Polish? That's very interesting. All those water demons and savage monsters – a very rich mythological culture you bring with you to this remarkable place. It's a powerful combination! Perhaps Janey will tell me more about her experiences if I come back.'

I nod and agree that this may be a possibility, though I fervently hope by the time she returns Janey will be ensconced in the local school and rooted in a far more normal childhood.

The scholar is taken up to the village to discuss with Keziah and Ariadne hares and moons and Celtic crosses and the wounds inflicted upon the people and landscape, and comes back fizzing with new thoughts and theories. When they start enthusing about the hills on either side of the valley representing the goddess's legs, 'the joyous gushing of the stream' between them, and all the 'vulval openings in the trees' I cover Janey's ears and walk her upstairs...

The house is so full that some of the archaeology students helping with the dig end up having to sleep in the tent, and feeding everyone taxes me to the limits of my creativity and resources as I produce all manner of breakfasts, sandwiches and shareable dinners: vast cottage pies and stews, roasts, endless pies and pastries.

Occasionally, Bella Lanyon comes down to help, as she used to when Jack was a boy.

'Just like the old times.' She grins at him when he walks in as we're making pastry, planting a big kiss on him and leaving flour on his cheeks, so that he makes an excuse and escapes before she can embarrass him further. She winks at me. 'He's a lovely lad. It's good to see him smiling again.'

Bella is smiling a lot more too. The archaeological find has proved to be something of a goldmine for the Lanyons. They've taken visitors in for bed and breakfast at the farm, and we are taking huge quantities of the eggs and milk and bacon and clotted cream from them every day to feed the archaeologists.

'I do feel as if the Lady is smiling on us again,' Bella confides in me. 'Perhaps after that poor woman were unearthed in the graveyard. I think that pleased her. We're going to leave the top field fallow this year so that her folk can breed safely. Hares love the wild grass that grows up there. Funny thing is, I was talking to my cousin, who's got the farm east of the village, Boleigh way. He's been having a rough time these past years, but he says his early potatoes are coming through lovely this year. Reckons he'll have a bumper crop.'

'That's good,' I say. 'Because I think we're going to need every potato we can lay hands on if this lot stays here much longer.'

They don't stay much longer. The finds are all catalogued and taken away for safekeeping while the county coroner makes his investigations. The young policeman who wanted to be an archaeologist explains to me that the coroner will make a ruling on whether the hoard had been hidden with *animus revocandi* – deliberately stashed away with the intent of recovering it later – or whether it had been lost or abandoned. If the latter, it would belong to us, as the finders and owners of the land on which it had been discovered, according to the 'law of finders'. But if it had been deliberately hidden, then it becomes a 'treasure trove' and by rights belongs to the Crown, or the Duchy of Cornwall.

'Well, that's something,' I say. 'There's still a chance we may get something.'

I had written off any chance of earning from the hoard, but Mother seems to have been counting on it, and is downhearted. 'So much for saving Josie's house,' she says gloomily. 'It was clearly hidden under the bridge – no one could've "lost" it there.'

'But not all of it was stashed under the bridge,' I remind her. 'Some of it was near the well. That might just have been dropped.'

It's been thrilling to have had such a remarkable hoard discovered in our grounds, but if we are being totally honest, being able to raise some money from the finds would be extremely welcome. It's clear from our first foray into catering for a large group that the guest house is likely to be a success. But it's never going to raise the funds to unknot all of Josie's problems and save the manor house. Magda spends more and more time up there with Josie, uncovering lost fireplaces and original panelling, even finding previously unexplored rooms. Every new discovery adds probable cost and complexity to the project.

'Now, the manor house is a real treasure,' Mother tells me morosely. 'All those centuries of history just mouldering away. Some more people came to look at it last week, sent by the bank. They walked around with notebooks, working out how many rooms they could get by partitioning the larger spaces and turning it into a modern hotel. A disaster – not just for the house and for Josie and for local history, but for our business here too.'

We wait for further news.

When it comes to Casworan Martin, Jack is proved right about the way these things work. The whole affair has indeed been hushed up and no charges have been brought against the vicar. Instead, following some sort of rumoured deal between the Church, the local magistrates and the MP, he has been shuffled off to a retreat near Herodsfoot.

When he comes back, Jack is grey in the face and looks completely wrung out. It's a long drive – a couple of hours in each direction – but it's the hour spent with the vicar that's really done him in.

'Honestly, I've never seen a man squirm so much. He didn't want to talk about it at all but he'd promised the bishop to tell me everything I wanted to know as part of his atonement. Not that I'm allowed to do anything with it, and, actually, not that I'd want to. But it was like getting blood out of a stone.'

I make him a big mug of cocoa containing a hefty slug of Mother's whisky and he cups his hands around it as if the warmth is a lifesaver.

'He said it was my father who killed my mother, and when I asked Martin why he didn't stop him, he just looked really shifty. Kept kneading his hands together as if trying to find an excuse, but in the end, it came down to the fact that he was scared of my father.' He goes quiet for a long moment, as if remembering his childhood. 'Well,' he says at last, 'I can't really blame him for that. Father's tempers were… titanic. He said my father didn't mean to kill her – he was just so furious that she'd seen them together and wanted to scare the life out of her. Those are the actual words he said. Can you believe it? "Scare the life out of her."'

'He certainly did that,' I say softly. 'How horrible.'

'He put his hands around her neck and shook her so hard that he…' Jack swallows. 'He broke her neck.' I see his jaw tighten as if he's trying to control his own emotions. 'Imagine the force that must've taken.'

Of course, we already know that poor Agnes Prideaux had a broken neck. The coroner had said as much in his report. The question of how her injuries had been sustained, though, was conjecture, and without witnesses the death had been ruled as 'misadventure', which had made Jack howl with rage. It was what had driven him to go and see Casworan Martin. He called it 'confronting my demons', which felt apt.

He looks up at me now. 'Martin said that when my father realised she was actually dead he broke down and wept. Kept shaking her and crying her name over and over. And the vicar said that made him feel furious, and jealous of Agnes.'

'What an utterly bizarre thing to say, and totally self-centred.'

'Love makes us do bizarre things,' Jack says so quietly that I hardly hear the words. 'I do believe Martin was in love with my father. He kept going on about how charismatic he was, how handsome, how he was completely in thrall to him.' He sighs. 'Anyway, when it became clear my poor mother really was dead, they carried her body up to the car and apparently her coat fell off while they were trying to do so, and Jory wouldn't go back for it because he'd got it into his head that someone – or something – was watching him, and was coming for him.

'They sat her body upright in the passenger seat so that if anyone saw the car it would look as if my parents were driving off somewhere together. And then my father drove like the clappers – he was a fast driver at the best of times – but he really seems to have scared Martin by the way he was driving. He kept saying, "I thought I was going to die!"

'Then, as they went through the woods, he said this white light enveloped them, like a luminous mist descending, and my father started screaming and raving about a giant hare. Casworan Martin said he saw nothing but mist and thought Jory had gone stark raving mad. He tried to take the wheel – said it was only by a miracle that they got to the village alive.'

'A miracle?' I shake my head. 'That man has no shame at all.'

'He said the mist swirled around the car all the way up to the church, but it didn't go into the graveyard, and that was when he thought about putting the body in the open Vingoe grave that was ready for Hepzibah's funeral the next day. So they...' He swallows and closes his eyes.

I don't reach across the table to comfort him as I know his tears will fall, so I sit there rigid, my hands gripping one another compulsively, till he masters himself and carries on.

'So that's what they did, without ceremony. Just dumped her body in the bottom of the grave like a bit of a rubbish.

And then my father got back in the car and drove off, leaving Martin to shovel enough earth back in to cover her up.

'He said he never saw my father again. Never heard from him either. It was as if he just "vanished off the face of God's earth",' he finishes, quoting the vicar.

'But the guardianship document? You recognised your father's handwriting on it.'

'He said it wasn't hard to forge Jory's signature. They were all taught the same style of cursive penmanship at public school. He just shrugged, as if it was nothing, and said, "What else was I to do with you? You were just a problem to be got rid of."'

'Oh, Jack.' My eyes burn.

His brows draw together, his expression dark. 'No one wanted to deal with an abandoned child. It suited the authorities to accept the document as valid, just as it suited everyone to accept the story that my father had been called away 'on official business' and his family had joined him. He was a pillar of the community, after all. The local Conservative MP. The master of the hunt, married to a girl from a landowning family with roots in the area going back hundreds of years. How could such a man possibly have committed such a terrible crime?

'And then he laughed and sat back in his chair and called for tea and cake, as if he was in some fucking hotel. His last words to me were that if I ever tried to pursue any of this in a court of law, he would deny everything, and the Church and authorities would band together to shut the door in my face. And the worst of it is that I know that's true.'

'What an utter bastard. But surely you can't let it go at that?'

'I don't think I have any choice in the matter. And anyway, I am so tired, Mila. What would I gain from battling with these people? They'll just do everything they can to destroy me, to keep me quiet. I've done my fighting. I know the truth. I just need to come to terms with it, and to honour my mother.'

He drains the cocoa, long gone cold, and after a while says, 'I feel the need for some neat whisky. Join me?'

We take our glasses to the drawing room and watch the moon rising over the ocean, laying her silver path from horizon to land. It is so windless, so still, that it looks as if you could walk upon it, right out to sea, without even getting your feet wet.

'Lovely, isn't it?'

'It really is. And so are you.'

Jack puts an arm around me and we stand with our bodies pressed together, side to side, hip to hip, gazing out over White Cove while the tension drains out of him, drop by drop, and the ice in our glasses melts into the fiery malt.

We marry in the early autumn, after the end of our first tourist season, during which we have been run off our feet. Janey and two of her new friends from school are our bridesmaids; Jack has had his hair cut and in his beautifully tailored suit he looks like Cary Grant. My dress is a strapless white satin Balenciaga worn with an elegant bolero sewn with seed pearls. Mother has spared me no expense, and no escape, having dragged me up to London to be fitted out. I find out later that she sold some of her jewellery to ensure there was a fund for the wedding, a discovery that stuns me to silence and reduces me to tears. She will not let me thank her. 'It's small recompense,' is all she will say.

We stand in the September sunshine on the steps of St John's Hall in Penzance while the photographer takes picture after picture and, instead of confetti or rice, the guests throw handfuls of rose petals that Keziah has collected from all the gardens in the village, with the permission of their owners. The air smells of attar and tobacco and *L'Heure Bleue*, and I stand enveloped in the fragrant moment, bursting with happiness.

It's a pity not to have been able to marry in a picturesque church, but Eglosberyan's church will remain always tainted by terrible memories, even though there is now a perfectly nice new vicar installed there. Nor did we feel we could disrespect the spirit of place represented by the White Hare, to celebrate our union in a building raised to oppress her followers, with a rood screen that glories in the hunting and death of wild things and the sundial outside that spells out the Latin threat *Lepus currere paulo*.

Run, little hare…

We have had Jack's mother – Agnes Prideaux, née Laitie – reinterred in the family plot beside the chapel at the manor house, an exquisite, tiny structure that had been swallowed by the woods. Before we go inside for the reception, Jack and I stand beside her grave and lay our wedding flowers down upon her and bow our heads in silent prayer.

The manor house is in the throes of refurbishment. The old wet-laid slate roof has been replaced, the towering chimneys repointed and the structure is now watertight ahead of the winter to come. Next week the new window frames are going in. They were due to be fitted last week, but when a Cornish carpenter tells you they'll be ready 'dreckly', it's never a good idea to interpret that as a specific deadline. No matter – a profusion of flowers has been draped around the doors: roses for love; blowsy pink dahlias for a lasting bond; chrysanthemums for long life, luck and health; and masses of greenery.

Inside, Magda has been given her head, and it is clear from the first glimpse that her refurbishment of the house at White Cove has been her apprentice-work; the manor house is her masterpiece. Everywhere you look: gleaming wood, shining tiles, spotless paint. The paintings have been professionally cleaned, to reveal deep colours and unexpected details. My particular favourite is the portrait of Katharine Laitie, an Elizabethan heiress who poses solemnly in her jewels and French hood and her lace-bordered ruff, cradling an enormous rabbit with glowing eyes as if it is some sort of lapdog.

The guests wander around, champagne flutes in hand, running their hands across the glossy wood of the King Charles chair, and sometimes taking a crafty seat in it; craning their necks to take in the timber beams and frets, the Tudor strapwork, stucco roses and decorative plaster bosses. Great care has been taken to find artisan restorers, though Magda has handled the budget with exceptional care, and a grant has been made by a heritage organisation.

The archaeological finds were referred by the county coroner to the Lords Commissioners of the Treasury who ruled that we should, as both the finders and landowners, be paid the full antiquarian value for the items in the hoard and the pure gold lunula, so long as the items are retained for the national and regional museums. And so, suddenly, as if out of nowhere, we were presented with a truly significant cheque, which has completed the decoration and provisioning of the house at the cove and bought Jack and me a second-hand Austin Healey (which I am currently, and rather terrifyingly, learning to drive). The rest has been poured into the Laitie family house and sent the bank packing. It's not a magic wand; the manor house will require so much more than even the archaeological funds or the grants will provide, but it's an excellent start. Relieved of so many, if not all, of her worries, Josie has turned into the funniest person I know. Whether we're at the manor house or down at the guest house, the rooms ring with raucous laughter. We're up at the big house a lot, not least because Magda has moved in there, released from the bustle of the busy guest house to focus her talents on the renovations and repairs, and appointed by Josie as the general manager of the manor house, while Kit Lanyon has become her estate manager, charged with caring for the grounds and woods. My mother has discovered her metier and, thank heavens, her sense of humour.

I can hear her now, hooting with laughter. Ariadne and Keziah and Josie are gathered in a knot with Magda and my old friend Daphne, down from London, arrayed in the latest fashion, the highest of heels and the most shocking scarlet lipstick. We are all minor local celebrities now, after coverage of the discovery of the hoard at White Cove in the newspapers, what people are now calling 'the goddess well', and the carved memorial stone outside the churchyard wall in Eglosberyan. All manner of historians and antiquarians – as well as plenty of cranks – have headed down to this corner of West Penwith in the months since the finds were first reported. The Church won't allow the churchyard wall to be disturbed and have prevented a dig beneath the stone that sits outside it, so rumours have run rife. It marks the grave of the goddess herself; of a Celtic princess, a local Boudicca who led the Cornish in a doomed last stand; an Irish missionary who was abducted and raped, then saved by St Piran – or was carved in more modern times. No one knows the truth, and the space for invention has allowed a hundred different theories to thrive.

I stand on tiptoe to gaze over the heads of the wedding guests to see where my daughter has got to, and eventually locate her and her two little friends, Gemma and Mary, on the threshold of the modern kitchen, feeding little bits of wedding cake to their dolls.

Janey looks up, radiant. 'Mummy, Mummy, look! Tansy and Rabbit have got married too!'

Rabbit (who has been restored to Chief Toy, if only for the wedding) wears a red carnation pinned onto his waistcoat, and Tansy – one of the other little girls' dollies, all hard pink plastic – a dress fashioned out of a lace-edged white handkerchief and an ox-eye daisy tucked into her springy platinum hair.

I laugh. 'They look very happy together.'

Gemma immediately forces Tansy upon Rabbit, making loud kissing noises, and they all squeal and giggle, then Mary grabs the doll and runs off through the crowd, with Gemma in noisy pursuit.

'Poor Rabbit,' says Janey, hugging him close. Then, 'Ow!' she cries, and drops him. She sucks her thumb, which has started to bleed.

'What have you done? Let me see.'

She pulls away. 'You'll get blood on your dress.'

'That doesn't matter.' I catch hold of her and examine her hand. There's a puncture in the top of her thumb, but already the wound is closing. 'What was it that pricked you?' I pick up Rabbit, but she tries to grab him away from me. Unsuccessfully.

Under Rabbit's waistcoat there's something hard, and evidently also sharp. I open the button and find that what is pinning the carnation in place from the inside is a rough gold lozenge.

I unpin it carefully, and stare in disbelief at the spare lines of the design.

Then I quickly look around to see if anyone has seen my discovery. No one is watching us. I close my fist around the brooch, then tow Janey outside into the garden.

We go around the side of the house where the woods come right up close, away from the wedding guests, and I hitch up my rather fitted dress so that I can sit on the grass beside Janey.

'Where did you find it, Janey?'

She won't meet my eyes or answer.

I hand Rabbit back to her while I examine the brooch more closely. Maybe it isn't what I think it is, maybe it's just a bit of cheap modern tat. But really, I know it isn't. The design is exactly the same as all of Janey's drawings. The same as the designs running along the walls of the room, the same as the inscription on the stone outside the churchyard: the sublimated Lepus that runs across the starry sky.

Elongated, stylised almost out of recognition, it is nevertheless clearly a running hare, made from pure, deep gold – a depiction that falls halfway between the figurative and the abstract so that it resembles its subject in much the same way as does Jack's beloved White Horse of Uffington, which I have now seen for myself, making Magda detour to the monument. It is clearly ancient and authentic. There is both grace and power in its simple lines – reverence too. The pin is long, jointed on the unseen side of the animal, the end still sharp enough to pierce cloth and flesh.

Someone wore this, I think, turning it over in my palm. Close to the heart, to pin a cloak or shawl, for luck, for good fortune, to ward off evil, to honour whatever it was the hare represented to them. What was the word the folklore expert used? *Apotropaic.*

'Was this with the things under the bridge?' I remember her sly manner when we came back from examining the well.

I see her go pink.

'You're not in trouble, darling. Just tell me.'

'I found it in the stream near the bridge when Rabbit was lost, ages before I showed you and Jack where the treasure was.'

I cast my mind back. That was before she started drawing all her Lepus sketches, wasn't it? It was, I'm sure it was.

'Will they take it away from me?' she asks in a very small voice.

I know that 'they' probably will, even if they pay us for it. I hesitate. 'We could have a copy made, just for you,' I suggest.

'That's no use!'

The pink in her cheeks becomes an angry red and I am horrified to see tears begin to roll down her cheek. I don't want this special day spoiled. 'Tell me why it's so special,' I coax, brushing the tears away.

Around us I can hear birdsong – robins and wrens, dunnocks and blackbirds, the chatter of jackdaws. The sunlight filtering through the leaves above is dappling the ground. The scent of the newly mown grass and honeysuckle nectar hangs heavy in the still air.

'I can't. I don't know. I can't explain what I don't know.'

'I think,' I say after a long pause in which ginger-bottomed bees buzz lazily past to inspect the towering foxglove spires, 'it was worn by someone a very long time ago. For luck, and to honour…'

'Her world.'

'Our world?'

'Yes.'

I pin the hare brooch carefully beneath Rabbit's waistcoat once more, then hand him back to Janey.

'This is our secret.'

'Our secret.'

Her eyes shine.

Epilogue

Berianu runs and runs and runs, as if hounds are after her. Down through the woods, leaping the stream, the hem of her cloak sopping up water, her long red hair flying in the wind. Bracelets and bangles rattle on her arms, necklaces knock her collarbones, the coins in the pot she carries clink against the clay. The enemy is gathering; fleetest of foot, she has been sent to hide the family treasures.

The enemy regard the people of the Land as godless and barbaric. But that is no more than an excuse. The local tribes honour deities large and small – the sun and moon, the spirits of the earth. What these men really want is subjugation, to strip the Land bare of its people, its gold and its tin.

At the clapper bridge, she kneels among the golden butter-cups, whips off the hare brooch that closes her cloak, and in her haste drops it into the stream as she concentrates on bundling all the jewellery – her mother's chain, her aunts' bead necklaces, her sisters' skeins of silver, the bracelets and bangles – inside the cloak. She pushes the bundle deep into the darkness under the bridge. In goes the pot of coins. The hare brooch washes a little way downstream through the dappled waters until it is trapped between two rocks.

And there it will lie for a thousand years and more.

Without her burdens she feels light as a bird, as insubstantial as a bee.

She runs to the sacred well. Berianu serves the White Lady, for whom she is named – the goddess who watches over this valley, maybe watches over all this world.

Goddess, see me
Goddess, hear me
Goddess, be with me...

She sees, and she hears, and she is there. The young woman's prayer is a plea for safety from the men who are coming with their iron swords, their helmets and armour. Their feet beat upon her skin. Her birds bring news of their passage – raven to crow; crow to jackdaw; jackdaw to gull.

They bring death. Theirs is a cult of death; hers a cult of life. But death is a necessary part of the cycle. All things must be born, must live, then die; she cannot break that pact. But where is the balance in slaughter and pillage? It is hatred personified. It is anti-life.

Soon she feels the blood flowing. The blood of the people of the Land. She gathers it where she may, channels it within her valley, cups it like a chalice, in a kind of rage. Down to the sea it runs, staining the land, soiling the network that links all living things. It flows over the stones in the streambed and beneath the bridge that even then is ancient. It seeps into the water-table to poison her own well; it debouches onto the beach, running between the white boulders, leaving rusty-pink tidemarks. It forms a widening pool around the figure lying on the shore, one arm flung up above its head as if to draw the attention of any onlooker.

But there are no onlookers now. The raiders' ships bob at anchor in the shallow waters. They have come by sea, as well as overland. The young woman who has been dedicated to her service all her short life stood bravely brandishing her belt-knife at the invaders, but they just laughed and gutted her like a fish, leaving her to bleed into the sand. Bruises have flowered like dark roses upon her pale limbs. Her long red hair is spread on the shore like seaweed and her empty blue eyes gaze up into empty sky. Sandflies are already beginning to gather.

Angry at the waste of this young life, she follows the invaders now, gathering her forces as she goes. The men feel awareness focused on them as they run up through the woods. They sense, with a chill down the spine, the antipathy of the trees towards them for the murder they have done on the strand below, as their comrades are still doing on the fields above. They feel the anger of the rooks, the loathing of the bees and the flies buzzing around them, and when the white mist envelops them, their sword hands tremble and their shield arms weaken.

These men will never forget this place; they will be plagued by nightmares – of burning eyes and a running white hare – for the rest of their lives, and they will never return here.

She is the gold of the bursting gorse buds; she pushes through the moss and soil with snowdrops in her wake.

Her spirit slips like a speckled trout down the soil-flecked stream, between the ferns and the butterbur; her breath stirs the feathers of the night-time owls, which open wide their moon-sheened eyes and blink, and shiver their wings into place again. She smooths the granite river stones as she passes; she soars among the calling rooks. In the fields, she runs with the March hares, dancing on their hind legs.

She is wind through the grass, which ripples and flickers at her passing. White is her colour – the white of snow, or breaking surf, or a winter hare – or a frightened eye.

Turn your head quickly as you walk the Cornish coast path and dip down into her valley and you may glimpse her among the bluebells and wild garlic, the ash and thorn, just a flash of white light, where the world thins.

This is her realm. You are only visiting, but she will continue.

Tread carefully. You may be trespassing.

Author's Note

The kernel of this story came out of something my husband Abdel experienced on one of his long peregrinations along the Cornish coast path. He is a keen walker, who thinks nothing of setting off from our home in Mousehole to head for Land's End and back again, a distance of some forty kilometres (twenty-six miles), up and down the most rugged and spectacular terrain. He would sometimes return from these excursions quiet and subdued, which I would put down to quite understandable exhaustion; but one day when friends were visiting and the subject got onto matters of the uncanny, he told us that something 'strange' had happened to him a number of times at the same location while he'd been out walking. He'd been descending into a steeply wooded valley between Treen and Lamorna – a rare, cool respite on a hot summer day from the sun beating off the granite crags – when he felt his skin horripilate and the hairs rise on the back of his neck, and he had a sudden intense awareness of another presence, which broke in upon the meditative state he'd entered into as he walked. And as soon as he sensed this, there was a brief whoosh of white light which passed through the leaves of the tree canopy down towards the sea – then nothing but stillness. This happened to him in the same spot on three or four occasions. He did not sense any hostility in the presence – if anything, the opposite. He says he often slips into a meditative state when walking and will channel healing thoughts towards close friends or family experiencing hardship as he paces along, losing himself in the landscape. He said the sensation he felt was like a manifestation of power and aid in this meditation, almost a response to a form of prayer.

Now, I have to say that Abdel is one of the most down-to-earth people you could ever meet. He's a cook and a gardener, a solver of problems – hands-on, practical, funny and irreverent – the last person prey to attacks of wild imagination. But this old connection had touched him, disturbed him, made him thoughtful. It had taken him many weeks to come to terms with it, which was why he had only mentioned it now, as Hannah and Phil and I related curious things that had happened to us over the years.

When he told us about his experience, I shivered. I had also felt this valley to be an unquiet sort of place, with its own strange, restless atmosphere. It reminded me of an uncanny sensation I'd had when climbing at Paviland, on the Gower Peninsula. My climbing partner and I had made our way down to the wave-cut platform to tackle a route called Middle Earth, on the way to which we passed an enormous cave hollowed deep into the limestone cliff. Of course, you can't pass such a cave without going in, so we did. I had only gone a few steps into the cold darkness when I felt the urgent, overwhelming need to be outside again, followed by an almost physical sensation, as if someone was pushing me back. Out in the sunshine once more, I trembled from head to toe. The only way back up to the footpath was to climb out. I went up that route fast and nervy and would not go back down to do another one, so powerful was the feeling that I was not wanted there. I knew nothing about the human bones that had been uncovered there (which were dubbed the Red Lady) or that one school of thought held that Paviland had been a *locus consecratus* – a sacred place – for more than five thousand years. There was a distinct presence there, and it did not feel welcoming. The wooded Cornish valley did not feel threatening in the same way as that cave, but it felt 'full' to me, as if a lot of things had happened there, not all of them good, and become concentrated in the deep, shady cleft that ran down to the sea, building up like an alluvial deposit or a geological moraine.

After I had finished *The White Hare*, a friend in the village lent me a copy of a book written by one of her family members about the area in which I had notionally set the story. Of the valley it says, *If you are afraid of ghosts, keep out of the woods at night!* There are a number of ghostly tales associated with the old manor house and the coastal land in which it sits. A roaming apparition may grab you by the upper arms and *rattle you till your bones shake*. A broken-hearted young woman is said to be seen wandering the woods; Ann Paynter drowned herself down in the cove in the eighteenth century, setting a curse upon the house. Tales tend to accrue around uncanny places.

Cornwall wears its ancient history close to the surface,

often on full view. Being wild and remote, West Penwith has been less developed than many other places in the UK, so there is a myriad of stone circles, standing stones, burial chambers and fogous, sacred wells, Celtic crosses and ancient villages left in the landscape to be seen and explored. And possibly as a result of this deep history infusing the atmosphere, it is also a place that embraces its myths, legends, folklore and superstitions. I was raised here, my mother's family rooted in the turf and mineshafts and granite, right the way back to the twelfth century, and probably beyond into a time before annals and parish records. Those stories and superstitions have been passed down the generations from grandmother to mother to child, and no doubt my mother's absolute certainty that she had seen and felt the presence of an Iron Age man in the ruins of Chysauster (a Romano-British settlement just outside Penzance that can boast the oldest recognisable village street in Cornwall, and into that foreign land beyond – England) made quite an impression on the seven-year-old me.

I thought about all this – Abdel's story of the presence in the woods, my own uncanny experiences in ancient places, and the history and tales that run through the crystals in Cornwall's granite, and soon *The White Hare* started to coalesce.

I started writing the first draft during the first Covid lockdown. The pandemic played havoc with my usual creative processes – travelling to research, walking, even writing, since I write outdoors in longhand, and at the outset I was unable to do much of any of this. As a result, I was forced to draw from a deep internal well, and that's why this is a different book to most of my other novels. But

I really hope you have enjoyed it and have come to sense a little of the unknowable and alluring mystique of Cornwall.

Now onto some more specific notes about location, history and archaeology.

When I write about the region in which I live, I try to avoid unambiguous, fully identifiable locations, preferring to make my settings notional, and just as Porth Enys in *The Sea Gate* is a sort of Mousehole but not actual Mousehole, so Eglosberyan and its valley draw on a number of different inspirations. You will find an immense church in the village of St Buryan which was built by King Athelstan in AD 931 after bloodily crushing an uprising of the Cornish Celts, and the nearby battleground was indeed known as Gwel Ruth – the *Red Field* in Cornish. Inside the church there is an impressive carved rood screen depicting the Wild Hunt, which was later Christianised and said to symbolise the Devil hunting for souls. The church is built on the site of a Romano-British settlement enclosure, which in turn was almost certainly built on the site of a pagan temple. The village is named for Saint Beriana/Buriana, who may well have much deeper pagan roots than the Irish Christian missionary healer of whom the tales tell (abducted by the lustful King Geraint and briefly saved by St Piran) – for her saint's day is 1 May, which is of course the Celtic feast of Beltane, when the sexuality of life and the earth is at its peak, when the maiden goddess has reached her fullness. And the name of the Irish Celtic goddess is Anu, whose name became Christianised in many places as St Anne – including St Anne's Church at Whitstone in Cornwall, where there is a sacred well with a crudely carved face just like the one in *The White Hare*.

One of the reasons I made Magdalena and Mila Polish in origin – apart from the fact that they are outsiders, indeed 'furriners', entering a closed community – is that they come from Old Europe, whence Neolithic people travelled to Britain, bringing with them their religious beliefs and superstitions, and I liked the idea of there being a convergence of cultures in which the pagan past is a crucial part of the character of the people of the present.

There are stone wayside crosses to be found all over Cornwall, marking or protecting ancient crossing points. Many were erected in the early medieval period, but of the older crosses it is believed that most of them are Celtic and some of them even pre-Christian, and that whatever design is inscribed on them was revised at a later date into the symbol of the cross.

There have been many significant archaeological finds in Cornwall and Scilly, including an Early Bronze Age gold lunula found at Harlyn Bay, Padstow (in the Cornwall Musuem), another at Gwithian (in the British Museum) and a third at St Juliot (Cornwall Museum). Two thousand Roman coins were unearthed from a farmer's field near Hayle in 2017. Gold hoards have been found at Morvah and Towednack, and on Scilly the hoard included a crude Venus or goddess figurine.

And at last, to the matter of the White Hare herself. Cornwall is full of white hare legends, but most are variations on a theme of the revenant souls of women and girls, rejected and betrayed by lovers, who roam the cliff-tops, portending doom to any who see them. The sexual symbolism is there, but it has been sublimated and watered down into a more palatable form for the eighteenth- and nineteenth-century audience for folk tales. Taking a deeper dive into history and mythology, you'll find that the hare was sacred to many ancient cultures, associated with the Moon Goddess and the Celtic goddess Ostara, because of hares' fertility.

Hares are portrayed as tricksters and messengers, because of their fleetness and guile, and as shape-shifters, changing form and colour as they marked the transition between winter and spring. Witches were often believed to adopt the form of hares when attempting to escape pursuers. There is an early British taboo against hunting hares – if you did so, it was believed you would be struck down by cowardice, hence the legend that Boudicca carried a hare into battle with her, hoping her Roman enemies would strike at it and lose their courage.

Ambiguous, liminal, uncanny, bridging the human and divine world, the White Hare seems to me to be a perfect manifestation for all those things in life we sense but cannot know.

Jane Johnson
October 2021

Further Reading

THE WHITE GODDESS – Robert Graves (Faber & Faber, 1961)

CORNOVIA – Craig Weatherhill (Halsgrove, 2009)

CELTIC BRITAIN – Thomas Charles (Thames & Hudson, 1986)

THE CHALICE AND THE BLADE – Riane Eisler (Pandora, 1993)

PAGAN CORNWALL – Cheryl Straffon (Meyn Mamvro Publications, 1993)

GHOSTWAYS – Robert Macfarlane, Stanley Donwood and Dan Richards (WW Norton, 2020)

BOSKENNA AND THE PAYNTERS – Jim Hosking (1999)

And do have a look at Terri Windling's wonderful Myth & Moor blog online, the evocative art of Jackie Morris and Catherine Hyde, and the art and jewellery of Hannah Willow, who has crafted me many a protective silver hare over the years.

Acknowledgements

It may seem weird accrediting Covid in my acknowl-edgments, but I think I must admit that had I not been confined to Cornwall during lockdown this novel might never have been written, let alone permeated by the claustrophobia and unease that made the perfect atmospheric backdrop for the story.

More traditionally, let me send love and thanks to my husband, Abdel – his curious experience on the coast path was the corm from which this story grew. And to Helen, for generously donating a wild stretch of her clifftop allotment to us, which provided not only exercise, vegetables and a much-needed escape from television news and other people, but also the perfect tucked-away spot where I could write longhand in my notebooks with the sound of the waves and the cries of seabirds in my ears.

Warm thanks to Philippa, Hannah and Phil for their sympathetic and helpful readings of early drafts, and to my lovely publishers, who helped me stay sane by providing a framework, a deadline and a much-needed sense of purpose. Special thanks to Charlotte Greig and Nita Pronovost for civilised and uplifting conversations, and for their excellent edits; to Emma Rogers for a gorgeous cover design; and to Nic Cheetham, Maddy O'Shea, Anna Nightingale, Jessie Price, Laura Palmer, Sophie Whitehead and all those in the sales, marketing and publicity teams who work so hard to get my books into the hands of readers.

Love and thanks must also go to my agents, Danny and Heather Baror, for all they do, and lastly to my native Cornwall, for seeding its stories in my bones.